"TOUCH ME, PRINCESS"

Wrapping his arm around her waist, Lance pulled her closer. He moved her palm over his chest, compelling her to feel the smooth naked flesh there, the flexing muscles of his rib cage, the hard, flat plane of his abdomen.

Summer closed her eyes. "Please, I don't want this . . ."

He gave her no choice. Catching her wrist again in his grip, Lance moved her palm downward.

"Do you feel what you do to me?" he whispered against her mouth. "Haven't you ever wondered what it feels like to be with a man."

Wondered? How could she not wonder? Ever since their wedding night, she hadn't stopped thinking about what had happened to them, what Lance had left unfinished. What it would have felt like to become fully a woman. His woman . . .

Praise for
THE SAVAGE

"A hero beyond compare . . .
A JOY TO R[...]
Re[...]

THE SAVAGE

NICOLE JORDAN

AVON BOOKS NEW YORK

THE SAVAGE is an original publication of Avon Books. This work has never before appeared in book form. This work is a novel. Any similarity to actual persons or events is purely coincidental.

AVON BOOKS
A division of
The Hearst Corporation
1350 Avenue of the Americas
New York, New York 10019

First Avon Books Printing: July 1994

AVON TRADEMARK REG. U.S. PAT. OFF. AND IN OTHER COUNTRIES, MARCA REGISTRADA, HECHO EN U.S.A.

Printed in the U.S.A.

RA 10 9 8 7 6 5 4 3 2 1

*To Ann Howard White,
for her unfailing instincts
and generous shoulder.*

*The time and my intents are savage-wild,
more fierce and more inexorable far. . . .*

WILLIAM SHAKESPEARE

Prologue

Texas, 1860

His kiss was more than she bargained for. His hot mouth bore little resemblance to the polite attentions of a gentleman. Instead, his caress was like the man: hard, intense, forbidden.

There was no tenderness. The intimate intrusion of his tongue was like a fiery brand in her mouth, marking her as his ... demanding, possessing. Emphasizing that he wasn't quite civilized.

But then, he was *not* quite civilized, Summer remembered in a daze. Lance Calder was the sort of man no lady would ever associate with, much less allow such intimacies. He was a half-breed. Part savage Comanche. Raised white, true, but nonetheless a savage.

It excited her, the fierceness of his kiss. And frightened her. She was afraid of the raw sensuality, the barely restrained savagery she felt in him. She should have known better than to flirt so close to danger. Yet she had gotten precisely what she'd wanted. After months of trying, she had finally broken his iron control—and discovered herself unprepared.

She tasted hunger and desire and anger in his kiss. She hadn't expected the anger. He was furious at her for driving him to this. Neither had she expected her own reaction. The frantic thudding of her heart. The acute breathlessness. The weakness flooding her limbs. She hadn't anticipated the overwhelming sensations ... especially the heat. The heat of his mouth, the heat of her flushed skin, the heat kindling low in her body. A heat that had nothing whatever to do with the warmth of the August night. She'd never experienced anything like it. She felt as if she had never been kissed before

in all her life. As if she'd never known what kissing was
about.

She could feel herself trembling . . . or was it he? She felt
his arm hard at her back, the rough texture of his work-
callused fingers against the side of her throat as he hungrily
angled his mouth to get closer.

Summer heard him groan softly, and a thrill of triumph
surged through her. It gave her a heady feeling of power to
think she could affect a man so, could affect *this* man so,
could make him tremble and lose control.

It startled her when Lance abruptly ended their kiss, dragging his mouth from hers, half pushing her away. His breath
sounded harsh in her ears, and she felt him fighting for restraint as he leaned his forehead against hers. The strength of
his fingers hurt faintly as he gripped her bare arms below the
puffed sleeves of her gown.

"Are you satisfied?" His voice was low, gruff, hoarse.
"Did it excite you, ma'am? Did it make you hot, kissing a
fierce Injun?"

Confused, Summer drew back and raised her gaze to his.
Even in the semidarkness she could see him well enough.
The lamp she'd left burning on the back porch spilled a
golden light over the yard, illuminating his harsh, strong-
boned face bronzed the hue of sunbaked earth. His coal black
hair was slicked back from his high forehead and still damp
from washing at the pump. He smelled of shaving soap and
leather and horses. Obviously he had spruced up for his
meeting with her, on the occasion of her seventeenth birthday.

Yet it was his eyes that held her spellbound. There was
something dangerous and untamed in his eyes. They were
black as ink, deep and hard and fearless, with a smoldering
intensity that made her wary. It was like looking into the
heart of a brewing storm.

"Well, ma'am . . . was it different? Did being kissed by a
savage feel different from your fancy gentlemen?"

He drawled the word *ma'am,* his tone holding faint derision,
with little of the respect due the white daughter of a powerful
Texas landowner. And yet it was his contemptuous use of the
word *savage* that made her wince. "Please . . . don't . . ."

"Don't, Miss Weston?" He pulled her closer, till her corseted breasts pressed against his hard chest. "Isn't this what you wanted? What you asked me for?"

Summer shivered. Lance was going much too fast for her. She couldn't handle him the way she could her other beaux, that much was becoming clear. He wasn't much older than she—perhaps four or five years, that was all. He looked to be in his early twenties. And yet Lance Calder was a man, with a man's hard experience. Nothing like the boys she was accustomed to having flock around her, the mere boys she had learned to flirt with and charm since she was old enough to let down her skirts.

There was nothing soft or polite about him. He was whip-cord-lean, hard as saddle leather, with a broad, deep chest that dwarfed her slender frame. She could feel the solid resilience of muscle as she clung to him, could feel the coiled tension in his body, in his strong hands as they gripped her bare arms.

With a show of bravado, she gave a faint laugh. "Well, yes. I was curious, I admit it. But just because I let you steal a kiss doesn't give you—"

"*Steal?*" He expelled a harsh breath. "That's not how I remember it. Seems to me I only fulfilled your birthday wish."

He was right, of course. He would never have dared touch her if she hadn't encouraged him, Summer knew. She'd spent months trying to get this man to notice her, trying to get him to break. She'd teased and taunted him all summer, subtly casting out lures and covert glances and secret smiles, flirting outrageously with her other beaux in front of him in a vain attempt to make him jealous.

Lance might have been a stone statue for all the attention he paid her.

He had ignored her until she was ready to scream, until her feminine pique had become a desire for retribution, a driving need to have him pay her homage. She was determined to conquer his stoic reserve, to bring him to his knees . . . if she could. Only, taming this fierce, half-civilized male no longer seemed as easy as her fantasies had led her to believe. The challenge of having him succumb to her feminine charms had backfired, if the breathless trembling of her body now was any indication. With a single kiss Lance had left her feeling shaken and uncertain and defenseless. *Her* knees were the weak ones, Summer discovered to her dismay when Lance suddenly released her.

She reached out and clutched at the rope swing that hung from a pecan limb overhead. Watching him turn away, she wondered if he meant to abandon her.

"Don't go," she was surprised into saying.

For a moment she thought he meant to ignore her plea. But he merely leaned a muscular shoulder against the trunk of the pecan tree, as if he planned to stay a bit longer, even against his will.

Summer let out her breath in relief. Unsteadily she lowered herself into the swing, carefully spreading her wide hooped skirts over the wooden seat. Her party gown of pink organdy and gros point lace was fabulously expensive and quite grown-up, but Lance hadn't said a single complimentary word about her appearance. Not that she'd expected him to. He spoke rarely, although she would never have called him a quiet man. It was more like he was holding all his anger, all his violent thoughts and feelings, inside, waiting to explode.

"I'm a damned fool," she heard him mutter. "Your pa wouldn't stop with taking a horsewhip to me if he caught me here with you."

He was right about that, too, Summer thought, glancing over her shoulder at her family's big, white frame ranch house with its slender wooden columns gracing the lower story. Papa would have an apoplectic fit if he knew she was out here in the dark with a "murdering savage."

Papa called all Indians murdering savages. Ever since Mama had died so horribly in a Comanche raid thirteen years ago, he hadn't been able to bear the sight of one. Ordinarily not even the fact that Lance Calder was probably the best mustanger in Texas would be sufficient reason to let him set foot on the Sky Valley Ranch. Nor even the recommendation of one of Papa's most respected friends, the Texas Ranger who had looked out for Lance after his mama passed on.

But Lance had saved her brother Reed's life last spring during a stagecoach ambush, which had earned him the chance to hire on as a wrangler. Papa raised horses, and so far Lance had proven his worth a dozen times over—but that didn't mean he would ever be accepted as a civilized man.

His looks were a strike against him, Summer thought with a covert glance at him from beneath her lashes. Not that he wasn't handsome. That wasn't the case at all, despite the harsh angles and planes of his bronzed features. His complexion was not overly dark, either—no more than if he'd been burned by the sun. But there was no doubt he was part Indian, with his skin pulled taut over high cheekbones and his wild mane of coal black hair streaming beyond his shoulders. He wore his hair long—out of sheer defiance, she suspected. Broadcasting the fact that he was an Indian. And Texans didn't take kindly to uppity Indians.

Certainly Lance hadn't been invited to the party celebrating her seventeenth birthday. Her papa would never have allowed an Indian inside the house, especially not a Comanche, even a half-breed who claimed to be white. She had been willing to risk her father's rage, however, for the chance to put a notch in Lance's invincibility.

Her birthday festivities had ended an hour ago, the well-wishers returning to their farms and stock ranches. This morning Summer had promised to save Lance a piece of birthday cake if he would come up to the house after the party, yet she hadn't known if he would. She'd waited anxiously throughout the interminable day and evening, hoping fervently that he wouldn't be able to resist the temptation of the sweet confection she'd promised, not daring to believe that her own allure might draw him.

Whatever his reason, he had come.

Still, he had barely glanced at the napkin-wrapped package before putting it in his vest side pocket and, with a quiet "Thank you kindly, ma'am," turning to go. That was when she had made her scandalous suggestion—that he grant her birthday wish and kiss her. He had looked at her long and hard before pulling her into his arms and complying.

"You never did answer my question, ma'am," he said, interrupting her thoughts as she swayed absently in the swing.

"W-What question?"

"About my kiss. You never said how it was different from all your other gents'."

Without volition, Summer loosened her grip on the rope and edged her fingers to her lips. They were tender from Lance's passion, still dewy from his mouth. The taste of him still lingered on her tongue. He should know the answer to his question. His kiss was nothing like the chaste, gentlemanly pecks she had sometimes allowed her suitors. *He* was nothing like them. Lance Calder had fascinated her from the moment he'd arrived in Sky Valley this past spring.

She couldn't explain her enthrallment with him, unless it was the allure of danger he represented. It most *certainly* was not his charming personality that attracted her. He was as friendly as a wounded wolf, and twice as wary. He was quite obviously sensitive about being thought of as a savage. Yet he made no apologies for his mixed blood. Indeed, he wore his defiance like a shield, his smoldering look daring anyone to call him a breed.

Add to that his knack for making her feel young and naive and absurdly awkward, and she couldn't understand her attraction for him. He didn't even seem to like her. She always wondered if he could see right through her with his sharp ebony eyes. He was watching her now with that piercing gaze, his look hard and intense. Or rather he was watching her mouth, as if he would like to kiss her again but wouldn't let himself.

"I really couldn't say," she replied unsteadily, remembering the taste of his kiss, the powerful feel of his lips moving over hers. "I don't have the experience to compare."

His soft huff of laughter was more like a snort. "You collect men's hearts for the sheer challenge of it, Miss Weston, ma'am. You won't make me believe that whopper about no experience."

"Will you *please* quit calling me *ma'am* in that odious tone of voice?" she demanded, thoroughly unsettled now by the brooding way he was looking at her.

"Yes, indeed. Whatever you say, Miss Weston."

Humility did not become him, Summer decided with asperity.

Clenching her teeth, she turned her head and lifted her gaze, looking beyond the canopy of pecan leaves. It was a beautiful night, with myriad stars blazing overhead in the vast black-velvet sky. She could hear the low chorus of chirruping crickets, the mating song of bullfrogs down by the creek. A perfect setting for her plan—except that this interview was not going at all as she'd intended. Lance's kiss had overwhelmed her, making her feel like a naive child playing with fire. And now he seemed intent on picking a fight. She didn't know why, except that maybe he was mad at her for winning their months-long battle of wills, for finally proving her power over him.

"Maybe you're right, Miss Summer. 'Ma'am' doesn't suit you. How about 'princess'?"

She gave him a sharp glance, certain that he was scoffing at her. "I'm not a princess."

"Sure you are." He waved a hand expansively, indicating their surroundings. "You live here in your ivory tower, sheltered and protected, showered with luxuries. Never known a real hard knock in your life."

"If you only meant to insult me, then why did you come here tonight?"

"Like I said, I'm a damned fool."

With one silk-slippered foot, she gave herself an abrupt push on the swing. It was true that she'd been spoiled and petted by her father and her three adoring older brothers, as well as courted and admired by the single gentlemen in three counties. She even admitted to behaving a bit wildly of late, since the one steadying influence in her life was gone: her older sister, Amelia, who had raised her from a baby. Amelia had married a farmer last year and moved to a new settlement in north Texas with her husband's family. Summer missed her sister dreadfully. Without her, growing up was harder, lonelier. But it was more than that. Now she had no one to ease her restlessness, her fears.

Lance was right. She *had* lived a sheltered life, pampered and loved and indulged. But her safe world was changing before her eyes. All during the long, hot summer there had been rumblings of war and talk of secession by the southern states, accompanied by vigorous debates on whether Texas should join in. Her own brothers were bitterly divided on the subject. The political tension straining her family was being played out all over the state, and seemed to be gathering momentum like a runaway team. Truthfully, her pursuit of Lance had begun merely as a way to forget her worries, to give herself something else to dwell on other than her fears. Once she'd started, though, she hadn't been able to stop.

She wondered what Lance thought about the possibility of war. He was as much a true Texan as anyone—more so, actually. She'd heard his story from her brother Reed. Lance was originally from Austin; his mama had been one of the first American settlers in the area before being taken captive by the Comanche and suffering untold degradations. They'd been rescued when Lance was just a baby, but even though it had outraged their neighbors, Charlotte Calder wouldn't give up her child.

It must have been a hard life for a single woman trying to raise a child of mixed blood born out of wedlock, especially in Austin, which had been a bastion of rectitude back then. It must have been harder for Lance, a defenseless child, growing up in the face of all that hostility. Texans never did anything by half measures, and they hated the Comanches with a passion. And Lance, with his rebellious nature, only made matters worse. When he was twelve, his mama had died and he'd run away to live with the Comanches for several years—his father's people, Summer understood—and some whites never forgave him for that, either. Afterward he'd lived in Round Rock, five miles or so from the Westons' Sky Valley Ranch, with Tom Peace, the Texan Ranger who'd offered Lance a job when he'd returned to civilization. The past several years Lance had spent catching and breaking wild mustangs farther west—an experience that made him an extremely valuable hand on a stock ranch.

"I would never have taken you for a fool," she replied with certainty.

"Well, fool or no, I don't aim to act like all the other in-fatuated males, fawning all over you."

Summer tossed her head, making her glossy dark ringlets sway. She was young, but not so young as to be unaware of her effect on men. She was the Belle of Williamson County, and as such, she deserved the respect due a lady. At least she'd always thought so until tonight, when Lance had confused her with his fierce kisses and made mock of her attempts to charm him.

"Do you mean to say you don't find me attractive?"

He shrugged a lean shoulder. "I don't mean any such thing. But you don't need me to tell you how beautiful you are. Or to feed your vanity."

But she did. Her feminine heart needed reassurance. "You didn't like kissing me?"

"I liked it well enough, princess. What I didn't like was you using me for your play toy."

Flushing, she looked away. "I didn't."

"Sure you did. Why else would you invite me up here except to try your wiles out on me? You've been waiting for a chance to corner me all summer."

What could she say in her defense? That she hadn't spent the past five months watching Lance and wondering what it would be like to have him attracted to her, to have him look at her with desire? To deny it outright would be a lie. But Lance wronged her if he thought she was only testing her own power when she had asked him to kiss her. She had wanted his kiss, more than she'd wanted anything in a long while.

"Well, nobody forced you to kiss me. You didn't have to if you didn't want to."

"I wanted to, princess. I wouldn't be a man if I didn't want to." His half smile was hard, self-mocking. "But I don't aim to become part of your collection."

Summer felt the bittersweetness of that smile arrow straight to her heart. She had never really seen Lance smile. Not a true smile of pleasure or joy. She wondered what it would take to coax a real smile from him. What it would take to make him look at a woman—to look at *her*—with love in his eyes instead of that rebellious, brooding stare that was so much a part of him. She thought she might like to try.

Tilting her head to one side, she softened her expression, giving him a questioning look of appeal. "Do you truly think me so vain and shallow?"

"I don't think you want an honest answer to that."

She bit her lip. "Well, *I* think it mean-spirited of you to blame me for my circumstances. I can't help it if I've never had to suffer life's misfortunes."

His deliberate silence spoke volumes. Uncomfortable, Summer thought it best to change the subject—and to satisfy her curiosity at the same time. "You ridiculed me for my experience. What about yours? Where did you learn to kiss like that?"

"You don't want to know."

"Yes, I do so. And please quit telling me what I might or might not want."

"Okay, then. I learned it from one of the whores in Georgetown who didn't mind bedding down with a redskin."

"Oh." Her tone was faint.

"You asked, princess."

"Well, you didn't have to tell me! You shouldn't say such things to a lady," she protested, even as she recognized the silliness of her rebuke.

His hard mouth curled at the corner.

"Have you kissed a lot of ladies?"

"If I had, it would hardly be a gentlemanly thing to admit,

now would it?" He paused. "That's what you want, isn't it?
A gentleman?"

"I like a man to be gentlemanly and polite, yes. My sister
raised me to value good manners."

"I'm sure she did. Miss Amelia always put great store in
such things. Why, she could write a book on manners, I'll
bet. I remember when I was a boy working at the livery,
when your pa brought your family to town. Miss Amelia always looked straight through me, just like I didn't exist. I
was beneath her notice, like horse manure she didn't want to
step on. Set a prime example of fine manners, I'd say."

Stiffening at his sarcasm, Summer came to her sister's defense. "Amelia didn't mean anything by it. She was just
afraid of you being part Comanche. She couldn't forget how
our mama died."

"And you could?"

Summer thought about his question. "I was young when it
happened, so I don't remember it as well as she does. And I
don't think it's fair to blame you for what someone else did."

"So why are you bothering with the likes of me, princess?
Taking pity on the savage breed? Or trying out your latest
tricks, to see if you can make me dance to your tune?"

Summer flushed, uncomfortable with Lance's discernment.
She took refuge in righteous indignation. "Will you *please*
stop calling yourself that?"

"What, breed? Why? That's what I am."

"Perhaps, but you don't have to keep flinging it in everyone's face as if it were some sort of badge of honor! Or a red
flag in front of a bull!"

She could tell by the way his obsidian eyes narrowed that
she had made him angry again, but she didn't care. If Lance
was intent on plain speaking, he deserved to hear a few home
truths of his own.

"Besides," she added more softly, relenting, "I don't think of
you as a savage. It doesn't matter to me if you're part Indian."

"It would matter if I was to come courting you."

The smile she had started to offer faded at his remark. It
was one thing to indulge in a stolen kiss or two with a man
she had no business even looking at. It was quite another to
contemplate a courtship. "Well, yes . . . in that case, it would.
Papa would never approve—"

"What about you? What would you say?"

She remained silent. What she thought made no difference. Even if the forbidden notion appealed to her, even if she secretly wondered what it would be like to experience passion at Lance's hands, even if she thought it might be exciting to try and tame a man like him, she would never be allowed the opportunity. It just wasn't done.

"I won't always be just a hired hand," he said into her silence. "Someday I'll have enough for a stake in some land. But"—his voice grew quiet—"that wouldn't be enough, would it? A man like me could never aspire to winning the hand of a princess like you."

She heard the soft acceptance in his voice, the bitterness, the regret, and wanted to deny it. But there was nothing she could say. It was a simple fact of life that young ladies of good family did not marry men of mixed blood, no matter what their connections in the white world, no matter how much either of them wished things might be different. She gazed up at him in mute sympathy.

"I guess a man can always dream," he murmured, almost as if he'd forgotten she was there.

He laughed then, harshly, humorlessly, and shook his head, as if to deny his wistful reflection. "What do I want with your highfalutin white ways?" he muttered. His tone was cynical, self-mocking, and yet she couldn't help thinking he just didn't want her to know how much he really cared about his position in society, about being as outcast. He looked at her again with that damn-your-eyes stare, and yet suddenly somehow she knew, with an elemental feminine instinct, that his mockery was a mask of bravado he'd adopted for the world to see, to cover up his vulnerability.

The silence stretched between them for a score of heartbeats. It was odd, but she could almost sense what Lance was thinking, what he was wishing. His dark face might have been carved from stone for all the emotion he showed, and yet she could feel his pain.

Slowly then, as if sleepwalking, he pushed himself away from the pecan tree and, with the silent stride of the true Indian, moved to stand before her. Reaching out a hand, Lance stopped the lazy motion of the swing. Summer sat silently looking up at him, a question in her eyes.

In response, he reached down and drew her to her feet.

Disquieted by the intensity of his gaze, she placed a slender hand on his chest to ward him off.

"You wanted a birthday kiss," he said in a low voice.

"Yes, but . . . you already . . . I've been out here too long as it is. Someone might come looking for me."

"Losing your nerve, princess?"

She didn't reply. She couldn't, for her breath had suddenly caught in her throat.

Lance raised his hand to her bosom, where several mahogany curls rested in teasing disarray. Gently, almost reverently, he brushed them aside, baring her throat to his hand. His fingers lifted, spread along the edge of her jaw.

"If I can't have the real thing . . . if all I can do is dream . . . I want a memory I can build on."

She could see the desire in his eyes, the longing, and felt the same overwhelming sensation flowing into her. Hesitantly, hungrily, she raised her face to this, offering her lips. She wanted it, his kiss. She wanted to give him a memory to take with him. She wanted a memory of her own to hold.

She felt the erratic beat of his heart beneath her fingertips as his warm lips covered hers, as they began to move with hard insistence. This kiss was not gentle either, but neither was it savage like before. This was hungry and lonely and raw, with a poignant edge of tenderness that had been entirely missing in his first kiss.

A shiver of yearning and pleasure swept through her. *This* was what she had hoped for from him. This bittersweet bonding that made her feel like a woman, made her feel desired by this hard, forbidden, intensely proud man—

"What the devil?" The sharp exclamation behind her startled Summer so badly that she jumped. Breaking off the kiss, she looked back to see her brother Reed barrel down the porch steps toward her.

She had no time to protest or explain, though, before he reached her, before he grabbed her arm and pulled her from Lance's embrace with a strength that made her stumble.

From the corner of her eye she saw Lance take an abrupt step in her direction, heard the soft oath he voiced, but Reed shoved himself between them and let his fist fly, connecting squarely with Lance's jaw and felling him to the ground.

Lance didn't stay down. With incredible agility he rolled to his feet and balanced in a defensive crouch, his arms slightly raised to allow the greatest freedom of movement. The long knife that had suddenly materialized in his right hand gleamed wickedly in the lamplight.

Summer screamed in fear. She wanted to do something, to intervene between the two hostile men, but she found herself frozen in horror as she watched to see what Lance would do.

Reed stood his ground, his fists balled in protective fury. "How *dare* you touch my sister!"

"R-Reed, stop!" she cried breathlessly, finally finding her voice. "Don't! I can explain—"

"Summer, get inside the house! Now."

"No! You don't understand—"

"Stay out of this, Summer," Lance interrupted, just as her brother retorted, "I understand plenty. He put his hands on you."

"No—" Her denial turned into a gasp as Reed took a step toward the wicked knife—but then the sound of the back door slamming open made them both fall silent. Frantic, Summer glanced back to find her father standing at the head of the porch steps, her two other brothers, Jamison and Tyler, directly behind him.

John Weston took one look at the combatants, at the knife in Lance's hand, and stiffened with rage. "I should have known better than to trust you, you devil. I want you to clear out, do you hear me?"

She saw Lance go rigid, saw his fingers clench as he gripped the knife more tightly.

"Papa, no!"

"Be quiet, Summer. You have ten minutes, Calder. Get your gear and get off my land, or I'll haul out the bullwhip and give you the thrashing of your life."

"Papa—" Summer started to protest, but felt her brother's fingers dig into her arm in warning as he hissed in her ear, "Shut up, Summer! Pa's mad enough as it is. If he finds out Lance touched you, he'll kill him."

That made her hesitate. Another look at the irrational fury on her father's face made her realize the danger. Papa had an insane hatred of Indians after what they had done to his wife, and he wouldn't stop at a simple whipping if she told him that Lance had kissed her, even if it was at her request.

"Dammit, did you hear me, you red bastard?" John Weston demanded.

Lance slowly straightened, any hint of emotion wiped from his copper-hued features. His face looked as if it had been carved from stone.

"You're finished here. And I'll make sure you don't work anywhere in this part of Texas."

Summer turned pleading eyes on her brother. "Reed, you have to do something!"

Looking uncomfortable, Reed spoke up. "Pa, maybe you're being hasty. We just had a difference of opinion—"

"He pulled a knife on you. That's reason enough to fire him."

"But maybe it—"

"Shut up, son!" John Weston snapped. "I won't have a murdering savage threatening to slit our throats whenever he takes a notion. Get going, Calder. You have nine minutes left."

Recognizing the finality in her father's tone, Summer knew she was powerless to change his mind. It would be futile to try. At least right now, when he was in such a towering rage. Perhaps tomorrow she might be able to persuade him. . . . She sent Lance an agonized look. He stood alone, apart, in the darkness, his fists clenched in defiance.

It was all her fault, she knew. She hadn't considered the consequences of her actions. Her vanity, her selfishness, her blind pursuit of her own desires, had led to this. She'd cost Lance his job, his pride, had hurt him dreadfully. She hadn't meant for this to happen. She couldn't blame him if he hated her. She held out her hand in a helpless little gesture of pleading.

He was watching her, his expression shuttered. Abruptly he turned and headed for the bunkhouse.

"Lance, please!" she cried after him.

He stiffened at the sound of her voice, halting in his tracks.

"I'm sorry. I'm so very sorry. . . ."

He glanced back briefly, and his eyes could have chipped flint. "Don't bother with your pity, princess. I should have known better than to play your little games."

"Summer, get inside!"

She ignored her father's order. In turmoil, she stood staring after Lance as he walked away, her fingers held to her lips, remembering the taste of his kiss and the bitter hatred in his eyes before he turned from her in anger.

Chapter 1

~~~⟡⟡~~~

Texas, 1865

Dreams had a hard way of dying, no matter how impossible.

His jaw set rigidly, Lance Calder turned his sorrel horse off the rocky trail and rode slowly toward the Weston ranch house. He'd sworn never to set foot here again, but Summer's letter had drawn him against his will.

I don't expect you to forgive me, but I hope you will find it in your heart to listen to my plea.

His mouth curled in self-mockery as he pulled his horse up. Was he about to get caught in her silken snare again?

Except for the fading paint, the house looked much as he remembered: a graceful two-story white colonial, with slender oak columns supporting a veranda in front and rear, and finished with weatherboard hauled all the way from Austin. Beyond, in the near distance, he could see the sprawling hills of Sky Valley. The rugged land stretched forever, raw and beautiful, dotted with clumps of woodland and pockets of rich pasture, teeming with wild game and herds of half-tame range horses.

Lance tried to survey the scene with cold detachment but failed. This was the kind of land that buried deep in a man's soul—and it had gotten into his.

He tilted his head back, looking up at the cloudless stretch of blue heaven, warmed by the September sun. John Weston had called this spread Sky Valley because the vast Texas sky seemed so close, you could reach up and grab a piece.

John Weston was dead now. A bad heart had taken him after his two oldest sons had died fighting for the Confederacy.

Lance felt no grief for the man. Weston had considered him no better than dirt . . . a murdering savage. The shaming

15

words still echoed in his ears; the indignity of being run out of the county still stung. He'd dared to touch Weston's white daughter and been made to pay for it.

And Summer . . . It was unlikely she could have changed her father's mind, Lance knew, even if she'd tried to defend him. But she hadn't tried. She'd left him to hang.

The bitter resentment still burned in his gut.

He'd had a dream. He'd vowed that one day he'd have enough money, enough power, enough respect, that his Comanche blood wouldn't matter. That one day he'd be able to claim his princess . . .

"Damned fool," Lance muttered to himself. Dreaming made a man vulnerable, weak.

And yet he couldn't stop his thoughts from returning to a warm August night and the girl he'd held in his arms for a fleeting moment. Her kiss was a blurred memory, but it still had the power to leave him shaken.

He stared blindly across the valley, his distant thoughts all wrapped up in the past and the desire he'd once felt for Summer Weston. Summer . . . a girl with skin as soft and white as magnolia petals, a voice as sweet and soothing as honey, laughter as lilting and musical as wind in the trees. She was all the things he'd never had, all the things he'd always wanted. She represented everything he'd ever hoped for in life: a home, family, position . . . acceptance. She symbolized everything he hated—the white world that had shunned him, made his mother's life hell.

As a kid, he used to care for her father's horses when the Weston family came to town for the day. Even then Summer'd been a charmer, all decked out in ruffles and bows, so feminine and delicate, it made his heart ache to see something so pretty. She hadn't spoken much to him then, but she'd smiled sometimes. And she had never looked at him with contempt the way other whites did. Whites like her father, her sister, Amelia.

Later he'd gone to work at her father's ranch and discovered just how shallow and cruel she could be.

He'd known better than to let himself get mixed up with her. At sixteen, Summer was headstrong and beautiful, with a well-deserved reputation for breaking hearts. He'd watched for months as she'd charmed and flirted and teased her way past anything male. He'd seen her holding court with her starry-eyed, lust-stricken beaux—and then stood in line just like the rest of them. She was spoiled and self-centered and childish, but he wanted her bad, he ached with it.

Did a man ever get over his first love?

He was staggered when she deigned to notice the breed hired hand. She was bored, no doubt. Probably curious to see if she could work her wiles on someone with his heritage. Her flirtations were all quite innocent—and as cruel as any taunt or insult flung at him by bigoted whites over the years. She didn't know that she was carving up his heart inch by inch, dangling out hope, making him yearn for things he could never have, dreams he could never realize. She played her heartless little female games without regard for the consequences, without caring who she hurt—and he'd been fool enough to let her.

He'd known the risk he was taking, meeting her at night, letting her taunt him into kissing her. Even then his only defense against her had been anger. He'd been mad as hell at himself for being unable to resist the temptation. He'd hated himself for his weakness, for giving her such a hold over him, for letting her enchant him, drive him crazy with desire for her, for letting her manipulate him with her alluring female tricks in a way no red-blooded man could resist.

Well, he damned sure wasn't going to make that mistake again, Lance swore. He wasn't going to let her sink her claws into him again. He'd learned his lesson. And he'd gotten over her in the five years since he'd been driven away.

Even so, he didn't want to push his luck. Ever since he'd returned to Round Rock four months ago to take over the livery stable Tom Peace had left him, he had done his level best to avoid Summer.

He'd seen her from a distance, though. Summer Weston was no longer a girl. She'd grown into a fine lady. She was not so proud now, either.

A cynical smile twisted his mouth. *Now that she needed him.*

Lance raised a hand to cover his breast, feeling her letter burning a hole in his vest pocket.

I don't expect you to forgive me, but I hope you will find it in your heart to listen to my plea.

She was willing to speak to him now that she needed

something from him. Five years without a word, and she expected him to come running.

His anger swelled again. Anger at his inferior station. Anger at the blind bigotry that'd kept him on the outskirts of the white community, looking in, all his life. Anger at being driven off this ranch five years ago.

Anger had a way of twisting a man, hardening the heart—

His horse snorted just then, splintering his brooding thoughts into fragments. With a heedless jerk on the reins, Lance turned the sorrel gelding, heading for the side of the ranch house.

He knew what Summer wanted from him. He just didn't know how he was going to reply.

He circled around the house and approached from the rear, near the creek, his narrowed gaze taking in his surroundings. The outbuildings necessary for a prosperous stock ranch— barn, corrals of both stone and split rail, bunkhouse for the vaqueros, chicken coop, dairy, and tool sheds—all showed signs of neglect. But then, he would have been surprised to find it otherwise. Most able-bodied men had gone off to fight the war, leaving their women to forge on alone.

A lot of those able-bodied men now filled the yard in back of the main house, perched on wagon seats, sitting in buggies, riding horseback.

Keeping his distance, Lance drew the sorrel to a halt. From the sound of it, he had interrupted an argument. He recognized the man with dark brown hair, supported by crutches, who held forth on the back porch, making an impassioned plea to the crowd for support. Reed Weston was missing half his left leg— which hadn't garnered him as much sympathy as might be expected, since he'd lost it fighting for the Union while hailing from a state that had declared for the Confederacy.

After a single glance, though, Lance only had eyes for Reed's sister. Summer stood beside him, looking regal and strangely vulnerable in a long-sleeved black gown that showed she was still in mourning for her brothers and father.

Despite his best intentions, Lance couldn't stop the fierce acceleration of his heartbeat. Even from this distance he saw that the beautiful girl he'd known had grown into a stunning woman. His memories, even as potent as they were, didn't do her justice.

But there were differences.

Her hair, the color of mahogany, gleamed with red and gold highlights in the afternoon sun, just as rich and lustrous as he remembered. But instead of ringlets, she wore it swept back into a chignon, bound by black net. The wide-spaced green eyes that could flash with the brilliance of emeralds held no laughter now; instead they were solemn and somber as she gazed out over the crowd. She looked as if she'd lost weight. Her hands were slender and white, but she held them clasped before her in an attitude of nervous anticipation. Her lips—the soft pink lips he'd once been allowed to kiss on a warm August night—held no seductive, mind-bewitching smile.

Remembering the feel of those lips, Lance involuntarily dragged his gaze away to focus on the tall pecan tree that stood to one side of the yard. The wooden swing was still there, unmoving and lifeless, a silent testimony to all that had happened since that night—

"Thanks for coming."

Lance stiffened at the quiet sound, not liking the fact that he'd allowed a man to approach him without his even being aware of it. Turning in the saddle, he met a pair of grave blue eyes whose corners were lined and weathered by the sun.

Dusty Murdock had once been a hired hand but was now the foreman of the Weston ranch. Tall and lanky, with dirty-blond hair, Dusty was older than Lance by some ten years. Fair, easygoing, nonjudgmental, he was also one of the few men Lance respected without question.

"Miss Summer will be glad you could make it."

Lance nodded curtly, acknowledging the comment, but turned his attention back to the crowd and the argument that was taking place.

"It isn't goin' too well, I'm afraid," Dusty went on in his quiet voice. "Nobody quite sees it like we do. They're sorry and all, but Miss Amelia isn't their kin. What with the war finally over, all anybody wants is to get back to living their lives."

As if to underscore Dusty's comment, an older man who seemed to be the leader of the opposition spoke again. "Reed, you have to understand. All we want is a chance to put our lives back in order, fix up our farms, start rebuilding again."

Lance recognized the older man as Harlan Fisk, one of the

acknowledged leaders of the community, but there were others he didn't know who obviously shared Fisk's view.

"You're asking us to leave our families," another man added. "These are dangerous times. Who's gonna protect our families from all the vagrants roamin' around while we're gone?"

"Yeah. We'd likely be gone a long while," someone else chimed in. "It's near three hundred miles to Indian Territory."

"I hate to dash your hopes, Reed," Harlan Fisk said, "but the likelihood of finding her isn't very good, even if she's still alive. And getting her back is going to be nigh impossible. Once the Comanches take a captive, they won't give 'em up easy. We could get killed just trying."

"I know the attempt will be dangerous," Reed replied with strained patience. "And you have a right to be afraid. But—"

"I ain't scared of no Injuns," one man interrupted. "I rode against them savage devils once for a massacre they done. But that don't mean I'm stupid enough to go courtin' trouble with 'em."

"Besides, it's so far away. We can't afford to be gone for that long, not on some wild-goose chase."

Harlan Fisk spoke again. "Reed, son, you're just asking too much."

"Is it too much?" Reed demanded. "I'd do the same for you if it were your sister who'd been taken."

"Says the man who turned on his own kind during the war," somebody muttered.

Reed visibly stiffened, even as his eyes narrowed. "I did what I felt was right, which is what every one of you did. You followed the dictates of your conscience. Still, if you won't do it for me, then do it for the memory of my father and brothers. They were on your side."

The silence that followed his impassioned speech told its own tale.

After a long moment his sister spoke, the anguish in her quiet voice clear. "We are leaving tomorrow for Fort Belknap. I can only ask that some of you will find it in your hearts to join with us."

Slowly, pointedly, Summer searched the individual faces of the crowd, moving from one to another to another, focusing on men who abruptly lowered their eyes, apparently uncomfortable with meeting her green gaze.

Lance's mouth twisted sardonically as he watched. Some of these men were the same ones Summer used to lead around by the nose as boys, the ones who used to pant after her, eager to do her bidding. Lance had little doubt that she could persuade them to help her now if she put her mind to it.

Beside him, Dusty muttered an oath. "Miss Summer was going to ask you to lead the posse, but at this rate, it doesn't look like they'll be able to raise much of one."

Lance didn't answer, for Summer had suddenly caught sight of him. He saw her give a slight start—and then recover—before her gaze moved on. But her action caused some of the others to finally notice his presence.

"Well, if it ain't our resident Injun," a sneering voice remarked.

All eyes turned in Lance's direction.

"Yep, sure is," he drawled in return. "You gonna make something of it, Prewitt?"

The man he'd recognized as Will Prewitt glared back at him.

Harlan Fisk was the first to interrupt the suddenly tense silence. "You should ask Calder to go after your sister, Reed. He's likely to have better luck than the rest of us, what with it being his people who took Amelia."

"I intend to," Reed replied slowly, evidently choosing his words with care. "I appreciate the fact that Mr. Calder was kind enough to respond to our invitation to come here today. Welcome, Mr. Calder."

"So it's *Mister* Calder now, is it?" Will Prewitt jeered. "You making deals with savages now, huh, Reed?"

"Shut up, Prewitt!" Reed snapped back. "I'd deal with the Devil himself if I thought it could help get Amelia back."

Prewitt gave a harsh laugh. "Well, maybe it ain't such a stupid notion after all. Only an Injun would be crazy enough to ride into Injun Territory an' face them Comanche devils."

Lance felt his fact stiffen, drain of all expression. As usual, the sting of the slur wasn't as bad as hearing them talk about him as if he weren't there, but both made the lifelong resentment flare in his gut.

He surveyed the crowd with a cold stare, returning the same contempt they'd offered him. "You let me know when you're ready to deal with the Devil."

Picking up his reins, he backed the sorrel a few steps, then turned abruptly, riding away without another glance. He heard Dusty utter another oath, thought he heard Summer cry out his name, but at the moment he didn't give a damn. Let Weston and his ilk figure out how to solve their problems, and leave him out of it. Sister Amelia could rot in captivity for all he cared. At the moment he just didn't give a fucking damn.

Summer went after Lance; she had to make amends for the inexcusable way he had been treated, especially if she had any hope at all of persuading him to help her. Instead of taking the long route around back, however, she cut through the house, hoping to intercept Lance on the main road.

Picking up her crinolined skirts, she raced down the front steps and across the overgrown lawn of bluestem prairie grass. She could see his retreating figure on horseback disappearing around the line of post oaks that flanked the road.

"Lance! Wait! Please . . ."

At first she thought he meant to ignore her, but when she cried his name again, he tugged on the reins and halted his horse.

He didn't turn, though. He sat rigidly in the saddle, his back to her. From the looks of it, he was in no mood to listen—or to forgive.

She was panting for breath by the time she reached him; her corset was too tight for such exertions. She stood there beside his horse, one hand held to her heart as she tried to catch her breath.

"Lance . . . please . . . I'm sorry. . . ." she managed to get out. "Will Prewitt had no right . . . to say those hateful things."

He turned the full force of those black eyes on her, and she could see the smoldering anger there. It was the same look he'd given her five years ago, the same anger. Apparently he hadn't forgotten what she'd done—luring him into a reckless embrace and then getting him fired for it.

She winced at the impact of that fierce gaze. He had every right to be angry with her. Her father had been justifiably incensed at him for pulling a knife on Reed, but it was *her* fault Lance had done it. She had caused the fight, and then hadn't defended him. She hadn't stood up for him with enough fervor, hadn't protested his dismissal strongly enough. She had tried later to find Lance and apologize, but by then he had left town for good. She'd asked both Reed and Dusty to let her know if they discovered where Lance had gone, but it was nearly a year later before she learned he'd taken up driving stages again somewhere out West.

She hadn't meant to hurt him. She had wanted to bring him to his knees, yes, but not that way.

"You interested in making a deal with the Devil, too, princess?"

His handsome face was dark, hard, unsmiling. Harder than she remembered, but just as compelling. The coal black hair beneath his hat was a bit shorter, more civilized, but he still looked at her in that same intense, brooding way: part resentment, part contempt, part desire for her as a woman.

She was feminine enough to recognize that desire. And respond to it. No man but Lance had ever made her knees go weak with merely a look. She still felt the pull of sexual attraction between them.

It gave her reason to hope. As long as he felt something for her—even if he was fighting it—she still stood a chance of persuading him to help her.

"Reed . . . didn't mean it the way it sounded. You have to understand . . . he's out of his mind with worry for Amelia."

"Oh, I understand just fine. Treat the savage redskin gentle-like as long as he can be of some use. Your pa felt the same way."

Lance heard the hostility in his voice, but he couldn't stop it, didn't want to try. He couldn't hold Summer to blame for everything the white world had done to him. Still, there was a part of him that bitterly resented everything she stood for, that wanted revenge for every slur, every insult, every hateful word thrown at him and his mother over the years.

She bit her lip at his retort. "I tried to convince Papa to change his mind, but he . . . I'm sorry, Lance. I never meant to cause trouble for you. I wanted to apologize to you, but you left town so suddenly. . . . When I looked for you, you were gone."

Lance clenched his jaw. Had she really tried to find him? Had she defied her father for his sake? Her look of pain and regret was so real, he almost believed her.

"I've been back in town four months now. Plenty of time for you to look me up."

She knew exactly when Lance had returned to town; Dusty had informed her, just as she'd asked him to. But she hadn't known quite how to approach Lance after all this time. And she'd spent most of her energy nursing her brother, Reed, after his terrible injury. "I know. . . . It's just that the war . . . Things have been difficult lately."

"Have they now, princess? Well, isn't that a damned shame."

She shook her head in denial at his tone, at his scornful diminutive for her. She was a princess no longer. It had taken that terrible injustice to Lance to make her realize just how shallow and selfish she'd been, but she *had* changed. She'd been forced to. The safe, sheltered world she'd known was gone, collapsed in devastating ruin around her during the interminable war. She was older now, both in years and experience. She'd aged a decade since the war began. Facing hardship and loss had made her grow up. Out of necessity, she'd learned the meaning of hard work, of pain, of dashed hopes. Indeed, it made her ashamed to think what a spoiled, worthless darling she'd once been.

"Please . . . I said I was sorry."

He clenched his jaw so hard, a muscle jumped. Wishing she could make him think better of her, Summer gazed up at him, searching his harsh, strong-boned face for any sign of softness. "I heard that after you left, you drove a stagecoach for a time. The Overland Route. It must have been dangerous."

He shrugged. "It was a living. Better than getting shot on a battlefield."

"You didn't join the Army?"

"The Confederacy? Nope. Couldn't agree with their politics. Something your brother, Reed, and I have in common. I went back to breaking horses again. Sold them to the Union Army."

"I'm glad you came home."

His dark eyes narrowed in suspicion at her soft tone. "I only came back here because Peace left me his livery."

She nodded as if she understood. "I was sorry about Mr. Peace. He was a good man."

"A lot of good men died in the war."

"I know. My brothers . . ."

Her green eyes suddenly shimmered with tears, and Lance felt his gut tighten. There was nothing feigned about her anguish, the way her lower lip trembled. He could have kicked himself; he had no call to be so cruel, reminding her of her loss—even if cruelty was his best defense against her.

"I was sorry to hear about your brothers," he said gruffly, grudgingly.

"Thank you." She swallowed with effort and forced a tremulous little smile that pierced his heart like an arrow. "I'm glad Mr. Peace left you his livery stable."

"You're the only one, then." His mouth twisted in that bitter way of his—half-sardonic, half-defiant. "Came as a shock to the good citizens of Round Rock to have to consider me one of their own. A savage *and* a Union sympathizer."

She wished he wouldn't be so hard on himself, or on the people around him. Hurting for him, she raised her hand to touch his denim-covered thigh in mute appeal. He flinched visibly, and made his horse sidle away from her, out of reach.

"Lance . . . I . . . I wanted to ask you—"

"The answer is no."

"Please, won't you just listen to what I have to say?"

He averted his gaze, looking down the road, impatient to leave. He'd be a damned fool to get involved with her again, to leave himself open to the kind of hurt he'd suffered five years ago. He'd lied to himself about why he'd come here today. He'd told himself he was simply curious to see Summer after all this time, that he only wanted to hear her ask him for a favor, to have her admit that she needed him. But he was wrong. Dead wrong. He still wanted her as much as ever, damn her. If he could just keep away from her, though, he'd manage all right. "I know what you're going to say. I'm not interested."

"But I need your help in finding my sister."

"Get somebody else."

"I have no one else to ask."

"Sure you do, princess. I'll bet any one of your countless beaux would be glad to help."

She smiled sadly. "I think you overestimate my appeal. I don't have that many beaux any longer. As you said, a lot of men died in the war."

"It's not my problem."

"I know, but I thought perhaps ... I have no one else to ask," she repeated quietly. "There's no army to call on. The Confederate troops have been disbanded. ... All the frontier forts are nearly deserted."

His grim silence didn't hearten her. Summer took a deep breath and continued doggedly. "Able-bodied men are scarce, and ones who could go— You heard what they were saying. They don't want to leave their homes after just returning. They don't want to leave their families unprotected, either, with all the lawlessness in Texas just now. In any case, no one is eager to help Reed because he fought for the Union. Some consider him a traitor. He did what he thought was right, but he's paying for it now."

"I have my own life to live, too," Lance said grimly. "Or maybe you hadn't thought of that. I'm trying to make a fresh start, get my business on firm footing. I'm no different from anybody else, even if I'm not white."

She bit her lip, not answering. Lance tilted his hat back restlessly, avoiding her gaze.

She tried again, as he feared she would. "We can't do it alone, Lance. Reed is crippled. He couldn't make such a long journey easily. I'm not sure he could find Amelia, even if he were whole again."

"I might not be able to find her, either. Indian territory covers a lot of ground."

"You would stand a better chance than anyone else."

His mouth tightened rebelliously. "You're asking me to risk my life for a woman who wouldn't give me *spit.*"

"I ... I'm asking you to do it for me."

He glanced down at her upturned face then, and wished he hadn't. The pleading look on her beautiful face was almost more than he could stand. But he'd seen that look before when she wanted something from a man. He'd seen her turn those luminous green eyes on some poor helpless fool and near lure his soul from his body.

"What about her husband?" he asked finally. "Wasn't your sister married?" He saw the eager hope that sprang to Summer's eyes at his question and wished he had kept his mouth shut. He shouldn't encourage her. He didn't *want* to get tangled up with her and her problems, devil take her.

"She was, to a farmer, but Amelia is a widow now. Her husband died two years ago of the grippe. She wanted to return home to Sky Valley, but she stayed on with his family because they needed her. She could have come home . . . where it was safe."

Hearing the quaver in her voice, Lance set his jaw, grimly fighting the sympathy for her that was trying to build inside him. He shouldn't care. It shouldn't make one bit of difference to him if Summer Weston was in trouble way over her beautiful head. He ought to be able to steel himself against the fierce longing she still had the power to arouse in him. If he was smart, he would get the hell out of there, right now, before she could say another word.

He didn't move.

"She's my *sister*, Lance. She practically raised me after my mother died. Perhaps you don't understand since you don't have a sister of your own, but—"

"I have a sister." At her quizzical frown, his mouth curled at the corner. "Nobody you would acknowledge, princess. She's a full-blood Comanche."

"Oh."

Summer lowered her gaze, feeling singed by the look of scorn in his eyes. Fumbling in the pocket of her skirt, she drew out a folded letter, dog-eared and worn by countless readings. "This came yesterday by stage. . . . The attack happened last week, north of Fort Belknap. Amelia was visiting neighbors. A raiding party struck the farm."

She offered him the letter, but he wouldn't take it. Disappointed, she put it back in her pocket while she went on. "They killed two men and one of the women before burning the place. One of the children hid and saw what happened. They took Amelia and a child and went north; that's all anyone knows. But the longer we delay, the less likely she'll be found. And I can't help thinking . . . about what she must be going through . . . the horrible things the Comanche do to their captives."

He knew about those things. He'd seen firsthand what his father's people did to white captives. He knew what they'd done to his mother.

But he also knew what he'd let Summer Weston do to him five years ago. Tie him up in knots and hang him out to dry.

He sure as hell wasn't going to fall for her practiced charms again. No way was he going to let her play her seductive little games with him.

Deliberately he forced himself to meet her pleading gaze, making himself remember all the times he had seen the shallow charmer persuade some worshiping male to do her bidding. From the cradle she'd effortlessly ruled those around her, never giving a thought to anything save her own comfort and enjoyment. She wasn't going to rule him like that again. She wasn't going to use him and then cast him aside with his heart sliced to ribbons.

"Like I said, princess. Find somebody else."

He nudged his horse forward, planning to ride away, but her soft little cry brought him up short. When he turned, he saw that she had raised one hand to her brow and was standing in the road, swaying like she was about to swoon.

Lance cursed under his breath. He knew he was being played for a fool; Summer was no more about to faint than he was. She had reached into her bag of feminine wiles and pulled out the first trick that was likely to keep him from riding off. Well, by God, he would call her bluff! He would teach her she couldn't manipulate him now the way she had so easily five years ago.

Hauling back the reins, he threw one leg over the saddle and dropped to the ground. In two strides he had reached her and bent down to catch her legs behind the knees. Bracing his other hand behind her back, he swung her up in his arms, forcing her to clasp him around the neck to keep from falling.

"Oh!"

He ignored her startled exclamation and stalked across the road, plunging down the rocky embankment without breaking stride.

"W-What are you doing?"

"Why, nothin', Miss Summer, ma'am. Just takin' you down to the creek. Have to get some water for your temples, doncha know? Isn't that what you're supposed to do for faintin' women?"

His savage tone with its exaggerated drawl made a mockery of his chivalry.

"You don't have to do that. . . . Lance, I'm all right, honestly."

"Honest? You wouldn't know the meaning of the word, princess."

"Lance, please . . . you're frightening me."

"Good. Then maybe you'll think twice before playing your damn tricks on me again."

He shoved his way past a thicket of redbud and wild plum bushes and reached the bank of the slow-moving creek, low after the hot summer months of little rain. It was cooler here, shaded from the sun by the tall cottonwoods and hickories that grew along the creek bottom.

Without ceremony or much care for his burden, Lance bent a knee to the ground and roughly laid Summer on a bed of ferns. When she tried to sit up, he held her down with a firm hand on her shoulder and proceeded to unfasten the front buttons of her gown's bodice, completely ignoring her shocked gasp.

"Lance . . .? W-What. . .?"

"Hush, princess, don't try to talk. A woman in your condition has to save her breath."

Her fluttering hands were frantically trying to close the buttons that he'd just undone, but he pushed them aside as a mere nuisance and finished his task. Catching her right wrist in his grasp, he drew the bowie knife he kept strapped in a sheath at his waist.

Her eyes widened in alarm.

"We have to loosen this contraption, ma'am, so you can get some air."

Not waiting for her protest, he lowered the point of the knife to her waist and, with several quick upward slices, cut the laces of her corset.

The sudden freedom from restriction made her rib cage expand, allowing air to rush into her lungs, yet it only had the effect of stealing away what little breath Summer had left.

Frozen in fear, she could only stare up at him. Lance had guessed right; she'd only been pretending weakness before in order to gain his attention. But she truly felt faint now. Lance was leaning over her, his fierce black eyes boring into her, as if any moment he might lose whatever tenuous hold he had on his control, as if he might unleash his most violent primal instincts.

Then his gaze dropped suddenly to her bosom.

The soft white swells of her breasts, pushed up by the stiff buckram padding of her corset, practically spilled over the lace edge of her chemise, leaving her indecently exposed. Summer felt his hot gaze move over her like a burning brand, felt her nipples tighten in response. She wanted to cover herself, but she couldn't move. Her lips parted as she tried to speak, but no sound came out.

Just as suddenly, he let go of her wrist and sat back on his heels. "Goddammit to hell!" In a furious motion, he snatched his hat from his head and flung it away.

Summer scrambled to sit up, to edge away from him, putting a safer distance between them.

Seeing her frightened gesture, Lance expelled a harsh breath and ran a hand roughly through his black hair. *What the hell had gotten into him?* He never let himself lose control like that, never let his anger explode. He'd learned the hard way how vital it was to keep a rein on his temper. Control often meant the edge needed for survival, and yet he had turned his violence loose on a woman, on *her*. And God help him, it was just one more proof of Summer's power over him.

She was clutching the open edges of her bodice together, watching him with those tear-filled eyes, eyes edged with fear.

Cursing himself, he looked away.

"I wouldn't hurt you," he said finally, his voice low, gruff. Her silence made him feel lower than dirt.

Untying the red bandanna around his neck, Lance pushed himself to his feet and then side-slid down the creekbank. He dipped the cloth in the water, wrung it out, and climbed back up to her. Keeping his movements slow, he hunkered down before her.

She was watching him warily with those big, green, shimmering eyes. Tentatively, awkwardly, he raised the damp cloth to her face, brushing it over the soft white skin of her cheek, wiping away the tears.

It was torture being this close to her. Her lower lip trembled, and all he could think of was how much he wanted to kiss her mouth, and how much he hated himself for wanting to. He didn't know how to handle all the feelings roiling inside him: lust, tenderness, regret, self-contempt, anger. What he felt most of all was anger, because she was still beautiful, damn her, and because he still wanted her.

Even so, he knew he owed her an apology. "I'm sorry I got riled," he muttered. "It's just that . . . you and your damned female tricks. I don't like being played for a fool."

She bit her lip in an obvious struggle for composure, which only had the unwanted effect of drawing his gaze to her mouth.

He clenched his own jaw. "You weren't really swooning, were you?"

"No." Summer lowered her gaze in shame. He had seen through her. She had tried to manipulate him, tried playing the same sort of calculating games she had been so good at as a girl, just as she had five years ago. She felt ashamed of herself—until she remembered Amelia.

"I . . . I'm sorry. I shouldn't have tried to trick you. It's just that I didn't know what else to do. I've been so afraid . . . so helpless. I *hate* feeling this way."

Finishing with his task, Lance sat back, draping his forearms over his spread knees. He didn't like feeling this way, either. He hated knowing all Summer had to do was look at him and he lost control. She still had the power to turn his insides to jelly. It scared him, how helpless he was against the emotion he'd thought long vanquished. He wouldn't let her see the power she held over him, though.

He looked away, watching the rippling creek water for a time, before finally saying in a low voice, "It's a fool notion, thinking you can save your sister."

She swallowed. "Perhaps so, but I have to try. I can't give up without at least trying."

He was silent for another long moment. "You can't just waltz into Indian Territory. You're liable to get your pretty scalp taken—or your body used to warm some warrior's bed."

"I know . . . I couldn't. But you might be able to." She hesitated. "Couldn't you, Lance?"

He plucked at a fern, tearing off a leaf and shredding it between his fingers. "I don't know. I guess I'd go to my father's people first. There's no way I could find your sister without their help."

"Would you try? *Please?* After Reed, Amelia is all the family I have left. Please . . . I won't play any more games. I'm asking honestly for your help, begging you."

He hesitated so long, she thought he wasn't going to answer.

"I might consider it," he said finally. He turned his dark, brooding gaze on her. "On one condition."

Her heart leapt with elation. Eagerly Summer rose up on her knees. "Whatever you want, whatever it takes. I'll give you anything I have."

"There's only one thing you have that I might want."

"What is it? Money? We're not rich, but we weren't hurt as badly by the war as some. We could pay you."

He shook his head. "Not money. I have enough for my needs."

"Well, what, then? Land? The ranch is part mine. Papa left me and Amelia each a quarter of the valley, and Reed the rest. I'll give you my share. It's worth a lot."

Agreeing silently, Lance let his gaze drift upward, over the rolling horizon. Among the hills of Sky Valley lay plenty of prime grazing pasture, with abundant water from the countless springs, where horses could grow sleek and swift and surefooted. He had dreamed of this land. Coveted it. Ached to have it.

"I know. It's good land. But that's not what I want."

"What is it then?"

He squinted off in the distance. "You, princess."

Her heart felt as if it had suddenly stopped beating. "Me?" The word was a breathless murmur of sound. "W-What do you mean?"

"I want you. For my wife." The corner of his mouth curved in a faint smile. "All legal-like. I wouldn't want you to think I'd ask you to do something indecent."

Summer stared at him. His soft tone held such mockery that she didn't think he could be serious. "You can't mean it. . . ."

His expression hardened. "Oh, I mean it, all right. I want you to marry me before a preacher. That's all I want. A wife that can help me become a respected member of the community."

Her silence clearly proclaimed her shock.

He tossed the bit of fern away. "Course, I don't expect you to like the idea, what with my Comanche blood and all. A bastard half-breed isn't exactly what every fine lady wants for a husband."

He wouldn't look at her, afraid to see the disgust he was

sure would be written on her face, but he could feel her eyes searching his own face.

"Is this . . . your way of getting revenge? Is this punishment for what I did to you all those years ago?"

He winced, realizing how low she thought him. "What do you think?"

"I . . . I don't honestly know."

"It isn't revenge, Summer," he said quietly. "If you were my wife, I'd stand a chance of living down my past, my Comanche blood. You have standing, respectability, wealth, land, a place in the white world. All the things my mother never had."

"I . . . just can't believe . . . You're really serious? Do you know what you're asking of me?"

"Do you know what you're asking of *me?*" He smiled coldly. "I'm good enough to do your hired jobs, risk my life for you, but I'm no one you'd want to associate with otherwise, is that it?"

She heard the bitterness in his tone, but didn't know how else to reply.

"You told me once"—his voice dropped, yet she caught the edge of scorn over the ripple of the creek—"it didn't matter to you that I was half-Indian."

"Yes, but . . . marriage . . . It's . . . such a high price."

"Maybe so, but that's what I want."

He paused for an instant.

"Before you say no, you ought to consider one thing," he said slowly, carefully, so she would understand, so she would have plenty of thought to chew on. "My people wouldn't take kindly to my helping whites against my own kin, but if we were married . . . it would change things. By Comanche law, a man is obliged to protect his wife's family. If you were my wife, it would be my duty to rescue your sister. There's not a Comanche alive who would argue with that."

Slowly then, he stood and went to retrieve his black slouch hat from two yards away, where he'd flung it earlier. Slapping it restlessly against his thigh, he finally looked down at her.

"That's my condition, princess. You think on it and let me know what you decide."

Chapter 2

Marriage was the price for saving her sister. Marriage to a hard-bitten, unforgiving stranger. A man she had once wronged. A bastard half-breed within whose veins flowed the blood of the most vicious race ever to ravage the Texas plains.

Marriage to Lance Calder. It was unthinkable—and yet Summer had thought of nothing else during the past five hours.

She had needed every moment of that interval for sober reflection, every moment to conquer the feelings of shock and denial Lance's ultimatum had aroused in her. The condition he had put on his services—while dumbfounding, contemptible, perhaps insulting—deserved careful consideration. The stakes were too high to do otherwise.

Summer had postponed telling her brother until now, though, waiting until after supper before following Reed to the west parlor, which had served as his bedchamber since his wounding rendered him unable to climb stairs. As she'd expected, he'd turned livid. For the last two minutes Reed had vented his helpless fury in a roar loud enough to make her wince. Summer clasped her hands together now as she watched her brother, feeling the same impotence, the same anger, but trying to draw courage from the simple need to calm him.

Too outraged to sit still, he paced the floor with as much vigor as a one-legged man could summon, his crutches thudding dully on the rose-patterned carpet.

"The nerve of that bastard! Who in God's name does Calder think he is?"

"I expect," Summer murmured with more equanimity than

34

she felt, "that he knows exactly who he is. No one will let him forget it. *He* won't let himself forget."

"The devil, he won't! He dared propose to you."

"Well, actually . . . it wasn't much of a proposal. He was more interested in the respectability that marrying a Weston could bring him. And I suppose he's right. As his wife, I could give him a better chance at acceptance than he has now."

Stopping abruptly, Reed turned to stare at her in horror. "You can't *seriously* be considering his offer? Good God, Summer! The man's an Indian!"

"Half-Indian—who was raised white."

"Dammit, you're splitting hairs!"

"Five years ago you weren't so troubled about his race," she pointed out reasonably. "You were the one who convinced Papa to hire Lance in the first place."

"Only because I thought he got a raw deal. I took him in because I felt sorry for him."

"You took him in because he was the best mustanger in Texas, and because he saved your life."

"That debt's paid now," Reed snapped. "And just because I might hire him as a ranch hand doesn't mean I want him marrying my sister!"

Summer took a calming breath, striving to present an argument that would persuade her brother as well as herself. "What choice do we have? How many volunteers did you get to help us search for Amelia? Three. That isn't nearly enough, Reed, and you know it."

"With the vaqueros who offered, we'll have eleven," he muttered.

She shook her head. "Eleven hundred wouldn't be enough if we don't know where to look. Lance said he would ask his Comanche relatives for help if he were to take on the job."

"But . . . *marriage* . . . It's absurd, impossible! The whole notion is scandalous."

She tried to smile. She'd had five hours to accustom herself to the notion, while Reed had only had five minutes. "It isn't as if we would be living in sin. He offered to marry me."

Reed clenched his teeth at her failed attempt at humor, as if not trusting himself to speak.

"Perhaps it won't be so bad."

"Not bad? You'll be shunned by everyone we know. No one will receive you—"

"No one receives us now," Summer interrupted him tiredly. "They can't forgive you for your political persuasions. Besides," she added doggedly, her voice suddenly unsteady, "I hardly think our social calendar should concern us more than Amelia's safe return. In any case, if—*when*—we find her, her reception is likely to be far worse than mine. What kind of treatment do you think she'll get from our neighbors? Have you thought of that? Have you thought of what she might be suffering at this very moment?"

The agonized look in her brother's blue eyes told her that her shaft had struck home. "That isn't fair," Reed retorted hoarsely. "I've though of nothing else for the past two days."

He turned abruptly to resume his pacing, but his right crutch caught on the edge of the carpet, causing him to stumble and swear foully. He righted himself before he fell, and Summer stopped herself from going to his aid. Reed hated to be made to feel like a cripple, and he wouldn't take help from her unless he was in the direst pain.

"Damnation, if only I weren't a cripple!"

She saw the frustration, the fury, on his face, and her throat closed over the ache of tears. *If only.* How many times had she voiced those same helpless, hopeless words since the war began? But she fought down the urge to say them again. She couldn't afford to dwell on wistful "what ifs," or indulge in the luxury of tears.

She watched silently as Reed gave up pacing and sank onto the velvet settee, his head bowed.

His voice, when he finally spoke, held a wealth of quiet anguish. "I'm your brother . . . a man. I'm supposed to be able to protect my sisters."

"Reed . . . you can't blame yourself for what happened to Amelia."

"Perhaps not. But I *would* blame myself if I stood idly by while you made such a sacrifice and married Calder."

For a moment Summer didn't answer. Then she asked in a low tone, "Do you remember Bart Mobly?"

"The fellow who moved to Austin a while back? Amelia's beau?"

"Yes, him. Amelia could have been his wife, Reed, but she wouldn't leave me, so he found someone else. She gave up her future to help raise me—and I was too young and spoiled even to realize it, much less appreciate it. But I understand her sacrifice now. How can I ever forget what Amelia did for me? How can I *not* try to repay her? How could I possibly consider my future more important than her *life?*"

"I . . . I know." Reed rubbed his hand roughly down his face. "I just . . . can't bear the thought of Calder touching you. If he's your husband— You're still an innocent, Summer. You don't know about the things that go on between a man and a woman. It isn't like the stolen kisses you used to give your flirts. It's more . . . physical. Sometimes it's . . . painful for a woman. I wouldn't want to think what a man like that might do to you."

She didn't want to think of it, either. Involuntarily her hand went to the hollow between her breasts. She could feel the constricting press of whalebone beneath her bodice, reminding her of what had happened this afternoon by the creek. She'd replaced the corset laces Lance had cut, but she hadn't forgotten the primal look in his eyes. That heated look alone had told her there was more to carnal relations than chaste kisses and gentle petting. Indeed, his kiss five years ago had told her that much. She might still be an innocent, but she was less naive than her brother gave her credit for.

"He said he wouldn't hurt me," she answered finally, her tone less certain than she would have liked.

Reed gave a scoffing snort of disgust but didn't reply for a long moment. "It's sheer blackmail, you know."

"I know."

"It's despicable, dishonorable."

That, too, was true. Lance had taken advantage of her vulnerability, her powerlessness, approaching her when she was at her most desperate. She fiercely resented his forcing her to make such a decision. And yet railing against his brazen ultimatum would not help rescue her sister. Nor would moral arguments. It would only waste time and energy that she didn't have.

"Honor won't bring Amelia back," Summer said quietly. She could feel her brother's blue eyes searching her face.

"Comanches killed Mama. Have you forgotten that?"

She shook her head. "No." She hated the savage Comanches as much as anyone. No one who had witnessed the terrible depredations the Comanches committed against innocent settlers year after year could help but feel hatred for them, in addition to horror and fear. And yet it wasn't right to hold Lance responsible for every atrocity his father's people had perpetrated.

"I haven't forgotten. But Lance didn't kill Mama. You can't blame one man for all the terrible things that an entire race has done to another."

A soft knock sounded on the door just then, interrupting Reed's reply. When Summer bid entrance, the door opened and a dark-skinned Mexican woman peered inside the parlor.

"Do you need me any longer this evening, *patrona?*"

"No, Consuala, thank you. You may go."

The woman smiled tentatively and shut the door once more. Consuala was one of several Mexican house servants John Weston had brought to live and work on the ranch twenty years ago. She was married to one of the vaqueros who worked with the horses.

Alone again with her brother, Summer would have continued the conversation, but Reed shook his head. "Go on up to bed, Summer. We'll discuss this further in the morning."

She hesitated, recognizing the stubborn resistance in his voice. She wouldn't succeed tonight in persuading him to reconsider. She wouldn't even try.

Going to him, she bent and kissed Reed tenderly on the temple, wondering if this would be the last time she bestowed such an affectionate gesture on her brother. If she made the long journey to Fort Belknap as she intended, there was always the chance she wouldn't survive the dangers she might have to face.

"Yes . . . we'll talk in the morning." She brushed back his sable hair, so like her own. "You should try to sleep yourself, Reed. You've been driving yourself far too hard. You have to save your strength."

With one last look, she left him and made her way slowly along the hall and up the front staircase to her bedchamber. She felt incredibly weary all of a sudden. Weary of the responsibilities and worries that had dominated her life for so long.

The war had wholly ravaged the Weston family. They weren't poor exactly. During the war she had managed to sell enough of the horses to keep the ranch going. The comfortable, privileged way of life she'd been born to might be gone, but they were better off than most. Wealth no longer meant as much to her as it once had, though. She would have given it all up instantly if she could have her brothers back, her father alive, if Reed could be whole again, if Amelia could only—

But she'd sworn she wouldn't let herself dwell on Amelia's fate. It would only drive her mad.

Forcibly Summer straightened her shoulders. She'd never mastered stoicism, but she'd long ago learned that she had a stronger will than she'd ever imagined. For years she had faced the devastation unbowed. She'd had no choice. And she had no choice now but to carry on. Still, she was tired, so very tired of being strong.

Slipping inside her bedchamber, Summer shut the door softly and leaned back against the cherry-wood panel. This was the room she had once shared with Amelia. Her gaze swept the airy chamber with its feminine furnishings: white lace curtains at the windows, crocheted doilies embellishing polished wood surfaces, the thick featherbed that drew you down into sweet slumber, with its cheerful yellow counterpane that her sister had lovingly fashioned. Amelia had tenderly tucked her into this bed at night—

Hush, now. I'll stay with you till you fall as asleep, Summer.

But what if the Indians come, like they did for Mama?

You don't have to be afraid, love. I'll protect you. I'll always be here for you.

At the poignant memory, Summer closed her eyes, unable to stop the tears that suddenly spilled down her cheeks. She had only a dim recollection of her mother, but Amelia had more than filled that yawning need in her life. She owed her sister so much. . . .

With a fierce gesture of impatience, Summer dashed a hand across her eyes. Going to the armoire, she reached up and took down a carpetbag in order to pack. Dusty would drive her into town. She was capable of driving herself, for that matter, but it would only be asking for trouble, a lone woman traveling at night, what with the lawless vagrants roaming the hills since the war's end. Once she reached Round Rock, Lance would protect her. From others, at least. She trusted him to do that much, even if she had little faith in his willingness to protect her from himself.

Summer paused as she pulled out her traveling suit of brown and gold striped grenadine from the armoire. The memory of Lance staring down at her so fiercely this afternoon, his dark, hawkish face so close, made a tremor run up her spin. *What in heaven's name was she letting herself in for?*

He was still the hard, unforgiving man she'd once wronged. And God help her, he still held the same fascination for her that she'd felt as a girl: dangerous, forbidden, exciting. He had awed her then. Left her tongue-tied and absurdly nervous—she who had the ability to charm anything male. Lance had only to look at her and she felt weak.

He'd done it to her this afternoon, but with a difference. His look this afternoon had been calculated to frighten her, to drive her away. When his eyes had deliberately roamed over her, she'd felt as if he'd stripped her naked and assessed her body—and was contemptuous of the conclusions he arrived at. And yet she was woman enough to recognize the lust in his eyes and to realize that part of his contempt had been reserved for himself. He didn't want to want her.

She was grateful for his masculine susceptibility. It was the only trump card she had to play, the only leverage. That, and the respectability of her Weston connections.

Reed was right. Lance was blackmailing her into marriage—a despicable, dishonorable act. But at least he wanted something from her, enough to lay out his terms for coming to her rescue.

Absently Summer raised a sleeve of her traveling suit to her damp cheek, trying to take comfort from the softness. *What would marriage to Lance be like?* She tried to picture him enveloping her in a loving embrace, but her mind utterly failed her. All she could remember was the way he had held her this afternoon when he'd carried her down to the creek, his arms like steel bands. She couldn't imagine any love in those arms. No gentleness or warmth at all. Only hardness and anger.

Do you still hate me, Lance?

He still harbored a bitter anger toward her, certainly. His wounded pride wouldn't let him forget what she'd done to him. She couldn't blame him. A man didn't forget that kind of hurt.

Their situations were entirely reversed from five years ago. Lance wasn't dependent on her father's goodwill for a job. He wasn't dependent on anyone. He had the upper hand now. He had caught her when she was at her most vulnerable.

All she had left was pride—but she was willing to swallow it whole if it meant he would help her find her sister. She would stifle all the feelings of impotence and rage she felt at being forced into marriage with a man whom her father had refused even to allow on the ranch. She wouldn't let herself think of the devastating consequences that a marriage to a half-breed would have on her own future.

She wouldn't tell Reed until after the deed was done, either. He would try to stop her, and she couldn't afford the delay.

No, she would go now, tonight. As soon as she could pack and get some money together. Before she could change her mind. Before she lost her nerve entirely.

One arm behind his head, Lance lay on the cot in the livery stable office, staring at the rough wood ceiling and the flickering patterns made by the low-burning lantern. The tiny room, tucked in the front corner of the livery, doubled as his sleeping quarters. The place was cramped and crudely furnished, but better than bedding down in a stall or outdoors with the elements and wild critters to contend with.

Lance hardly noticed his surroundings, anyway. His mind was too wrapped up in thoughts of a green-eyed enchantress and the hell his conscience was giving him—and the resentment he felt toward both.

He should never have gone out to the Weston ranch today. And he damned sure shouldn't have stuck around long enough for Summer Weston to fix those pleading green eyes on him. If he'd had the sense to ride away, maybe now he wouldn't be torturing himself this way—one part of him hoping feverishly that she might actually consider *thinking* about his offer. Another part cursing his foolishness for opening

himself up to rejection. Still another flogging himself for adding to her troubles.

"Damned, stupid ass," Lance muttered fiercely.

He should have stayed away from her, from temptation. He
should've known what would happen the minute he got close.
His gut had twisted when he'd seen her standing on her back
porch facing that unsympathetic crowd, looking so defenseless and alone. And then later, looking so defenseless against
him. He'd gone and scared hell out of her by almost attacking
her.

His conscience hadn't stopped hounding him since. He
should never have let his temper get so out of control.

A real bastard, that's what he felt like. A bastard and a
fool.

He'd gambled big this afternoon. Laid himself open for all
kinds of hurt. A fine lady like her would no more marry a
man like him than she would suddenly take up employment
in a whorehouse. He'd been fantasizing even to think up such
a harebrained proposal.

But then, he'd been fantasizing a lot lately. Ever since
coming back to Round Rock, he'd thought of little else but
Summer Weston.

You didn't remember her right, though. The potency of his
recollections, no matter how vivid, paled in comparison to the
real thing.

How could his memory be so faulty? For years he'd
dreamed about Summer. He'd lain awake nights, deliberately,
self-destructively, forcing himself to recollect every haunting
detail about her, recalling the cruel kisses she'd given him,
reminding himself that he was just one in a long line of hapless males whose hearts she'd so carelessly trod on. She was
so good at playing the coquette, at teasing and leading a man
on.

Yet she hadn't always been like that. Maybe that was why
he'd felt so betrayed when she'd started her damned little
games with him. As a young girl, she'd been kind and
gentle . . . never looking down her pretty nose at a half-breed,
bastard kid. God, how he'd waited anxiously each week for
her to come to town with her pa, hoping she would notice
him, longing for her to smile at him. That smile of hers . . .
so sweet and fresh and innocent, unsullied by the harsh real-

ities of life, untarnished by the knowledge of her own feminine power.

That smile, bestowed on him like a precious gift, had somehow eased his terrible loneliness. He'd discovered he could bear all the taunts and insults that whites hurled at him, knowing there was someone out there who didn't hate him. Believing Summer could see past his birth and blood kin and look at him as a real person with feelings and dreams of his own.

His hopes had turned out to be pure fantasy. Still, he couldn't crush the image of Summer he'd kept hidden in his heart, or the memories he'd cherished.

He couldn't crush the want.

Dammit to hell, he wanted her. This afternoon he'd nearly lost control of himself. He'd wanted to touch her and run his hands over her and fit his mouth to hers and thrust himself between her spread legs and bury himself so deep in her softness, he wouldn't know where he ended and she started.

Just remembering made him ache.

Lance shifted restlessly on the hard cot. Why, after all this time, was he still so smitten? Why did he still need her so bad? He should have gotten over his infatuation with her by now. He'd been just a boy when he'd fallen for her. He was a man now.

Trouble was, he also had a man's lusts, a man's hunger. The minute he'd laid eyes on her, all the old needs and desires had come stampeding back with twice the force. It didn't help a damn knowing that his reaction was only natural. Summer Weston was the kind of woman who drove men beyond reason, the kind of woman a man could die for.

And his case was worse than most. What he felt for her was more than just simple lust. She'd always meant more to him. She'd always been a symbol to him, of all the things he wanted to have but couldn't, wanted to be but wasn't. She was proud, queenly, so far above his touch, he might as well be wishing for the moon. She wasn't for him.

He had no right to dream such dreams. He knew what he was. A man no decent woman would keep company with. Decent women, when they passed him on the street, crossed over if they could. If not, they brushed their skirts aside to avoid any contact with him.

He could never be good enough for a princess like Summer. His Comanche blood made him inferior. And there was damn little he could do about it. He'd had that bitter lesson pounded into him over the years. A man couldn't fight against blind prejudice.

Nobody could. His mother had tried.

His ma's people were nothing to sneer at. They came from good English stock, moving from Tennessee to Texas in search of a better way of life. Charlotte Calder hadn't found the good life, though. She'd suffered plenty as a Comanche captive, and then later, because of *him*. The Comanches had been bad, but her own folks had been even crueler. If she'd been willing to abandon her son, if she'd shown proper remorse for bearing a bastard child and inflicting him on the white world, then she might have been forgiven. But she'd held her head high and tried to ignore the insults and slurs, the contempt, the hurt of being shunned. And then she'd made the hardest sacrifice, turning herself into a whore in order to feed and clothe her bastard son.

Involuntarily Lance's fists clenched with the old rage. Sometimes as a kid he'd hear her crying at night, and he wanted to punch his fists through a wall, or take out his knife and carve out the innards of the bastards who held themselves so high and mighty above her—his savage Comanche blood at work, Lance thought without humor.

But his savage instincts hadn't been enough to save her. He hadn't been able to protect her when she most needed him. Bile rose in his throat at the twenty-year-old memory, when he was almost eight.

She was hanging out laundry in the yard behind their small cabin when the three white men caught her and dragged her into the house. Her scream of terror and pain brought him running from the woods where he was checking his traps, sent him bursting into the cabin. She was sprawled whimpering across the bed on her back while a bearded frontiersmen pumped away between her legs.

He remembered the smell most, the stench of unwashed male bodies and filthy buckskin. He remembered the largest man's hateful laugh as he raped his mother. Remembered his own violent, impotent rage.

He flew at the giant's back, but one of the others caught him and held his scrawny, writhing body.

"Lookee here, will ya?" his captor taunted. "If it ain't the puny little breed. Don't get so riled, breed. We're just havin' us a little fun with yer ma. She don't mind. She's used to having them Comanche bucks fuckin' her. Ow! Shit, the little savage bit me!"

He fought with every ounce of strength he possessed, trying to kill all three of them, while his mother sobbed and pleaded with them to leave her son alone. Only the powerful fist that finally caught him across the face had silenced him.

He'd come to in a daze to find his mother rocking him, her tears wetting his face. He'd cried with her, cried for her pain, for her shame, for his own shame in being unable to save her. She tried to tell him it wasn't his fault, but he knew better.

She'd taken Tom Peace as her protector after that. As her permanent lover. She needed a man who was strong and powerful enough to keep away the scum who thought she deserved to be raped because she'd once been a Comanche captive—and because she'd kept her half-breed son.

Lance squeezed his eyes shut at the memory. He'd hated Peace for that, when he should have been grateful his mother had someone to protect her. He should have been grateful to Peace for teaching him to fight and to defend himself and to kill when necessary, too. Instead he'd been bitter at his own failure. She'd died before he was old enough to help her much.

She'd never complained about her lot, though. She'd even done her best to make him see that he should hold his head high, too.

You shouldn't pay them any mind, my love. I'm proud of you, and that's all that matters.

Deep down, though, he was ashamed of what he was. And ashamed of being ashamed. No matter what his mother said.

He'd tried to believe her. As a kid, he'd tried not to care what whites thought of him. He'd learned to bottle up the rage and not let himself feel the hurt. But that didn't ease the lonely feeling of never belonging anywhere.

That loneliness had carved an emptiness inside him. He wasn't a part of any place. He'd gone in search of his Comanche father, trying to find somewhere to put down roots, but he hadn't belonged to that world either. The savagery, the killing, had been too fierce for him to live with himself. So he'd come back to Round Rock, thinking maybe he could fill the emptiness here.

He didn't want all that much. A piece of land where he could raise good horses. A woman who stood beside him and looked at him with pride. Some friendly neighbors who didn't act as if they wanted to spit on him when he passed by. Not much, but he wanted it.

He wanted it to bad, he could taste it.

Lance cursed softly in the silence. He was setting himself up for a hard fall, letting himself hope too damn much. There was no way Summer would ever agree to become his wife. Not even to save her precious sister. And even if she did agree, only because he'd given her no other choice, there was no way she would ever see him as a husband to be proud of. He was a fool for even allowing himself to hope.

Round Rock was hardly large enough to be called a town, but it boasted a supply store and a combination livery stable/ stage stop, since it was directly on the road north from Austin to Dallas. Many of the locals still called the settlement by its earlier name of Brushy, after the creek that ran through the county.

In '48, when Brushy/Round Rock was first established, Tom Peace had given up rangering in order to start the livery stable. In his will, he'd left the business to Lance Calder.

Summer eyed the livery now as the buckboard approached. The rough log building was faintly illuminated by moonlight, while a glimmer of yellow shone between the chinks in the shutters, indicating that someone was home.

Her ranch foreman, Dusty Murdock, drew the team to a halt and turned to her. "You sure you want to go through with this, ma'am?"

"No . . . but I don't think I have any choice."

"I could maybe try to talk to him for you. He used to consider me a friend—at least, as far as he let anybody be a friend to him."

She tried to smile. "I appreciate the offer, but I doubt in this case he would listen to you."

"I'll wait for you, then."

"Thank you, Dusty."

Summer allowed him to help her down from the buckboard and then went to the livery door. She could feel her heart pounding as she raised her gloved hand to knock. If Lance was here, he would have heard her arrival, yet he hadn't come out to greet her. Perhaps he meant to make this as difficult as possible for her.

When she rapped softly, there was a long pause before she heard him call out in a low voice, "It's open." Lifting the latch, she pushed open the door and stepped inside.

Lance was lounging on the narrow bed, his back propped against the wall, his arms folded across his chest. She didn't think he'd been asleep. He still wore his boots, and he was watching her, his eyes alert and wary.

He didn't get up in her presence, didn't offer her a place to sit down. Closing the door behind her, Summer stood awkwardly, uncertain how to deal with his rudeness, or this situation. She could feel his hard gaze roam over her as he took in her appearance: her traveling suit, her sturdy half boots, her kid gloves, her serviceable narrow-brimmed bonnet.

"You came all this way to call on me, princess? I'm honored."

At the sarcasm in his voice, she felt her temper flare, but she tamped it down. In her circumstances, she couldn't afford wounded pride. Besides, sparring with him would get her nowhere. "Yes, I came to call," she said quietly.

"I'm surprised your brother let you."

"Reed doesn't know I'm here."

Lance's eyes narrowed. "You made that trip alone?"

Hearing the sharp disapproval in his tone, she could almost believe he was concerned for her safety. But no, he would care only that his terms couldn't be met if something happened to her. "I wasn't alone. Dusty brought me. He's waiting outside."

"You always did have Dusty wrapped around your little finger, along with half the other males in the territory."

"I didn't have you," Summer was stung into retorting.

"Yeah, and that's what galled you, didn't it? You had to have me on your string. You had to have me dancing to your tune. And when I wouldn't, your pa had me run out of the county."

The fierceness of his eyes made her wince. Summer bit her lip, unable to defend herself. It hadn't happened quite that way, but she was still responsible.

The silence stretched out for a long moment.

"So have you made up your mind, princess? You gonna sacrifice yourself for your sister?"

"I . . . I can't convince you to change your mind?"

"No."

The single gruff word shriveled her last hope. "If . . . If I agree to marry you . . . you'll find Amelia?"

"I can't promise I'll succeed, but I'll do my level best, yes."

She wanted to ask what would become of their marriage if they never found Amelia, but she couldn't allow herself to voice the possibility for fear it might come true. "And afterward? When Amelia is safe? Where . . . would we live?"

Lance's glance swept briefly around the room, and his eyes took on a sharp gleam of amusement that had little to do with humor. "Your place is a bit fancier than mine, I'd say. Wouldn't you rather live on your ranch?"

"Yes, but I didn't know if you would."

"I think I could force myself."

"Would we . . . What about . . ." Summer could feel her cheeks flushing. "Marital relations."

"Would we share a bed, is that what you're asking?" Lance's black eyes traveled over her, touching her more intimately than his hands had ever dared. "What do you think?"

"I . . . didn't know if you were . . . interested in me that way."

Swinging his legs slowly over the edge of the bed, he rose to his feet with the grace of a wild animal and moved to stand before her. Reaching out, he caught her wrist, ignoring her startled, questioning gaze. With careful determination, he drew her gloved hand toward him, placing it directly over his groin, making her feel the hard, swollen ridge of his masculinity.

Summer flinched and tried to pull back, but Lance wouldn't release her.

"Does this feel interested?"

With a twisting jerk of her hand, she finally managed to

break free, but only because he allowed it. In anger, she retreated a step and averted her gaze. He was trying to shame her—and succeeding. *How did he manage to unnerve her so?* He left her feeling off balance and entirely too vulnerable. "Are you trying to frighten me?" she demanded unsteadily.

"No, ma'am. I just want you to know what you're letting yourself in for. If you're not willing to share a bed with me, let me know now. We'll call the whole thing off."

Lance saw the struggle on her face but steeled himself against giving in. The truth was, he wanted her so bad that he was willing to take whatever Summer was willing to let him have. But he'd be a fool to let her see his weakness for her. And he'd already been enough of a fool for one day.

"Look at me, Summer." His whisky-rough voice held a command she couldn't ignore. When she lifted her gaze, he held it with hard determination. "You'll be my woman, not a princess in some tower. You'll sleep with me. And take me into your body. And let me do things to you that no white woman would ever think of letting a savage do. You won't deny me when I want you. Even if you aren't willing, as my wife you'll come to me when I tell you."

His explicitness, his slow enunciation of exactly what he would require of her, made her squeeze her eyes shut in mortification. "Why . . . why are you making this so difficult for me?"

Lance clenched his jaw at the plea in her tone. He knew better than to let himself soften. She wasn't beyond using her wiles to make him feel sympathy for her. And once he let that happen, it was only a short step till he was panting to do her bidding. "I just don't want you holding the notion you can walk all over me once we're married."

Summer's own slender jaw clenched. She resented the terrible position he had put her in, resented his forcing her to make such a decision. But she made herself open her eyes. "I . . . I scarcely know you."

"You'll get to know me a lot better when I'm your husband."

"I . . . expected to marry well."

His expression hardened even more, if that was possible. "I know. I'm not what you would consider a 'desirable prospect.' Five years ago I wasn't good enough for you, and I'm not good enough now. But I'm all you've got."

And that was the cold truth. They both knew it.

Summer searched the dusky, compelling face so close to hers—the broad forehead, the high cheekbones, the sharp nose, the hard, merciless eyes. His eyes were so dark, she could see herself reflected in them. So unfathomable, she could read nothing there but determination. He wasn't going to change his mind. She swallowed and wet her dry lips, accepting the inevitable.

"I want to leave tomorrow," she said, mustering her own determination. "The longer we delay, the harder it will be to find Amelia."

He frowned at that. "Who said anything about you going?"

"I always meant to accompany Reed to Fort Belknap."

"It's a long, dangerous trip for a woman."

"I don't care. Amelia is my sister and she needs me. I'll travel as far as her in-laws' farm with you, so I can be as close as possible when you find her. I can stay with the Truesdales while you search for her," Summer said, refusing to be dissuaded or to consider the possibility of failure. "The stage comes through here at half past ten. Reed checked."

The set of Lance's shoulders relaxed the slightest degree, she thought. "I know what time the stage comes through town," he replied dryly. "I supply the teams for the line, remember?"

"Oh. Yes . . . well . . . what will you do about the livery while you're gone?"

He shrugged. "There's a kid who helps out sometimes. Molly Jenkins's boy. I can get him to stay here full-time to look after the horses and meet the stage."

When she remained silent, Lance pinned her with his gaze. "You're not gonna change your mind?"

Summer shook her head. She wanted to do it now, before she lost her courage. "No. I'd like to get it over with. Perhaps we should find a minister."

His expression never changed, yet she couldn't help but believe that some of the wariness, the hardness, had faded from his eyes. It was relief she saw there, she would swear it.

"Yeah," Lance said tonelessly. "I'd like to get it over with, too." He reached out and took her elbow. "Let's go find ourselves a preacher."

Chapter 3

Her wedding was nothing like she'd ever dreamed it would be, with none of her family in attendance and only Dusty and the minister's wife to act as witnesses. Indeed, Lance had to rouse the circuit-riding Methodist minister out of bed, who then balked at performing the ceremony for a white woman and a half-breed under such suspicious circumstances.

When Reverend Baxter insisted that he first talk with Reed, Summer retorted that she didn't need her brother's permission to marry. Lance settled the issue by saying they were leaving tomorrow on a long journey to Indian Territory, and that unless the good Reverend wanted Miss Summer to live a life of sin, he would make their union legal.

Summer managed to repeat her vows in a credibly steady voice—not at all like a woman whose life had just been thrown into turmoil—and listened tensely as Lance did the same.

An awkward moment followed. Lance didn't have a ring, and it was left to Dusty to fashion a substitute of braided leather taken from a horse's bridle.

Summer watched with a sense of unreality. That she should be reduced to this . . . She might have laughed if the reason for her marrying hadn't been so sobering. As it was, the strangeness of the ceremony hardly touched her. She felt light-headed with fatigue and the strain of the past two days, and all she wanted was for it to be over so she could get on with finding her sister.

It was only when Lance turned to kiss her to seal the vows that Summer seemed to waken. He bent his dark head and brushed his hard masculine lips over hers briefly, and she suffered an attack of nerves so strong, it was near panic. She was married to this man. This hard, unforgiving stranger. For better

51

or for worse. And she would have to honor those vows . . . tonight and every night, if Lance could be taken at his word. He had made it perfectly clear he didn't want a wife in name only.

The ride back to the livery was made in silence. When the buckboard drew to a halt, Lance sprang down and raised his arms to help Summer descend. She felt his fingers firm on her waist, all business, while his dark face remained shuttered, devoid of all emotion.

When he set her on her feet, Summer found her gaze drawn to the rough log building that was the livery stable and office—the place where she would spend her first night with her husband.

"Go on inside," Lance said quietly as he hefted her carpetbag from the back of the buckboard.

Wanting to delay the inevitable as long as possible, Summer turned and looked up at Dusty, who sat twisting the reins in his hands.

"Thank you, Dusty. For everything."

"Sure, Miss Summer . . . Mrs. Calder, I mean. I hope to God you find her."

She gave a start at the strange new title, but managed to nod and say with determined conviction, "We will. Tell Reed . . . Tell Reed this is for the best."

Dusty tipped his hat solemnly.

Forcing her feet to move, Summer entered the office, where an unwelcoming darkness greeted her. She fumbled for the lantern and matches Lance had left on the table beside the door, and busied herself lighting the wick while she tried not to think about what was to come.

She heard Lance's low voice outside as he spoke briefly to Dusty, then the rattle of the buckboard as it moved off into the night. Lance's booted footsteps behind her as he entered the room sounded like gunshots. When the door shut softly behind him, panic welled up in her again. Summer shivered violently.

"Are you cold?" she heard him ask gruffly.

With effort, she shook her head. "Just nervous."

Without comment, Lance set down her bag on the bed and began to build a fire in the cast-iron stove in the corner.

"You want some coffee?"

She started to say no, but then changed her mind. Hot coffee might help settle her nerves, and at the very least, occupy Lance for a few more minutes. "Yes, please. That would be nice."

She watched as he filled the coffeepot from a bucket of water by the stove. His home apparently boasted none of the amenities the Weston ranch house had. If there was a water pump, it was outside.

Glancing around her at the crude furnishings, she found her gaze fixed on the narrow bed that was little more than a wood-and-rope frame covered with a straw mattress and a wool blanket. Hanging above it on a peg was a buffalo hide, which probably provided extra warmth in winter.

Tearing her gaze away, Summer forced herself to say calmly, "Tomorrow will be a long day. Perhaps we should get some sleep."

"Maybe we should go to bed."

The tone was cool, hard, inexorable. She couldn't possibly mistake his meaning. Lance intended to claim his rights as her husband.

Lamely Summer turned to look at him. He had paused while grinding a measure of coffee beans, and was watching her narrowly. The force of that black gaze nearly took her breath away.

"Your brother may come looking for you," he said grimly in explanation. "I don't want to give him any reason to say we're not married."

She thought she understood his reasoning. He was determined to consummate the marriage so it couldn't be annulled. But that didn't make her feel any calmer.

Silently she nodded.

Lance seemed to take her agreement for granted, since he resumed the task of grinding. Summer didn't know what to do with herself. She was aware of the fragrant aroma of coffee mingling with the odor of woodsmoke from the stove, aware of the heavy thud of her heart.

"Do you need to use the privy? It's out back."

Embarrassed at the discussion of such a private function, Summer shook her head without answering.

"Then you better take off your clothes."

There was a pause the length of a heartbeat. Then, obediently, she reached up and fumbled with the strings to her bonnet. When she had set it on the table, she stood there awkwardly.

Lance spoke again. "All your clothes, princess."

Her heart started pounding erratically as she realized what he was demanding; he didn't intend to give her any privacy at all. Summer turned to stare at him. He had gone quite still, as if waiting for her answer.

"This is what you agreed to when you married me," he reminded her sharply.

"I know . . . It's just that . . . shouldn't . . . we put out the light?"

"No. I want to see you." At her shocked hesitation, his mouth twisted. "You might as well get over your modesty now, princess. I'm going to know your body well enough in a little while, in any case. And you're going to know mine."

The thought of learning about his body made her pulse suddenly skip several more beats. Tense with nerves, Summer walked the three steps to the bed and fished in her bag for a nightdress. When she pulled it out, Lance cut into her whirling thoughts.

"You won't be needing that. I want you naked when you're in bed with me." When she froze, he added defensively, "I'm not like your polite starched gentlemen, sleeping in a nightshirt and hiding beneath the covers to rut in secret. I wasn't raised that way."

No, Summer thought wildly. He was raised a savage. His ancestors were cold-blooded killers who raped and murdered white women like her.

"No," she retorted, resentment flaring at her fear, at Lance's high-handedness, his insensitivity. "I wouldn't expect someone of your background to behave like a gentleman."

She regretted her outburst instantly. She saw his grim mouth harden, saw his narrowed eyes spark with fury, and chastised herself for a fool. Taunting him about his heritage would hardly endear her to him, or encourage him to treat her with gentleness and concern for her inexperience.

Shivering, she let the nightdress drop from her shaking fingers. This was nothing like what she had expected for her wedding night. This tense skirmish of wills with a cold, hard stranger, unvarnished by tenderness or love. But she'd made a bargain with Lance: marriage in exchange for his help and protection. It was the same bargain women had made with men for centuries, and she would find the strength to keep her end of it. She had no other choice. If she changed her mind, then Lance might change *his*. No, if he insisted on making her undress in front of him, then she would do it. The cost to her pride, her modesty, was nothing when stacked up against Amelia's life.

She risked another glance at him. He was watching her, his features taut, his muscles coiled with the vital, dangerous energy that was so much a part of him, his smoldering eyes so dark, so intense, so . . . hungry that it frightened her.

She couldn't think with him looking at her that way, not when she could feel this fear dancing inside her stomach, not when she was fighting against an unnamed emotion that she didn't want to call excitement.

Not daring to look at him, she shrugged out of her jacket bodice and began to unfasten the buttons of her lawn blouse. It felt so wanton to be taking her clothes off in front of him. Her body felt flushed and hot, her nipples puckered and tight beneath her chemise. She kept her back to him as she drew off the blouse and folded it nearly in the carpetbag. Then she reached for the buttons of her full skirts.

Lance watched her undress, hardly daring to breathe. The anger, the want, the need, were like a fist inside him, twisting his innards. He was so hard, he could pound fence posts. So swollen, he thought he might explode if he touched her. If he *didn't* touch her.

Forcing himself to look away, he finished the mundane task of fixing coffee, adding the grounds to the water and setting the pot on the stove to boil. That gibe of hers about him not being a gentlemen had cut him to the quick. He'd hoped to make her forget his Comanche blood, his bastard birth. He'd wanted to make her forget that he wasn't good enough for her—

Realizing where his thoughts were headed, Lance muttered an expletive even as the old resentment came surging back. He couldn't change who he was. It was stupid to feel the old gnawing inferiority. Summer was his wife now. He had the right to take her if he wanted to.

More than the right. It was a necessity. He had to consummate their marriage; tonight, on their wedding night. And not just because her damned brother would be breathing down their necks as soon as he learned what they'd done, although that alone was a good enough reason. No, it was because of Summer herself. She'd be less likely to renege on their bargain if she was fully his wife. If she lost her virginity to him, if he branded her as his, then she couldn't back out of her vows so easily—like she was obviously thinking about doing right this minute.

Slanting a glance at her, Lance let himself look his fill as she stood there in crinoline petticoat and camisole, her throat and shoulders and arms bare. Seeing her so nervous was unpleasantly satisfying to his soul: the proud, pampered Belle of Williamson County brought to her knees by the savage half-breed.

She was looking at him, her green eyes wide, wary, her lips slightly parted. She looked afraid. He didn't want her afraid of him.

Then again, Lance consoled himself, maybe he was being too hard on himself. Maybe that was Summer's game—making him feel sorry for her, playing on his sympathy so he wouldn't carry through tonight with making her his woman. He knew better than anybody how good she was with games. Which was what he had to remember, he told himself fiercely. He would be damned if he'd fall for her wiles again. He wouldn't give her reason to really be scared of him. He would show her more mercy than his mother had received at the hands of all the white men she'd known.

"You gonna take all night, princess?" He voiced the taunt with a slow, calculated Texas drawl and watched Summer's chin snap back up to an imperious angle. It made him feel a little better, seeing the defiance in her eyes. It appeased his own fear a smidgen.

Summer was his now. His woman. She belonged to him. There was no way in hell he would let her go. He would bind her to him the only way he knew how, by making her share the most intimate act that could happen between a man and a woman, by making her take him into her body. He would try to make it easy for her, though.

Without watching her remove her petticoat, Lance pulled off his vest and hung it on a wall peg, then his chambray shirt, baring his torso. He felt Summer's gaze touch him: his hairless chest, his bronzed skin, his lean frame corded with ropes of muscle developed during countless hours of physical, backbreaking labor taming wild mustangs. Lance felt himself tighten, his skin grow hot. He wanted her to look at him, wanted her to become familiar with his body so she would lose her fear of him.

As she took off the camisole, he sauntered over to the bed, trying to ignore the way Summer flinched when he squeezed past her, trying not to curse when she backed away a few steps.

Sitting on the edge of the mattress, he tugged his boots off, one by one, and then leaned back, propping his shoulders against the wall.

Maybe he should try to get her to talk, so she wouldn't think so hard about being afraid of him.

"Do you know what's supposed to happen tonight?"

"N-No . . . not really." She bit her lip as she untied the laces of her corset. "I once saw a stallion cover a mare. It looked . . . awkward."

"It won't be that way for your first time. We'll be face-to-face."

"You're . . . going to have to show me what to do."

An unexpected tenderness crept through him. He felt suddenly like a low-down snake. She was so innocent. He would contaminate her purity just by touching her. She was too good for him; bright and decent and fresh. . . . Maybe he *was* a savage. For sure the hot storm of lust streaking through him felt savage. Being so close to fulfilling his fantasies had a lot to do with his brutal hunger. Knowing Summer was his for the taking made him ache with need. The things he'd dreamed of doing to her . . . Having her go wild beneath him. Feeling her wrap those long, slender legs around his hips as he thrust hard and fast into her. Hearing her cry out with pleasure as she bucked and writhed and arched against him. The image was strong enough to make him break out in a sweat. Sinful enough to make him unsure of himself.

Hell, he didn't know how to make love to a lady. It was beyond his experience. He'd never had a true lady. The few whores he'd mounted who didn't mind getting tossed by a half-breed had all been willing and wild, as eager for a good tumble as he. He knew how to give a woman pleasure. He'd learned on purpose, so they would have good reason to let him in their beds. He could hold his own with the most practiced whore.

But he didn't know how to treat a lady . . . let alone his wife. And soon he would have her beneath him. His wife . . . Summer. The notion made his mouth go dry. If there'd been time, he would have asked the saloon girl in Georgetown who'd taught him about women what he should do. He wanted it to be good for Summer. He would try his damned-est to make it good.

"Everything, princess," he said, seeing her hesitate. She had removed most of her underwear and stood shivering in her drawers and chemise.

Summer clenched her teeth as she sat in one of the two rough wooden chairs by the table to remove her boots. Then standing again, she shimmied out of her lace-edged drawers.

When that was done, there was no more reason for delay. She felt Lance watching her, felt those hot, smoldering eyes touching her scantily clad body in all the most intimate places. She wanted to sink through the floor, and yet the tur-moil roiling inside her was not just embarrassment or fear. There was heat and wonder and nervous anticipation, too.

"I'm waiting," Lance said softly, giving no quarter.

Hesitantly, rebelliously, she reached for the edges of her chemise and drew the garment over her head. Letting it drop to the table, she heard Lance's sharp inhalation and closed her eyes in shame. This was how slave women must feel on the auction block. Naked. Quivering. Heart wildly pulsing. The object of base male speculation and desire.

A sensual shiver raced through her.

The small room grew hushed, only broken by the quiet crackle of wood in the stove and the soft bubble of simmering coffee. For the longest moment Lance said nothing; he couldn't have managed it just then if his life depended on it. His breath had hissed from his lungs at the sight of her. She had high, rounded breasts with tight pink nipples ... slender, graceful shoulders that tapered to a waist so narrow, he could span it with his hands ... sweetly curving hips and slender legs. Be-tween, at the junction of pale, slim thighs, lay a bush of dark, curling hair that hid the portal to her womanhood.

She was a thing of beauty, and after a lifetime of ugliness, his soul craved beauty.

For a full minute his hot gaze took her in, while the tension in the little cabin swelled. Her chin was raised at a stubborn angle and she'd opened her eyes, as if determined not to be cowed. He wondered how a person could look so proud and vulnerable at the same time.

"Come here, Summer," he said gruffly, huskily. "I can't touch you if you're all the way across the room."

Since the room was barely ten feet wide, there could be no great distance between them, but she bit back the retort and forced her feet to move till she reached the narrow bed where he was sitting and stood over him.

"Lance ..." Her voice was hoarse, shaky. "You said ... you said you wouldn't hurt me. ..."

He felt his gut tighten at her soft plea; unwanted tenderness squeezed his throat and roughened his voice. "I won't ... not on purpose ... but it may hurt a little. I hear sometimes it hurts a woman the first time. But I'll try to make it easy. I'll do my best to pleasure you."

Summer stared down at him, biting her lip as she considered the possibility. She hadn't thought that Lance would want to give her pleasure after what she had done to him. For that matter, she didn't want to feel pleasure, not when Amelia might be suffering torment. Still, his assurance relieved her mind. He wasn't going to fall on her and rape her like a beast.

She watched blankly as he patted the mattress beside him. "Sit down here next to me. I'm not going to hurt you."

Reluctantly she obeyed, turning to sit rigidly on the edge of the bed.

Lance felt every muscle in his body clench at her nearness. She was so beautiful, it made his chest ache, his manhood throb with painful need. He couldn't quite believe this was happening, that Summer Weston was really about to become his wife in fact as well as name. Almost reverently he reached out a finger to stroke her tight, naked back. She flinched at his touch, but didn't move away.

"Summer ..." He swallowed against the hoarseness of his throat and began again. "Can I take down your hair?"

The quiet question startled her. She hadn't expected him to ask her permission for anything. She had simply expected him to take. She nodded slowly.

She felt his hard fingers, cautious and gentle, in her hair, searching for the pins that held her snood in place. He could have dropped them on the floor, but he handed them to her one by one—and she was grateful. It gave her something to do, something to cling to. She was aware of how smooth the carved wood felt against her palm, how soothing his fingers felt against her scalp as he slowly raked the knot at her nape, loosing the tangled tresses.

Again Lance said nothing; he was too caught up in the wonder of what he was doing to try to speak. He hadn't remembered her hair right. How it glowed dark and lustrous as a sable pelt. How it shimmered with red and gold highlights. How silky and soft it felt against his fingertips. It was more beautiful than any memory he'd held on to. And her skin . . . so soft and white and silky . . .

His hand was shaking as he raised it to stroke her bare shoulder; all his senses felt sharp and hungry and raw. Slowly, so he wouldn't scare her, he moved his hand around her shoulder and downward . . . to cover her right breast, cupping it with his palm.

He waited for the panic, the rejection, but Summer sat frozen, completely rigid. He moved his hand slowly, cupping, stroking, trying to tell her with his quiet touch that she didn't have to be afraid of him. He wanted to bury his face in her breasts, to suck so hard on her nipples that she cried out in pleasure and pain, begging him to suck her elsewhere. But if it took every ounce of willpower he had, he would force himself to hold back. She had been his dream for as long as he could recall, and he wasn't going to destroy this chance. He would prove to her he wasn't the savage she feared.

At his gentleness, Summer closed her eyes in wonder. The lean, callused hand was so hard, so very strong. Frighteningly strong. *Shouldn't I be afraid?* she thought with bewilderment. But there was nothing startling about Lance's touch. Instead, the heat of his palm against her flesh was stirring, arousing, exciting. Her budded nipple throbbed almost painfully. She wanted to press her breast into his hand, to offer him more of herself.

As if he could read her mind, Lance brought his other arm around her body, to fondle her left nipple. Summer gave a soft, involuntary murmur of approval. She could hear his breath in her ear, as shallow and rapid as her own, feel the pulse of his heart against her back, the scalding heat of his bare chest against her skin. The quiet heat affected her strangely. Slowly, moment by moment, she felt her tense, rigid muscles soften, grow weak.

With a breath of a sigh, she relaxed back against him. She

was so tired . . . so tired of fighting, of being strong. But she had someone to lean on now. She closed her eyes.

When, a moment later, through a daze, she heard Lance say in a husky half whisper, "Lie down, princess," she didn't protest. Obediently she did as he wanted.

Lance shifted so that he was wedged against the wall, giving her room on the narrow cot, and gently turned Summer to lie full length on her back. Her naked body was fully open to his gaze, his for the taking.

Slowly, though, carefully, he stretched out on the cot beside her. He was half-afraid to do more for fear he'd attack her. The way he was feeling right now—his body throbbing, his erection stiff as a poker and on fire for her—he was liable to explode. God, he wanted her. But he had to go slow, he had to force himself to wait.

Lassoing his control, he searched her upturned face. Her eyes were green and questioning, her lips soft and parted and vulnerable. He'd had so little softness and warmth and beauty in his life, he didn't know what to do with it now. He didn't know how to show a woman tenderness. . . .

If Summer had been a mare, he would know how to act. He knew how to gentle a wild mare. In taming a mustang, a Comanche would breathe into her nostrils, make her learn his breath in order to claim mastery. He could make Summer learn his breath, accept his touch.

With quiet determination, Lance bent his head and covered her mouth with his. When his tongue slid between her lips, he felt her stiffen for the barest instant, but then she parted for him, letting him thrust deeper.

He kissed her for a while, letting her grow accustomed to the taste of him, letting her feel the press of his body now and then, the caress of his palm as he kneaded her breast. In a while, when he finally felt she was ready, he moved his lips from her mouth to her chin, the slim column of her throat, the delicate line of her collarbone, and lower.

She made a gasping sound deep in her throat when his mouth claimed her nipple, but she didn't try to pull away. He set to work suckling her, first gently, then harder . . . then soft again, changing the rhythm, the method of torment . . . drawing back to blow on the wet, glistening bud, raking the pebbled peak lightly with his teeth, his tongue licking and soothing where he'd hurt. She was breathing hard by the time he let his hand move down her silky body, to cup between her legs.

Her sharp gasp made him raise his head and whisper against her lips, "No, don't tense up. I'm just going to touch you. . . . This'll make it easier for you to take me."

She seemed to relax against her will, and lay there passively as he stroked the feminine cleft between her thighs. In a minute, though, he could feel the sexual tension begin to grow in her body.

He kept up his tender assault, readying her for him . . . probing her secrets gently . . . thrusting his middle finger slowly inside her, deeper, deeper . . . then withdrawing, only to thrust again . . . wetting his finger with her pearly dew and letting it glide over the aching center of her womanhood . . . rubbing the hard little nub with exquisite concentration. After a few moments the hairpins in Summer's grasp slipped unheeded from her fingers, and she raised her hands to clutch his shoulders.

When finally he heard her soft whimper of pleasure, Lance felt a surge of desire so powerful, he thought he might shatter. He shifted his weight then, moving his denim-covered knee to ride intimately between her thighs, pressing hard against her crotch. As he'd wanted, her hips began to thrust erratically against the pressure.

"Lance . . . ?" Her voice was a whisper of confusion. "What . . . are you doing to me? I'm so hot. . . ."

"That's okay, princess," he said hoarsely. "What you're feeling is good. Move against my leg . . . ride me."

Summer closed her eyes against the fierce heat flaring within her, consuming her, against the fierce, unbearable ache between her trembling thighs. She felt so feverish, so wild. She had to get closer to him or she would die—and Lance seemed to know it. He had gripped her squirming hips in his powerful hands, forcing her to accept the hard pressure of his rocking thigh, the rasping friction that was driving her mad.

Suddenly, helplessly, her entire body went rigid. Desperately she clutched at the muscles of his sleek shoulders and let out a strangled cry at the brutal rush of feeling, the savage fire that streaked through her, but she was powerless against the fierce sensations, the passion that seemed to be tearing her apart. Frantically she arched against Lance as her body shuddered violently.

"Easy . . ." she heard him whisper roughly in her ear. "Easy, princess."

She couldn't possibly have responded; her breath rasped in her throat as she tried to draw in air.

Lance didn't say a word; he only held her, his damp forehead pressed against hers as he waited for the explosion of ecstasy to pass.

Eventually, when she regained awareness and could feel again, she realized his lips were feathering over hers, across her cheekbones, her eyes, her temple. All the while he was murmuring to her in a strange tongue, whispering to her softly. It had to be Comanche. She might not understand the words, but she couldn't mistake the tone . . . his voice tender and caressing as a lover, not the cold, heartless stranger she had feared.

Still dazed, she felt his hard body shift as he reached down and unbuttoned his pants and drawers. Felt the thick pulsing heat of him as his rigid flesh sprang free of the confining denim and knitted cotton.

Summer knew a moment of panic as that swollen granite shaft brushed against her bare thigh, but then she realized Lance was looking at her, demanding in a hoarse voice that she look at him.

"Summer?" His hot, dark eyes holding her gaze, he ran his fingers slowly, deliberately, over her lips, dipping in between, making her taste her own essence. "I didn't hurt you, did I?"

"No . . ." She could barely get the rasped reply past the dryness in her throat.

"You know we're not finished?"

Mutely she wet her parched lips with her tongue and nodded.

"You're not afraid of me, are you?"

Slowly she shook her head. She was less frightened of Lance than of the intense pleasure he had made her feel. And more than a little confused by her own wild response, the devastating way he had shattered her control. "No . . . I . . . I'm not afraid of you."

"That's good. A wife shouldn't be afraid of her husband."

Wife. She was Lance's wife now. Summer tensed involuntarily at the reminder, and yet Lance seemed to understand her unease.

He was still watching her, his obsidian gaze smoldering and intense as he began whispering to her again in that strange lover's tongue. And then he began stroking her again with his hands—his unexpectedly, wonderfully gentle hands— arousing her taut nipples, moving over her belly, her naked thighs, making fresh desire kindle inside her.

Surrendering helplessly, Summer closed her eyes and let her head fall back. When his fingers tangled in the thatch of her woman's mound, her legs parted wide to give his searching fingers access. He meant to do it again ... make her come apart in his arms. And she wanted him to.

The fevered throbbing between her thighs grew in intensity, till it seemed like unbearable fire licking at her womb, along her limbs, through her veins. Summer whimpered mindlessly, caught up again in the same storm of passion that had swept her away only moments before. She clung to Lance, hardly aware of what she was doing, what he was doing.

The flow of foreign words had stopped, that much she knew. He was kissing her while his fingers worked their magic. She could feel his mouth grinding against hers, his tongue thrusting deep as she writhed against him in a frenzied attempt for deliverance.

A score of pounding heartbeats later, her frenzy erupted in a shattering explosion.

The long moments afterward were filled with her rasping breaths, with her violent tremors.

Keeping himself still, Lance held Summer as she quieted, savoring her response ... her shaking body, her naked skin sheened with sweat, the erotic scent of feminine arousal mingling with the aroma of coffee. His own desire was like a firestorm raging inside him, but he was willing to accept the delay. Just now it was enough to have Summer clinging to him in the aftermath of passion—the fulfillment of one of his cherished dreams.

After a while, though, when she remained unmoving, Lance shifted his weight to his elbow and raised his head. Her face was flushed, her lips slightly parted and still, her eyes shut.

Her eyelids fluttered open even as he watched, and he caught his breath, seeing the emerald depths shimmering with tears.

"You okay?"

Vaguely Summer returned his gaze, nodding mutely. She didn't want to talk; if she did, she might break down completely. She closed her eyes, suddenly assaulted by a tremendous weariness. She was so tired, so tired of being afraid, tired of being alone, of being proud.

She drew a deep, shaky breath that incredibly, helplessly, turned into a sob; she couldn't stop it. She felt a loosening, a melting inside her, and suddenly the tears were running down her cheeks.

"Summer?" His voice was rough with alarm.

"I'm fine. . . ." She shook her head, trying to swallow, trying to smile through her tears. "I don't know why I'm crying. . . . It's just the last two days have been so hard. I'm just tired. . . ."

Lance felt his thudding heart settle down a notch. Tenderly he gathered Summer in his arms, pulling her close against him. He thought he knew what had happened. She wasn't playing games with him this time. She was simply exhausted after the strain she'd been under, and the powerful sexual climax she'd just experienced had sparked a physical release of tension, like a dam letting loose.

He needed badly to feel the same kind of release . . . needed to feel the hostility, the resentment, the fierce anger, draining out of him as he poured himself into her. And yet somehow he needed more to offer her comfort.

Gently he pressed his lips against her temple. "We'll find her," Lance said softly, in understanding. "We'll find your sister."

Summer swallowed hard, gulping back her sobs, and buried her face in his throat. That was what she'd needed to hear. She needed to believe she wasn't alone. That Lance would ease her burden of fear.

"Go to sleep," he said, regretting the words but knowing he had no choice. He couldn't take her now. Not with her weeping for her sister. Not when she was so utterly vulnerable.

"Yes," she murmured shakily, and closed her eyes.

It was several moments, though, before her convulsive sobs lessened. Sometime later, Lance felt her quivering body relax, heard her breathing grow slow and even. He lay there, her forehead tucked under his chin, cursing his nobility while primal feelings of desire and hunger and protectiveness swirled through him.

He hadn't taken her, and yet he was almost glad. He didn't want Summer to think of him as a brute, didn't want to force her or leave her afraid of him.

Hell, if it weren't for the circumstances, he would have been willing to give her time to grow accustomed to being his wife, instead of demanding she sleep with him tonight. He wasn't a savage—even if he felt like it at the moment. His groin was ready to burst, but he could live with the pain.

If for a single instant he considered easing himself between her thighs, sinking his shaft deep within her shivering warmth and taking her while she slept, he ruthlessly crushed the notion. Even if he had to lie there and ache all night as punishment for having scruples, he wouldn't claim his right like that. Not when Summer might hate him for it in the morning.

Lance tightened his hold on her—and suddenly realized how cool her skin had grown. He frowned at the ceiling. He ought to let go of her long enough to cover her with the blanket. He needed to put out the lantern, too. Needed to get up and take the coffee off the stove so the pot wouldn't boil dry.

But he needed more to hold Summer in his arms and savor the feel of her body, soft and willing and helpless, against his. Needed time to get used to the idea that she was really lying here with him, innocent and trusting. To grow accustomed to the wash of tender emotion, alien and strong, that was lodged like a pain in his chest.

He couldn't believe all this. He'd spent years yearning for what he couldn't have. And now, suddenly, incredibly, it had come true.

Summer was his woman. His wife. His fantasy.

Well, maybe not entirely. She wasn't fully his wife yet. Not until they consummated their vows—and even then he couldn't count on her keeping her word. He could still lose her at any moment. Especially if he failed to find her sister. Or even if he managed to bring Amelia back alive. Either way, there would be nothing to tie Summer to him then.

Deliberately Lance forced himself to let out the breath he'd unconsciously been holding. He wouldn't let his fear get the better of him.

Summer was his for the moment.

And he would fight to his last breath against anything or anyone—including Summer herself—in order to keep her.

Chapter 4

Summer awoke alone and disoriented. Wincing at the bright sunlight streaming through the chinks of the shutters, she lifted her head slowly from the pillow. Lance. This was Lance's home. His livery stable. His office. His bed.

A powerful rush of awareness assaulted her. She was naked, wrapped in only a blanket, lying on the hard cot where she'd been introduced to passion by the ruthless stranger who was now her husband. The scent of him clung to her skin, more powerful even than the smell of fresh coffee that permeated the small room.

With a silent groan, Summer buried her face in the pillow, yet she couldn't shut out the insistent images that shimmered darkly behind her eyes. Lance making her undress for him. Lance initiating her to pleasure and bringing her to ecstasy. Lance holding her in his hard arms while she sobbed in fear and weariness.

He hadn't claimed his rights as her husband, and yet what he had done seemed somehow worse. He had bonded them together with intimacy, at the same time proving his mastery over her. He had *seduced* her, using tenderness and passion as weapons instead of threats of rape and physical coercion.

The realization left Summer in a welter of confusion. Lance had threatened to take her by force, but he had shown her nothing but gentleness . . . and incredible, incredible pleasure.

The sharp memory streaked through her, sending warmth pooling between her thighs. She hadn't known what lovemaking would be like. She'd never imagined any feelings could be that . . . intense, that overwhelming. She had never expected to respond so strongly to any man, even Lance, who'd always had the power to stir her blood with merely a look.

67

She'd always known he was dangerous, but last night had actually frightened her. She knew she couldn't control him the way she could her other beaux, but never before had she lost control of *herself.*

When Amelia had once warned her of the possibility, she had scoffed. She could almost hear her sister's voice scolding her in exasperation at one of her flirtations. *Mark my words, young lady, one of these days you'll meet your match. And then you'll see how much it hurts to have your affections toyed with.*

Was this what Amelia meant? Had she met her match in Lance?

Summer raised a trembling hand to her temple. Her head felt fogged by too many hours of exhausted sleep, her naked skin overly sensitive to the scratchy wool of the blanket, the hollow between her thighs throbbing with a tender ache. . . .

At least Lance had left the office. She didn't want to face him just now. She didn't want to remember the shameful things he had done to her, the way she had come apart in his arms, how she had broken down in tears afterward. Her pride was in tatters, her nerves a state of raw confusion. She didn't want to be so vulnerable to him.

And when he returned? What in heaven's name was she going to do? She had surrendered to him with pure wantonness—

A sudden realization made Summer's chin snap up. She was Lance's *wife* now. There was no dishonor in what she had done. She had accepted his conditions in exchange for his help, simply that. Her weakness last night had been the result of strain and weariness, nothing more. She had turned to Lance for comfort—and he had responded with more tenderness than she'd thought him capable of, holding her and stroking her before she'd succumbed to exhaustion.

Today she would be better prepared to handle herself, to face the difficult future. This morning they would take the stage for Fort Belknap. Shortly, in fact. From the brightness of the sunlight, the morning was well advanced—

With a sudden exclamation of dismay, Summer whipped her head around to stare at the shuttered widow. *Dear God, Amelia!* How could she have forgotten her sister even for an instant?

Throwing off the blanket, Summer jumped up from the cot and searched frantically for her watch, which was pinned to the bodice jacket of her traveling suit. Prying open the gold case, she felt relief flood her. It was scarcely nine o'clock. There was still ample time to catch the stage if she didn't dally.

Hurriedly she washed and dressed, then brushed her hair. As she secured it into a simple knot at her nape, she couldn't help remembering how Lance had removed the pins last night. The thought made hot color flood her cheeks.

Trying to ignore the insistent recollections, she gave her skirts a final smoothing and stepped outside the office, intending to make use of the privy behind the stables. It was a cool, fresh early September morning, sunlit and sparkling. A dozen horses moved restlessly in the corral beside the building, but there was no sign of Lance.

She had returned to the office and was eating a hasty breakfast of biscuits and coffee when she heard the plod of horses' hooves outside. When the door latch lifted, Summer froze, not daring to look behind her, not knowing how to act.

The door swung slowly open and Lance stepped inside the room; she knew it was he from the way her skin suddenly started to tingle. She was palpably conscious of his presence in the small cabin. His nearness had always affected her powerfully, but this time the effect was magnified tenfold after what had gone on between them last night.

This man was her husband, the husband who had become familiar with her body last night, who had held her through the night, lending her his strength. The thought of facing him unnerved her.

"I went to fetch Molly Jenkins's boy," Lance said gruffly into the silence. "And to pick up some supplies."

As he set down on the table the parcels he carried, Summer raised her head and their gazes collided. The shock was like plunging into an icy swimming hole on a hot summer's day; it stole her breath away. When he looked at her with those hard obsidian eyes, her thoughts scattered. All she could remember was Lance's mouth on her breasts, his fingers stroking between her thighs.

He broke the spell first. Carefully avoiding touching her,

Lance moved past her and began filling his saddlebags for the journey ahead.

Summer sat awkwardly sipping her coffee, wondering what she should do or say. The tension was back between them; she could feel its presence, alive and distancing. And Lance's silence disturbed her as well.

"Do you need me to help?" she asked after a moment.

"No. I can take care of it."

"It ... it feels so strange ... to be married."

When he glanced up from his packing, his ink black eyes looked wary, the guarded look of a wild animal prepared for danger. "We're not really married yet. Not completely."

His caution struck her as odd. Was it possible that Lance was as uncertain how to act toward her as she was toward him?

The notion of Lance Calder—arrogant, rebellious, hard-as-nails Lance—exhibiting uncertainty at anything amazed her. And consoled her at the same time. For an instant Summer forgot her confusion and resentment, forgot the strange circumstances of their marriage, in the need to reassure him, to ease the tension between them.

"I want ... I should thank you, Lance ... for being so considerate last night."

The swift play of emotion that crossed his face was gone in an instant, to be replaced by the familiar hard remoteness. "Just don't expect to get around me so easy next time."

"Next ... time?"

"We didn't finish last night, princess. Stop pretending to be so ignorant."

"I wasn't pretending. I know we didn't finish."

He made a sound that was almost a grunt and returned to his packing.

Summer watched him, having difficulty reconciling the hard stranger with the tender lover he had become last night. "Are you always such a bear first thing in the morning?" she demanded in irritation.

He looked up at that, focusing narrowed eyes on her. "Only when I'm left hot and aching by a damned tease."

She flushed. "I wasn't ... I didn't mean to tease you."

"Sure you did, princess. That's always been your game. Arouse a man till he's half-crazy with lust for you and then sashay away." His dark eyes swept over her with that characteristic hard stare of appraisal and challenge. "But you better understand now that you're not going to treat me like that. You're my wife now. When I want you, I intend to have you."

Summer felt her resentment swell again at his highhandedness. She appreciated Lance's consideration last night, but just because he hadn't raped her was no reason for her to grovel in gratitude. He had forced her into this disreputable marriage, but she hadn't agreed to be his doormat—or his trollop.

Her chin rose. "I consented to become your wife, Lance Calder, not your ... your fancy woman. And I won't be treated like one!"

His gaze hardened. "Are you already trying to get out of our bargain?"

"I wasn't, but if you mean to be such a boor, perhaps I *should* reconsider. Perhaps I was too impulsive—"

Lance cursed out loud. His temper was raw as fresh meat from the lack of physical release. He had an erection the size of a fence post, and it was all he could do to keep his hands off his bewitching bride. And now Summer was threatening him with what he feared most: her defection.

He had clenched his fist and opened his mouth to reply when he was interrupted by the rattle of wagon wheels outside. Lance immediately went rigid, while Summer tensed. She couldn't mistake the sound of her brother's voice cursing and telling his team to "Whoa!"

She rose from the table, smoothing her skirts and straightening her shoulders. She had hoped she wouldn't have to face a confrontation with Reed this morning, but he must have learned from Dusty about her marriage and come after her.

Avoiding Lance's gaze, she went to the door and opened it. She wouldn't make Reed climb down from the buckboard on only one leg. She stepped outside where he waited in the sunlit morning.

His gaze swung at once to her, his eyes pinning her, but otherwise he remained where he was.

For a long moment Reed sat unmoving, his hands clenched on the reins, his handsome face tight with conflict, his blue eyes filled with feeling: fury, anguish, regret.

"You did it," he said, finally breaking the silence.

"Yes," she said simply. "We're married."

She felt Lance come silently to stand behind her, felt his hand settle possessively on her shoulder. Summer flinched involuntarily at his touch.

She saw Reed notice the gesture, saw the way his mouth tightened. "Are you . . . all right?"

"Yes, I'm fine. Truly."

He digested that in silence. "There's nothing I can do, is there." It wasn't a question.

"No. I'm Lance's wife now, Reed. *Completely.* It's too late to annul our marriage."

She felt Lance's startlement in the tightening of his fingers. Quite possibly he expected her to rescind her marriage vows after the quarrel they'd just had. But her reasons for marrying Lance hadn't changed. She wouldn't go back on her word. And she didn't want her brother holding out false hope.

"We're leaving for Fort Belknap in a little while," Summer said into his silence. "The stage should be here shortly."

"You were going to go without a word to me."

She heard the hurt in his voice. "I had to, Reed. You would never have approved, otherwise."

"Well . . ." The word was expelled on a harsh breath as he looked away, staring off in the distance. "If I can't change matters . . . I guess the only thing I can do is try to help."

He reached in the side storage box beside the driver's seat and withdrew a small leather pouch. Quietly he held it out to Summer. "Here. It's all the money we have. Three thousand and some dollars, Union bills. I've heard the Comanches are sometimes willing to ransom their captives." He looked directly at Lance for the first time. "You may need it to buy Amelia back."

Summer's eyes filled with tears. Reed hated what she had done, but he was resigned enough not to fight it. And hopeful enough of their chances of success to donate the Weston savings to aid in their sister's rescue.

She started to move forward, but Lance prevented her by tightening his grasp on her shoulder. When she glanced back at him in question, she found him staring belligerently at her brother.

Lance spoke then for the first time, his tone gruff, hostile even. "I have money. I don't need yours, Weston."

His blue eyes narrowing, Reed stared back. "It's *my* sister you're trying to save."

"It's my *wife's* sister as well. I'll take care of it."

There was a wealth of possessiveness in the way he said "wife," but Summer didn't think it had much to do with her personally. Lance was only stating the code Westerners lived by: a strong man protected his woman, his woman's family. He had taken Reed's offer of money as an insult, as an insinuation that he couldn't provide for his wife . . . his white wife.

She watched helplessly as Lance's smoldering gaze locked on Reed, as Reed glared back at Lance in frustration: two proud males fighting over the right to protect their women.

Reed must have seen the absurdity of it, though, for he suddenly shook his head and let out his breath on a huff of unwilling laughter. His blue eyes held a grim gleam of humor when he said, "I'm not offering you charity, Calder. I'm responsible for Amelia, and it's my duty to pay for her release. You'll not make me any more beholden to you, either. I'll be damned if I'll let you risk your life in my place without me doing all I can to help. Besides, you may need every penny."

When Lance remained silent, Reed thrust the leather pouch toward him again. "Blast you, take it! We're in this together now, whether or not you and I like it."

Beside Summer, Lance nodded once, stiffly, and released her shoulder. Moving to the buckboard, she accepted the pouch, but instead of stepping back, she climbed up to the seat and embraced her brother.

"This is for the best," she murmured, pressing her cheek against his. "You'll see."

He returned the gesture, holding her tightly. "You be careful, Summer, do you hear?"

"I will."

After a moment, she felt Reed look over her shoulder at Lance. "You'll take care of her?"

"Yes."

Reed let her go then. Holding her elbow, he helped her gently to the ground. Summer knew how much it cost her brother to surrender his duty; it went against every gentlemanly instinct, every family feeling he possessed, to entrust the safety of both his sisters to the care of a man like Lance. But he had no choice, and he seemed to know it.

His fingers clenched around the reins once more as he looked at Lance. "I'll be obliged to you ... if you can bring Amelia home." His voice was low, unsteady.

Lance nodded. "I'll do my best."

With a last glance at his sister, Reed flicked the reins and urged the horses forward. The buckboard made a wide circle and rolled away with a rattle of wheels, heading back toward the Weston ranch.

Summer waited until her brother was out of sight before wiping away the tears on her cheeks. Turning to Lance, she handed him the pouch of money. "You'd better keep it."

It startled him a bit that she would trust him with so large a sum, just as it had stunned him when she'd told her brother they were married for good. He hadn't expected her to stretch the truth that way. In fact, he'd prepared himself for just the opposite. They hadn't consummated their marriage last night, and if Summer meant to renege on their bargain, this was the time. His heart only just now had stopped pounding. Did she really mean to accept him as her husband?

When she would have returned to the office, Lance stayed her with a hand on her arm. "This is a lot of money. You're not afraid I might ride off with it?"

She gave him a puzzled glance, as if uncertain whether he was jesting or goading her. She swallowed once hard, as if it were impossible for her to speak just then with the tears clogging her throat. Shaking her head, she moved past him, going inside the cabin.

Lance stood there a minute, trying to get control of himself. The relief he'd felt clearing the hurdle of her brother was fierce, but not as strong as the guilt he felt when he looked at Summer, at the shadows under her eyes, at her lips slightly bruised with passion, at the tearstains on her pale cheeks. Damn, he felt like a heel. Even if he hadn't forced her last night, he'd taken advantage of her weakness, added to her troubles by making her marry him. Last night he'd marked her as his, and he wanted like hell to do it again.

The memory of what he'd done to her wouldn't go away. He kept remembering how it felt to have her silky-skinned body pinned beneath him, her slender legs open wide to him, her hard-nippled breasts pushing against his bare chest. He kept thinking about what it would have felt like if he hadn't stopped. To have her go wild for him. To have her clawing at his back and arching her hips against him as he rode her. To have her moaning with need for him.

Dammit to hell, Summer belonged to him. She was his wife now. He'd had every right to take her. Trouble was, she looked worn-out, as if she was only holding back the tears by sheer force of will. As if she might break if he touched her. God, he wanted to touch her.

He'd given her pleasure last night, he knew that. He'd discovered the hidden fire in her, kindled a passion in her body that she'd never felt before.

And the thought of doing it again made his mouth go dry. He was conscious of a fierce urge to follow Summer inside the office and lay her down on his bed and thrust himself so deep inside her, he became part of her, to devour her mouth and fit himself to her body, to totally claim his ownership. But she didn't need some horny bastard rutting on her, husband or no.

Lance clenched his teeth, trying to stifle his primal urges. Last night had shown him without a doubt just how damned vulnerable he was to her. And the way his body felt just now, he was likely to attack her if he so much as touched her. His stiff sex hurt, squeezed by the pressure of his denim pants. He wanted her bad; as hard as he tried, he couldn't stop wanting.

But he had more control than that, more pride. He wasn't going to let Summer lead him around by his groin. He would have to spend the next several days cooped up in a stage with her at the mercy of his own lust, so he'd damned well better learn to live with it.

Unless he wanted to prove himself the primitive brute she'd always believed him to be.

The stage arrived a half hour late, well within the four-hour leeway the stagecoach company warned its passengers to prepare for. Until then, Summer and Lance said little to each other, both trying to ignore the other and the tension raging between them.

The lad whom Lance had hired to look after the livery while he was gone, Nate Jenkins, made short work of changing the team for fresh horses, eager to prove his worth. Meanwhile, the passengers, four in all, and the two burly drivers stepped down to use the facilities and to gulp down the fresh coffee waiting in the office.

While they were inside, Lance stowed Summer's bag in the boot along with his own gear, and told her to wait till the stage was ready to pull out before boarding. "The trip will be long enough as it is. You'll be glad of every chance you get to stretch your legs."

When she nodded, he turned to help Nate finish harnessing the horses.

Summer watched, grateful that Lance was going well armed. He had packed two Henry carbines—a new type of short-barreled repeating rifle. The guns could each fire sixteen rounds without reloading. He'd also strapped on a sixshooter—a Colt Navy .36 revolver—at his thigh, and she knew Lance always carried a knife. He'd scared her witless with it yesterday—God, was it only yesterday that she had asked him to help her?—and brandished it at her brother five years ago. The small single-shot derringer she carried in her reticule hardly compared to Lance's arsenal, but still it made her feel safer. Her father had taught her to shoot when she was small—in Texas even the youngest child knew how to defend against Indian raids—but when the war started, he'd made her start carrying protection whenever she left the house.

Less than ten minutes later, the drivers and passengers filed out of the stage office. Lance handed his and Summer's tickets to the large, red-bearded man in charge.

"*Two* passages?" The driver raised his shaggy eyebrows. "You riding with us, Lance?"

"Yeah, Shep. We'll be going as far as Fort Belknap."

The well-dressed blond lady in the group—the only other woman besides Summer—paused in the act of being assisted inside the stagecoach and turned to stare at Lance. "Surely you don't expect us to travel all the way to north Texas with *him?*"

From the nervous look on her face, it wasn't just snobbery that caused her outburst, but fear. Summer could partly understand the woman's trepidation; there was something restless and dangerous about Lance, even when he was at ease. His hard, hawkish gaze warned people away, and just now the smoldering anger was back in his eyes, the quiet hostility. His look was enough to give any gently bred female palpitations. Even so, that woman had no right to treat him with such sneering disdain, Summer thought indignantly.

Another of the passengers—an elegantly dressed man, perhaps the lady's husband—glanced pointedly at Lance, a sneer on his face. "I assure you, we're not traveling anywhere with any murdering savages."

Casually, almost lazily, Lance reached down and drew his Navy Colt from the holster at his hip, causing the woman to gasp, and Summer herself to catch her breath.

His bronzed brow furrowed, Lance inspected the action of the revolver's chamber, studying it intently. "I haven't murdered anyone recently, as I recall. As for savage ..." His mouth twisted in a cool smile. "I reckon that's what I am, all right." His black gaze lifted to the man, piercing and deadly.

The red-haired driver's chuckle sliced into the tension. With an accusing look, the woman lifted a shaking hand to her heart. "I refuse to ride in a coach with someone like that."

"Suit yourself, ma'am, mister. But I ain't puttin' Lance Calder out for nobody."

The guard who rode shotgun turned to stare at Lance. "You're Lance Calder?"

Lance's shuttered look gave none of his feelings away. "That's my name."

Breaking into a sudden grin, the guard wiped his right hand on his pants and offered it to Lance. "I've heard tell about you, 'bout the job you did for the Butterfield. I'm mighty honored to meet you, yessiree. I'm Petey Nesbeth. I hired on with this line last week."

After the slightest hesitation, Lance accepted the offered hand and allowed Petey to pump his arm in a show of unbridled enthusiasm. "This fella," Petey announced to the group, "was the best damn driver the Butterfield Stage ever had. Saved a lot o' hides, never lost a passenger." He turned back to Lance. "You're welcome to ride up top with me. Shep told me about that time you kicked the Frazier boys off your route an' then outran their ambush, but I shore would like to hear it from the horse's mouth."

Lance looked from Petey to the passengers, then to Summer. "Will you be okay?"

Something hard and bleak in his eyes tugged at her. She would have preferred to have his company, but apparently he was willing in the interest of peace to spare these good people his presence. Or perhaps he simply didn't want to be subjected to their bigotry.

Summer forced a smile. "I'll be fine." Yet she couldn't help but wonder, as she allowed Lance to help her inside the stagecoach, if this was what it was like for him, day after day, enduring the slurs and insults, the contempt of whites like her. She hadn't realized it was so vicious. She was appalled that he had to suffer such treatment. No one deserved to be treated like filth. Especially a man as skilled and valuable as Lance.

She settled herself in the forward-facing seat beside the other woman. Then the remaining passengers climbed on board—one of the men beside her, the other two men facing the rear—and the drivers took their places. In another minute, Shep whipped up the fresh horses, and the stagecoach rolled out of the yard, picking up speed rapidly.

The deplorable state of the Texas roads, which often were no better than dirt trails, soon became apparent. Summer had to clutch the leather strap overhead to keep from being thrown from her seat, and soon the dust hung thickly in the air.

For a time no one attempted any conversation. Summer watched the Texas Hill Country flash by in a rolling blur of rocky outcrops and clumps of woodland, interspersed with grazing land that was beginning to rebound with green after the hot, dry August they'd just had. With her thoughts so absent, it was a moment before she realized the blond woman had addressed her.

"That Indian man . . . what does he call himself?"

A swift stab of anger arrowed through Summer, and she found herself leaping to Lance's defense. "Why," she said sweetly, "he calls himself Mr. Calder. And my husband."

"Your . . . *husband?*"

The look of horror on the woman's face reminded Summer

forcibly of her new circumstances. A white woman who had married a man of mixed blood could hardly expect to be treated with the same respect and deference that the Belle of Williamson County had been accorded.

Indeed, such a reaction was even reasonable. She herself held conflicting emotions on the subject of Indians. Her own prejudice was deep-rooted. She'd been taught to hate the red man almost from the time she was born, ever since they had killed her mother so brutally, and her father had nearly gone mad with bitterness and grief. Few Texans who had carved homes out of the wilderness had escaped the atrocities committed by the various Plains tribes, particularly the Comanche: neighbors and beloved relatives murdered, captured, enslaved, outraged. It was only a few years ago that the last of the Indians had been driven from Texas, forced to live farther north in the Indian Territory. The fact that Lance still remained, that he hadn't allowed himself to be driven out, only testified to his grit.

She would have to adopt some of that grit now, Summer realized bleakly. His own private battles would now become hers. She could tell by the way the other passengers were observing her—with faint contempt and undisguised speculation. The man directly across from her eyed her with a boldness that he would never have dared use if she had been protected by her father or brothers.

Abruptly Summer turned her face to the window. She couldn't worry about that right now. She would have to deal with her marriage to Lance once Amelia had been safely returned, yes, but until then, she simply couldn't let herself think about it. Until Lance succeeded in his goal, she would have to control her dismay and turmoil over her relationship with her new husband.

What mattered most was finding Amelia and bringing her home alive.

Chapter 5

The two-hundred-plus-mile journey by stage to Fort Belknap took three and a half exhausting twelve-hour days—and then only because the weather remained good. The trip, though dusty and dry, was blessed with sunshine, moderate daytime temperatures, and cool evenings, with none of the rains that could turn the Texas prairies into fields of mud and the streams into dangerous torrents.

After leaving Round Rock, the stage stopped in Georgetown to pick up two more passengers, and then headed north through the hills, eventually spilling out into more open country bordered by forest known as the Cross Timbers. Mile after endless mile of undulating terrain—half prairie, half woodland—rumbled by. Seas of wild gamma grass followed the dip and roll of the land, melding with clumps of scrub cedar and thickets of post oak and pecans, broken here and there by willows and cottonwoods that grew along the sandy creek beds. Occasionally pounding herds of buffalo thundered by in great clouds of dust to alleviate the monotony, and sometimes there were signs of civilization—farm acreage whose sandy soil was planted in corn or melons, or ranches that raised cattle or horses.

From the very beginning of the journey, Summer received a firsthand taste of the rejection and scorn that Lance had lived with all his life. While nothing overt occurred, the grim silences and the bold sneers of the other passengers served to clearly emphasize her changed status. Before the end of the first day, she had begun to understand Lance's anger at white prejudice and his own inferior position in society. It was no wonder that respectability and acceptance were so important to him, if he'd had to face this sort of bigoted hostility day after day.

For the first time she could imagine what his life had been

like. Lance carried himself with a kind of hard self-awareness and defiance—a combination that had always dangerously fascinated her before, but now seemed to be entirely justified. The remoteness, the damn-your-eyes attitude, had no doubt been bred into him by years of being shunned. As a child, he would have learned from painful experiences not to expect approval or acceptance. As a man he would have learned to fight for every inch of respect and acknowledgment he could muster, even while pretending that the rejection, the rebuffs, the contempt, didn't matter—a strategy with which she was quickly coming to sympathize.

She had few chances to speak to Lance alone initially. The relay stations where they stopped for the night boasted primitive accommodations that afforded little privacy. The first night was the best. The small stone building doubled as an eating establishment and bunkhouse. The men slept in the hard, cramped bunks, while the two ladies shared a bedtick stuffed with prairie feathers—wild grass—near the fireplace. The second night there were no bunks, only a dirt floor and blankets that hadn't seen a good washing in months. The fare for every meal never varied—salt pork and cornbread.

Neither night did Lance attempt to claim his rights as her husband, as Summer feared he would, or even try to remain near her. He bedded down outside in the open air, along with Petey, not pushing the issue of his acceptance.

Summer didn't know whether to be relieved or offended by his neglect. She could sense that his withdrawal was as much emotional as it was physical, and it left her feeling acutely alone and somehow abandoned. The naked intimacy they had shared on their wedding night might as well never have happened—except for the sharp memories that frequently assaulted her. The feel of his hands on her breasts . . . the heat of his mouth covering hers . . . his steel-hard body pressing her down . . . his fingers moving in hungry, quickening rhythm between her legs . . . the fierce pleasure he had given her against her will.

The memories of pleasure conflicted with other, darker feelings toward Lance. Her resentment at his forcing her to wed had been repressed temporarily by her determination to get on with the difficult task ahead, but during the endless weary hours of the journey, it returned full force. Lance was greatly to blame for the silent treatment she was receiving at the hands of the other passengers. If he hadn't demanded their marriage in exchange for his help, she would still be Miss Weston, admired and courted, accepted unquestioningly—Summer shook her head fiercely at the ignoble thought. She didn't want to return to being the spoiled, pampered darling she'd once been, but having to deal with the disapproval, the silent scorn of the other passengers, was unnerving. Despite her contention with Lance, it comforted her to know he was near.

During the lonely, numbing hours of travel, jostled by the unrelenting rock and sway of the stagecoach, lulled by the monotonous landscape, she even found herself wondering what it would have been like if they had met under different circumstances. If they had married without the tension between them, without the resentment of the past, the uncertainty of the future. If Lance were white—

But then, that was a moot issue. If Lance were white, he wouldn't be the man he was now, and she wouldn't need him to rescue her sister. Indeed, if Lance were white, there would be little question of his acceptance. He would probably have women fawning all over him. The ladies who shunned him now would be the first to flirt with him and seek his attention. He might not be a gentleman, but there was something primal and intently masculine about him, an attraction that drew a woman against her will, that led her to imagine dark, forbidden fantasies. Fantasies that entailed Lance making love to her, hungering for her, looking at her with the hot gleam of desire and arousal in his midnight eyes. Fantasies where she held him to her breast and tamed the savage within, softened the hard, unforgiving man he had become.

She certainly wasn't immune to such feelings—despite Lance's Comanche heritage, despite his dishonorable demands that had forced her hand, despite her determination to forget what had happened between them in their marriage bed. Indeed, that night had only served to heighten the physical attraction between them.

Lance had initiated her to sexual intimacy. She had experienced passion at his hands ... rough, tender, incredibly arousing. ... She couldn't possibly ever forget that.

Summer told herself it was loneliness, not desire, that caused her to seek him out the third morning of their journey. Loneliness and nerves. Even more than she wanted to share his familiar company, she wanted the reassurance that his steadying presence gave her. The blond woman had disembarked yesterday afternoon with her husband, leaving her alone inside the coach with only the male passengers. One man's stare—the brown-haired Mr. Yarby's—had grown bolder, more brazen, to the point of making her acutely uncomfortable.

It was barely daybreak when she left the station building and went in search of Lance. Her muscles ached from the hours of sleeping on the hard floor and the longer hours of being cramped in the coach, so it was a relief to be able to stretch her legs.

She found him in the stone corral, checking the soundness of one of the stage horses, while Pete and Shep rigged the others. For a moment she watched Lance ... watched his lean hand moving carefully down the animal's left foreleg. She stood mesmerized by the sight, remembering the feel of those same long fingers stroking, probing, her body ... remembering the heat of his bare skin beneath her own clutching fingers ... his naked torso that was so different from her own ... the hard sculpted muscles, the broad, deep chest, the taut, flat belly. . . .

He must have sensed her presence, for he glanced sharply over his shoulder to find her watching him. Summer was grateful for the morning air, cool and crisp, that wafted over her heated cheeks.

"I thought that was the drivers' job, to handle the horses," she murmured conversationally.

Lance's jaw hardened at what he took to be a criticism. "I don't like to be idle. And I don't want one of the team pulling up lame before we reach Fort Belknap. We can't afford the delay."

He heard her push open the picket gate and step inside the corral, felt her move to stand behind him. His muscles tensed with awareness as they always did when she was around, all his senses becoming acutely alert.

"When you finish with that, would you mind ... would you tie my bonnet strings? I have no mirror."

Lance frowned, wondering what game Summer was playing now, even as a sharp memory from five years ago assailed him: a laughing Summer rigged out in Sunday finery before a buggy drive, gazing teasingly up at one of her countless beaux as he adjusted the bow under her chin. A flirtatious, beautiful Summer casting sideways glances beneath long eyelashes to see if the breed was watching, smiling when she realized he was. Her suitor's name was Albert. Lance had hated that prissy name with a passion ever since.

Clenching his teeth as he finished with his inspection, he gave the bay's shoulder a final pat and turned to his wife. His hard look was skeptical, but he grasped the ribbons of the low-crowned velvet bonnet she'd placed on her head and tried to tie them.

To his disgust, he found his fingers unsteady. Her upturned face, kissed by the rays of the breaking sun, looked as beautiful as he'd ever seen it, the pale skin flushed rose and gold, her green eyes soft and uncertain.

"There," he said gruffly, straightening the bow and stepping back.

Summer regretted that he had finished the task so soon. With Lance so close, she'd fought the need to turn her face in to the cradle of his palm. Yet such a public display of intimacy, of need, of weakness, would do her reputation with the other passengers no good, nor did she think Lance would appreciate it.

"Thank you," she murmured.

When she didn't leave, Lance eyed her impatiently. "You want anything else from me?"

She smiled faintly, almost wistfully. "Well . . . yes . . . actually there is something."

Without warning he felt hot desire pulsing to life within him, unwelcome but undeniable. That flush of heat, that pure raw wanting, was powerful enough to make him catch his breath.

Lance cursed himself. He'd done his damnedest to control his powerful need for her. For the past two endless day he'd kept his hands off Summer, leaving her alone even though it had near killed him.

Yet all she had to do was smile at him now and he swelled up like a randy stallion. All she had to do was look at him with those pleading green eyes and he was ready to do nigh anything she asked.

"Would you ride inside the coach with me today? I'd prefer your company to the others'."

He didn't want to deny her anything—except that. Slowly Lance shook his head. "That'd be a mistake. I'm not exactly welcome in white society, or hadn't you noticed?"

He saw her mouth tighten briefly. "So? Those people have no right to object to your riding inside. You've paid your money just like everyone else."

He heard the edge of anger in her voice and wondered if Summer was incensed for his sake or her own. Probably her own. She'd never before had to deal with rejection from her own kind, the kind of rejection she'd been faced with the past two days from the other passengers.

"In any case," she added, "our drivers would take your side, I'm sure of it."

Remembering Shep's response when the blond witch had tried to keep him off the stage the other day, Lance looked away restlessly. He didn't need anybody sticking up for him, but he wasn't sorry Shep and Petey had. His brief career driving the Butterfield Mail cross-country, over thousands of miles of hostile territory, had earned their respect, and he was proud to have something he didn't have to be ashamed of in front of Summer. But he also knew what a liability he was for her with the other passengers.

"I wasn't just thinking of me," he said finally, in a low voice, "but you. It'll only be harder on you if they see you with me. It's best I keep away."

Her brow furrowed as she looked at him sharply. For a moment she gazed at him intently, her eyes filled with an unspoken accusation he thought he could read: *You should have thought of that before making me marry you.*

She opened her mouth as if she might argue, then hesitated. "I just wish . . ." But then she shrugged her slender shoulders. "I wish this would be over."

She turned and let herself out of the corral, but Lance could have sworn he'd seen disappointment in her eyes because he'd turned her down. Reluctantly he watched her go, wishing she would see he was trying to be noble.

The past two days had been hell. He'd wake up thinking about her, hard and aching for her, but then he'd remember the circumstances. Seeing how the other passengers treated her—because of *him*—had awakened him from his fantasy of a peaceful future with Summer. Reality had come rushing back to punch him in the gut. He'd had time to see exactly what he'd done to Summer by forcing her to marry him. He'd turned her own kind on her.

It was an unwritten rule in her society. A white woman who willingly kept company with a half-breed was no better than a whore.

Worse, he would wind up repeating the past if he wasn't careful. He'd been so damned anxious to consummate their marriage—because he'd wanted her so bad, and so her brother wouldn't have grounds for an annulment—that he hadn't spared a single thought to the future. He'd been thinking with his groin instead of his head—a common event where Summer was concerned.

He hadn't considered the likelihood of making her pregnant. The whores he'd had carnal relations with knew how to use those little sponges soaked with brandy to keep a man's seed from taking hold. But Summer was a lady. She didn't know anything about stopping babies, or about keeping herself safe from a man like him. And he wasn't sure he had willpower to control himself. If he ever got inside her, he didn't know if he could pull out in time to keep from spilling his seed in her.

Summer wouldn't want to have his kid, he was sure of it—and he wouldn't want her to, either. Their child wouldn't be a bastard like him, but it'd still be part Comanche. He didn't want to do that to a poor helpless kid. Make it suffer like he had.

He didn't want Summer to suffer because of him, either. Riding into Indian Territory to rescue a Comanche captive wasn't the most dangerous thing he'd ever done, but it could get him killed. If he died, she would have to bear a mixed-blood child alone, and he knew from his mother's bitter experience what hell that could be.

He couldn't let that happen to Summer. By marrying her he had won the right to protect her—which meant protecting her from himself as well as from anything else that could cause her harm. No matter how much he wanted her, no matter how fierce this burning need to take her, he had to keep his hands off her.

God, he would be glad when they reached Belknap and he

could turn Summer over to her sisters in-laws. Another day and a half and he would be removed from temptation. Surely he could keep away from her until then.

Until then he wouldn't try to make love to her . . . not until he returned from Indian territory . . . *If* he returned. It would be the hardest thing he had ever done, but he owed her that much.

His noble vow lasted all of twelve hours. That night, at their last stage stop, Lance found Summer out back of the station, alone, crying quietly in the darkness.

His heart contracted in alarm at the sound of her soft sobs; his fists clenched in helpless rage as he remembered all the times his mother had cried to herself when she thought he was asleep.

"Summer?" he demanded sharply. "What's wrong?"

She went rigid at his approach and hastily fumbled for her handkerchief. "Nothing . . . I'm f-fine."

The bleak despair in her voice gave lie to her words. "You don't sound fine to me."

"I am . . . honestly. I was just . . . worried about my sister."

Which was party true. Summer inhaled a shuddering breath, trying to calm herself, not wanting Lance to see her in such a state. She didn't understand what was wrong with her. Despite the difficulties of the past few days, she should have had more control over herself. She'd known what to expect: the weariness, the fear gnawing at the edge of her consciousness, the ever-present terror for her sister, her nerves rubbed raw by uncertainty.

What she hadn't expected, though, was the terrible loneliness. She felt so alone, as if she were fighting unarmed, single-handedly, against the world. And Lance's remoteness only made it worse.

How she wished she could go to him . . . that he would put his arms around her and comfort her tenderly the way he had on their wedding night. But he was keeping his distance from her.

Wiping her eyes, she glanced over her shoulder at him. His hard-planed, hawkish face, silvered by moonlight, was tight with concern. And so was his voice when he tried to reassure her.

"Crying about it won't do any good, princess. You can't let it get to you."

"I know."

"I told you I'll do my damnedest to find her."

"I know you will." She bit her lip. "I don't suppose ... I could go with you ... to Indian Territory."

His gaze searched her face for a moment, but then he shook his head. "I can't let you. It'd be too dangerous for you. Not to mention too difficult a ride."

"I'm stronger than I look."

"I know," he said gently.

"If we find Amelia—*when* we find Amelia—she might need me ... another woman."

"Maybe so, but she'll have to settle for me. You'd only slow me down."

Summer wanted badly to argue, yet she knew Lance was right. She had no business accompanying him beyond the settled frontier. A white woman traveling through hostile Indian country would be subject to countless dangers. Even Lance might be unable to protect her. And the last thing she wanted was to impede his search for Amelia. Her own need to be with her sister, to comfort and help her, would have to wait.

Her shoulders hunched in frustration. "I just feel so helpless."

Lance didn't reply, not knowing what to say. Awkwardly he took a step closer, his hands hovering at his sides.

At his silence, Summer turned to gaze up at the faint stars overhead. "Amelia taught me about the constellations. She used to make up stories ... about our mother. Do you see Cassiopeia there? Melly says Mama lives there. ... *Mama's up there in heaven, Summer.*"

Her vision blurred at the memory, her throat filling with tears. "Oh, Lance ... I can't bear it. ..."

Summer turned blindly toward him, her voice catching on a sob. She heard him take a swift breath, felt his arms come around her, and then she was clinging to him helplessly. Gratefully she buried her face in his hard shoulder and wept, letting the sobs come.

Lance held her shaking body tightly, and yet he had never felt so useless. He hated to see her like this, hurting and helpless. He hated the guilt he felt, even knowing it was unreasonable. His own people were responsible for her grief; the Comanches had killed her mother, taken her sister captive. He hadn't taken part in either atrocity, and yet he still felt somehow to blame. And it *was* his fault the other stage passengers were treating her like a leper.

Lance gritted his teeth, both in rage at the situation and frustration at the feel of Summer's slender body shaking in his arms.

He shouldn't be touching her like this. He was liable to lose control any minute, which he'd sworn he wouldn't do. And yet he wanted, needed, to offer her comfort. She was his woman now, his wife. It was his duty to console her, to take care of her. He felt his heartbeat thunder in his ears as he tightened his hold.

It was several minutes before Summer's tears let up, and longer still before her shudders subsided and she became aware of Lance's embrace. She felt his body, hard and reassuring, offering her strength, felt his cheek, warm and gentle, against her hair. His voice was a low murmur, whispering to her in the same strange language he'd used on their wedding night, when he had demanded her innocence as the price of his cooperation. Hearing it brought back a rush of memory so powerful, it weakened her knees.

How could he affect her so intensely? How could he shatter all her defenses so easily? Like then, she was taking comfort from him again, trying to burrow inside him in an effort to feel safe. It amazed her how safe she felt in his arms. She'd never expected to react to Lance in such a way. She should hate him, should despise him for the difficult position he'd forced upon her. Instead, she hated herself, for her acquiescence, for her show of weakness.

Yet she was helpless to deny herself the solace he offered. When she felt his lips brush her cheek, Summer didn't push away. When he nuzzled the corner of her mouth, she tilted her head back to give him better access. When his lips settled on hers in a gentle caress, she could only sigh, wanting to surrender.

His taste was warmly familiar, the scent of his heated skin so exquisitely tantalizing. Then suddenly Lance shuddered. His kiss deepened, turning hard and hungry and overwhelming.

Summer felt the swift, responsive rise of heat inside her, the raw, coiling tension—and for an instant she even welcomed it. For a dozen heartbeats, she yearned to be swept away from the fear and despair, carried away on a primal rage of desire.

And then Lance's splayed hand tightened around her bottom, drawing her hips roughly against him, letting her feel the blatant bulge at his loins, reminding her where this was leading.... She felt the danger in his kiss, the seeking, the need, the wildness like an explosion. Felt the fierce hunger in his embrace ... brutal, lustful ... hot and primitive.

Summer froze suddenly, assaulted with guilt and confusion and fear. How could she allow herself to feel such pleasure when her sister wasn't safe? How could she let her passion get so out of hand? Frightened as much by her lack of will-power as the intensity of her feelings, she tried to draw back.

"Lance ... no, we can't ... we can't do this ... please!"

Almost frantic, she pushed at his chest, until he abruptly let her go. Summer took a stumbling step backward, holding up her hands to ward him off.

He was breathing hard, his eyes molten, his face a dark, taut mask of confusion and desire. "You're my wife, Summer," he said unevenly, the strain in his voice apparent. "We have every right to 'do this.' "

"I know ... but maybe we shouldn't ... not until this is all over ... until Amelia is safe.... The others ..." Her voice trailed off lamely at the way Lance had stiffened, at the harsh look that had taken hold of his features.

"You don't want your white friends to know you're hump-ing a scum breed, is that it?"

"No ... that isn't it.... I mean ..." Weakly Summer raised a trembling hand to her forehead. "You don't under-stand. I just can't ... deal with this just now."

His jaw went rigid; she could see the clenched muscles even in the dim light. "Oh, I understand, princess," he re-torted with lethal softness. "Better than you know. You want me to risk my life for you, but I'm supposed to keep my filthy Injun hands off you in the meantime."

Summer closed her eyes and swayed. "Lance ... I didn't mean ..."

His mouth curled. "Don't worry, princess. I'm not going to rape you. You couldn't pay me to touch you again." Lance's scornful gaze flickered over her. "You'd better get inside where your fancy white friends can protect you. It's dangerous out here in the dark, what with a savage breed roaming around."

With that he turned abruptly on his heel and walked away, leaving a bewildered, regretful Summer to stare after him in the darkness.

Chapter 6

Summer gazed uneasily out the stage window late the following morning, counting the miles until the end of their journey and trying to ignore Mr. Yarby's leering glances.

She wished she were safely at home with Amelia. The dry, dusty landscape of north Texas held little of the raw beauty that typified the Hill Country of Sky Valley, while the jolt and sway of the stagecoach only made her head ache.

She had never been this far north before, but because of her sister's letters over the years, she knew something of the area. Fort Belknap had once been a thriving military post and a hub for travelers and settlers. Before the war, the Butterfield Overland Mail had passed through there on its way west, connecting St. Louis and San Francisco. While the war raged, the governor of Texas had billeted a civil force there—two companies of Frontier Regiment Riders—to protect settlers against Indian depredations, but when the Confederacy fell, Fort Belknap was abandoned, leaving the settlers to fend for themselves.

The stage trail, after crossing the Brazos River at Miller's Crossing, passed close enough to the actual fort for Summer to see that it had already begun falling into decay.

A quarter of a mile farther on, the road widened into the main street of Belknap, the frontier town that had sprung up near the fort. The stage station, with its corral fence of stacked stone, resembled the ones where they'd stopped previously, except that this one enjoyed the company of other buildings, including a courthouse and a church and a small hotel.

All of which, Summer noted with dismay, were boarded up and deserted.

Still, she was grateful when the stage rumbled to a halt with a creak of leather and jingle of harness. She would be glad to

91

reach the Truesdale ranch and take refuge with Amelia's in-laws. Lance's cold silence this morning had been almost hostile.

He had good reason to be angry with her, she knew; he had only tried to comfort her, and she had pushed him away. Yet she hadn't known how to apologize to him for last night, or to make him understand that she had been rejecting his sexual advances and not Lance himself.

How could she explain that she'd been frightened—she, who'd never been frightened by any man but him? That when the consoling brush of his mouth had changed to raw hunger, she had panicked? His voice afterward had held withering scorn, and yet she'd clearly heard the raw wounded edge. She had hurt Lance without ever intending to.

Summer bit her lower lip. The idea that she still had the power to hurt Lance Calder was distinctly unsettling, but even more unnerving was the power he'd begun to wield over her. Lance had only to touch her and she lost control. She would be vastly relieved when he rode away in search of her sister. Perhaps a separation would give her time to accustom herself to their new relationship, to determine just how to handle the complicated, dangerous man who was her husband and the disturbing, helpless way he made her feel.

She would also be glad to see the last of Mr. Yarby. His bold stares had degenerated into outright leers, and worn on her already shaken nerves.

Yarby managed to be the first to dismount and, to Summer's dismay, insisted on helping her down. His hands squeezed her waist with insulting familiarity and held her far longer than necessary, while his tall body crowded her menacingly.

"Sorry our pleasant little trip's gotta end," he whispered, his breath hot on her face.

Breaking away, Summer drew a deep breath and moved close to her husband, seeking his protection. Lance's black eyes flickered over her, then narrowed on Yarby, but he didn't say a word as he took her elbow and shepherded her to the rear of the stagecoach.

While Lance retrieved her bag and his gear from the boot, Summer watched the other passengers disperse. Yarby was greeted by another tall, lean man whose features were so similar, they might be brothers or cousins.

The newcomer was dressed as a rancher but wore a saber and

six-shooter, as well as a gray forage cap of the Confederate Army. Looking over Yarby's shoulder at Lance, he elevated his nose and grimaced. "I smell Injun."

Beside her, Summer felt Lance stiffen, but he held his tongue, not taking the bait.

"Yep, wind's in the right direction, I can smell a stinkin' Injun a mile off."

"Now, Frank," she heard Yarby say good-humoredly, "don't be rude. That pretty lady's married to that stinkin' Injun."

"You got to be shittin' me."

She felt both pairs of leering eyes focus on her, felt her own face flame with color.

"Hey, Pale Face," Frank called to Lance. "Who the hell do you think you are, puttin' your hands on a white woman?"

Seeming to ignore them both, Lance hefted one of his Henry repeating rifles and held it out to Summer. "Carry this for me?"

She forced a smile. "Certainly," she agreed with gratitude. Not only did she feel better being armed in the presence of those two crude men, but relieving Lance of some of his burden would give him a free hand to carry the second rifle unencumbered.

They waited inside while the station master changed the team and sent the stage on its way. It was the first time Summer had been alone with Lance since last night, and yet whatever he felt toward her wasn't showing on his hard features. He was all business when he questioned the station master about the raid on the Grice ranch and Amelia's capture.

Jeb Burkett knew Lance from his Butterfield days and was more than willing to share what sketchy information he had. He had known Amelia and liked her, and thought her capture "a terrible shame." She had been visiting the Grice ranch when it was attacked and burned to the ground. The Grices were all killed except for two children, one of whom had supposedly been taken with Amelia. Martha Truesdale, Amelia's mother-in-law, had hoped Summer would bring some able-bodied men to add to a rescue party she was arranging.

"Thing is," Burkett said, "folks around here are pretty worn-out, fighting the Comanches and Kiowa, and they could use some help. You going after Amelia, Lance?"

"Yeah. But alone."

Burkett nodded slowly. "Well, if anybody can do it, you can. What can I do to help?"

"I'd like to hire some saddle horses to visit the Truesdale farm. And I'll want a good mount to take me into Indian Territory. Later I may need you to supply some horses for trade. If I find Miss Amelia, the Comanches will probably want payment in horses."

"Sure, Lance, whatever you need. I'll start getting up a herd. But I've got to warn you. Miz Truesdale won't like you calling on her place. She hates anything to do with Comanches, and I mean anything."

Lance nodded brusquely and asked to be shown some mounts.

When he and Jeb went out back to the corral, Summer stepped outside to the front porch, needing to escape the feeling of being shut in. Hearing about Amelia had rekindled all the pain and helplessness she'd struggled so hard to repress during the past few days.

It was only a moment later that a strange sound disturbed her morbid thoughts.

"Pssst."

Moving cautiously to the end of the porch, she shielded her eyes from the hot afternoon sun and peered around the side of the building—only to give a start of alarm to see a man's broad chest. The next moment was a blur. Hard hands grabbed her shoulders and pressed her back against the stone wall with a force that made her gasp. Her heart pounding, she looked up to find Frank's leering face looming over hers.

"Howdy, girl. We never got a chance to be introduced proper-like, with that Injun buck hanging around your skirts." The hot gleam of lust in his pale gray eyes made Summer shudder.

Yarby was lounging against the wall, watching with a grin. "Hey, now, Frank, don't hurt the little lady."

"She's no lady, Jimmy."

"She pretends pretty good. She kept her snooty nose in the air all the way from Round Rock."

"She's only an Injun's squaw, big brother. That right, girl? You his squaw?"

When he tried to take her chin between his fingers, Summer jerked her head away. "I'm his *wife.*"

Frank grinned at his brother. "A mite touchy, isn't she?"

Summer drew a shaky breath, trying not to panic. "You'd better . . . release me at once. Lance will be back any minute."

Yarby chuckled. "He makes a fuss, we'll offer him a horse for you. Horses and women are all the same to a Comanche."

"You just settle down," Frank said as he gave a tug on her bonnet strings and dragged it from her head, tossing it in the dirt. "We're gonna have us some fun."

Real fear filled Summer when his hand reached up to stroke her left breast. She gave a cry, which caused Frank to clamp his hand tightly over her mouth.

Unable to breathe, Summer squirmed, trying to break free, but his lean body pushed against her, pressing her back.

"Easy, girl." His hand kneaded her breast hurtfully. "You should be grateful to us. After having that stinkin' buck between your legs, you're gonna love the taste of a real man."

Summer whimpered in pain and fury, hating him for what he was doing.

"That's right, pretty thing. Sing for me. You like me, don't you? Soon you're gonna be begging for it."

Struggling against his touch, against the sweaty hand that was smothering her, she managed to twist her head and open her mouth far enough to sink her teeth in the fleshy part of his palm.

"*Ow!* Goddammit to hell— You bitch—"

Frank drew back his fist to strike her, but his howl of outrage was drowned out by his brother's sudden surprised grunt. From the corner of her eye, Summer saw Yarby go sprawling face-first in the dirt. The next second Frank was suddenly pulled off of her and shoved face-first into the stone wall.

She heard the crunch of bone, heard Frank's sharp cry, even as she drew a rasping breath in an attempt to draw air into her aching lungs. As she stumbled sideways, she realized Lance had come to her rescue. He stood at Frank's back, one hand twisting a stranglehold on the man's shirt collar, the other pressing the razor-sharp blade of a knife against the side of his neck.

Frank's right hand made a desperate half-formed movement toward his holster before Lance's savage growl in his ear stopped him. "Touch it and you're a dead man."

Frank made a choked sound. Blood was spurting from his broken nose, and his mouth had opened wide in a silent shriek of agony.

In relief, Summer sagged against the wall, holding her stomach and gasping for breath, trying not to gag on the sour bile that had risen to her throat.

Lance ran an assessing eye over her. "You okay?"

She forced herself to nod.

His mouth tightening, he glanced over his shoulder. Yarby had rolled over on his side and was reaching slowly inside his frock coat.

Abruptly Lance jerked his hand and threw. In a blinding flash of silver the knife went flying to land with a soft *snick* in Yarby's right shoulder. With a scream, he dropped the derringer he'd had hidden and clutched at his wounded shoulder.

Unconcerned, Lance drew his six-shooter and held it to Frank's head.

"You touch her again," he said softly, his tone lethal in its controlled savagery, "you come within a thousand yards of her, and I'll gut you, do you understand me? I'll carve out your innards while you're still alive and leave them for the buzzards to fight over . . . just the way the Comanches do. They know how to make death slow and painful. By the time I'm finished, you'll be begging me to kill you. You got that?"

Frank whimpered and nodded once, twice, while Summer shuddered. She had no doubt Lance meant exactly what he said. His bronze face held absolutely no emotion, but his black eyes smoldered with hate.

"You need some help here, Lance?"

Summer started. She hadn't even heard Jeb Burkett come up.

Lance nodded. "You could take this scum away and hold them till we ride out of here. And get him a doctor," he added, gesturing with his head at Yarby, who lay on the ground, moaning.

"The only doc left town four months back," Burkett replied grimly, reaching down to help Yarby to his feet. "But I'll see he gets patched up."

"Just a minute, Jeb," Lance drawled. "I'm a mite fond of that knife."

Bending over the wounded man, he grasped the knife handle and drew it out swiftly, ignoring Yarby's gasp of pain as he wiped the bloody blade on the sleeve of the man's fancy frock coat.

His own pulse was still pounding in his ears, the need for

vengeance still surging through his body. Yet grim satisfaction had begun to calm him. He was no longer seven years old, watching with impotent rage as those stinking bastards raped his mother. This time he had handled it. This time he had protected his woman.

When Burkett had led the two wounded men away, Lance looked uncertainly at Summer, who was scrubbing her lip furiously with the back of her hand, trying to obliterate the suffocating taste of Frank's sweaty palm.

"I've got some soap in my saddlebags, if that'll help."

She wouldn't meet his gaze.

"Or I could hold your head under the pump for a while. Drowning's a good way of getting clean."

She began to laugh, the sound caught somewhere between a giggle and delirium. Lance was trying to make her feel better, she realized. Her voice catching on a sob, Summer closed her eyes and leaned weakly against the wall.

For the span of several heartbeats, while she tried to compose herself, Lance didn't move. Remembering the last time he'd tried to comfort her, he kept his fists clenched tightly at his sides, not daring to touch her. It had cut him like a knife last night when she'd pushed him away; he wasn't going to bare himself to that kind of hurt again, or give her another chance to spurn him. And yet, as if possessing a will of its own, his hand came up to tenderly brush her cheek.

Summer flinched, an involuntary reaction to her recent assault, yet her action shattered the fragile moment; Lance went completely still.

Awkwardly aware of the fresh constraint between them, Summer tearfully fumbled in her skirt pocket for a handkerchief. Lance stepped back, as if withdrawing from her physically, distancing himself emotionally, putting his own defenses back in place.

And yet as he raised an eyebrow at her, his tone remained gentle—and even held an edge of humor. "It must be hard, going through life being the object of so much admiration. We haven't even saddled up yet, and already you have fellows fighting over you."

She sent him a startled glance as she wiped her damp eyes. It was the closest she'd ever seen Lance come to teasing. Usually his sarcasm held a bite that stung even the toughest hide.

Drawing a breath, Summer gave a shaky, watery laugh. "I suppose we should go."

"You sure you're okay?" His mouth was unsmiling, but his dark features had softened; the smoldering fire in his eyes had eased.

"Yes, I'll be fine."

It might be a lie, Summer thought, but it was a lie they both needed to hear.

Covertly Lance watched Summer as they rode north through the hills toward the Truesdale farm. Outwardly she had recovered from the assault; she looked as lovely and poised as usual. But although she mostly avoided his gaze, he saw the wariness, the fear, in those emerald eyes of hers whenever she happened to glance his way.

For the dozenth time, Lance cursed himself. He still felt a violent rage at seeing that scum put their filthy hands on her, but much of that rage was directed at himself. He should have known better than to leave Summer even for an instant. He'd known those two bastards were hovering around like buzzards. A man with any brains or experience didn't let down his guard for a second. A man who deserved to be called a man protected his woman.

That was a big part of the trouble. He had made Summer his woman, his wife. As such, she was the target of the hatred and bigotry that had always been directed at him, that he'd always been helpless to prevent. Goddamn, but he'd wanted to spare her that. He'd never expected it to be so bad. He'd thought her breeding, her background, would shield her from the worst.

He wished like hell he could stop it. Maybe he'd made a mistake, forcing her to marry him. Would he do it differently if he had the chance? Would he give up his dream?

It might be beyond his power to control now. If Summer had to face that kind of humiliation and degradation day after day, she would come to hate him—if she didn't hate him already. He didn't want that. Jesus, he didn't want that.

That was the second part of the trouble. He wanted too much. He wanted Summer body and soul, every way there was to want a woman. He wanted her writhing in pleasure at his touch. He wanted her eyes soft and liquid with need. Her mouth—ah hell, he'd give his right arm for another taste of her mouth. He couldn't stop remembering how it had felt under his last night, warm and soft, quivering just a little. He'd wanted so bad to stop her trembling, to take her inside him and ease his craving, to keep her safe.

Trouble was, as long as she was married to him, she would never be safe. And as long as she had to suffer because of him, his conscience would continue to flay him with guilt.

Burkett had given good directions to the Truesdale farm, as well as a timely warning. Summer and Lance hadn't gotten within a hundred yards of the stone house before two fiercely barking dogs raced out to greet them, scattering the chickens pecking in the yard. A second later a male voice shouted out, telling the newcomers to "Hold up right there!"

Squinting against the glare of the sun, Summer could see a young man half-concealed by the corner of the barn, aiming the barrel of a shotgun in their direction. Hurriedly she introduced herself as Amelia's sister.

He told the dogs to shut up and called them off.

"You're Billy, aren't you?" Summer asked. "Amelia wrote me about you."

Before he could answer, an elderly woman with graying hair came out on the porch. She was dressed in black-dyed calico, and also held a long gun. Summer hoped it was Amelia's mother-in-law.

"Mrs. Truesdale?"

"Yes? What do you want?"

"I'm Summer Weston, Amelia's sister."

Rather than offer a welcome, however, the woman gestured with her weapon. "Who's that with you?"

"This is Lance Calder. He's . . . He brought me here, and he means to go after Amelia, to try and rescue her."

Mrs. Truesdale's thin mouth twisted with bitterness. "That won't bring my Mary back. Those dirty, stinking killers butchered her."

Summer nodded sorrowfully as she urged her horse closer. "I know, your letter said so. I'm so terribly sorry."

"Those stinking Comanches have Amelia," she added dully as Summer and Lance rode into the yard. "God pity her soul. She was like a daughter to me—" Her eyes narrowing suddenly, she broke off in midsentence and gasped. "You're an Injun!"

Lance abruptly halted his horse, but Martha Truesdale's face twisted in an expression that was part terror, part horror.

Her eyes grew wild as she raised the gun in her hands. "You dirty Injun with your Injun ways. Get out! Get outa here, before I put a bullet through your godforsaken guts."

Billy hurriedly left his place beside the barn and ran toward the house. "No, ma! Stop! He didn't do nothing. Nan, get out here! Ma!"

But his mother was beyond reasoning. "Murderer! You killed her, you bloody murderer!"

"He isn't . . ." Summer began helplessly.

A young woman came rushing through the door while Billy made a grab for the waving shotgun. Finding herself thwarted, Mrs. Truesdale burst into tears and bent over, clutching her stomach. *"Merciful God . . ."* Her anguished wail pierced the bright afternoon. "Why'd you come back to torment me? Haven't you done enough?"

"Ma, go inside! Nan, take her, for Crissakes. I'll handle it."

Nan hesitated, sending a worried glance at Lance.

"Go on! I'll take care of it."

Making soothing noises, she shepherded her sobbing mother inside the house.

Billy turned back to the visitors. "It's only her grief talking. Our sister was killed by a Comanche lance in the same attack that Amelia was taken in." The words were apologetic, but the tone held a hostile chill.

"I'm sorry," Lance said quietly.

He shook his head. "We don't want your sympathy, mister. I think you'd better get off our land. You're only upsetting Ma."

"Billy," Summer said sharply, unable to help herself, "Lance isn't here to harm anyone. He's my husband."

The silence that followed her admission resonated with shock. Billy studied her for a long moment, his consternation apparent. "Then you better go, too."

"Billy . . ." She gave him a pleading look. "Please. We can't leave just yet. We need to know what happened to Amelia."

"We told you everything we know in the letter."

"Then . . . perhaps we could speak to the child who survived, the little Grice girl."

"They sent her back east to her kin."

Summer looked at Lance, not certain what to do, but his face was as expressionless as a stone. She turned back to Billy. "I had hoped to stay here with you while Lance is searching for my sister."

He frowned, considering. But then he slowly shook his head. "I don't think that would be such a wise idea, ma'am, not if you're . . ." He left the words unsaid, but his meaning was clear enough: *Not if you're a half-breed's squaw.* "Ma's nerves are shaky at best—you saw what happened. She needs to try to forget about Mary, and havin' you around . . . well . . . it would only remind her. Might even drive her over the edge. No, I'm sorry, Miss Weston . . . I mean Missus. . . . I know you came all this way, but I think it'd be best if you found some other place to stay. The hotel's closed, but maybe somebody will put you up."

Summer started to reply, but Lance raised his head. "Come on, let's go."

He turned his horse abruptly, leaving Summer no choice but to follow him.

"If you find Amelia," Billy called after them, "she's welcome to come back here . . . no matter what those red devils have done to her. We'll take her in."

Neither Summer nor Lance looked back.

They rode the two miles to the Grice ranch in silence. Summer accompanied Lance mechanically, paying no attention to her surroundings as her mind battled weariness, fear, outrage.

She hadn't expected to be turned away from the Truesdale farm. She'd been prepared for discomfort on the part of her sisters-in-law, yes, perhaps even contempt. But not outright repudiation. Her instinctive ire at being judged so unfairly vied with her dismay at her own impotence—and neither surpassed her dread for Amelia.

No matter what those red devils have done to her. Billy's words echoed in her ears with terrifying clarity. She had only been fooling herself, trying to pretend that Amelia would be all right. Even if her sister could be rescued quickly, even if she could be *found,* there was every likelihood she'd been subjected to the horrible ordeals Comanche captives usually suffered.

She had to prepare herself for that eventuality, Summer knew. Just as she had to brace herself for a future as Lance's wife. People's reaction when they learned the truth would be no different from Billy's, or the Yarbys of the world: revulsion and contempt. She might have to face a lifetime of such rejection—but that wouldn't matter if she could save Amelia. She could deal with rejection as long as Amelia was safe.

She had to find her sister.

She didn't know what course to take now, though. She hadn't thought that far ahead, couldn't think that far. Her mind wouldn't seem to function.

Lance watched Summer in smoldering silence, cursing himself as much as the circumstances. She looked numb, disoriented, as if she hadn't recovered from a deep shock. And he was to blame.

He'd known he was making her life harder by forcing her to marry him, but he'd been wrong. He hadn't only made her life harder. He'd branded her an outcast like him. And all the old rage came boiling to the surface, making him want to explode.

The Grice ranch had been burned to cinders. The gaunt, soot-scarred chimneys of the main house stood silhouetted against the sky, while the blackened stone walls bore silent testimony to the brutality of the attack. An acrid stench of fear and flames still hung in the air, as dense as the cloud of flies hovering over a grimy mat of chicken feathers and the carcass of a cow the buzzards had picked over.

Lance sat his horse for a long moment, grimly observing the devastation. Beside him, Summer stared in mute shock. When he dismounted, saying he wanted to have a look around, she nodded, yet she hardly noticed when he bent to inspect the ground.

She couldn't stop imagining the horror of what had happened here. Three people had lost their lives, and she couldn't help but picture it. She could almost hear the screams of the dying, the barbaric war cries of the Comanches as they circled ever closer, the crackling flames of fire as it licked the walls. Had Amelia suffered before being taken? Dear God . . .

Shuddering, Summer buried her face in her hands. Seeing this destruction made it harder to believe she would ever see Amelia alive.

She didn't know how much time passed before Lance returned, didn't hear his footsteps at all. She only became aware of his presence when he reached up and touched her arm.

Summer started, her gasp of alarm loud in the silence as she stared at the broken shaft of an arrow which he'd found during his search. Raising a hand to her pounding heart, she met his fierce gaze—and wished she hadn't. His black eyes glittered as he looked up at her. His harshness frightened her, and yet not as much as the reflection that suddenly occurred to her. Lance had lived with the Comanches. Had he participated in such raids as this? Had he killed innocent settlers and their families? Had he butchered women and children and carried them off into captivity?

The thought made Summer recoil in horror, even though she instantly rejected the possibility. Of course he hadn't partaken in such savagery. Surely not.

Lance noticed her reaction, the uncertain fear in her eyes, and his jaw clenched. He'd seen that look enough countless times before to recognize it—that combination of doubt and apprehension and accusation that whites often showed toward halfbreeds.

His gut knotted with renewed wrath. Summer's fear was probably only natural, instinctive for a lady of her class and upbringing. For sure her suspicion was no worse than most he'd been subjected to. But it galled him more than acid.

He expected such mistrust from well-bred women who didn't know him. He'd just never thought to see it in his own wife.

"Where are we going?" Summer asked some time later, interrupting the grim silence of their ride.

"Back to town. I'm sending you home on the stage."

"No," she said quietly.

His eyes flashed briefly as he turned his head to give her a narrow look. "I'm not giving you a choice."

"No," she said again with unwavering determination. "I won't go home. Not without Amelia. I won't abandon her."

His mouth tightened. "You heard Truesdale. You aren't welcome to stay with them. And I can't leave you here alone, not with those two jail-buzzards still running loose. I may be gone for weeks."

Summer shuddered in remembrance. She didn't want Lance to leave her here alone, either. His own civilized conduct might be questionable, but she would feel far safer with him than remaining here for Yarby and his brother to prey on. "Then take me with you."

He gave her a look of scorn. "Like hell."

"I'm serious."

"So am I. The answer's no."

She hesitated, regarding him with a troubled expression. "Why not?"

"That's a fool question if I ever heard one. Because I couldn't guarantee you'd come out alive, that's why. I might not be able to protect you if we ran into trouble. You might even wind up in worse shape than your sister."

"I don't think so. You would protect me. And even so, I'm willing to chance it."

"Well, I'm not."

"I would be safer with you than staying here alone."

He didn't try to argue the point—which gave Summer reason to hope.

"You said you would visit your family first, to ask them for help. Couldn't I stay with them?"

The notion that she would consider living with his Comanche relatives frankly startled Lance. For a full minute he didn't even answer.

"Lance ... please ..."

"No, dammit! It'd be too dangerous for you."

"It will be dangerous for you, too."

"Yeah, but I'm used to it."

"I'm not as helpless as I look."

He shook his head. No, Summer wasn't helpless by a long shot. She'd developed a quiet, resilient strength in the years he'd been away, the same kind of strength his mother had been forced to learn. And he had to admire her devotion to her sister, her courage in wanting to help. But that was entirely beside the point. He couldn't risk Summer's life; it would kill him if something happened to her because of him. "You'd only slow me down," he said, hedging.

"I'll try not to. Please ... you promised to help me find my sister."

"I never promised to take you into Indian Territory."

She bowed her head, biting her lip. "I'm not going home," she said in a low voice. "I can't leave Amelia. I *can't* turn my back on her. If it were your sister who'd been taken, you would understand." Her voice quavered as she turned tear-filled eyes to him. "I married you, Lance. . . . I kept my part of the bargain."

And now it's your turn, Lance knew she meant.

He cursed, low and fluently. The hell of it was, she was right. She would be safer with him than with her own kind. He'd give his life before he'd let any harm come to her. And it was entirely possible they could make it to his brother's camp without encountering any trouble. If he was careful, if they hugged the hills as long as possible, if he kept a sharp lookout, he should be able to keep her out of danger.

In fact, once they reached Indian Territory, the risk would lessen. He planned to turn into a Comanche warrior as soon as he crossed the border, and Comanches didn't attack their own kin.

And as she'd suggested, he could leave Summer with his family. He could trust them to look after her while he was searching for her sister. Summer would probably be shocked to the roots of her gleaming chignon to find herself in the midst of such a brutal society, but it might do her good to see the culture he came from.

Then again, it might give her a disgust of him forever.

Still, he didn't have many good choices.

"I'll think about it," he said gruffly, reluctantly, before urging his horse into a lope, leaving her to follow as best she could.

She kept up with him. With grim determination, Summer spurred her horse after Lance and refused to eat his dust. By the time they reached the stage station at Belknap, she could tell he was wavering. And when Jeb Burkett told them it would be two more days before the stage for Austin came through, Summer glanced at Lance and released a long breath of relief.

She could tell by the grim set of his mouth that, for better or worse, she had won.

Chapter 7

They set out from Belknap that afternoon, heading due north through the Cross Timbers, and rode long past dark by the light of a half-moon. Lance wanted to make as many miles as possible that day so they could reach the trading post on the Red River by the next evening. He intended to buy presents for his family there, and led a packhorse for that purpose—which was all the communication or explanation he offered Summer.

Uncomplaining, she kept up with him, even though she was unaccustomed to riding astride, even though her stiffening muscles protested every grueling mile. She was too grateful for being allowed to accompany him.

They finally made camp in the shelter of a sandstone bluff, near a small spring. Feeling rather useless, Summer watched as Lance unsaddled the horses and fixed a meal of bacon and beans. She was too weary to have much of an appetite, though, and she fell asleep as soon as supper was finished. Lance cleaned up and lay back on his bedroll, cradling his rifle and wondering if he'd made a huge mistake bringing her with him. Wondering if he'd miscalculated the danger.

Not the physical peril. He could handle that, he was pretty sure. Summer was his responsibility now, and he would give his life before letting a single hair on her head come to harm.

But the risk to his own self-preservation was far more lethal. Day after day, having Summer so close by, and yet so far . . .

Lance squeezed his eyes shut. Dammit to hell, why'd he have to go and let himself get involved with her again? He'd been doing fine until then. Now he hurt, and seemed to be hurting all the time.

That look in her eyes today ... like she didn't know whether to trust him not to murder her own kin.

And even if she did someday realize he'd rather cut out his own heart than cause her pain, he would never be good enough for her ... a scum half-breed with the disposition of a mountain wildcat. No white woman would want to get near him, let alone take him to her breast and cherish him as her husband. Summer would never be able to overcome her instinctive fear of him, her disdain at his background, her revulsion at being forced into marrying a man like him. What a damn fool he'd been to think she could ever come to look at him with desire, with love in her eyes.

He had his emotions fiercely under control by morning—although Summer remained oblivious to the battle. When he woke her at dawn, she groaned and burrowed deeper beneath her blanket. Her body felt like one huge ache. The prospect of facing another day of hard riding made her quail, but when Lance calmly threatened to leave her behind, she forced her sore limbs to move.

By the time she had performed a quick toilet at the spring and pulled on her gloves, Lance had struck camp and was preparing to mount up. She flinched when he tried to help her into the saddle, more in pain than in startlement, but from the way his hard mouth curled, she realized he'd taken it as a rebuff.

He dropped his hands from her waist as if he'd touched hot coals, and said in a drawling voice, "Don't worry, princess. I told you I'm not gonna rape you."

"I didn't think that. . . ."

The apology she'd been about to make died on her lips when he turned on his heel and left her to struggle into the saddle on her own.

They ate breakfast on the move. Summer chewed awkwardly on the dried beef jerky and hardtack, which tasted a lot like sawdust. As the morning wore on, she eyed Lance with growing annoyance. She resented his masculine strength, resented his easy adaptation to such difficult conditions. He sat his roan like he was part horse. But then, that wasn't much of an exaggeration. Comanches were the greatest horsemen alive, and Lance had obviously inherited the trait.

Irritated, Summer tore her gaze from him and faced forward in the saddle. There'd been a time when she might have tried to impress Lance with her own equestrian skill, or at least have tried to interrupt his brooding silence to make him notice her. But she couldn't afford to indulge in such nonsense how. All she cared about was finding her sister. Still, she couldn't help thinking what a spoiled little fool she had once been.

After a few more hours, though, she didn't even have the energy to waste on unproductive thoughts. It was all she could do to keep her numb body in the saddle. Lance seemed driven, allowing only two brief stops to rest and water the horses.

They reached the Red River at sunset, just as the western sky turned a breathtaking crimson and gold. The shimmering rays glinted off the sinuously winding current, making it look like it stretched forever. A large log building stood by the river ford, fortified with stone walls and blazoned with a cedar sign proclaiming the place to be Deek's Trading Post.

They were barely in sight, however, when a huge grizzly bear of a man came out to greet them. "Hot damn, if it ain't Lance Calder!" the bearded giant exclaimed, tossing his rifle aside. "Where you been keeping yerself, boy?"

To Summer's surprise, Lance's hard mouth split into a grin of genuine pleasure. He slid down from his horse, straight into the waiting arms of the bear, and suddenly both men were on the ground, rolling over and over each other. Summer watched in alarm as they wrestled in the dirt. They sprang to their feet to warily circle each other . . . and then suddenly the game ended as abruptly as it had begun. Laughing, the two men embraced and pounded each other on the back, before Lance finally pulled away and slapped at the dust on his denims.

"I went back home and turned respectable," he said in reply to the earlier question.

"You? Naw, you're pullin' my leg."

"Well, believe it, it's true. I have my own livery now. And . . . this is my wife, Summer."

Deek turned to stare at her. *"Wife?* Goldamn, you don't say." Evidently recollecting his manners then, he whipped off his hat and ran a hand through his shaggy hair. "I'm right pleased to meet you, ma'am."

"This is Deek McTavish," Lance said to Summer, in a cool tone. "I've known him since I was twelve." His features had turned expressionless, as if he were waiting for her response.

Summer summoned the charming smile that had never failed to win male hearts. "I'm pleased to meet you as well, Mr. McTavish."

Almost imperceptibly, Lance relaxed, while his friend shook his head. "Just Deek. Everybody calls me Deek."

"Deek, then. If you would help me down, Deek, I would be eternally grateful. I fear I'm stuck to the saddle."

The bear threw back his head and roared, but he hastened to her rescue, swinging her down and supporting her elbow while she recovered her balance.

"I still cain't believe yer hitched," he said to Lance. "How'd somebody as ugly as you ever wind up with somebody so purty?"

To Summer's surprise, Lance laughed, a slow, rusty sound that caught at her heart. "Who are you to be calling me ugly?" he retorted, avoiding an explanation as well as his wife's gaze.

"Well, come on in and set. Topusana's fixing some stew. You'll stay the night, o' course," he said to Lance.

Without waiting for a reply, Deek ushered them inside a room that was crowded with every imaginable kind of merchandise. A small Indian woman was bent over the fireplace, and when Deek made the introductions, Lance's scrutiny of a moment ago was repeated, with him watching Summer closely to see how she would react. He expected her to shun his friends, she knew, and she was determined to prove otherwise. Her greeting to Deek's wife, Topusana, held as much charm as she could muster, and she was pleased when the Comanche woman shyly returned a smile.

When Lance excused himself to see to the horses, Deek settled her at the wooden table and poured her a cup of coffee without asking if it was wanted, then kept her entertained by telling her his life history.

He had been trading here for twenty years, Summer learned, with the Comanches and Kiowas as well as white settlers. The Comanches pretty much left him alone, since he was married to one of them.

When Lance came in, he found Summer and Deek laughing together over one of Deek's exploits against a bull buffalo. The spear of jealousy that shot through Lance was as sharp as the hatred he'd felt toward the Yarby brothers—which was inexplicable, considering that Deek was likely the dearest friend he had. But maybe it was because his wife was laughing with another man, sharing an easy moment with someone else when his own relationship with her was so strained. Maybe it was because her laughter faded as soon as she set eyes on him. Maybe because he remembered how she'd let Deek help her down from the saddle a while ago when she didn't want her own husband touching her.

Clenching his teeth, Lance poured himself a cup of coffee and settled himself at the table.

"So what brings you here?" Deek finally got around to asking.

"I need to buy a few things from you, presents and such."

"Always glad to take yer money, son. Just tell me what you need."

Lance began by explaining why they intended to journey into Indian Territory. Deek shook his head sorrowfully when he heard about Amelia, and pronounced it wise to get help from Lance's kin.

"Last I heard, Fights Bear was camped out on Otter Creek, but that was more'n a month ago. They're likely getting ready to move for the fall hunt by now."

"Probably. But Otter Creek's a good enough place to start."

Deek glanced skeptically at Summer. "You ain't gonna take her with you?"

Lance shrugged. "It's her sister. She wants to go."

Flushing under the trader's scrutiny, Summer said lamely, "Amelia might need me."

"Well, you better rig her out in somethin' besides that fancy dress. She'll stand out like a red flag, otherwise."

"I intend to. I thought Topusana might agree to loan her one of her deerskin dresses."

Deek nodded. "Fights Bear know you're coming?"

"No."

Summer looked from one to the other. "Who is Fights Bear?"

Deek frowned at Lance. "Didn't you tell her nothin' about yer kin?" Without waiting for a reply, he explained, "Fights Bear is Lance's brother . . . half brother, actually. He's a war chief of the Panataka Comanches. They're Honey Eaters. Topusana comes from the same band."

"Honey Eaters?" Summer asked blankly.

"Lord, don't you even know that?" His scowl was for Lance, though. "You better let her know what she's in for, ridin' into a Comanche camp, or she's gonna have one hell of a shock."

Lance's mouth hardened with the first defensiveness he'd shown Deek since arriving. "If she wants to know, all she has to do is ask."

The uncomfortable subject was dropped then, while the trader questioned Lance about his search plans.

The two men discussed strategy over a meal of venison stew. Summer, surprised to find herself famished, ate every bite on her plate, and didn't protest when Topusana piled on another helping. But she listened intently to everything Lance had to say—which was far more than he'd ever volunteered to her. She resented his forthrightness with his friend, especially when he'd been so surly and closemouthed with her, yet it was clear Lance valued the older man's advice, while he probably thought explanations to her were only a nuisance and a waste of time.

Not wanting to be a burden, she offered to help wash the dishes after supper, but Deek wouldn't hear of a guest being put out, and Lance wanted to turn in early, so they could get an early start.

First, though, he wanted Summer to try on one of Topusana's dresses. From the conversation Summer gathered he meant to dress her as a Comanche woman and don his own Indian garments, so they would pass for natives. Hence, she wasn't surprised when Deek's wife approached her with a bundle of clothing. Carrying a lamp, Topusana led her into a small storage room that apparently doubled as a spare bedchamber for passing travelers.

Summer had left her crinoline petticoats behind at the Belknap station so she could ride without hindrance, but now she discarded her traveling suit and camisole and corset as well. When she would have kept on her chemise and drawers, though, Topusana shook her head vigorously, saying in broken English that so many clothes would make her too hot when the sun shone.

Reluctantly Summer jettisoned the last remnants of civilization and covered her nakedness with a long, shapeless deerskin dress that reached below her knees. The fringed bodice was a bit too small for her bosom, and pushed against her naked breasts in a way that made her feel indecently exposed. Like any lady, she was accustomed to wearing layers and layers of undergarments beneath her voluminous gowns, and a single layer of soft deerskin hardly felt like being dressed. The thigh-high leggings and moccasins Topusana gave her didn't seem to help much, either.

When the Comanche woman suddenly left the room, Summer felt deserted. But then Lance appeared in the doorway. He stopped short when he saw her, his black eyes narrowing.

Nervously Summer smoothed the skirt of her new costume. She had no mirror, but she knew she must look a sight, if Lance's odd expression was anything to judge by. "Do I look that bad?" she asked uncertainly.

He didn't answer at once. He couldn't, and keep his voice steady. She didn't look like the spoiled, regal Miss Weston now. The plain, primitive garment stripped her of pride and pretense, making her seem as simple and innocent as any shy Comanche maiden. Except for the color of her complexion, that is. Her face was flushed with sun from the long hours of riding, since her bonnet hadn't protected her fully, but it looked like the flush of passion. Lance wished like hell it were.

He swallowed hard, wishing also that he could quell the sudden swelling ache in his loins. Ever since Yarby's assault, he'd managed to conquer his brutal lust for her, not wanting to add to Summer's fear of him. But the temptation now to give in to it was riding him hard.

"Don't I look all right?"

Lance gritted his teeth. He could tell Summer how beautiful he found her, how desirable, but she knew that damned well already. He hadn't kowtowed to her vanity five years ago, and he wasn't about to start now.

"You look okay," he answered gruffly. "Except for your hair. Comanche women don't pin it up like that. They wear it short and hanging free, or long in a braid."

"Oh."

"Take your hair down."

His voice had softened perceptibly. Obediently she reached up and pulled out the pins. Shaking the chignon free, she let the long, dark mass fall down her back, feeling Lance's hot eyes on her all the while. His command reminded her of their wedding night, when he'd made her undress and stand naked before him. Except that this was somehow more intimate, more powerful. Then, she hadn't known what to expect. Her carnal knowledge then had been limited to stolen kisses. Now she knew how it felt to find pleasure in a man's embrace, to experience passion at his hands.

Summer found herself quivering at the memory, at the sensations that memory aroused. Much of that night seemed like a dream, yet she could still vividly remember the feel of Lance's fingers threading softly through her hair, stroking it, stroking her body.

She knew for a moment he must be sharing the same thought, for he took a step toward her, a harsh look of need on his face.

Afraid of what she saw there—the searing intensity, the naked glitter of want in his eyes—Summer took an involuntary step backward. Lance looked like he might assault her right there, like he might tear off her clothes and take her body as he'd almost done on their wedding night, regardless of the present circumstances. But they weren't alone. There were other people—strangers in the next room.

"Lance . . ." She glanced nervously toward the open door.

He stopped abruptly and slanted a look over his shoulder. When he turned back, his eyes not only had lost their molten heat, they'd gone cold. For a moment, Lance stared at her, his gaze transmitting the silent message: *You're my wife. You should be sleeping with me.*

Yet he made no move to enforce his rights.

His features hardening, he turned to go. "Get some sleep. We've got a hard ride tomorrow," he growled before shutting the door forcefully behind him.

Alone, Summer stared in bewilderment and frustration and

rising irritation, wishing she had handled the situation better, had handled Lance better. Wishing she didn't feel such keen disappointment at her husband's abrupt departure.

She took Lance's advice, though. After making use of the wash water Topusana had provided her to take a quick sponge bath, Summer donned her nightgown for what she feared might be the last time and curled up on a mattress covered with buffalo robes. She fell asleep almost before her head touched the pillow.

It seemed like only a few moments later when she felt someone shaking her awake. Squinting in the dim light of a lantern, Summer saw a shadow looming over her, an ominous, violent figure that resembled the terrible specters in her nightmares.

She sat up abruptly, but her choked scream died to a breathless gasp as she recognized Lance. He stood over her, his legs spread slightly, his hard face a mask of defiance.

He was naked from the waist up, except for a necklace made of bear claws that hung halfway down his smooth bronzed chest. Below the waist he wore only moccasins and a long breechclout that left the sides of his legs bare and showed powerful horseman's thighs rippling with muscle. His straight black hair was held back from his face with a headband of red deerskin, which only emphasized his high cheekbones and broad forehead.

His eyes traveled over her contemptuously as she clutched the covers to her breast. "Get dressed, princess. We're riding out in ten minutes."

Her pounding heart settled down a degree, but her temper flared as she realized he had deliberately tried to frighten her. "Damn you, you did that on purpose!" she hissed rather hysterically.

"Did what?"

"Dressed up like an Indian to frighten me."

His mouth curled at the corner. "Better get used to it. It's what I am. Get dressed—wear the clothes Topusana gave you, and put a scarf or something over your head to protect you from the sun. Hurry up. I won't wait for you."

He turned on his heel and disappeared as quietly as he'd come. Willing her heartbeat to slow down, Summer clenched her teeth. "You don't scare me, Lance Calder," she muttered beneath her breath, determined to make it the truth.

To her dismay, however, she found Lance just as disturbing when she went outside a short while later, where he was loading the packhorse with the various goods he'd collected. In the dawn light he seemed even more threatening, if that was possible. Most of his bronzed body was exposed to her gaze, his limbs and torso rippling with hard muscle, and he moved silently, with the raw power and grace of a predator.

Was he naked beneath the loincloth?

Flushing, Summer silently cursed herself for entertaining such a shameful thought, and for feeling such a powerful attraction. Such confusing sexual urges alarmed her. This wasn't like her—this couldn't be her. She was a lady ... a gently bred virgin. And yet she couldn't deny the weakness that had stolen over her limbs, the aroused heat that pooled between her thighs at the sight of Lance standing half-naked in front of her.

Forcibly Summer clasped her hands together as she fought back the shocking urge to touch him. For the first time in her life she wanted a man, truly wanted—wanted his body, wanted him to touch her and take her in his arms and join with her. To teach her the secrets between a man and a woman that she had only glimpsed on their wedding night.

Determinedly Summer ground her teeth until they ached. Perhaps it wasn't so reprehensible, desiring Lance; he was her husband by law, after all. But it was entirely inappropriate under the circumstances to be lusting after him. She had to remember her sister's terrible plight.

"Do you suppose you could put on a shirt?" she demanded irritably, even as she avoided his gaze.

"No," Lance answered just as curtly. "I like being free of civilized clothes. And I'm not going to suffer from the heat just to satisfy your notions of modesty."

Without waiting for permission, he lifted her into the saddle and vaulted onto his horse's back. He'd exchanged her Mexican saddle for an Indian one—a wooden frame tree covered with buffalo hide, with a high pommel and cantle—but he rode bareback, with only a loop of plaited buffalo hair for a bridle. His roan horse was loaded with weapons, though—

his Henry rifles and a bow and quiver of arrows he'd gotten from somewhere.

She had no trouble picturing Lance as a Comanche warrior. At the moment he looked just as savage. Indeed, he looked supremely dangerous, a danger that beckoned and taunted.

She was grateful when Deek and his wife came out to see them off. She had already thanked Topusana for the use of the dress, but she repeated her thanks and accepted with gratitude the hide pouch the Comanche woman handed her which she was told contained food for their journey.

As they set out, Lance gave her a single warning. "We run into trouble, you do exactly as I say, do you hear me?" Then he lapsed into the same smoldering silence that had punctuated their previous day's journey.

The land they traveled was beautiful in a raw, lonely sort of way. They might have been the only two people on earth for all the company they encountered.

As they crossed the river valley, they hugged the hills at the eastern edge of the flat prairie, taking the high ground if given a choice. It provided better cover, Summer suspected.

Once, when his horse snorted, Lance held up a hand in a gesture to halt and lifted his rifle. A few minutes later he moved on.

"Panther," was all he said.

She wondered how he had known, but sensing his disinclination to talk, she asked only one question. "How long will it take to reach your people's camp?"

"Two days, if they're at Otter Creek. More if we have to look farther."

It was several hours later before Summer realized Lance had a purpose in taking this route. Detouring through a gully, he led her to a dead end at the base of a ridge. When he dismounted and pulled away the brush and thicket, however, she could see a crevice in the wall.

Telling her to wait, he entered the cave and shortly emerged carrying a long lance whose red cloth covering was decorated with eagle feathers, and a round shield of buffalo hide painted with a primitive picture of racing horses.

"Are those yours?" Summer was surprised into asking.

"No, I stole them from a passing sailor," Lance replied sarcastically.

"Well, excuse me for wondering!" Summer snapped back.

He gave her a sharp glance, but offered a gruff explanation as he grabbed a handful of mane and swung up on his horse's back. "I hid them here when I left my people. I didn't think the good citizens of Texas would take too well to me carrying Comanche weapons."

She wanted to ask why he had left, but doubted he cared to discuss it. She bit her tongue as they set off again.

As the day wore on, they headed northwest across flat open prairie. Watching him mile after mile, Summer couldn't help comparing this Lance to the one she'd been acquainted with most of her life. She wouldn't have known him if she met him on the street. He looked every inch the fierce Comanche warrior, as if he belonged to the land and the wind. And she was too fiercely attracted to him for her peace of mind. All too frequently she found herself staring spellbound at his barbaric handsomeness, fascinated by his primal masculine beauty.

Late that afternoon, Lance found a place that offered shelter and fresh water and forage for the horses. A slight rise in the terrain had been hollowed out by a stream to form a gully and was protected by a cedar brake. He halted the horses, saying they would stop there for the night.

"You feel well enough to make yourself useful?" he asked as he dismounted.

Summer nodded. She had ridden just as hard today as yesterday, but surprisingly she didn't feel quite so terribly exhausted.

"Good. I'm tired of pampering you."

She might not be as physically drained as before, but three and a half difficult days of traveling in a stagecoach, and two harder days of riding horseback through wilderness, had made Summer's temper raw. Her anger flared at his gibe. "I never asked you to pamper me!"

Lance snorted. "No, you just expect it as your due."

Summer gritted her teeth as he came around to her side. "Just tell me how you want me to help."

"You know how to cook?"

"Some. We have household servants at home—the vaqueros' wives—so it isn't often necessary."

Lance's mouth curled as he lifted her down from her horse. "When we reach my brother's camp, you're going to have to pitch in. Women perform all the work in a Comanche village, and they won't understand if you don't."

"I'll do my fair share."

His gaze scornful, he lifted one of her hands and peeled back the glove to inspect it. The palm was soft and white and obviously unaccustomed to hard physical labor or anything but the light chores expected of a lady. "What do you do every day if you have all those servants? Play lady of the manor?"

Irritated by his smug look of triumph, Summer jerked her hand back—and saw a muscle in Lance's jaw tighten. "Actually, I've spent the years since my father died running our ranch—which happens to entail more brains than brawn."

"Fix us some supper while I see to the horses," he said brusquely as he turned away.

"Should I make a fire?"

"No, I don't want to risk it."

Involuntarily Summer cast a worried glance around the small clearing. "Is it dangerous here?"

"No more dangerous than any place else, but there's no need to advertise our whereabouts. I don't believe in inviting trouble."

They worked in silence for a time. Lance unloaded the supplies, then watered and hobbled the horses while Summer searched through the provisions. By the time he returned, she had arranged a blanket beside the stream and laid out a meal of dried beef and apples and the last of the cornbread Topusana had made them.

Lance settled himself cross-legged on the edge of the blanket, far enough away that Summer had to lean over to hand him his food. Just then the angle of the fading sun caught her face, highlighting the vivid bruise on her jaw. The sight sent fury streaking through Lance.

He'd vowed not to touch her, but he couldn't stop himself. Raising his hand, he gently brushed the vicious mark with the pad of his thumb. "That bastard hurt you," he breathed.

Wincing at the memory of Frank Yarby's fist gripping her

chin, Summer drew back abruptly. She saw the swift anger that claimed Lance's features before a cold wall slammed down to shutter his expression.

Without comment he took a bite of the sandwich she'd made him, but he was seething inside. Every time she flinched from him, it made him madder than hell—and it was damn well time he put a stop to it.

"You better learn not to jump out of your skin every time I touch you, princess, or you won't have any skin left."

"I don't do that."

"Sure you do. You're scared to death I'm going to do something to you that you won't like. But you'd better get used to me touching you."

His tone was so harsh, so threatening, that Summer had a hard time swallowing her food. The look she sent him was anxious, wary. "You wouldn't . . ."

"Force myself on you?" He smiled coldly. "I told you not to worry, princess. I'm not gonna ravish your pure white body."

Summer glanced again around the secluded clearing. They were all alone, out in the middle of nowhere. There was no one to prevent Lance from doing anything he wanted to her. He could throw her down on the ground and take her if he wanted to. Legally, he even had the right.

He must have read her thoughts, for his mouth twisted. "I'm not the unprincipled brute you think I am."

"I . . . I don't."

"Sure you do."

No, Summer reflected in confusion. At times she thought Lance boorish, ill bred, bad-tempered, and uncivil, but she knew he had principles of a sort, even if they didn't always match hers. And while he might have a belligerent disposition, she didn't think he would deliberately hurt her.

"You can rest easy, princess," Lance said, watching her. "I'm not even going to try to bed you."

His grim declaration surprised her so much that she blurted out her reply without thinking. "Why not?"

He met her gaze with a hard one of his own. "You mean why won't I claim my lawful rights, even though you're my wife?"

She hadn't meant to start this indelicate conversation, but

now that she had, she wanted an answer, to know what Lance expected of her, of their marriage. "Yes. Why haven't you . . ." She flushed and fell silent.

Because I can't bear seeing the fear in your eyes when I touch you. Because if I touch you, I'll lose control, Lance said viciously to himself. *I get too close, and my pride will shatter.* He looked away. Losing control was something he wouldn't permit himself to do; relinquishing his pride was something he couldn't allow. Pride was the only defense he had against his magnolia-skinned, honey-voiced wife. Summer might turn him inside out, but wild horses couldn't make him admit it to her.

Lance clenched his teeth, renewing his determination not to feel the things she made him feel, to want the things she made him want.

But there were other reasons, too. Reasons that went beyond lust or pride.

"I don't want to make it any worse for you," he answered finally. "You're having a hard enough time as it is."

"What do you mean?"

"I'm an outcast. I've branded you the same."

She couldn't dispute that. The whites she'd come in contact with since her marriage had shown her nothing but contempt.

"Besides," he said, his voice dropping, "I don't want to leave you breeding. If something happened to me, you'd have to raise my kid alone, and I'm not going to do that to some poor little devil."

Involuntarily Summer moved a hand to her abdomen. She hadn't let herself think about having Lance's baby. Hadn't let herself think about the consequences of bringing a mixed-blood child into the world. She didn't want to think about such a thing.

Lance saw the dismay on her face, the faint look of horror, and smiled bitterly. "Yeah, I thought that's how you'd feel."

She didn't try to deny it. She couldn't. "I hadn't thought much about it," she said lamely. But perhaps she should think about it. "Lance? On our wedding night . . . what you did to me . . . Did that make me pregnant?"

He wanted to curse . . . at the same time he wanted to reassure her. "After the way you left me hurting? There's no way, princess. Not when you're still a virgin." His eyes seared her. "Surely with all your experience with men, you know that. Don't tell me you're that ignorant."

"Well, I am." Her chin lifted. "A lady isn't raised with knowledge of such things."

"No, I don't expect so." Lance looked off in the distance. "There are ways around a woman getting pregnant."

Surprise widened Summer's eyes, while acute embarrassment flushed her cheeks. "How?"

"Just . . . ways. A proper wife would know about them."

His emphasis on the word *proper* annoyed her. "I hardly think the usual standards apply in this instance. Our marriage isn't exactly . . . This isn't the sort of marriage I expected."

His huff of laughter was loud in the growing dusk. "I don't suppose it is. I'll bet it's one hell of a shock for you, princess. No lady would want an uncivilized breed for a husband, and you're more finicky than most."

"I am not."

"Sure you are. You want a pale-skinned, soft-handed pansy to do your bidding."

Summer bristled. "I want a gentleman for a husband, yes."

"Well, you damn sure didn't get one."

"That is altogether too obvious!"

"Well, I didn't get what I wanted, either," he lied. "I want a woman who'll be honest with me, not try to work her wiles on me every time she wants something."

Glaring at him, Summer rose up on her knees. "You should have thought of that before you forced me to accept your proposal! You were the one who insisted on this marriage!"

"Yeah, and it's high time you remembered you're my wife!"

By now Lance had risen to his knees also, and his face was cruel when he reached out for her and caught her arms. Summer's flashing green eyes suddenly sobered with wariness, and perhaps a little fear.

Sliding his right hand down her arm, he closed his fingers around her wrist. When she tried to pull away, he held it captive. Slowly, inexorably, Lance forced her hand up and pressed her palm against his bare chest.

"Touch me, princess."

"Lance, no . . ."

"Oh, yes. You're going to learn not to be afraid of me."

Wrapping his arm around her waist, he pulled her closer, even as she tried to push him away. Giving no quarter, he moved her palm over his chest, compelling her to feel the smooth naked flesh there, the masculine nipples, the flexing muscles of his rib cage, the hard, flat plane of his abdomen.

Summer closed her eyes. "Please, I don't want this . . . ."

"On our wedding night you wanted it."

"I . . . I didn't. . . ."

Releasing her wrist, his hand rose to cover her breast, and Summer gave a soft gasp. "You remember our wedding night? What I did to you?" His fingers flexed, kneading the soft deerskin, until her gasp turned into a whimper.

"Your breasts are real responsive, princess." His mouth sought her lips, brushing the corner. "You like my hands on you, don't you?"

Summer shook her head, not wanting to surrender to his intimidation, or to the heated need that suddenly spiraled through her.

He gave her no choice. Catching her wrist again in his grip, Lance moved her palm downward, over the waistband of his breechclout, beneath the front flap. A layer of deerskin wrapped his loins, but she could feel the stiff bulge beneath the supple leather, the hard ridge of his masculinity.

He pressed harder. "Do you feel what you do to me?" he whispered against her mouth. "Don't you want to know what it's like to have this buried inside you? Haven't you ever wondered what it feels like to have a man moving between your legs?"

Wondered? How could she not wonder? Ever since their wedding night, she hadn't stopped thinking about what had happened between them, what Lance had left unfinished. What it would have felt like to become fully a woman. His woman.

"No," she whispered in protest.

"You don't even know what you're missing, princess." His voice was rough and silky . . . seductive and threatening, all at once. "What you felt before—what I made you feel—that was only the beginning."

He moved their clasped fingers, edging beneath a fold of the loincloth, bringing her in direct contact with his manhood. Summer gasped at the feel of the hot, rigid flesh beneath her hand, and immediately Lance took advantage. Covering her parted lips with his, he thrust his tongue deeply in her open mouth.

His kiss was a simulation of sexual possession, shockingly graphic, intensely and deliberately erotic, while he forced her to touch him, molded her fingers against his hot sex.

Summer was panting for breath when she finally managed to pull her mouth away. "No ... please ..."

Lance suddenly let her go. Muttering a violent oath beneath his breath, he abruptly stood up.

Quivering, she looked up at him. He was staring down at her, his black eyes alive with an emotion that was stronger than hunger, more intense than want.

Shaken, she could only stare back at him.

When he bent to pull off his moccasins, she jumped.

"Settle down, princess. I told you, you don't have to be afraid of me."

"What ... are you doing?" she half spoke, half whispered, as she watched him reach for the front flap of his breechclout.

"What does it look like? I'm getting undressed. I mean to cool off. I'm so hot for you, I'm about to burst. I need a cold bath."

"You're going to ... bathe *here?* Out in the open?"

"You have a better place to suggest?"

He had loosened the front flap from the rawhide strip around his waist and started unwinding the deerskin from around his loins. In shock, Summer lowered her gaze, realizing he meant to bare his body in front of her.

"Look at me, princess!"

His sharp command brought her eyes up. Crimson color flooded her face as full comprehension dawned, while her heart began to pound in slow, painful strokes. He meant to force her to view his nakedness.

Her breath went shallow as he tossed the breechclout aside. She wanted to look away, but her shocked eyes clung to him, to the dark lean body towering over her. Against her will her gaze traveled over him, taking in his powerful form with its clean lines of muscle and sinew—the strong, bronzed shoulders and arms, the lean, tapering waist, the narrow hips, the athletic thighs, the long, jutting arousal that thrust out from a sprinkling of crisp black hair at his groin.

The sight of his huge, swollen sex caused her throat to go dry, her stomach to contract.

"My body is no different from any white man's," Lance declared harshly.

No, he was wrong, Summer thought dazedly, her heart thundering in her ears. His body was far more beautiful than any other man's. Virile, masculine, hard, corded with powerful muscle. Despite her genteel upbringing, regardless of the demands of modesty, she was captivated by the beauty of his nakedness.

"You better get used to it," Lance added gruffly as he turned away. "If we get through this alive, you're going to get to know it real well."

If he meant to threaten her with carnal knowledge of his body, though, he missed the mark. Summer only felt a shameful excitement at the thought of knowing him more intimately.

She watched helplessly as Lance stalked over to his gear and bent down to fetch something ... watched the powerful play of sleek muscle in his back, the hard, lean buttocks flexing with sinew. His skin was almost as dark there as the rest of him, she realized with appalling curiosity.

He pulled a cake of soap from a buffalo hide pouch and strode down to the stream that was little more than a trickle. Deliberately turning to face her, his legs spread wide, he scooped up a handful of water and let it trickle over his chest, over his groin. The chill, although providing a shock, did little to ease the throbbing heat he felt. He'd been in a state of painful arousal for the past week, lusting after his beautiful wife, and not even ice water would be able to cool him down for long.

Gritting his teeth, Lance started soaping his body, running his hand over his chest, down his abdomen, over his groin. . . . When he cupped his balls, he inhaled a sharp breath. It was a mistake to have touched himself there. He was so hard, he was near to bursting. His throbbing cock felt like it might explode.

He cradled it gently, moving his soap-slick fingers along the length—and he heard a soft gasp. He was still holding his heavy shaft in his hand when he raised his head.

His innocent wife was watching him, wide-eyed, horrified, captivated, unable to look away. She was as fascinated by him, by what he was doing, as he would have been had she been the one bathing, touching herself.

He met her shocked green eyes, held them, as deliberately he curled his hand around his turgid length and squeezed. Stiffening, Lance nearly groaned at the sensation that was more pain than pleasure, yet he didn't release himself; instead he tightened his grip. He needed relief from the fierce hunger he'd suffered for the past week, needed to ease the ruthless swelling, no matter how temporary the release.

It wouldn't take long to bring himself to the bursting point. All he had to do was picture Summer naked like he was, and he was ready to erupt. All he had to do was remember what it had felt like on their wedding night, remember stroking her lush breasts, her tight nipples, imagine gripping her soft buttocks as he thrust deep into her, over and over and over again.

Baring his teeth, Lance let his head fall back, his fingers kneading himself hard, sweeping up and down his tumescence in swift, jerky motions. He could hear his breath, harsh and uneven in his ears. Feel himself shaking as he arched against the pleasure-pain.

A guttural moan sounded deep in his throat as the tremulous explosion built inside him. Another instant passed, and then he was coming violently, his body convulsing. His seed shot out, hot and pulsing, spurting in ever-diminishing arches to land in cloudy pools on the grass.

When finally he opened his eyes, it was to find Summer staring at him, her lips parted, her breath shallow. Bending to scoop up a handful of water, he rinsed off his body, starting with his groin.

When eventually he came out of the water, she was still staring at him. Lance's mouth curled with self-mockery. His little exercise in self-satisfaction hadn't helped much. His flaccid length was already swelling again, and knowing that Summer was watching him only made him that much harder.

But then he made the mistake of approaching her blanket. With a start of alarm, Summer edged away from him.

Lance stopped abruptly, his bronzed body naked and dripping as he stood over her. His eyes took on a hard gleam as they swept her shrinking form. "I told you, wife, I'm not going to touch you. You're safe from me. At least until we find your sister. Until then you don't need to worry about a savage breed rutting between your legs."

Chapter 8

Lance was as good as his word. That night he neither touched her nor made the slightest attempt at intimacy. Indeed, the only time he spoke was to order her tersely to get some sleep. Summer was still tossing and turning on her bedroll long after Lance's even breathing told her he had nodded off.

Her resentment of him only swelled, if that was possible. She could scarcely believe he hadn't shown the slightest shame or remorse for the carnal act he'd performed on himself. It was as if he had dismissed the incident from his mind, dismissed *her* from his mind as well.

Summer couldn't forget, though. Her cheeks grew hot every time she remembered Lance standing naked in the stream, his hand massaging his erection. Each time she closed her eyes, she remembered the magnificent sight he made coming naked up out of the water like some pagan god. *Damn him for confusing her!* His scandalous action had disturbed and aroused her, despite all her efforts to the contrary. But while Lance had found relief for himself, he'd left her to struggle with her bewildering feelings alone, offering no respite for the powerful, shameless yearnings he'd incited in her.

The following morning was worse. Lance ignored her entirely as he broke camp, and when Summer went down to the stream to perform her morning ablutions, the memories followed her. More disquieting, when she drew the slippery soap over her skin, all she could think about was Lance's slick hands on his body—and what her own were doing just now.

What if it had been my hands on him, touching and arousing him? Bringing that painful look of ecstasy to his face?

Scandalized by the thought, Summer flushed to the roots of her hair. And yet the images wouldn't go away.

Lance's hands had pleasured her on their wedding night— and last night had pleasured himself that way. Could she do the same to him? *Should* she be doing that to him? Was that what he'd meant when he had taunted her about not being a proper wife?

Her cheeks hot, Summer cast a vexed glance over her shoulder where Lance was saddling the horses. His cold silence only heightened her pique. The Belle of Williamson County was *not* accustomed to being ignored by a man. But then, Lance Calder was not just any man. Nor was their relationship like any marriage she had ever envisioned. She was a bride, but not a bride. She was his wife, and yet she remained celibate. Which was her own fault, of course. Lance had made it clear in a dozen ways that he wanted her, even if he was treating her like a pariah just now. She had felt his desire yesterday, in his every hard look, every restrained gesture, every angry, heated caress.

Abruptly Summer splashed a handful of chilly water over her burning cheeks. Honestly, she should feel grateful for his abstinence. Any child of Lance's would likely suffer the same cruelties growing up that he had, and she didn't want that for her children—or for herself, for that matter. It was too late for her, perhaps; her marriage to Lance had no doubt made her an outcast in her own society. But her situation would only be made worse if she were left with a mixed-blood child to raise alone. If Lance didn't return from this mission— But she couldn't consider such an alarming possibility She couldn't bear to think Lance might lose his life trying to help her.

Besides, she might not become pregnant. He had said there were ways around it . . . ways a proper wife would know.

Hotly, Summer dried her face on a scrap of a cloth and then began rebraiding her tousled hair. Perhaps she deserved Lance's coldness. He was right about one point at least. She had to learn not to flinch every time he looked at her with those smoldering, yearning eyes.

She didn't fear Lance, precisely. He had never hurt her, even if he did have a temper like a wounded bear. Indeed, he had often treated her with astonishing gentleness for so hard a man.

What she feared was the overwhelming feelings of confusion he aroused in her, the feeling of being swept away, of losing control. And yet ... would it be so wrong to allow Lance to sweep her away? To forget just for a short while her terror over her sister?

Biting her lip thoughtfully, Summer gathered her toiletries and slowly rose. Perhaps she was being selfish. Considering the risk Lance was taking for her sake, he deserved better from her. She should at least *try* to be the wife he wanted. She owed him her best effort. If what he wanted was a proper wife, then she should comply.

Indeed, that was what she'd promised when she agreed to their bargain. She couldn't claim ignorance, either. Lance had warned her what to expect in their marriage bed. He had been honest—brutally so—from the first.

It shouldn't be a hardship, though, letting Lance make love to her. He'd shown her what a considerate lover he could be. And her surrender might help soothe his brutal temper. Perhaps he simply needed the physical release. Her sister had always said men felt carnal urges more strongly than women. And Lance was more man than even *she* knew how to handle.

Drawing a deep breath, Summer returned her toiletries to her saddlebag and stood watching as he loaded the packhorse, twisting her fingers together with uncharacteristic uncertainty.

"Lance?"

"What?" He didn't even turn to look at her.

"I've ... been thinking about what you said. About the risk you're taking for me ... And you're right. You do deserve a proper wife."

"So?"

His curt replies weren't helping her at all. "So you can ... if you want ... you can make love to me."

That brought his head whipping around. His black eyes pinned her, while his lips thinned. "Don't do me any favors, princess."

Summer flushed. "It isn't a favor.... I wouldn't mind if you ... Honestly."

"I don't want your damned charity."

"It isn't. You have the right, just like you said."

"Sure, but maybe I don't want what you have to offer."

That was a bald lie; they both knew it. A man didn't look at a woman the way Lance sometimes looked at her if he didn't want her. Even now his smoldering glare gave her reason to hope. Desire was there, hot and shimmering between them; she could feel it.

Before Summer could challenge him, though, Lance added tersely, "Maybe I just don't enjoy feeling like trash every time I touch you. Maybe I don't care to have you looking at me like I'm going to attack you."

"Lance ... I'm sorry ..." She smiled at him tentatively, with imploring sweetness. "I was frightened at first. It was all so new to me ... We've been married barely a week. But I've had time to grow accustomed to you ... to us. And I'm not afraid of you. Can't you forgive me?"

With an angry jerk, he tightened the cinch around the horse's girth. "Thanks, but no thanks."

When he turned and walked away, Summer stood there, half-stunned, half-piqued, by his rejection.

Lance busied himself with the rest of their gear, clenching his teeth and cursing under his breath. Her magnanimous offer grated on every nerve he owned. *You can make love to me if you want.*

Like hell he would. He would chew nails before he let Summer make such a sacrifice. He didn't want her turning herself into a martyr. He wouldn't play the wicked villain to her helpless, swooning maiden, He didn't want her that bad.

Or maybe he did. But that wasn't what kept him from taking her up on her offer. It wasn't even his conscience holding him back. He knew it would be a fair exchange, his risking his life for Summer's body.

The trouble was, he didn't want just Summer's body, no matter how willing. He wanted *her.* All of her. Wanted her smiling at him the way she once had—with that sweet, open smile that had snared his defenseless kid's heart. Wanted her green eyes going all soft and liquid with tenderness when she looked at him.

Dammit, he wanted her to care. He wanted—needed—her to see him as somebody worth having as her husband, a man she could look up to.

And that was about as likely as pigs flying.

* * *

That day they rode in silence across mile after mile of flat open prairie. If it had been any other man, Summer might have tried to charm him out of his ill temper, but with Lance she didn't dare. He seemed determined to resume hostilities, committed to remaining immune to her appeal.

Indeed, exercising the normal social graces seemed only to anger him more. She had merely to smile at Lance and he assumed she was practicing her feminine wiles. He mistrusted even simple courtesy, coming from her. The one time she attempted an apology by placing a placating hand on his arm, he pulled away as if burned.

She tried to tell herself she wasn't upset that he had spurned her offer, that she wasn't disappointed, but the voice of her conscience upbraided her for thinking like a fool.

She *wanted* Lance to make love to her, wanted him to desire her. She wanted to know what she had missed on their wedding night—and every night since. It wasn't hard to imagine the pleasure he could give her. Every womanly instinct she possessed told her his lovemaking would be raw and fierce and exhilarating, like dancing with lightning.

By late morning, though, Summer was hot and weary enough not to care if her actions angered him, as long as she could end the brooding silence that her husband had subjected her to lately.

Deciding it would be a fitting revenge to force Lance to talk to her, Summer brought her horse alongside his and bestirred herself to ask about his Comanche relatives. "You said you had a brother named Fights Bear. Is that who you intend to ask for help?"

Lance gave her a sharp glance, as if suspicious of her intent.

"You said I had to ask if I wanted to know about your family. Well, I'm asking."

He didn't reply at once, yet she couldn't blame him for his hesitation. No doubt he thought she would look down her nose at his heathen relatives. She intended to try to keep an open mind, though, and not sit in judgment of a way of life she didn't understand. "I would like to learn about your family. I want to know where we're going, what to expect when we get there."

Lance shrugged. "I'm not sure what to expect."

"Do you think your brother will help us find Amelia?"

"I don't know. Maybe. I didn't leave under the best of circumstances."

"What do you mean?"

"I rejected the Comanche way of life. I'm no longer considered a member of the People."

Summer searched his face in the harsh sunlight. "You rejected it? Why?"

Lance averted his gaze, staring straight ahead between his horse's ears. "It's a long story. You wouldn't be interested."

"But I would." When he didn't reply, Summer decided perhaps it would be wiser to use a less direct approach if she expected to pry out any information from him. "Does your brother blame you for leaving?"

He nodded curtly. "Like any warrior, Fights Bear only has scorn for a Comanche who would attach himself to the white man. I've only been back to visit twice since I left, and my reception wasn't too keen then." Lance gave a faint smile, as if recalling a private memory. "My grandmother and sister were the only ones glad to see me."

"Your grandmother?"

"My father's mother. She's a real terror. She has more power than most Comanche women because of her medicine skills."

"Your father, he isn't still living?"

The shuttered look came down to claim Lance's expression, and his terse "No" was all the answer he gave.

When he fell silent, Summer let the subject rest for the time being, realizing she might be probing painful memories.

And yet her curious questioning seemed to bear fruit. Lance didn't seem as angry with her when they stopped at noon to rest the horses and eat beneath the questionable shade of a mesquite tree, nor did he snap at her when she asked him what he was doing. He had fished in his saddle pouch for several items and was now sitting cross-legged, braiding two long ropes of what looked to be horsehair and buffalo sinew into his own hair.

"Yeah, it's horsehair," Lance replied evenly. "A Comanche's hair is his pride, and mine's too short." His mouth quirked. "I'm not just doing this out of vanity. I'll fit in better this way, wearing braids."

She had to smile at the notion of Lance doing anything out of vanity. She had never met anyone so hardened to public opinion, or so determined to ignore what other people thought of him. If he was concerned about his appearance, it had to be because he considered it important to their chances of success. It struck Summer as rather sad that he should have to go to such lengths to be accepted by his own family. But then, that was the same dilemma Lance had always faced. He was an outcast in two societies; he fit into neither.

Just now, though, he looked very much like a Comanche warrior. Today he wore fringed buckskin leggings as well as his breechclout and moccasins, but his chest was still bare except for the necklace.

Summer watched curiously as he tied an eagle feather to a lock of hair high on his scalp. "Shouldn't you wear paint on your face?"

Lance's white teeth flashed in a grin, the first real smile she'd seen since they left his friend Deek's trading post. "Comanches only paint their faces when they raid or hunt, or when they have something to celebrate."

At the mention of raiding, Summer was the one to fall silent. It was during a raid that her sister had been taken captive. A massacre where three people had lost their lives.

Her unguarded mood abruptly vanished. Lance might jest about Comanche customs and even make light of their brutality, but the Comanches were killers who hated whites with a blind passion. She couldn't forget that. Her fear had diminished somewhat over the past few days—partly, she was certain, because Lance had downplayed the danger, and partly because they had encountered no trouble. But they were deep in Comanche territory now, and the risk of death was real.

Biting her lip, Summer forced herself to begin gathering their belongings for what she hoped was the final leg of their journey. Perhaps she'd been foolish to insist that Lance take her with him, but it was too late to turn back now. Besides, she still would prefer to entrust her fate to Lance Calder than be left behind as prey for the Yarby brothers. Even if at the moment her husband was looking less and less like the stranger she knew, and more and more like a hostile Indian.

* * *

Her tension grew as the afternoon wore on, as did her headache. The heat didn't help. The air had turned sweltering, with little shade and no water in sight, only endless miles of flat grassland sparsely dotted with mesquite. Lance had made her take off her head covering since no Comanche woman would be afraid of sunburn, and the September sun beat down on her mercilessly.

She was grateful when he allowed them to stop a few minutes to rest. Lance had vowed not to spare her any sympathy, but when he saw the way she was wilting, he evidently took pity on her and poured some water from the leather water bag onto a cloth, telling her to hold it to her brow and throat.

It was midafternoon when they entered the hills again where it was slightly cooler. Shortly after that, Summer became aware that the atmosphere had suddenly changed.

"We've got company," Lance said quietly. "Just keep riding till I tell you to stop."

Alarmed, Summer sat upright in the saddle and gazed around her, but all she could see was a hill up ahead. It was at least ten more minutes before Lance's theory proved out. Without warning, an Indian warrior mounted on a painted pony suddenly appeared at the rise of the hill.

Summer couldn't quite manage to stifle a gasp as he rode down directly in their path and halted, his feathered lance raised as if daring them to proceed.

"He's likely a scout for a band camped near here," Lance murmured to her. "Don't worry. If he'd meant us harm, he would never have shown himself. He would have shot us first."

His reassurance gave her little comfort.

"Stay here, and don't say anything," Lance ordered. "Keep your eyes lowered, and let me handle it. I'll see if he knows where Fights Bear is camped."

Handing her the reins of the packhorse, Lance rode forward with a gesture of greeting, a gesture that, to Summer's immense relief, was returned. She sat rigidly waiting while they held a conversation, using a mixture of speech and hand signs.

Finally Lance looked over his shoulder at her and motioned curtly for her to join him. Swallowing the dry fear in her throat, Summer nudged her mount into a walk, leading the packhorse.

When she reached the two men, Lance brought his horse alongside her and kept riding. Summer could almost hear her heart pounding as they passed, and she could feel the warrior's fierce black eyes following them all the while.

"Relax, princess," Lance said when they were out of hearing. "He's not going to hurt you. A Comanche won't attack another Comanche unless it's for blood vengeance."

She didn't bother reminding him that *she* wasn't a Comanche, but he seemed to understand her fears.

"He thinks you're my white slave," Lance explained, his tone holding an edge of amusement.

"Oh, well," Summer said with forced gaiety, "naturally, that relieves my mind. As long as I'm your property, he'll spare my life."

Lance grinned. "Something like that. I didn't tell him he was in the presence of royalty. He wouldn't understand that you consider yourself a princess, or why a warrior would allow himself to be commanded by a mere woman, especially his wife."

Resenting his levity, Summer tossed her head proudly. "You have never in your life let anyone command you, Lance Calder, let alone me. And I am not a *mere* woman!"

"No, that you're not."

His rusty chuckle raised her hackles, but at least it served to stiffen her spine and make her momentarily forget her fear.

Which, Summer realized nearly an hour later as she silently seethed, was no doubt exactly what Lance had intended all along.

Her first sight of a Comanche village both impressed and intimidated her. Just as the scout had indicated, a few hour's ride north through the hills brought them to the camp of Fights Bear.

When a group of young boys raced out on their ponies to meet them, shrieking and waving their bows and lances, Summer went stiff with dread, but Lance greeted several of them by name and made them laugh with something he said. Turning, the youths provided them an escort into the camp.

The village itself was nestled between two rugged hills and

seemed to stretch forever. Scores of pale, conical tepees covered with sun-bleached buffalo hide stood laid out in a square, the curling smoke from the cooking fires rising to disappear into the blue skies overhead. An immense herd of horses grazed in the rich grass beyond the camp, tended by a few boys.

The noise and activity within the camp held Summer's attention: naked children frolicking and playing games, scrawny dogs scavenging for bones, women clad in buckskin garments hard at work over the cooking pots, ancient men smoking their long pipes at the entrances to their lodges, fierce-looking warriors standing proudly at attention as the visitors passed. For all its activity, however, the camp didn't have a look of prosperity about it. The racks that should have held strips of drying buffalo meat were mostly empty, while the dirty faces of the children had a lean look of hunger.

She and Lance were the subject of many curious eyes as they rode toward the center of the village. More than a few people offered greetings to Lance, Summer noted with relief. Perhaps he'd been mistaken when he'd said he might not be welcomed with open arms.

In the center of the camp was a clearing, ringed by the lodges of the most important leaders. Lance came to a halt before one of the tepees, where a Comanche warrior stood waiting, his arms crossed belligerently over his bare chest.

The defiant expression on his face, even more than his features, told Summer this was Lance's half brother. It held the same damn-your-eyes arrogance she'd seen so often on her husband's face. The physical resemblance was striking, as well. Lance's coloring was lighter, his features leaner and younger and less weathered, but they had the same high forehead, prominent cheekbones, sharp nose, and strong chin. The same fascinating, forbidden appeal.

It startled her, how attractive she found his brother. Fights Bear was a brutal Comanche, someone she should by rights hate and fear. Was she suddenly developing a passion for savage-looking, dangerous men? Or only those who resembled her husband?

The grim look on Fights Bear's face didn't diminish when Lance raised his hand and said something in Comanche that Summer assumed was a greeting. When Lance said a few more words, this brother's fierce black eyes turned on her for a long, uncomfortable moment. Lowering her own eyes politely, Summer tried to look appropriately meek and unassuming. Since Lance hadn't introduced her, she assumed it would be beneath the dignity of a war chief to formally recognize a woman, especially a white one.

When Fights Bear finally nodded and made a gruff reply, Lance turned to Summer and murmured in an undertone, "We're going to get down and eat. It's a Comanche law to offer hospitality to anyone who seeks it, so he's going to accept us as his guests tonight."

"Will he help us find Amelia?" Summer asked anxiously.

"I haven't asked him yet. It would be bad manners to talk before we're fed."

Lance swung down off his horse then, but left her to dismount on her own—perhaps, Summer suspected, because it would hurt his consequence as a warrior to be seen helping a mere woman. When he told her to bring the two pouches that contained presents, she didn't protest, not wishing to give Fights Bear any reason to turn them away. His reception already worried her. If his fierce expression was anything to judge by, his attitude toward Lance held more than reserve— indeed, almost an edge of hostility.

At the moment the two brothers were eyeing each other in grim silence. With the two men on level ground, Summer could see Fights Bear was several inches shorter than Lance, yet he possessed a commanding air of authority that she wouldn't want to cross.

It was only when Fights Bear barked something to the women standing behind him that Summer paid them any heed. Two of the women were obviously Comanche, but to her surprise, the third had features that appeared Mexican.

Fights Bear turned and disappeared into his tepee, and Lance followed. When Summer hesitated uncertainly, the woman who looked Mexican offered a shy smile and motioned for Summer to enter after the men.

The interior was dim, but when her eyes adjusted, she could see the dwelling was crowded with belongings. Hide bedding, willow-rod backrests, wooden and horn utensils, and parfleches made of buffalo hide nearly obscured the earthen floor, while weapons and other various objects hung from the slanting walls. A ring of stone occupied the center as a fire-place, but the hearth was cold—Summer assumed because it was too hot to cook inside.

Fights Bear had seated himself at the rear facing the entrance, with Lance on his right. Summer sat where Lance indicated, beside and slightly behind him.

In only a few moments one of the Comanche women entered with food. She served the men first, then handed Summer a leaf that wrapped a half-raw, half-charred strip of buffalo meat so hot that it burned her fingers. When she eyed it uncertainly, she found Lance giving her a stern glance over his shoulder.

"Eat it," he ordered harshly. "And look like you enjoy it."

Obediently Summer smiled and took a bite, finding the meat tough, stringy, and unsalted. She forced it down, though, in silence.

When they were finished with the scant meal, Lance reached for the bags Summer had carried in and began to speak in Comanche.

"I have brought gifts for you and your wives, my brother."

Fights Bear gave them a summary glance and nodded. "I accept. But you did not seek me out only to offer me presents, Kanap-Cheetu."

"*Haa*, that is true. I ask your help in finding my wife's sister. She was taken by the Comanche from Texas when the moon was last full. I have an arrow shaft belonging to one of her captors."

Lance rummaged in a pouch and brought out the broken arrow he'd found at the Grice ranch. He showed it to his brother, who studied the feathers and painted markings at the end. "This is not of your band, I think."

"No, the markings are not familiar."

"I wish your help in locating the owner of the arrow."

Fights Bear scowled. "You ask much for one who has turned from the ways of the People."

Lance returned his brother's hard gaze. "I follow the laws of the Comanche. This is my woman, my wife. It is a warrior's responsibility to protect and provide for his wife's family."

Fights Bear crossed his sinewed arms over his bare chest. "I do not wish to aid a white woman against the Comanche."

"Perhaps we can strike a bargain. In exchange for assistance, I would give you ten horses and a hundred Yankee dollars." He stopped at the other man's sneer. "I see your scorn, my brother, but the white man's money can be used for trade, to provide food for the young ones when the buffalo are scarce."

For a long moment, Fights Bear was silent. After a hard glance at Summer, though, he nodded. "We will hold a council and share a pipe to discuss the matter. But the woman will not be welcome."

Lance nodded dispassionately. *"Aho,* thank you." He turned to Summer, who had been listening without comprehension, and briefly explained that the tribal leaders were to meet to decide their action. "It may take a while. Go with Fights Bear's wives. They'll show you where you can sleep."

Grateful that their request hadn't been denied outright, Summer offered a tentative smile to his brother, and rose obediently. When she ducked through the entrance flap, she found the Mexican woman waiting outside.

"Do you understand Spanish?" the woman asked in that language.

"Sí," Summer replied. "A little. The nurse who raised me when my mother died taught me, but I am not fluent."

The woman grinned broadly. "My name is Kwasutu, Short Dress. I am the third wife to Wasape Naaohrutu, Fights Bear."

"I am Summer."

"You will share my lodge, Summer." Turning, Short Dress led the way to a tepee a short distance behind her husband's. Someone had taken care of their horses and picketed them outside, Summer noticed as she followed the woman inside. The tepee looked similar to the one she'd just left, except that this was smaller and more sparsely furnished.

She settled herself on the ground near the entrance, where Short Dress indicated, and watched as the woman unrolled a bundle of buffalo blankets and began fashioning a bed.

"How is it that you speak Spanish so well?" Summer asked.

"I came here from Mexico when I was a girl."

"You were a captive?"

She couldn't keep the horror from her voice, but Short

Dress merely nodded pragmatically. "Yes. They beat me at first, especially Wasp Lady, until I learned to work hard."

"Wasp Lady?"

"The grandmother of Fights Bear and Sharp Lance. Very likely she will visit here tonight. She wishes to observe you."

Summer noticed the use of the word "observe" rather than meet," but before she could ask about it, Short Dress went on chattering. "Fights Bear sometimes calls on me to speak to the whites who come to our village, for they often know Spanish, and he will not learn English. Fights Bear is a good husband—strong and brave and wealthy, with many horses. I have my own lodge with my two sons. Fights Bear summons me when he wishes to sleep with me. My sons will come soon, and you will see how they resemble their father—and their uncle, your husband. They will be happy to see their uncle, Kanap-Cheetu, for they have heard many stories about his bravery."

"Kanap ... Cheetu ..." Summer tried to pronounce the awkward words. "Is that my husband's Comanche name?"

Pausing in her task of building a fire of buffalo chips, Short Dress looked at her in surprise. "Why, yes. Did you not know your own husband's name?"

"Lance doesn't talk much about himself," Summer replied contritely.

Short Dress nodded in approval. "It is good. Men's deeds should speak, not their words."

"His name—what does it mean?"

"Sharp Lance, of course. What else?"

Summer smiled ruefully. "I feel so ignorant of Comanche ways."

"I could teach you, if you care to learn, señora."

"I would indeed be grateful, especially if you would tell me about my husband."

"What do you wish to know?"

She had so many questions, she didn't know where to begin, but before she could frame the first one, an ancient Comanche woman entered the tent silently.

Short Dress immediately rose to her feet, and Summer did likewise. The Mexican woman performed the introductions with great deference to the old woman, before finally murmuring to Summer, "This is Peena Waihu, Wasp Lady."

Not knowing what else to do, Summer curtsied politely, which elicited a giggle from Short Dress, but absolutely no response from the silent Wasp Lady. Her form was unimposing, small but plump, yet she possessed the same fierce black eyes as her two grandsons, the same hostile stare of a wild panther toward humans, or a Comanche toward whites. Finally she stepped forward and grasped Summer's hand, inspecting the palm intently.

"Payutyukatu!"

Summer looked questioningly at Short Dress.

"She says you are too soft to be the wife of her grandson."

Biting back the retort that she had never asked to marry her grandson, dismissing the fact the Lance held the same contempt for her softness, Summer forced a smile. She didn't want to antagonize his grandmother by arguing, especially if the old woman might have some influence over the decision to search for Amelia.

"I am strong enough," she replied pleasantly.

Wasp Lady returned a scoffing look. "We shall see," Short Dress interpreted. "My grandson does not appear to have made a wise choice."

Summer raised her chin. "Tell her I am the wife he chose."

"How many horses did Sharp Lance give for you?" the old woman barked.

"Why . . . none," Summer said, taken aback by the question. When Wasp Lady smiled in grim triumph, however, Summer felt the need to elaborate. "My family owns many horses and did not need more. Instead Lance offered money." Which was true, if stretching a bit. Lance had been determined to use his own money to ransom her sister. "Furthermore," Summer added staunchly, "he risked his life to save me from two evil men who attacked me."

For the first time since entering the tepee, the old woman's expression softened. "Yes, that is good." She added something else in Comanche, then turned abruptly and left.

Summer breathed easier, until she asked what the old woman had said.

"Tomorrow I am to test your boast of being strong."

"What . . . does that mean?"

"You must work with me, perform the tasks of a Comanche woman."

"I don't imagine I shall be very skilled."

"*Sí*, but I dare not defy her," Short Dress said uneasily. "Wasp Lady has much power."

Summer gazed thoughtfully after the old woman. "I thought females were not regarded highly by the Comanches."

"Yes, that is so, but Wasp Lady makes good medicine."

Their conversation was interrupted just then by the return of Short Dress's sons, who raced into the tent and stopped abruptly at the sight of the strange white woman. The boys were perhaps ten and eight, but already possessed all the swaggering arrogance of men twice their age, she realized at once. Refusing, however, to be intimidated by youths half her own age, Summer set out to charm them.

With Short Dress acting as interpreter, Summer told them about her family's horse ranch, embellishing only a little on her brothers' adventures when they were younger. By the time their mother ordered them to bed, the two boys seemed to have gained a marginal respect for the white visitor.

Both Short Dress and her two sons went quickly to sleep on their pallets, but Summer remained far too tense to follow suit. Instead she settled on her own pallet to await Lance's return, and listened to the unfamiliar sounds of the Comanche camp.

Once or twice she thought she heard voices raised in anger, but it was hours later before Lance quietly entered the tepee.

Summer was sitting on her bed of buffalo robes, her arms wrapped around her legs, her chin on her knees, but she immediately lifted her head. "What happened?" she demanded, forgetting to whisper.

Lance glanced pointedly at his sleeping nephews; she could see him in the faint glow of the smoldering fire Short Dress had lit for the night. "I thought I told you to get some sleep."

"I couldn't. Not until I learned what happened."

His mouth curved in a faint smile as he said quietly, "Fights Bear demanded twice the fee in money and horses, but he agreed to help. He means to send out emissaries tomorrow to search neighboring bands for Amelia."

Bowing her head, Summer felt a sob of relief well in her throat. It was a full minute later before she had control of herself enough to thank Lance.

"Thank me when your sister is safe." He sounded tired. When she looked up, she could see that he was removing his leggings. "Go to sleep, Summer. There's nothing more you can do tonight."

A vast weariness overtook her as she realized he was right. Obediently she lay down on the pallet and pulled a buffalo pelt up over her.

"Not like that, princess. Take off your clothes first."

She turned her head to stare uncertainly at him in the dim light.

"Kwasutu will think it strange if I let you share my bed fully dressed."

"What . . . should I wear, then?"

The faint curl of his mouth told her the answer she dreaded. And yet she wasn't prepared to argue. If following Comanche customs was the price she had to pay, even if it meant sleeping naked with her husband, she would do it.

Wrapping a robe around her as a shield, Summer awkwardly removed her moccasins and leggings and deerskin dress. Lance stood over her, waiting, but she refused to look at him, knowing he was completely naked.

Finally, unable to delay any longer, she stretched out again and lay there rigidly. In silence Lance slid in beside her and pulled the pelts up over them both.

What shocked her, though, was how, without a word, he compelled her to roll over on her side with her back to him, and curled his arm around her waist, drawing her tense body back against his.

Summer caught her breath in a soft gasp. His bare skin was sleek and hot as a furnace, his manhood hard and throbbing against her buttocks.

"Relax, princess," he murmured, his warm breath teasing her ear. "I told you you're safe from me. Go to sleep."

Summer forced herself to close her eyes. Lance wasn't going to claim his rights as her husband tonight. He'd said he didn't intend to make love to her until this ordeal was over, and he was a man of his word. Even if physically his body was clamoring for hers. Even if physically her body was beginning to feel the same wanton urges.

Summer exhaled slowly, trying to relax as he'd commanded. He'd said she would be safe from him. The only trouble was, that was no longer what she wanted, to be safe.

She could feel Lance's heat enveloping her, scalding her skin, could smell his hot, musky maleness. His thick shaft pressed blatantly against her buttocks, nestling in the backs of her thighs. Her pulse had quickened to a hammering beat, while desire curled like a coiled spring inside her.

Squeezing her eyes shut, Summer found herself wondering, scandalously, if Lance could take her from behind, like a stallion takes a mare. What would it be like to have him thrusting into her? If she moved the slightest inch . . .

Hardly daring to breathe, she shifted, pressing back against him, into his tantalizing warmth.

Her movement played havoc with Lance's control. Having Summer naked and restless in his arms was sheer hell, even worse than he figured it would be. Her twitching was enough to drive him wild; her tight little fanny rubbing against his groin was pure torture.

She was definitely aroused, he knew. And whether consciously or not, she was trying to arouse him.

Determinedly Lance ground his teeth. He wouldn't give in to her teasing. This was all a game to Summer. She was testing her power over him, pulling his strings like all the other fawning puppets she called her beaux. His body might be betraying his need, but he wouldn't give her the satisfaction of falling for her tricks.

Then again . . . maybe it was time she got a taste of her own medicine.

After another moment of deliberation—of enduring her silken bottom pressing against his throbbing erection—Lance reached his hand to cup her right breast in his callused palm.

Summer went rigid, her gasp loud in the firelit darkness.

Her nipple had peaked instantly, and Lance found incredible pleasure in running his thumb over the tight bud. His touch featherlight, his fingers closed over the quivering nipple, gently squeezing, pinching, torturing her until her breast pressed wantonly against his stroking palm, until she arched instinctively against his caress.

"Do you like this, princess?"

Her reply was barely audible, a breathless moan.

"Summer? You have to tell me what you like." His whisper was hoarse in her ear.

"Yes ... Lance ... yes." She could scarcely summon the power to think. His long, brazen fingers were lingering over her sensitive nipples, kneading, plucking, until they throbbed and pleaded for his touch, till they felt like points of fire.

Then one of his arms slipped beneath her while his other closed around her waist, pulling her tight against his nakedness. Summer shuddered at the feel of him: the hard, hot wall of his chest at her back, the powerful horseman's thighs cradling hers, the heated granite probe of his manhood.

And then his caressing hand moved lower.

Drawing a sharp breath, Summer held it as his hand crept downward, over her slim waist and flat stomach, seeking the soft mound of hair between her thighs, sliding intimately between her legs.

She was wet there ... hotly, invitingly, drenched with dew.

"Does this make you hot, princess? Does it feel good when I touch you here?"

He trailed his fingertips over the soft lips, probing the moist secrets of her.

A long, tremulous wave of longing racked her body. Yes, she was hot, flaming hot. Her whole body burned in anticipation. She wanted to be touched, wanted Lance to stroke her there.

She arched her hips feverishly against his fingers as he parted the quivering folds of flesh.

"Does this feel good, Summer?" she heard him ask.

Whimpering in answer, she clenched her hands as those fingers teased her, sliding inside her ... lingering, withdrawing, moving slowly in and out. Summer trembled at the sweet assault, the exquisite torture.

"Do you want me, princess?" Lance growled softly in her ear.

Yes, she wanted him. She wanted him with a fierceness that shocked her.

When she moaned a breathless "Yes ..." Lance replied with a terse "Good."

Abruptly withdrawing his fingers from between her legs, he gave the curve of her hip a condescending pat. He wouldn't give her the release her hot little body was craving.

Releasing his hold on her waist, he turned over on the pallet, giving Summer his back.

"Lance?" Her tone was bewildered, shaken, her body rigid with unfulfilled sexual tension as she raised herself up on one elbow.

"Go to sleep, princess."

"Sleep? You expect me to sleep *now?"*

Lance's smile was grim in the darkness. "Now you know how I feel all the time. I only left you aching like you do me."

In the stunned silence that followed, he was certain he could feel his wife's green eyes glaring daggers between his shoulder blades. It was a long, long moment before she lay back down on the pallet with a definite flounce.

Unsympathetically, Lance shrugged. Let her suffer a little while. It wouldn't hurt Summer to know what it was like to want someone so bad, it kept her up nights. Maybe now she would understand what her heartless teasing did to flesh and blood.

He wouldn't satisfy her craving for him—or his for her. He would live with his own deep ache.

And he would keep his hands off her if it killed him.

Chapter 9

The following week at the Comanche camp was one of the most trying of Summer's entire life. Besides the mental strain and uncertainty regarding her sister's fate, and the added tension of sleeping naked and aroused in Lance's arms each night, the physical effort expected of her nearly drove her to exhaustion.

Her every waking moment was filled with work—gathering firewood, carrying water, preparing meals, keeping the tepees in order, dressing and tanning hides, sewing clothing and robes, storing supplies for the winter months, all the thousand and one tasks that a Comanche wife was responsible for. To make matters worse, Short Dress was not only Fights Bears's third wife, but the *chore* wife, which meant she performed many of the menial tasks the other two wives didn't care to do. And Summer was required to help. Lance's grandmother saw to that.

A virtual slave driver, Wasp Lady oversaw her progress with a sharp eye for laziness or mistakes, frequently waving her gnarled fists. Once the old woman nearly struck her.

Lance's sister was scarcely any more friendly. Huwuni, which meant Dawn, had two sons of her own, as well as a daughter—a mere baby whom she carried on her back strapped in a cradleboard. Huwuni refused to let Summer look at the child, and laughed at her effort to make pemmican, which was concocted by pounding wild berries and walnuts together with dried meat and then adding tallow and marrow fat.

"You are a worthless wife," Dawn observed disdainfully, according to Short Dress's translation.

Fights Bear's other two wives said something similar, only their remarks were more subtle. Summer needed no translation, though, to know that she didn't measure up to their standards.

Their scorn made her feel so unworthy, so alone—and at the same time, more sympathetic toward Lance's struggle to gain acceptance in her world. Such blind bigotry was no worse than what Lance had endured from whites for so many years.

Yet Summer gritted her teeth and bore the adversity with grim fortitude. She was determined not to shame Lance before his people, or give his grandmother the satisfaction of defeating her. Besides, her sister was no doubt suffering worse as a captive, Summer knew. She could endure any hardship as long as in exchange she could expect help in rescuing Amelia.

To her infinite gratitude, the search had begun. As agreed, Fights Bear had sent out emissaries to various neighboring bands with the power to negotiate for Amelia's release. In the interim all Summer could do was wait—and work.

At least Lance seemed sympathetic. When he joined her in bed the second evening, he no longer appeared bent on revenge, thankfully showing no intention of repeating his mortifying, maddening, deliberately suspended seduction of the previous evening. And when she rolled nervously on her side to give him plenty of room and couldn't stifle a muffled moan, he reacted with concern.

"What is it?" he murmured in the darkness.

"Nothing." Summer shook her head ruefully. "Perhaps I'm not as strong as I thought. My muscles aren't accustomed to hauling water and wood, at any rate."

He didn't reply, but a moment later she felt his callused hand glide up her bare back. Summer tensed as his fingers closed gently over her shoulder, fearing a repetition of last night, with him leaving her aroused and unfulfilled. Instead Lance began slowly to knead her sore muscles. Summer stifled another groan at the discomfort, and yet his careful ministrations had an incredibly welcome effect.

She closed her eyes gratefully and let her head fall back, savoring the texture of his work-roughened palms massaging her skin, the feel of his long, hard, sensitive fingers tracing the curves of her shoulders . . . her arms, her back . . . pressing gently . . . lightly rubbing in slow, rotating strokes . . .

magically relieving the tight, knotted muscles. It was sensual and yet soothing, as if he wanted nothing more in the world than to comfort her.

After a time she could feel the tautness and tension draining out of her, the pain begin to dissipate . . . could feel her aching body relaxing enough to sleep.

She saw little of Lance during the days, although she knew he'd been hunting because he brought back two bucks for the women to skin and butcher. Comanche warriors, she learned from observation and from the loquacious Short Dress, bore the responsibility for hunting game and making raids, and that was about all. A warrior saw to the safety and well-being of his family and therefore his band, but the only duties he performed regularly were caring for his weapons and his horses.

Otherwise a warrior spent his time lazing about the camp, smoking and talking, playing games or engaging in sporting feats, or engrossed in personal grooming. A man might fill endless hours simply combing and greasing and braiding his long hair, Summer learned to her curiosity and resentment. She herself was afforded only moments each day for her own grooming. In contrast to a husband, a Comanche woman had little time to preen; her life was occupied by endless, back-wrenching work. And she received little appreciation for it. Indeed, a warrior seemed to show his horses greater affection and consideration than he did his wives.

Short Dress didn't seem to mind the inequities, however. "It is our way," she said with a shrug. "A horse carries a warrior into battle and to hunt the buffalo, whereas a woman is only good for unimportant tasks."

Working alongside Short Dress did at least give Summer the opportunity to learn more about Comanche customs, some of which made her wince—like eating the raw liver and heart of a freshly killed buffalo (considered a delicacy) and drinking its warm blood or curdled milk from its udder. The first time she saw the dozens of dried human scalps hanging from a lodge pole in Fights Bear's tepee, she recoiled in horror. The grisly sight brought home more than anything else just how brutal and ruthless a people the Comanche were—a fact she had momentarily forgotten while accepting Fights Bear's hospitality.

As a Texan she'd always deplored the Comanches and their murderous ways, yet after listening to Short Dress, Summer began to realize that from their viewpoint, they were fighting for sheer survival. Not a single person in the camp hadn't had at least one immediate family member killed by whites.

"Wasp Lady has lost many relatives," Short Dress said sadly. "Her husband and several sons, as well as two grand-daughters. Can you not understand why she looks at your white skin and sees only an enemy?"

Furthermore, acts that white society often considered barbaric, Comanche culture viewed as only natural and right, many of which were rooted in spiritual beliefs. The taking of a scalp, for example, wasn't done for the purpose of torture, but because it destroyed an enemy's soul and prevented it from returning to the world and plaguing the People, which was more effective than killing the body.

To the Comanche, their code of behavior was simple. They raided for horses to increase their wealth and prestige, took Mexican and white captives as slaves to make their work easier and to bear their children, and made war to avenge a wrong or to turn back the tide of white immigrants. They hated passionately the settlers who had overrun their hunting grounds and driven the buffalo from the plains, leaving their children to starve, and decimated their camps with epidemics of cholera and smallpox. They especially abhorred the Texans, who had dishonored treaties and claimed their lands and forced them onto crowded reserves. Texans were enemies to be fought to the death.

Lance's mother had discovered that bitter truth shortly after arriving in Texas, Summer knew from what her brother had once told her. Charlotte Calder's white family had been killed in a Comanche raid, while she was taken captive by their leader. Short Dress knew little about Lance's mother, however, since their rescue had occurred long before the Mexican woman's own captivity.

Working with the women, though, did allow Summer to learn more about the enigmatic man she had married. Her third day in camp, she was put to work with a bone knife, scraping a deer hide that had been staked out on the ground, a task that abraded her knuckles raw and strained her back. Kneeling beside her, Short Dress was softening another hide with a mixture of animal brains, tree bark, and grease as she explained how Lance had become a Comanche.

"I had been with the band three years when he arrived in camp," Short Dress said with a smile. "I remember Pakawa called for a feast to celebrate the return of his son to the People."

According to Short Dress, young Lance had come searching for his heritage and his father. He'd been accepted guardedly into the band, yet as a boy, he'd endured the cruel taunts and scorn of the other youths, for he couldn't ride half as well, or shoot a bow and arrow at all, or steal horses from under the nose of an enemy. He'd worked like a demon, though, to become a worthy warrior, practicing hour after countless hour until he could hold his own with all but the most skilled boys his age.

And he'd had good teachers. His father, Pakawa, which meant Kills Something, had been a great war chief, a position of leadership that was earned by deed, not inherited, in the Comanche culture. His older brother, Fights Bear, who had also accepted responsibility for training Lance, had eventually become a war chief.

"Lance wouldn't talk about his father when I asked," Summer admitted, "except to say that he was dead. Do you know how it happened?"

Short Dress glanced cautiously over her shoulder. "The People do not care to speak of the dead, but I will tell you since you ask. Pakawa was the bravest of warriors. *Sí,* the People still sing songs about his courage. One day he led a war party against the white soldiers, and allowed his son, Sharp Lance, your husband, to accompany him for the first time into battle. Kanap-Cheetu was not called Sharp Lance then. It is a name of honor, for only the bravest warriors are allowed to carry a spear into battle.

"But that day the evil whites had too many guns. Pakawa's medicine was not good. His chest was pierced by a white bullet. Kanap-Cheetu took up his father's lance and shield and stood over the fallen body of Pakawa to protect him from the blows of the white soldiers, until they could be driven away. It was a great deed—there is none greater to us. Sharp Lance's bravery was much talked about among our people. But he cared nothing for that. His grief was great when

Pakawa died. Afterward he had a powerful vision. It told him to return to the whites, his mother's people. Wasp Lady agreed he must follow his vision and gave her blessing."

Greatly intrigued, Summer mentally filed away the tale to ask Lance about when next she saw him.

The next time came that afternoon, although she had no chance to speak to him, for he was engaged in some kind of sporting contest on horseback with the men of the band. The entire village turned out to watch, and Summer was given a reprieve from her duties to admire and cheer with the other women.

The feats the warriors performed *were* incredible. In addition to simple horse races, they galloped back and forth over obstacle courses, showed off their skill at archery, picked up objects from the ground as they dashed past, and speared targets with their long lances.

The maneuver that impressed Summer the most—and seemed the most dangerous—was when a rider slid halfway off his mount, clinging to the horse's side with one heel across the back, his elbow braced in a rawhide loop plaited to the mane, and shot arrows from a bow beneath the straining animal's neck.

Lance came close to winning one of the obstacle races, but lost to his brother, Fights Bear. Yet Summer could tell that her husband was pleased by his performance. As Lance rode past her, he sent her a rare smile that touched his eyes with a soft sparkle. A sparkle, Summer realized with dismay, that had the ability to make her heart beat faster. It was the closest she'd ever seen Lance come to showing true happiness, and she thought the sight incredibly appealing. His hard features lost their fierceness, their harsh arrogance, and relaxed into striking handsomeness.

For a moment Summer wondered what it would take to make that expression permanent. She knew so little about the man she had married that she could only guess what Lance wanted or needed out of life, or what had made him the complex, guarded man that he was.

The next afternoon, however, afforded her the opportunity to discover more. Summer was working over the deerskin before the tepee when Lance rode up on a pinto horse and offered to take her down to the creek to bathe.

Surprised, Summer wiped her sweating brow and looked at him with misgiving. "You want me to bathe with you?"

He gave her a wry smile that made her suddenly aware of herself as woman; the curve of his lips stole the harshness from his features, added the sting of sensuality. "No, princess, I'll let you do it alone. I told you I'm not going to force myself on you. But I thought you could use the rest. And the chance to get clean."

Summer flushed, knowing she must look a sight. She'd scarcely had a minute to expend on her own grooming, and her hair badly needed washing. Yet she glanced uneasily over her shoulder. "Your grandmother might object if I stop work."

"I'll handle my grandmother. If you want to go, then climb on."

Summer didn't need to be asked twice. When Lance extended his hand to help her mount, she eagerly scrambled up behind him. It would be wonderful to escape, even temporarily, from Wasp Lady's tyranny. And she craved the chance to rid herself of the dirt and sweat of the past week—even if it meant being alone with Lance.

This would be the first time since arriving at camp that she had enjoyed his sole company . . . unless she counted the hours of warm, naked darkness she endured in his bed each night. Her cheeks colored hotly when she recalled that first night and Lance's shameful, infuriating, carnal taunting.

She supposed it was his way of punishing her . . . for all her earlier rejections of him, for all the times she had used her feminine wiles against him to gain her own ends. He had turned her own weapons against her, making her desire him—and it hadn't felt at all nice.

What was worse was the knowledge that perhaps she had even deserved it.

Lance rode north about a mile, where the hills were more rugged and the timber thicker. Summer clung to his waist, her chest brushing his bare back. Lance had won that point, she had to admit. Because of their close proximity during the last few days, she'd become more familiar with his body. She hadn't fully overcome her resentment at their unwanted marriage, or her natural reserve at the physical intimacy of their relationship, but she no longer went rigid every time he touched her or whenever she came in contact with his naked skin.

He found a protected area where cottonwoods and elms lined the creek, and a small pool between the rocks offered the perfect natural setting for a bathtub. Dropping the reins, Lance slid to the ground and helped Summer down, then hefted his rifle and the bundle he'd brought.

When he started down toward the creek, though, Summer glanced at the paint pony he had borrowed from his brother. "Shouldn't you tie him up?"

"He doesn't need to be tied. A Comanche horse is trained to stand with the reins down."

Lance had brought blankets and a leather parfleche that contained, to Summer's delight, soap, a cloth towel, and a porcupine-quill brush. He'd also supplied her with fresh clothing—a blue calico shirt and deerskin skirt that he said belonged to his sister. She'd seen some of the Comanche women wearing calico that they'd obtained from white traders, but that wasn't what surprised her.

"Your sister doesn't mind if I borrow her clothes?" she asked.

"She was the one who offered."

Summer looked at him in amazement. "I didn't think Dawn liked me very much."

Lance's smile held real amusement. "She didn't at first. But she says for a white woman, you show courage."

Summer smiled back at him, inordinately pleased at that dubious compliment. If his hostile sister had begun to soften toward her, then perhaps her exhausting labor and her genuine efforts to adapt to Comanche customs had been worthwhile.

Lance turned his back like a gentleman, giving her the privacy to bathe, and settled on a blanket, his shoulders propped against the trunk of a tree. Summer unbraided her hair and shed her heavy deerskin dress and moccasins with only a momentary concern for modesty. She'd lost much of her self-consciousness during the past few nights of having to sleep naked with Lance, and it seemed foolish to be nervous now. Indeed, one of the things she liked about Indian society was the physical freedom. After all the years of enduring constricting whalebone and horsehair and layer upon layer of undergarments, she enjoyed the license permitted by the primitive Comanche culture. Picking up the soap, she stepped cautiously into the pool.

The cool water was heavenly. Raising her face to the sky, Summer gave a sigh of pure bliss. She knew she shouldn't enjoy herself while Amelia's fate was so uncertain, but she couldn't help feeling pleasure at the simple chore of scrubbing herself clean.

She had washed her hair and was rinsing out the soap when she remembered Lance. He wasn't watching her, she noticed with a glance over her shoulder. Certainly he wasn't ogling her the way she had him when he'd bathed in front of her. In fact, he seemed to be ignoring her entirely.

His disinterest stung. For a brief moment Summer considered calling to him, just to gain his attention, to make him look at her—and yet she didn't want to push him too far. Lance had set the rules of their relationship; he was keeping his distance with an iron will. If she broke them, if she tried to exercise her feminine powers on him gain, he might never bring her back here. Or worse, he might pay her back the way he had the other night.

It was a long while before she reluctantly ended her bath. After wringing out her wet hair and drying off with the cloth, she donned the shirt and skirt and her moccasins. Then she went to join Lance on the blanket, settling beside him in the dappled shade of the cottonwood tree.

His black gaze traveled over her coolly, and yet she thought she could see approval in his expression.

"Feel better?"

She laughed. "Immensely. You have my undying gratitude."

"That so?"

His gaze dropped to her mouth, and suddenly the air was charged with a subtle tension. She could see desire in Lance's eyes, hot and smoldering, and the sight heartened her. For the past several days he had pretended total indifference, but he wanted her now; she knew it with every womanly instinct she possessed.

The knowledge soothed pride that had been stung by his previous rejection. She wasn't the only one so strongly affected. Yet she also saw the sudden hard clench of his jaw as Lance clamped down on his urges.

Self-consciously Summer picked up the hairbrush he'd brought. When she started to use it on her wet hair, though, Lance startled her by taking the brush from her.

"Turn around. I'll do that."

Tensely she did as he asked, presenting her back to him. She felt his fingers gently arranging her wet locks, felt the careful stroke of the brush as he pulled the quill bristles through her tangles. It was soothing and yet disturbingly arousing. His slow, sensuous ministrations reminded her far too much of their wedding night.

The silence between them grew. After a moment, Summer decided it might be wise to break it—before she did something foolish like testing Lance's restraint.

"Amelia used to brush my hair like this," she said tentatively.

She winced at the sudden, sharp tug on her scalp as the brush caught on a snarl. Perhaps Amelia wasn't the safest subject after all. Biting her lip, she tried again.

"Short Dress told me how you acquired the name of Sharp Lance—because you performed a great act of courage in battle—but she never said what you were called before then."

A moment went by before Lance answered. "It was White Woman's Son."

"That sounds like a Comanche name. Didn't you have a white name? One your mother gave you?"

"Yes, but I quit using it when she died."

"What was it?"

"It doesn't matter. That part of my life is over."

Summer hesitated, not wanting to pry, yet wanting to discover more about her husband and his complex past. "Was that part so painful, then?"

Lance gave a curt laugh. "You might say that. I sure as hell wouldn't want to live through it again."

"You were twelve when you went in search of your father, weren't you?"

"So what?" His tone suggested wariness.

"My brother Reed once told me what he knew about you. He said that when your mother died, you ran away to find your Comanche father."

"That's about right." She could almost feel Lance shrug. "When Ma died, there wasn't any reason for me to stick around Austin."

"You rode all the way to Indian Territory alone?"

"No. The Comanche still lived in Texas then. They hadn't been run out of the state yet. But I didn't know where to start looking for my father's band. Didn't know anything about him except for what little my mother had told me. But I'd heard talk about a man named McTavish who'd spent time with the Comanche, so I headed north to find him."

"Your friend at the trading post . . . Deek?"

"Yes, only he wasn't my friend at the time. I stopped there for supplies, but I didn't have any money to pay for them. I'd stolen a horse just to get that far." Lance chuckled as if remembering something amusing. "I made the mistake of trying to lift a gun off Deek, and he caught me at it. Nearly skinned me alive."

"He didn't hurt you?" Summer asked, concerned.

"Not really. Tore a strip off my hide, that was all. Then he found out what I meant to do and put a stop to it fast. Wouldn't let me set out on my own to find my father. He even offered to help."

"He must have known the danger involved."

"Yeah." She heard the reluctant smile in Lance's voice. "I didn't want to listen to him. Didn't want his help, either. I figured I had only myself to depend on, and I was determined to prove I didn't need anybody else. I was a hardheaded, fool kid back then, but Deek managed to knock some sense into me that time. Locked me in his storeroom and kept me there till I agreed to let him help. He probably saved my life. I likely would have died out here on my own, or at the very least been taken captive by another band. Deek found my father's camp without much trouble."

"And your father took you in?"

"Yes. Kills Something accepted me as his son. Children are cherished in the Comanche culture, especially boys. As long as I was willing to adopt their ways, they were willing to let me stay. In fact, my father was glad to get me back. He was away from camp hunting buffalo the day the white soldiers came—most of the village was, or I never would have been taken from him."

"That must have been when the frontier regiment rescued you and your mother."

"Yeah," Lance said dryly, "they rescued us, if you could call it that." His tone turned grim. "The soldiers destroyed the village, killed dozens of women and children. They would have killed my mother, too, except they saw her blond hair and figured she might not be a Comanche. Real smart of them."

"It must have been terrible for you."

"I don't remember anything about it. I was just a baby then. All I know is what Ma told me—and the stories I heard later from my Comanche kin. They had a bad time of it that winter. With all their stores and shelter destroyed, they nearly starved. My father had his revenge on the white man in the next battle, but he never forgot what they'd done. He never forgot me, either. He said he looked for me every time he went on a raid."

She caught the wistful note in Lance's voice and frowned. "You sound almost as if you regretted being rescued."

"Maybe I did. At least I would have belonged somewhere if I'd grown up Comanche. The whites sure as hell didn't want me back. And it might have been easier on my mother if we'd never returned to civilization."

"Easier?" After experiencing life in a Comanche camp, Summer couldn't believe anything could be more difficult than living as a Comanche captive. "You can't mean that."

"No?" He gave a bitter laugh. "The Comanches weren't any crueler to her than the whites were. In fact, her own people hurt her worse. At least my father took her as his wife when she got pregnant with me. He didn't have to do that for a slave. Her people only turned their backs on her. Made her into a whore."

Summer turned her head sharply to stare over her shoulder at him.

"You look shocked, princess. You didn't know my mother was a whore?"

"No," she replied unevenly, disturbed as much by Lance's accepting tone as the revelation itself.

"No, I guess you wouldn't have been told. It wasn't a tale fit for a lady's ears." Lance pulled the brush through a lock of her hair with more force than necessary. "But it's true. It was the only way she could support herself and a half-breed kid. She tried to fashion bonnets for sale, take in laundry and sewing and such, but nobody would give her work with me around—and she had to feed us. But she wouldn't give me up. She paid a steep price for keeping me."

Summer found herself trying to swallow a sudden ache in her throat. "She . . . must have been a brave woman."

Lance's fierce gaze softened, grew distant. "She was the bravest person I've ever known, man or woman."

She watched him for a moment, groping for something comforting to say. "I can only imagine how difficult her life must have been."

His mouth curled at the corner. "No, you can't, princess. You can't begin to imagine. You never had to face one tenth of the hardships she had to."

Lowering her gaze, Summer turned back around. He was right. She'd never experienced anything like the difficulties Charlotte Calder had endured.

"I hated the whites who'd forced her to live like that," Lance went on in a low voice, remembering. "Hated myself for being the cause of her shame."

"But you were just a child," Summer murmured. "Surely she didn't hold you responsible."

"No," he agreed. "She didn't blame me."

Lance fell silent as memories of aching loneliness washed over him. He could still hear his mother's voice trying to soothe his youthful fury, trying to calm his hatred. *Don't you worry for me, my love. I chose you over respectability, and I've never regretted it for an instant. Not for a single instant.* He tried to shrug off the memory.

"I guess after a few years it got a little easier for her. She took up with a ranger and became what they call a 'kept woman.' You knew Tom Peace. You thought him a fine, up-standing citizen."

"Yes, but I didn't know . . ." Summer faltered.

"No, his choice of mistresses wasn't something that would be talked about in polite company. And that was before he moved to Round Rock. But my mother was his woman for years. I guess she was thankful to have to service only one man instead of countless strangers. And she was grateful that he put up with me."

"Did he? Put up with you, I mean?"

"Yeah. He taught me how to defend myself from people who wouldn't let me be. How to use my fists and shoot a gun. That's all I ever let him do for me. I didn't want his charity." Lance's fingers tightened around the brush as he recalled those early years. Tom Peace had tried to be a father to him, but he'd been a wild kid hell-bent on self-destruction and revenge.

"I hated him," he said softly. "More than anybody else. I never forgave him for not doing more for my mother. He could have saved her a lot of grief by marrying her, but he was too damned proud to marry a whore, too worried about what people would say. He loved her, but he wouldn't help her when she needed him."

"Perhaps he regretted it," Summer offered.

Lance made a scoffing sound deep in his throat. "Sure he did. *After* she died. It wasn't till then that Peace decided he was sorry he didn't do right by her. Too late to do her any damn good. He felt guilty enough to offer me a home when she died, though."

"Did you take him up on it?"

Lance gave a harsh chuckle. "Hell, no. No way was I going to let him ease his conscience. He deserved to suffer a little bit. Course, it probably hurt me more than it hurt him. No doubt I was biting off my nose to spite my face. But right then I didn't give a damn. I was hurting too bad from losing Ma."

"How did she die?" Summer asked, hearing the pain in his voice even now.

"A wasting disease of some kind. Peace paid for doctors, but they couldn't do anything for her except try to ease her suffering."

"It must have been difficult for you to see her so ill."

Lance nodded silently. It had nearly killed him to watch his mother die, to watch her take her last painful breath. And in the end he'd gone half-crazy. "Ma, don't go!" he'd screamed, clutching her ravaged shoulders as tears poured down his face. "Don't leave me!" He'd held her to him in a fierce grip as he rocked her lifeless body—even when Tom Peace had tried to pull him away.

"Come on, son. She's gone."

"Get your hands off me, you bastard! And her! Don't touch her, God damn you! God damn you to hell!"

He'd struck out at Peace with his fists and managed to inflict some damage—a split lip, a bloodied nose—for even at twelve, he'd been wiry and strong. But Peace had grabbed him and held him tight, subduing his struggles while he sobbed out his grief. He'd hated Peace even more because of that. Because he'd dared to offer comfort. It was only years later that he realized Peace had been hurting, too.

"Peace didn't want to stay in Austin after that. He worked a stock ranch there, but he sold it and moved to Round Rock to start a livery. Offered me a job and a place to live if I wanted to come with him, but I wouldn't take it. I didn't want anything to do with him—or anybody white, for that matter."

Summer caught her lower lip with her teeth, more affected than she cared to admit by this unexpected, vulnerable side of her husband. She could picture Lance as a boy, alone, afraid, the one person in his life who had loved him, dead. And even then, he'd been too defiant, too proud, to accept help or comfort, or even simple human warmth.

"That was why you went in search of your father," she prompted gently.

"Yeah."

"Did you enjoy it, living with the Comanche?"

"Parts of it. I liked the feeling of belonging. The Comanche eventually accepted me as one of their own—although after all the scorn and insults I'd suffered from whites, I guess I would have taken acceptance anywhere I could get it. It was harder than I expected to become a warrior, though. I had a lot of catching up to do. I didn't know the first thing about what a Comanche considers important. I had to bear the taunts of kids half my age until I learned to hold my own. But my father and Fights Bear taught me, and they were the best. Nobody better."

"But if you wouldn't take help from anyone else, why would you accept theirs?"

"I guess because I wanted their respect. And it was a matter of survival. I'd thrown in my lot with them, and I was going to become a Comanche or die trying. Literally."

"Did you? Become a Comanche?"

"No. Not fully."

"Why not?"

His hand stilled in her hair, but for a moment he didn't answer.

"If you enjoyed living with them," Summer pressed, "then why did you leave?"

"I didn't fit in after all." Lance let out his breath in a long sigh. "Not like a true Comanche. I couldn't stomach the killing. You heard about that battle when my father was killed? We were on a war raid . . . my first. Some white settlers died. I helped kill them."

Summer clamped her lips together, trying not to exclaim in horror. Knowing that Lance had participated in the terrible atrocities committed against the Texas settlers—the kind of depredations her sister had suffered—appalled her. And yet he said he'd regretted it. He'd repudiated that life, which meant he wasn't beyond redemption.

She took a deep breath. Lance had gone still, as if waiting for her reply, yet she couldn't trust herself to make one. For a span of several heartbeats she thought he might say something more—perhaps to try and justify actions that couldn't be justified—but thankfully he didn't.

"My father had died by then," Lance added finally when she didn't speak. "There didn't seem to be as much reason for me to stay."

Summer swallowed, trying to keep the revulsion from her voice. "Short Dress . . . said your grandmother gave you her blessing when you left."

"Only because I'd had a vision. The Comanche put great store in such things, and she knew I couldn't go against it."

"And your brother? What did Fights Bear do?"

"He tried to persuade me to reconsider, but he couldn't change my mind. He felt betrayed when I left. He only had hatred for a Comanche who would fight with the white man against other Comanches. I promised him I wouldn't, though. I couldn't choose sides, anyway. I was too much a part of both."

And not enough of either, Summer thought silently. "What did you do then?"

"I took the job Peace had offered me, working at his livery."

"You had forgiven him by then?"

"No, I still hated him, but I figured he owed me for what he had done to my mother. I worked for him for three years—you saw me when you used to come to town, remember?" Lance laughed humorlessly. "It didn't go so well. Peace and I still had bad blood between us, and the good citizens of Round Rock didn't care too much for having a half-breed in their midst, you may recall. I got out of there as soon as I could. Went west and broke mustangs . . . used the skills I'd learned from the Comanche. I did that for a few years, until I hired on at your ranch."

Summer shifted uncomfortably, not knowing what to say.

"After your pa kicked me off his place, I swore I'd never return to Round Rock."

"But you did. You came back after Tom Peace was killed in the war."

"Yes. Peace left me his livery in his will. Just to spite me, I'll bet. I'd told him often enough I didn't want his damned charity."

"If you considered it charity, then why did you accept it?"

Lance gazed out at the horizon. "I guess I'd smartened up some by then. Enough to swallow my pride, at least. And it didn't look so much like charity by then. I'd always wanted a place to sink down roots, a place to call home. I'd never really had anything I could call my own. And I thought . . . maybe it would help me become part of the white world."

"Yet it didn't, did it? You weren't really accepted by the white world, either."

"No."

There was a wealth of pain in that single word; she could hear it—although she doubted Lance was aware of it, or that he would be pleased to know she'd noticed. Summer glanced over her shoulder at him, fighting the urge to touch him, to offer comfort for his nameless hurts, knowing that he wouldn't accept comfort from her.

How long had it been since anyone had touched him with kindness? He'd had to make his own way in a tough, unforgiving world, enduring experiences that had scarred him deeply. His past had left him hard and bitter to his very soul. But he was a survivor. He'd lived through trials that would have broken lesser men.

"It must have been lonely for you," she observed quietly.

"You don't know the half of it." He was silent for a moment. "Do you know"—his voice dropped, becoming so low, she could scarcely hear him over the ripple of the creek—"what it's like, always being dirt beneath a man's boots? Being spit on and shunned by folks because of who you are, no matter what you do, no matter how hard you try? Can you imagine what it feels like?" He suddenly looked at her and laughed softly. "No, of course you can't, princess. You've always had everything you've ever wanted."

"Not ... everything."

"Close enough. Your pa always shielded his little princess from the darker sides of life. You never had to hear your ma crying because she had to lie beneath some rutting bastard in order to put food in your belly."

Summer knew he had a right to criticize the proud, pampered belle she'd once been, but her life hadn't been all roses, either. At least not since the war began.

She raised her chin. "No, I don't recall ever hearing my mother cry at all. She was killed by the Comanches before I was old enough to remember such things. Your mother paid a terrible price, but at least she lived to do it. Mine paid with her life."

She regretted the words as soon as she uttered them. A shuttered look slammed down over Lance's features, abruptly ending the quiet intimacy between them. Even before he looked up at the sky, measuring the position of the sun, and announced tersely that it was time to go, Summer knew the interlude of sharing confidences was over. What she'd said wasn't really so bad, yet she hadn't needed to remind Lance of the vast gulf between them, or to say it in that accusing tone, as if he'd been responsible for her mother's death.

Suspecting he might throw an apology, no matter how heartfelt, back in her face, though, Summer did as she was told and finished braiding her hair while she watched Lance gather up their things.

Yet she wished she could take back her thoughtless comment. This afternoon she had felt closer to Lance than she'd ever dreamed possible. He had shown her more openness than she'd ever expected, telling her things about himself and his past that she never could have learned from anyone else.

He was unlikely to share more of himself anytime soon, she knew. And he probably thought she didn't fully appreciate what he was doing for her sister. She *was* grateful to him, more than she could ever say.

Summer gazed wistfully after him, her thoughts full of regret.

Lance felt similar regrets as he collected their gear and tied it on his pinto. He'd been a damn fool, baring his soul to her—even though that was mainly the reason he'd brought her out here. Summer had begun to relax around him the past few days, and he'd thought maybe it would help the process along if they could have some time alone together, if they could become better acquainted. He knew it would take her time to get used to the idea of being his wife, and she never would as long as she saw him as a stranger.

But his plan had backfired. He'd wanted Summer to realize he wasn't the savage she feared, but all he'd done was confirm it, telling her about killing Texas settlers. And he'd succeeded in letting her probe old wounds as well. She'd dredged up hurtful memories he had done his damnedest to forget.

Lance wrapped his fist around his horse's reins as he recalled those times. The pain hadn't lessened much over the years. Summer was right. All his life he'd been lonely as hell. Lonely, empty, angry. Moving from one battle to the next without having anything to show for his efforts.

He'd give a lot to change all that. He wanted to make something of his life. He wanted a woman to fill his arms and banish the emptiness inside him. Not just any woman. He wanted Summer. Her or no one.

It had always been Summer. It was always her face in his dreams. Her scent he remembered. Her honeyed voice he heard in his mind. He thought he might sell his soul if she would just look at him like she wanted him in return. If she could come to care for him the way she cared for her sister. If she would be willing to sacrifice her future, maybe even her life, for him.

Remembering the hurtful accusations he had thrown at Summer a minute ago, Lance gave a harsh, silent laugh and shut his eyes. He'd been lying when he'd said she didn't know anything about hardship or bravery. He could see a lot of his ma's grit in her. Summer had kept the Weston ranch going during the war when other women would have folded, for one thing. She'd shown incredible courage riding into Indian Territory with him in search of her sister. And she'd tackled the backbreaking work of a Comanche woman without a single word of complaint.

He wished he couldn't see how hard she was trying. How much she had changed from the spoiled belle who had cut out his heart. He wished he could have saved himself this time. But the past few days had destroyed the last of his defenses.

He'd been battling the truth for days now. He had fallen again for Summer, this time beyond hope. Tumbled heart-first into her silken web, despite his fierce effort to stop it from happening.

Against his will, Lance let his gaze seek her out. She was kneeling on the blanket, tying the end of her braid with a strip of rawhide, the way Comanche women did. But the sun had set just enough to bathe her in golden light, turning her sable hair to fire.

The sight just about took his breath away. He wanted Summer, more than he'd ever wanted anything in his life—but he wanted her to come to *him*. On her own. Without reservation. He didn't want to just have her. He wanted to protect her, keep her, guard her, love her. He wanted to win her, wanted to bind her to him. He wanted to make her love him.

It sure as hell didn't look as if it would happen anytime soon, though.

He didn't know how much more he could stand, how much longer he could keep his distance from her. His body burned with need, with a fierce possessiveness he'd never felt for any woman but her. His heart hadn't known one moment's peace in her presence. She had the power to turn his insides to jelly with her beauty, her sensual allure, the grace she had just breathing, damn her.

His torment didn't end, either, when a short while later he mounted his horse and pulled her up behind him. Having Summer pressed against his back, her slender thighs on either side of his hips, her warmth surrounding him, was pure agony.

They rode back to the Comanche village in silence, but every one of Lance's nerves screamed at him all the while. Every time the movement of the paint horse rocked Summer against him, Lance swore under his breath, cursing her allure and his damnable need.

Chapter 10

❦

His restraint shattered the following afternoon.

Lance was sitting in front of the tepee he shared with Summer, sharpening his weapons while she labored over the deer hide, when his brother strode up. Lance's grin of welcome, however, faded abruptly as Fights Bear stopped directly beside Summer.

The war chief wore little clothing but more decoration than usual. In addition to the eagle's feather dangling from a scalp lock, he had plaited clusters of shiny red beads into his long black braids, while a necklace of elk's teeth adorned his bronzed bare chest, and blue-painted shells hung from his ears. His finery had a purpose, Lance realized with a sense of foreboding.

Standing over Summer, Fights Bear reached down and lifted one of her braids. *"Nananisuyake tsop-yaapt."*

Summer froze like a startled doe, simply staring up at him. Lance could have translated, could have explained that his brother thought she had beautiful hair. But he wasn't inclined to encourage another man's appreciation of his wife. From the look of satisfaction on his brother's face, though, he suspected his caution might be too late.

A tight fist clutched Lance's belly, even before Fights Bear turned to him.

"I would speak with you, Kanap-Cheetu."

Returning his knife to the scabbard at his waist, Lance rose silently and entered the tepee, dreading what he knew was about to come. He offered his brother a seat in the rear of the lodge, the place of honor, and waited until Fights Bear initiated the conversation.

"We are still brothers, is this not true?" he said. "Even

166

though you now live with the whites, the blood of our father runs in your veins."

"I am honored to call you brother, yes," Lance replied warily.

"Then I claim the privilege of brothers, and ask you to share your wife, the white woman you call Tahma."

The fist in Lance's stomach squeezed tighter. He didn't answer, knowing he could never agree to his brother's request.

At his silence, Fights Bear grinned. "I offer you any one of my wives in exchange, all of them. You may have your choice, even of my favorite."

"Why—" Lance cleared his throat of the sudden restriction there. "Why do you wish this, Wasape Naaohrutu?"

"I would enjoy the novelty of sleeping with a white woman such as yours. I have taken white captives before, but none that were willing. I think I should like it."

Lance fought the need to ball his hands into fists, struggled to keep his voice low and not reveal the turmoil raging inside him. His brother would never understand the fierce possessiveness he felt for Summer. He could only explain her white background and hope Fights Bear would accept it as justification for refusal.

"But she is white, brother. She does not understand our customs. To her, sleeping with another man, even though that man is her husband's brother, is adultery. She only understands the white law that makes adultery a crime."

The congenial look on Fights Bear's face faded. "You consider the white laws stronger than the laws of the People? Perhaps you have turned traitor!"

"No," Lance replied grimly. "I still honor the laws of the People. But Tahma is not one of us, and I have given a vow to protect her. She would not wish to share your bed."

"Since when are the wishes of a mere woman more valid than those of a war chief!"

"They are not, of course, but my wishes are the same as hers. I do not wish to give you use of her."

"You are selfish, Sharp Lance!"

"Perhaps so. It gives me pain to refuse you, Fights Bear, but I regret I cannot share her with you."

His expression thunderous, Fights Bear rose abruptly to his feet. "You came to me, asking for my aid, to ransom the sister of your wife, and I agreed. But I will give you help no longer," he declared, his tone infuriated. "You choose to follow white laws over those of the People. You are not Comanche! You are welcome here no longer!"

With that, Fights Bear turned on his heel and stormed out, leaving Lance to grit his teeth in fury.

He wasn't aware that Summer had entered the tepee until he heard her ask softly, "What's wrong?"

Lance looked up sharply, and she caught a glimmer of something protective and fiercely intimate in his eyes, before his usual mask shuttered it. "Nothing that concerns you."

"Are you certain? You were arguing with your brother about something just now, I could hear you."

Without rising, Lance snatched up the nearest blanket and began fashioning it into a bedroll.

"Lance? What is it? What are you doing?"

"Packing," he ground out. "Fights Bear wants us to leave the camp."

"What?" Summer drew a sharp breath. "Why?"

"It isn't important."

"Not important? But—" She broke off in confusion. It was crucial they remain at the camp until Amelia was rescued— but before she could protest, Lance's growling voice interrupted her chaotic thoughts.

"Don't worry. Fights Bear can deny us the use of his lodging, but he can't force us from the village. He doesn't have the authority. Not even the peace chief does. We'll find some other place to stay."

Summer shook her head. She didn't want a lesson in Comanche protocol. She wanted to know what had put the seething expression on her husband's face. "But ... what about Amelia? How will we find her without your brother's help?"

"You let me worry about that."

"I ... Lance, I don't understand ... Why was Fights Bear so angry? What did he say to you?"

"He said," Lance replied through clenched teeth, "that I was no longer Comanche. That I wasn't welcome here any longer."

"In heaven's name, *why?*"

"Because I wouldn't share you with him, dammit, that's why!"

Uncomprehending, she stared at him. "What do you mean, share me?"

"He covets you, princess. He wants to sleep with you."

"What?" Her voice was a reedy whisper.

Lance threw her a hostile glance. "Do I have to explain it in graphic detail? Comanche custom allows a man to sleep with his brother's wife. Sleep as in 'fuck,' not 'slumber.' Fights Bear thinks it's his right to have you in his bed."

Feeling incredibly slow, Summer raised a hand to her forehead. "But . . . he already has several wives. Why should he want me?"

His lip curled. "Don't play innocent, princess. You always did have a way of attracting men like bees around a honeypot."

Summer thought the accusation totally unfair. She might have unwittingly caught his brother's eye, but she'd done nothing to encourage his attention. Her behavior toward Fights Bear had been entirely circumspect, nothing that could be considered even remotely flirtatious or enticing. Indeed, she had kept her distance precisely because she was half-afraid of the powerful Comanche warrior.

"I didn't deserve that," she said unsteadily. "I've never even spoken to your brother, much less given him any suggestion I might welcome his advances."

"Maybe not, but he wants you." Viciously he finished tying a rawhide string around the bedroll and started on another. "Fights Bear demanded my cooperation in exchange for helping find Amelia." Lance swore audibly. "I already agreed to pay him a fortune in horses. That's more than enough. I'm not giving him you, too."

Summer took a deep breath. "I don't believe it is only your decision to make."

Lance went suddenly still. He turned his head slowly, fixing her with his dark gaze.

Summer swallowed hard at the look in his eyes. "A-Amelia is my sister. I think perhaps I have a right to be involved in any decision that affects her fate."

"You're figuring on fucking my brother?" The question

was soft, almost casual, but it held a tension as volatile as gunpowder.

Summer winced at his crude language, yet she couldn't allow Lance's jealousy—if that was what it was—to concern her; the situation was far too grave. She needed instead to worry about how serious Fights Bear's ultimatum was.

Forced to consider the question, Summer closed her eyes. Could she do it? Could she give herself to a fierce Comanche warrior simply because he claimed it as his right? What if the alternative was losing Fights Bear's support? What if her refusal possibly cost her sister's life?

Bravely she raised her chin, trying to muster her courage. "If that ... is what it takes to insure your brother's support, then yes, I'll sleep with him."

In a single fluid motion, Lance surged to his feet. Summer took a startled step back, too late to prevent him from corralling both her wrists in one hand.

"You would *whore* for your sister?" he asked in that same lethal tone.

The question stung as if he'd slapped her. She realized Lance's fury had swelled to a dangerous level, but she couldn't allow herself to be intimidated, not with so much at stake. Tilting back her head in disdain, Summer returned Lance's gaze, measure for measure.

"I suppose you could call it that," she replied grimly. "I expect some people would say that is precisely what I did by marrying you. Whore for my sister."

For a full five seconds Lance stared down at her. A full five seconds that gave Summer the opportunity to regret her ill-judged assertion. A full five seconds before Lance's temper exploded.

His black eyes glittering and wild, he wrapped a hard arm around her waist and jerked her against him. Her heart gave a sudden lunge as she stared at his dark, rigid face.

"I won't share you!" He growled as he abruptly lowered his head.

His lips, hard and vengeful, slanted over hers, forcing hers against her teeth, assaulting her with a fierceness that stopped her breath.

Alarmed by his fury, Summer fought to be free, but Lance controlled her struggles by tightening his grip, so that her arms were crushed between them. When she tried to turn her head, his fingers clamped on her chin and held it so he could enter her mouth with his tongue. It swept inside, hot and fierce, brutally lustful.

His kiss was a ruthless act of aggression, a seizure that punished, that dominated, that ravished without ardor. He kissed her as if he were taking what belonged to him, roughly, hurting her, seeming to *want* to hurt her, his mouth violent with need against her unyielding one.

Summer pushed against his bare, muscles chest to no avail. Her world reeled. She whimpered a muffled cry of protest into his mouth, but his fierce tongue only plunged in more deeply, subduing her, forcing her to open wider, robbing her of breath.

Lance's rage was beyond control. She was *his* wife, goddammit; she belonged in *his* bed, not his brother's. He deepened the brutal kiss, determined to brand Summer as his own. She would feel him, taste him, think of him, when she gave herself to another man.

His eyes blazed when he suddenly raised his head. Dimly she saw the harsh, almost cruel look of arousal on Lance's face. The skin was pulled tight over his high, prominent cheekbones; his white teeth were bared like a beast's.

"You don't want my brother, princess. He won't be easy on you. He'll simply take you like chattel, spend his lust on you, and throw you back to me."

As if to graphically demonstrate, Lance's powerful body bent over her, forcing her back against his arm. His knee parted her legs, shoved hard against her femininity beneath her deerskin skirt, threatening her with his overwhelming strength. Yet somehow his assault did more to arouse than threaten. All Summer could manage to think about was their wedding night, the memory of Lance's thigh moving roughly between hers, giving her her first taste of ecstasy.

He bent her ruthlessly over his arm, but try as she might, she couldn't seem to care about the pain that shot through her. She felt terrifyingly weak, knowing full well she was at Lance's mercy. And yet, incredibly, at the same time she felt powerfully feminine, aware that she had driven this strong man to lose his rigid control. She could feel the hunger in his muscular body. His obsidian eyes were wild, fierce, naked in intent, his face dark and taut with both rage and physical need. He meant to take her; she could see it in his violent look, feel it in his brutal embrace.

And yet his possession was what Summer wanted, what she yearned for. It was all too possible that she would be forced to share his brother's bed, and she desperately wanted Lance to be the first. He was her husband. She wanted to belong to him.

Through a haze of awareness, she heard his threatening growl. "Fights Bear won't pleasure you beforehand. He won't do this. . . ."

In two swift seconds, Lance had ripped the buttons from the calico shirt she wore and pushed it open, baring her breasts. His hard fingers closed roughly over a soft mound in a grip that should have hurt but didn't. She could feel her nipple swelling painfully against the callused pressure of his palm, but she could only gasp at the sensations his touch awakened in her.

"He won't kiss you here. . . ."

Lowering his head, Lance closed his lips hard over her nipple, making Summer cry out in surprise as a jolt of fire ran from his mouth and streaked to every part of her body. It wasn't a caress but a branding. His plundering mouth was hard and hot and compelling, and made her tremble with helplessness.

She was dimly aware of a white-hot excitement flooding through her, of the tightness rapidly building in her lower belly. Her hands coming up to clutch the rough blackness of his hair, she arched against him, caught in a tangled web of need. Lance tormented her breast, suckling as though he would devour her, and forced a shuddering moan from her.

Then suddenly he was kneeling at her feet, shoving up her leather skirt over her pale naked thighs, up to her hips, to bare her lower body. Summer froze in shock as she realized she was completely revealed to him. Her heart hammered as he hauled her close and his hot mouth found the dark curls between her legs.

"W-What . . . ?"

She made a strangled, senseless protest, but Lance wouldn't stop his feverish assault. He blamed her for the violent need inside him, blamed Summer for this fierce wanting that ate at his reason. The yielding primitive scent of her made his groin grind, made him so hard, he thought he might explode. Fiercely he tightened his grip on her hips and pressed his open mouth against her succulent flesh.

She jerked, whimpering, as his probing kiss invaded her, as his hungry lips explored the heated center of her womanhood. Mercilessly his searching tongue stroked the most vulnerable part of her in a lash of pleasure that was almost cruel. Summer arched wildly under the sensation so exquisite and unbearable that her entire body quivered. She wanted to demand that he stop, that he cease tormenting her, but the dark head between her burning thighs was giving her the most frightening pleasure she had ever known. His face pressed into her, both hands gripping the curves of her hips, compelling her surrender, making the anguished pleasure inescapable. She screamed softly at the mounting, burning frenzy swelling inside her.

Lance could feel her passion building like a raging inferno, hot enough to match his own. A convulsive shudder shook him, and he cursed at the difficulty of tearing aside his loincloth. He was so swollen with need that he thought he might die if he didn't have her now, at once. Releasing his throbbing length, he lowered Summer on shaking limbs that could no longer support her, so that her knees straddled his thighs, her bare breasts rubbed against his naked chest.

He vaguely knew he'd once had reasons he shouldn't be doing this, shouldn't be taking her body, but he couldn't remember them just now. He had Summer, hot and willing in his arms, and his mind refused to function. There was no stopping him this time. The blood pounded so wildly in his ears that he scarcely head her startled cry as his hardness tried to impale her soft flesh. Her spine arched in shock as he thrust into her, as he encountered the fragile barrier to her womanhood.

Virgin! his conscience screamed at him. He had to go slowly—but God, he wanted her! And he knew that for this moment at least, Summer wanted him. Her breath coming in erratic, ragged gasps, she clung to him, her eyes closed, her teeth painfully clenching her lower lip as she waited for his claiming.

"Easy," he rasped in a raw, shaking voice. Jesus, he didn't want to hurt her.

Fighting for restraint, Lance forced himself to slow down. His own eyes fiercely primitive, he drew Summer's slim legs up to clasp his hips. Swiftly then, he rose up on his knees and laid her down on her back. His body covering hers, he eased his weight onto her, trying to hold back.

Summer went rigid as his swollen shaft again sought entrance to her body, but Lance was kissing her face, murmuring soft words of passion in his Comanche language, and she forgot to be afraid.

The moment she relaxed, he thrust into her, slowly, inexorably, sinking, squeezing his huge sex into her tight heat now slick with desire. The impact made her gasp. She knew a sharp, shocking moment of pain as he filled her to bursting . . . but then her flesh seemed to swell around him, her body to soften, molded by his. The pain slowly died away, leaving only a dull, full throbbing.

Panting, Summer held completely still, afraid of the strange arousing ache caused by having Lance deep inside her, part of her. He was so big, so overwhelming, and yet she wanted this pleasureful hurt . . . wanted him joined to her this way. . . .

He was watching her, his obsidian gaze smoldering and intense with determination as he slowly withdrew, then crowded into her again. For an instant her muscles tensed at the fresh invasion, but then her body closed around him with a long, desperate shudder.

Lance groaned aloud at the shattering relief as her hot, moist flesh tightly sheathed him. Vainly he clenched his teeth. His control was slipping, his rough excitement burgeoning beyond restraint. His hips began moving against hers, rhythmically, driven by an urgent, primal force.

In a daze of awareness, Summer arched instinctively against him. She was whimpering steadily now, but not in pain. Some primitive part of her nature had taken control. She writhed, frantic, her nails digging into his hard flesh as she tried to get closer.

Reveling in her helpless response, Lance reacted with violent hunger, his hips thrusting hard and rhythmic, his arms closing convulsively around her, his movements rawly frenzied. He had known desire before, but not this gnawing, tearing desperation. Where had it come from, this terrible need?

Summer felt it, too. She sobbed, bucking beneath him, striving to get closer, seeking escape from the fiery heat that was too fierce to be borne, but then his hands closed over her buttocks, lifting them so he could thrust harder, deeper, his shaft plunging in a savage claiming.

The inferno broke over her first. Something went wild inside her; she could no longer hold her body still as passion wrenched her, racked her. Her gasping cries filled the tepee moments before a low, rough groan burst from Lance's throat. With uncurbed, hammering wildness, he joined her, his body contracting, shuddering, as a throbbing white-hot orgasm exploded from him, filling her with his seed.

Afterwards—long moments afterwards—he sank against her, spent and shuddering, his breath coming in rasping gasps. Summer lay panting beneath him, dazed and weak, her face pressed against the smooth, sweaty silk of his bare shoulder.

Finally she heard him draw in a long, ragged breath, felt him rise up on his elbows, relieving her of some of his heavy weight.

"You all right?" His voice was low, still hoarse with passion.

Her lids lifted slowly. Deep in the obsidian eyes burning close above her was a fierce possessiveness.

"What . . . what if I said no?"

He stared down at her for a long moment. "Summer, I . . ."

She thought he might have started to make her an apology, yet he didn't complete whatever he'd been about to say. Instead Lance eased himself off her and rolled over on his back, draping his forearm over his eyes.

Awkwardly, with a trembling hand, Summer pulled her skirt down over her naked thighs. Her flesh felt raw and aching, but her body fulfilled, as if their joining had made her whole. Lance hadn't hurt her, precisely. Merely left her emotions shaken and raw, her thoughts in turmoil. She had wanted his passion, with a fierceness that shocked her. But she wanted more for him to understand.

"Lance . . . I have to . . . at least talk with your brother."

At first she didn't think he meant to answer. Then finally

he spoke, his voice raw and unsteady. "You go to him, and he'll think you're offering to sleep with him."

"Perhaps . . . I can persuade him to change his mind."

Lance's sharp huff of laughter mocked her.

"I can't just let Fights Bear withdraw his support. Don't you see? It could mean my sister's life."

"Yeah, I see. You're willing to do anything at all to protect her." His tone was bitter.

"Do you blame me?"

He turned his head to look at Summer; the black glitter had returned to his eyes. "You're my wife. You think I want to share you with another man? Even if he is my half brother?"

"Do you think I *want* to sleep with another man? Especially an—" She bit off the word *Indian,* not wishing to insult Lance by denigrating his Comanche relatives. They were his people, after all, and she knew how thin-skinned he was on the subject.

He was still looking at her, his features shuttered. "I guess the vows you took when we got married didn't mean a damn thing to you."

Summer had no answer for that. She hadn't wanted to take those vows, but she'd been forced to for her sister's sake, just as she might now be forced to barter her body if his brother demanded it.

"Those were vows recognized by a white society," she replied uneasily, "but we're here now, where different customs apply. You're half-Comanche. I would have thought you'd be anxious to uphold your people's customs."

Lance muttered an expletive under his breath at her reasonable argument.

"Lance . . . I've come this far," she said quietly, unsteadily. "I can't take the risk of hurting my sister's chances for survival, simply because I don't have the courage to make sacrifices." Summer's voice dropped to a mere whisper that threatened to crack with tears. "You said your mother was a brave woman. Well, I'm trying to be brave, too. And . . . and if I can . . . force myself to do something so naturally abhorrent to me, then I don't see how you have the right to prevent me."

Lance closed his eyes, struggling with the fierce urge to pull Summer into his arms and hold her possessively. He couldn't argue with her, that was the hell of it. The only reason she had married him was because of her sister. This wasn't much different. Summer only wanted to try and save her goddamned sister. What right did he have to stop her? Especially after the way he'd just acted. He was a savage bastard, just like he'd always been called. In his rage, he'd practically raped Summer, taking her like any experienced whore on the hard ground, instead of an innocent virgin.

What right did he have to prevent her? No matter how much it killed him to let her go to his brother, even if he felt like killing to keep her with him, he couldn't stand in her way.

Lance curled his fingers into fists as sick, impotent rage twisted his gut. He couldn't protect her. He was forced to stand by while another woman sacrificed in his place. It was a familiar feeling; he'd lived with it for most of his life.

When he didn't reply, Summer rose unsteadily to her feet. She could feel a throbbing twinge between her legs and the warm rush of Lance's seed down her inner thigh, but she wouldn't let herself dwell on what had happened between them. At least not now.

Fumbling to close her torn blouse, to smooth her rumpled skirt, she looked down at him. "Lance . . . I . . . I have to go."

Turning, she went to the entrance and raised the flap. She cast one brief glance over her shoulder at Lance, then slipped quietly through the exit.

His fists clenched, Lance refused to watch her go, dimly aware of a sweeping sense of desolation, of a sharp, aching aloneness that he'd never felt so forcefully, even in all his years of being an outcast.

Chapter 11

S he was shaking when she entered Fights Bear's tepee just before dusk.

The war chief was alone, having dismissed his other wives when Summer humbly begged an audience with him. She had brought Short Dress with her, not for protection, although that would have been welcome, but because she needed a translator. Even if Fights Bear had spoken Spanish, her own mediocre command of that language would hardly be adequate to support the delicate negotiations she hoped to conduct.

A swift glance at the Comanche warrior's dark features made Summer wonder if she was making a terrible mistake by thinking to persuade him to reconsider. Fights Bear's smoldering ebony eyes, so much like Lance's, held suspicion and anger, as well as his usual arrogance and the contempt he reserved for dealing with whites. He sat with his arms folded over his muscular chest in an attitude of complete disdain.

The thought of having to sleep with this man filled Summer with dread. Despite the resemblance his handsome copper features bore to her husband's, Fights Bear was a stranger, a warrior from a culture that seemed barbaric and cruel compared to white civilization.

Could she permit him to know her body carnally the way Lance had just done? Could she submit to the most intimate act between a man and woman? Would Fights Bear take her brutally, without compassion, or would he show her even a small measure of the tenderness she had come to expect from Lance? If she failed in her goal, she would have answers to those questions before the night was through.

Summer clenched her fingers together to hide their trembling, finding it difficult to concentrate. Her mind felt numb, distracted, as if a part of her had remained with Lance in their tepee. After his fierce lovemaking, her body felt strange, different, acutely sensitive. Flashes of remembrance kept assaulting her: Lance becoming part of her, moving over her, within her. He had made her fully a woman. He had finally asserted his rights as her husband, insistently, without mercy. He had bonded them together physically, if not emotionally.

The image was seared into her brain; the feel of him thrusting between her legs, filling her, claiming her body, was branded on her mind, her nerves, her skin. And yet she had no time to dwell on what should have been one of the most momentous events of her life.

Too much was at stake.

Summer took a deep breath as she stood submissively before Fights Bear. She would do whatever she had to in order to help her sister survive. Other women had managed in far more difficult situations. Lance's mother, for one. Charlotte Calder had been given no choice in the men she was forced to accept in her bed. It comforted Summer to remember Charlotte's bravery.

Deliberately she kept her head bowed, her eyes lowered. She spoke softly, infusing a deference into her voice that she didn't feel. "Short Dress, please tell him that I have come to clear up a misunderstanding concerning his brother, Sharp Lance."

Fights Bear's answer in the Comanche language came abruptly and held a stinging rebuke.

"He does not recognize Sharp Lance as his brother," Short Dress translated.

"I regret that is so," Summer murmured, "and so does Sharp Lance. He does not wish there to be anger between brothers. That is why he sent me to you," she lied. "If you wish to claim me as your sleeping partner, then that is your right."

When silence met her announcement, she stole another glance at Fights Bear and could see the harsh set of his features had relaxed somewhat, although the arrogance still remained.

She let her voice turn pleading. "Please, Fights Bear, I ask you to forgive him. He only wished to allow me to follow the ways of my people, but he knows that white customs mean nothing to Comanches."

The war chief said something and waved an arm imperiously at his third wife in a gesture that signaled dismissal, but Summer broke in quietly, hiding her alarm. "No, please, Short Dress! Ask him if you might stay for a moment. I won't know how to speak to him, otherwise."

The Mexican woman complied, and after a moment's consideration, Fights Bear grunted.

When he indicated for Summer to sit beside him, she knelt obediently, still keeping her head bowed. "I am honored to have been chosen by so great a warrior. Since coming to this camp, I have heard countless stories of your courage and your feats in battle."

The war chief nodded as if such flattery were only his due.

Summer ventured a tentative smile. "I would also like very much to thank you for helping to search for my sister. She means a great deal to me, and I can't bear to lose her. Sharp Lance has already promised you horses, but I would like to show my gratitude as well."

She held out her hand, palm up, offering him a small object. It was a lady's watch whose gold case was ornamented with delicate filigree.

"This belonged to my mother. I would like you to have it in appreciation for helping to save my sister. Perhaps you would care to give it as a present to one of your wives."

Accepting the watch, the Comanche chief studied it closely.

"If I may," Summer offered. "The clasp opens like so . . . ." Carefully she pried open the case to reveal the watch face inside.

Fights Bear grinned with genuine delight.

"The hands move with time," Summer explained. "You wind it like this . . . ." Demonstrating, she made the minute hand revolve, and then directed his rough fingers to do the same.

Suddenly, though, he frowned. Cautiously he held the watch to his ear, listening to the faint tick. His black eyes widening, Fights Bear dropped the watch as if it were a live coal. The shock and apprehension on his face were genuine.

When Summer picked it up and offered it to him again, he gave her a long stare before accepting it.

"It has a heart that beats!" Short Dress translated in awe.

"Well, yes," Summer admitted, not knowing what else to say.

"It is good medicine?"

"Very good," she prevaricated, praying he would believe her and that Comanche superstition would work to her advantage. "I have always worn it next to my own heart"—she indicated her breast where she usually kept it pinned—"and felt comforted by it."

For a while longer Fights Bear inspected the watch without speaking. Finally, though, he nodded regally.

"It is a present worthy of a war chief," Short Dress explained. "He will keep this for himself and use its medicine." Fights Bear added something else gruffly. "He thanks you for your gift, Tahma."

"I am honored that I, a mere woman, have pleased the mighty Fights Bear." Summer gave him a brilliant smile, the kind she reserved for flirting with her beaux, and she wasn't disappointed by the spark of interest in his dark eyes. The male ego, she suspected, was the same in any culture.

"I do not wish to be bold or impolite," she added softly, "but if I might explain why Sharp Lance showed reluctance to give me to you, then perhaps you would lose your anger with him."

The war chief's pleased look faded, but he did not prevent her from continuing.

Assuming her most charming manner, Summer raised her eyes to gaze admiringly at Fights Bear. "Your brother esteems you greatly and craves your respect. He has told me that you taught him the skills of a warrior."

"This is so."

"He would never willingly incur your censure. That is why he regrets angering you. He realizes that he was mistaken to deny your request. Sharp Lance said you wished to sleep with me, and he bows to your wishes."

The grunt the war chief gave was no more than an acknowledgment of the facts.

"And although your customs are not mine, I do not want to make Sharp Lance lose the respect of the Comanche People. I wish to honor my husband, as a wife should."

Fights Bear nodded approvingly. "This is good."

Summer took a deep breath. She was prepared to present

her reasons why their coupling would be a mistake—and to suggest an alternative. She only prayed she could make him listen.

"I don't wish Sharp Lance to be cast out from the Comanche people, and yet . . . he must also live in the white world. It is against white laws for a married woman to sleep with a man who is not her husband."

Scowling suddenly, Fights Bear looked every inch the dangerous barbarian that he was. "I care nothing for these white laws!"

"Of course not," Summer said soothingly. "Forgive me for implying such a thing. But truly, I was merely explaining the thoughts that ran through your brother's mind. He only hoped to protect me. Whites do not think highly of a woman who would give herself to many men."

Impatiently Fights Bear thumped his chest with his fist. "Not many men! One only! We are brothers. It is fitting for brothers to share wives."

"In the Comanche culture, yes. But it would shame Sharp Lance terribly before whites if his wife were to take another man as her lover."

"Whites are fools!"

Summer smiled. "I have often thought so. But that is another subject. My concern now is my husband. It would deliver a fierce blow to his pride if he could not protect his woman. Perhaps you can understand. A proud man suffers far more from shame than from physical wounding. And Sharp Lance is very proud."

To her relief, Fights Bear nodded slowly in agreement.

"I will do whatever you ask," she murmured. "If you wish to have me in your bed, then that is your right. Indeed, I am honored that so great a warrior as Fights Bear would favor a mere white woman. Still, it is a pity. . . ." She lowered her eyes sadly.

He barked something that she took to mean "What are you talking about?"

"It is a pity that Sharp Lance will suffer for adhering to Comanche law. In this case, it would greatly hurt his consequence in the white world."

"I tell you, I care nothing for the opinion of whites!"

"Yes, I know. Forgive me." She clasped her hands humbly.

"It is just that . . . I care for my husband. I don't wish for him to lose face with either people. I would do anything to protect him." She stole a glance at Fights Bear. "Is it wrong for a woman to wish to protect her husband?"

For the first time, Fights Bear cast a glance at their Mexican translator. "I would wish that my own wives would show such devotion," he replied in a tone that sounded almost dry.

Summer bit her lip. She hadn't wanted to cause a family squabble. "I'm certain they would do no less for you than I wish to do for Sharp Lance," she said quickly. "I worry greatly for his pride, for I know the scorn that the whites will show him if he allows his wife to sleep with another man. However . . . there is an honorable alternative, I think. One that would allow Sharp Lance to save his pride and still honor you as a brother."

Fights Bear looked at her narrowly.

"Perhaps you would accept horses in exchange, as proof of Sharp Lance's respect for you as his brother."

She held her breath as she let that sink in. Horses to a Comanche were like gold to whites; they symbolized wealth and prestige and power, and meant more to a Comanche than females ever could. She could only hope Fights Bear would rather have horses than her body.

The speculation on his dark features told her she had aroused his attention at least, and Summer went on hopefully, beginning with flattery. "I know that you already own many horses, and that you do not need more to improve your consequence, but you would spare your brother much pain by accepting the horses instead."

"It is not the usual way," the war chief said thoughtfully.

"No . . . but then, these are not usual circumstances. And you are wise enough to see the merits of this solution. Would you at least consider it, Fights Bear? You would make your brother very happy."

"Ten horses?"

Summer slowly let out the breath she had been holding. Ten horses was an exorbitant number, but she wasn't about to quibble or accuse Fights Bear of taking advantage of her position.

With a soft smile of agreement, she bowed her head humbly. "Thank you, Fights Bear, for your wisdom and your regard for your brother. I think Sharp Lance will think that a fair exchange."

She wanted to tell Lance of her victory at once, but when Summer returned to the tepee she shared with him, he was nowhere to be found. She wasn't allowed to go in search of him, either, for she had to help cook supper—more roasted meat, as usual—and then prepare the bedrolls for sleeping. By the time the camp settled down for the night, she still had seen no sign of her husband.

Restlessly Summer turned over in the bed they usually shared and pulled a buffalo robe more snugly around her body. The feel of the tanned hide rasping against her naked breasts made her wince with remembered pleasure. Embarrassed, Summer shut her eyes, recalling the heat of Lance's mouth assaulting her nipples, the wicked lash of his tongue between her thighs, the fierce passion that had exploded between them this afternoon. What in heaven's name had happened to her? One moment she was struggling in his arms, resisting his fierce caresses. The next, she didn't even recognize herself.

She'd been an entirely different woman in his arms—primal and lusting and oblivious to anything but the need to get closer to him. It frightened her, the wild way she'd responded to Lance, to his fury, his violence. She'd been raised a lady, and ladies did *not* behave like strumpets. Ladies did not allow their husbands to do such shameful, abandoned things to them, either.

What was more alarming, she had always relied on charm and beauty and the power of her femininity to control men, but Lance had proven invulnerable to all her usual maneuvering. She, on the other hand, was growing less and less certain in their relationship. It frightened her to contemplate a future with Lance as her husband. If she fell apart each time he merely touched her, then she would have no control over the marriage he'd forced on her, no control over him. And Lance was ungentlemanly enough to exploit her weakness if he could.

Still, her wanton behavior and her growing helplessness weren't her only concerns. It worried her even more that Lance was gone.

* * *

He rode into camp at midmorning the next day. Without a word, or even a glance at his wife, Lance dropped the deer he'd killed beside the working women and then dismounted to enter the tepee.

Summer wiped her hands on the grass to clean off the tanning solution, then rose and followed him inside. She found him hanging his bow and arrow quiver from a lodgepole.

"Where have you been?" she demanded without preliminaries. Her relief that he had returned safely was overshadowed by her anger that he had frightened her so.

The menace in his black gaze when Lance glanced over his shoulder at her took her aback. "I don't reckon that's any of your business."

Summer started to retort that where her husband slept was very much her business, that she was his wife—but she remembered the argument they'd had yesterday concerning his proprietary rights, and she bit her tongue. Theirs was not a normal marriage, by any means.

"I didn't sleep with him," Summer said in a low voice.

The silence that greeted her announcement stretched into a full minute as Lance settled on the ground with his back to her and began refilling his parfleche from the tepee's stores, replenishing the supplies he'd used up during his hunting trip.

"I'm afraid you are ten horses poorer, though."

If Summer hoped he would be curious enough to ask what she meant, she was disappointed. Lance went indifferently on with his task.

Trying to keep a rein on her temper, Summer moved across the tepee to stand before him. "I offered myself to Fights Bear. I told him that you sent me because you wanted to honor him as a brother. But then I suggested an alternative. I managed to convince him to accept another ten horses in exchange for *not* sleeping with me."

"Should I give a damn?" Lance asked finally.

Summer felt like stamping her foot in frustration. Why was he being so contrary? She had gone against his wishes yesterday, yes, but she'd had no choice. Couldn't he see that?

"You seemed to care a great deal yesterday. In fact, I distinctly remember you throwing a tantrum because I risked approaching your brother."

A muscle twitched warningly in his jaw, but he didn't abandon his smoldering silence.

Summer watched Lance in dismay. Did he truly not care? Or was he merely jealous because she'd been prepared to sleep with his brother?

If it was jealousy, then she was glad. He hadn't tried to hide his possessiveness yesterday—yet that could have been explained as mere male pride. A man held on to an object he possessed, and a wife belonged to a man much as an object. Or perhaps he wanted to protect his own consequence. Much of what she'd told his brother last evening was true. If his wife was shamed, then Lance would suffer. He had married her to improve his status in white society, or so he'd said.

Yet she wanted to mean more to him than simply an object, or a means for social advancement. She wanted . . . What did she want?

She wanted Lance to respect her, at least, Summer realized. She wanted him to see her as more than the shallow, vain creature she'd once been. She wanted to earn a measure of the same reverence Lance had used when he'd spoken of his mother.

This man was her husband; he had become part of her yesterday. She didn't want him to think badly of her because of what she'd been willing to do for her sister.

And whatever the reason for his anger, she was feminine enough to realize the wisdom of soothing his wounded pride.

Swallowing her own frustration, Summer knelt beside him and placed a gentle hand on his arm. His body went rigid at her touch, but he didn't pull away.

"Don't be mad at me, Lance," she pleaded softly. "I should think you would be pleased I persuaded your brother to change his mind."

Lance recognized her change in tactics immediately and wanted to curse. He had little resistance when Summer went into her "helpless belle" routine. "You trying to work your wiles on me again, princess?"

She gave him a smile that could have lit up a room with its warmth. "To be truthful, I'm trying to charm you out of your sulks."

"It isn't going to work," he declared gruffly.

"No?" Her green eyes skeptical, she eyed him thoughtfully.

"You've accused me often enough in the past of using feminine wiles to get my way, but in this case I think you should be grateful, for that's just what I did with your brother. I presented a reasonable argument that appealed to his masculine pride." Her smile turned wry. "Men are not so different in any culture that they're immune to flattery."

Lance grunted. "Yeah, and you've always been expert at playing us for fools."

"Not fools, precisely. Merely targets for persuasion . . . like wet clay susceptible to molding." She gave a rueful laugh. "I don't know why you are so sensitive about my methods. You've always been immune to my charms."

Despite his determination to withstand her assault, Lance found himself struggling to maintain his fury. Her wiles were working, damn her. But it was her success with his brother that had made his relief possible. For the first time since yesterday afternoon, he could breathe again; the jealousy that had clamped like a tight band around his chest had eased.

He hadn't been able to stick around camp and watch while Summer gave herself to his brother, so he'd stormed off in a jealous rage and gone hunting. But he'd been so clumsy and sick with fury that he'd only hit a single target. And he hadn't slept a full minute last night, either. Every time he closed his eyes, he pictured Summer lying beneath his brother's thrusting body and he'd wanted to kill.

Now all he wanted to do was haul her into his arms and shout for joy. And maybe take his brother's place.

The thought of having her again, hot and wild like yesterday, made Lance's mouth go dry. Not that he deserved the privilege. As rough as he'd been yesterday, he could have hurt Summer badly. He'd nearly raped her in his rage—and guilt had been eating him alive ever since. But apparently he hadn't hurt her too much. She was here now, smiling at him, teasing him out of his temper with her seductive charm. At least she didn't seem to hold his violence against him. His fierce relief at her forgiving attitude almost matched his gratitude over her deliverance from his brother.

At her playful smile, the corner of his mouth twitched; he couldn't help himself. "I'm not immune, dammit!"

She gave another ripple of laughter that was pure delight to hear. "Well, that is certainly reassuring! I had begun to think I'd lost my touch entirely."

Lance shook his head in exasperation, hardly believing he was sitting here joking about Summer's powers of manipulation, and loving every minute of it. "Your touch must have been working pretty well if you managed to get around my brother. He hates white women."

"It wasn't easy, let me tell you. And I'm not certain he's happy about it. If you are ever in a horse race with Fights Bear again, it wouldn't hurt to let him win. Bolster his male ego, you know."

Lance laughed in spite of himself, a gruff chuckle that was rusty with disuse. "Yeah, I know."

"I am sorry it cost you so many horses."

"I'm not. I would have paid ten times that amount to keep you away from him."

"Then you think I am worth a hundred horses?"

His eyes surveyed her with reluctant amusement. "Fishing for compliments again, princess?"

"Well, yes," she admitted shamelessly. "I don't believe it would hurt you to feed my feminine vanity once in a while. But I was also curious. Your grandmother suggested I was worthless because you didn't pay my brother any horses for me when we married."

His mouth curved in a wicked grin. "You're not worthless, at least."

Summer winced in mock pain and wrinkled her nose. Her saucy reply, however, was interrupted when Short Dress ducked beneath the flap of the tepee and entered, chattering urgently in Comanche and clutching Summer's arm.

"I'm sorry, I don't understand. What is she saying?" she asked Lance in alarm.

The grimness had returned to his expression. "The emissaries Fights Bear sent out have returned. They've found your sister."

Summer felt her heart lurch. "Amelia? She's *here?*"

"No. They weren't able to ransom her. Fights Bear wants you to attend a council to discuss the matter."

Chapter 12

The council meeting took place outdoors in the village arena, with all the warriors attending and the peace chief of the band presiding. He opened the proceedings by lighting a pipe made of engraved soapstone, filled with tobacco and crushed sumac leaves.

Allowed to watch, Summer sat behind Lance and war chief Fights Bear, her nerves ragged with fear. By the time a smoke offering had been made to the Great Spirit and the pipe had been passed around the entire group, she wanted to scream with anxiety. Only then did they begin deliberations regarding the sister of Sharp Lance's wife.

"Why are they taking so long?" Summer asked Short Dress, whose hand she was clutching fiercely.

The Mexican woman shook her head and told Summer to have patience. She had only been permitted to attend because she might be called on to speak, but she would be sent away if she interrupted the men—and she didn't want to shame her husband, did she?

"You must be brave," Short Dress admonished. "The People respect courage and have only contempt for those who show fear, especially whites."

Summer clenched her teeth and subsided, yet she considered it one of the most difficult tasks she'd ever performed in her life, to sit there for three interminable hours while Amelia's fate was deliberated.

The warriors spoke in turn, beginning with Fights Bear, who told of his promise to help his brother ransom Amelia. Then his emissary spoke—one of the young men who had gone in search of Amelia. He had eventually located her with a band of Antelope Eaters two days' ride northwest of here, but her owner would not return her for any price.

Lance, to Summer's immense gratitude, asked about Amelia's condition, and if she was fit to travel. The young man replied that she seemed like any white captive—cowed and groveling—which brought guffaws of laughter from the Comanche warriors around the circle, and made Summer taste blood, she bit her lip so hard. She could only console herself with the fact that her sister was still alive and that Lance would not abandon her.

He didn't. After more general discussion, Lance expressed his intention of rescuing Amelia himself, which sparked a good deal of argument from the Comanches. No one, not even a peace or war chief, had the power to prevent him from conducting a raid on his own, but they were not required to support him either, and he would likely need help if he meant to appropriate Amelia from her owner. Someone suggested that they try more diplomacy first, and Fights Bear waded in with a proposal that supported a diplomatic initiative.

The council meeting dragged on for what seemed an eternity, primarily because the decision had to be unanimous. Compounding the difficulty was that Amelia belonged to another Comanche band, and Comanches did not make war on each other.

Finally, though, the peace chief announced a plan of action that had heads nodding in agreement.

"What did he say?" Summer demanded of Short Dress in an anxious whisper.

"Fights Bear will lead a party to visit the camp of the Antelope Eaters, and will conduct the bargaining himself. When they see that a powerful war chief makes the request for ransom, they will likely reconsider their decision."

Closing her eyes, Summer almost gave a sob of relief. The battle for Amelia hadn't been lost yet. She could almost kiss Fights Bear for throwing his powerful weight behind his brother.

The council meeting continued for a while longer, but Summer scarcely cared what decisions were made. Short Dress paid more attention and explained that the People would hold a dance tonight to make medicine for the success of the venture. It was not a raid precisely, nor a hunting party, but Fights Bear needed medicine. Then the warriors would slip away at night, one by one, because it was bad medicine to begin a venture in daylight.

The discussion still wasn't finished when Short Dress gestured for Summer to leave. "Come, we have much work to do to prepare for our husbands' departure."

The preparations consisted of readying food and horses and weapons, and the women of the camp pitched in eagerly. Fights Bear's grandmother directed all his wives, and Summer as well, scolding them all to hurry and to take care in the packing.

Everyone knew of the venture, for as soon as the council meeting concluded, the camp crier rode through the village, heralding the decision. Shortly the volunteers who planned to accompany the party began bringing their shields to hang on a rack before Fights Bear's doorway to absorb the all-powerful medicine of the sun.

Summer was filling a parfleche with dried meat and mesquite bean meal when Lance returned to the tepee to take charge of his weapons.

To her surprise, he gave her a grin of reassurance. "Do you realize how big a victory you won today?"

"Victory?"

"When Fights Bear decided to take up your cause. I've never seen him take the side of a white before, especially a woman. But he swayed the council. Good thing, since I couldn't have managed it on my own."

"I'm glad he wasn't offended because I didn't want to sleep with him," Summer said in a small voice.

Lance's mouth twisted wryly. "Far from it. He admired your bravery for daring to approach him with your suggestion. And he was pleased to gain the extra horses. You impressed him, even if you are white."

She didn't feel impressive. All she felt was trepidation about the upcoming mission.

"Hey," Lance said softly, "why the long face?"

"Amelia . . ." Her voice broke on her sister's name and she pressed a hand to her mouth.

"She's alive, princess. Be grateful for that."

Her green eyes swam with tears. "I know. It's just that . . . I'm afraid. . . ."

"Fights Bear's negotiations should work. His name commands a lot of respect among the Comanches."

"What if it doesn't?"

Lance's gaze turned solemn. "I promise you, princess, I won't return without her."

Understanding his vow, Summer looked away. He would rescue Amelia or die trying. A hard knot of fear coiled in the pit of her stomach. Was she perhaps sending Lance to his death? Did she have a right to ask him to risk his life for her sister's sake?

"It . . . could be dangerous for you."

"Maybe. But I'm used to danger. For a half-breed, just being alive is dangerous. I quit worrying about it a long time ago. You'll be all right while I'm gone?" he asked, changing the subject. "My grandmother will look after you."

Summer tried to summon a smile at the thought of that witch-woman caring for her. "I'll be fine. I . . . I just hope you come back safely."

Lance grinned at her, making her realize he was relishing the challenge of the task ahead. "I intend to, princess. You're not going to get rid of me that easy."

The drums began shortly. A dance would be held that evening to send the warriors off on their mission, but they would leave in the dead of night, so as not to incur bad medicine.

Lance collected arms, lasso, food, clothing, and horses, then put on his paint and dressed for the occasion, wearing his finest trumpery in addition to his usual long breechclout and fringed leggings and moccasins. With the stripes of red paint streaking his cheekbones and forehead, and the necklace of bear claws adorning his bare chest, he looked so similar to the other Comanche warriors that Summer scarcely recognized him.

Just before sundown he went to join his brother. Fights Bear mounted his horse and paraded through the village to enlist volunteers to join his party. Lance rode double behind him—a distinction, Short Dress informed Summer, reserved for men who had performed the honorable act of carrying a wounded confederate out of battle danger, the Comanche way of giving public recognition for meritorious service.

The dance began after dark. The people of the village gathered around a fire to sing songs and make medicine. Only warriors leaving on the raid could dance, but they were aided by a woman partner. Wasp Lady bestowed the honor upon Lance since Summer knew nothing of the customs.

The spectators formed a circle outside the dancers and joined in the singing, some shaking gourd rattles, others shouting encouragement and chanting.

The primitive proceedings disquieted and fascinated Summer. The warriors performed when they wished to, unless they were ordered to dance by the whip wielder, who seemed to be in charge of the celebration. She watched with wide eyes as Lance joined the ritual, unable to take her eyes away from the lean, hard body leaping and gyrating to the pulsing beat of the drums. Once, after he had sat down, she caught him watching her in return, but his expression was totally unreadable.

Nearly an hour of the wild revelry had passed before one old warrior approached the drummer and announced that he wished to tell a story. When the crowd fell silent, he recited the details of a coup he had gained and took an oath that what he told was true. For Summer's benefit, Short Dress translated in a low voice:

"Sun, Father, you saw me do it. Earth, Mother, you saw me do it. Do not permit me to live until another season if I speak falsely."

At the conclusion, he received an enthusiastic ovation and the noise rose to a cacophony: barbarous whoops, beating drums, shaking rattles, stamping feet, and clapping hands.

Then the dancing resumed and the performance began all over again. Eventually, well into the evening, Fights Bear, who was to lead the party, rose and spoke to the crowd of the necessity of the mission and its aim, to ransom the sister of Sharp Lance's wife. Solemnly he appealed to his followers to display their accustomed courage while on the mission, that their people might be proud of them and not consider them cowards. When the drums and singing resumed, Fights Bear silently and without ceremony left the dance.

Short Dress told Summer he would say farewell to his family and ride to an appointed meeting place outside the camp to await the warriors who would accompany him. Lance would do the same.

"Go now," Short Dress said, giving Summer a push toward their lodge. "Return to your tepee and he will come to you. A warrior and a maiden must not be seen leaving together."

She made her way through the darkness to the tepee she shared with Lance. His horses stood picketed outside, ready for the journey. Ducking inside the lodge, Summer stirred the coals to give herself something to do.

She had her back to Lance when he entered, but she turned slowly to face him, her hands clasped to keep them from trembling. Sometime during the long hours of celebration, she had realized that she might never see him again. The expression on his features was unfathomable in the golden light from the fire, but she could see he was searching hers intently, as if trying to divine her thoughts.

"Lance," she whispered. She took a step toward him, then stopped in confusion, unsure how to say farewell.

He seemed to know. His eyes were hard and hungry as he closed the distance between them and took her in his arms. She could feel the heat of his body, smell the hot, musky maleness of his skin as he lowered his head.

His kiss was deep and hard, branding her with his ownership. He tasted of longing, harshly denied, of need, unwillingly leashed. Yet she welcomed his hunger as it forced out the fear inside her.

When he hauled her closer, bending her back over his arm, she responded willingly, surrendering to his fierceness, her fingers digging into the firm, vibrant muscle of his shoulders, clinging tightly, as if they might join their bodies with sheer pressure. His crushing embrace took her breath away, and yet she wanted it, wanted him. She knew Lance felt the same way, for the physical evidence was irrefutable. He was hard against her, the ridge of his manhood pushing against her softness even through their layers of clothing. He wanted her, and the knowledge set her heart thundering.

Yet with an abrupt movement, he broke off the fierce kiss and held her away.

Breathing hard, she searched his dark, painted face. "Please, Lance . . . take care."

Lance's harsh expression softened. Even if her concern was mainly for her sister, he could pretend it was for him. "I will."

And he would, Lance vowed silently. He would return. He wasn't about to get himself killed. Not now, when fate had given him a chance to fulfill his dreams, to win everything he had ever wanted, to fill the empty place in his soul.

Regretfully he forced himself to release Summer, to step back. He felt the savage ache of longing as he gazed at her upturned face, beautiful in the firelight, and her wet, passion-bruised lips still trembling from his kiss.

Lance cursed under his breath. If he didn't leave at once, he would never find the willpower. With one last look he gathered his shield and lance and left the tepee.

Summer didn't follow him outside. She couldn't watch him ride away, not when she might be sending him to his death.

Her throat tight with unshed tears, she buried her face in her hands, her thoughts on the man whose hard mouth she still tasted, whose rough hands she still felt on her body.

They rode fast, dismissing the hazards of the mountainous terrain, changing horses frequently to keep them fresh, sleeping little. For a full night and day Fights Bear's warriors traveled. The rugged mountains eventually eased into dry rolling hills interspersed with flat valleys, which allowed them to increase their speed. It was morning of the following day when they arrived at the camp of the Kwahadi—the Antelope Eaters.

Fights Bear was received by the band leaders with pleasure and respect, for he was well-known as a mighty warrior. The visitors feasted and shared a pipe and were honored at a council meeting afterward. Lance sat beside his brother and, when the time came, allowed Fights Bear to conduct the negotiations. Amelia's owner was present. His name was Tuhsinah, which meant Hanging from the Belt. Although a fairly young man, he had cruel features, even for a Comanche.

Fights Bear began by offering Tuhsinah thirty horses for Amelia, and then increased the number to fifty—an unheard-of price for a white captive—yet he had no more success than his emissary had. Tuhsinah refused to sell. The white captive could not have meant a great deal to him, but apparently he was intent on being stubborn. Still, no one could force him to give up a captive who had been earned honorably in a raid.

Fights Bear finally abandoned the attempt. His face showed no emotion, but Lance knew his brother was furious at being turned down. Grimly Lance forced back his own anger and bided his time. It would require more than wealth and prestige to win Amelia's freedom. What was needed was cunning and careful planning.

The Antelope Eaters gave the visitors lodging for the night and allowed their horses to graze with their own herds. Lance placed his gear and bedroll beneath a brush arbor built by the Comanches in summer to avoid the heat of the tepees, and had a brief word with his brother.

"I mean to walk through the village and have a look around," he said in a low voice.

"You will not attempt anything foolish, brother?"

Lance smiled grimly. "Not without discussing it with you first."

"It would not do to attract attention to yourself."

"*Haa*, I know."

Heeding Fights Bear's warning, Lance strolled casually through the camp, unobtrusively searching for any sign of Summer's sister.

He didn't expect to find her in very good shape, not after three weeks as a Comanche captive, especially the Antelope Eaters, who were known as the fiercest and most unsociable of all the Comanche bands. He knew the suffering she would have endured; his mother had experienced it firsthand.

Shortly after the raid, Amelia would have been tied to a horse or a mule and subjected to a grueling ride with no food or water, or if speed wasn't a necessity, bound and forced to run countless miles behind a rapidly moving horse or risk being dragged to her death.

Somewhere along the trail, if pursuit was not imminent, the spoils of the raid would have been divided by the party leader, depending on the coups each warrior had earned. Amelia would have been given to one warrior, most likely the one who had abducted her.

When they finally arrived at camp, however, her real horrors would begin. The first night she would have been raped repeatedly by the warriors of the band and beaten viciously by the women, who often were more cruel than the men. Comanche women took great pleasure in burning their white victims with sticks from the fire and lashing them till the skin bled, doling out the same treatment they themselves expected to receive at the hands of an enemy. If the captive quickly learned obedience, then the punishment would lessen—unless her new master and his wives were the vindictive sort who enjoyed torture for sport.

A half hour later he spotted Amelia lugging water from the stream. His heart clenched at the pitiful sight she made. She was half-clothed, her calico shirt so shredded that her breasts were partially visible, her bare legs and feet lacking the protection of either skirt or leggings or moccasins. It was a typical Comanche method, to humiliate their captives by keeping them nearly naked. Her body was filthy, her dark brown hair lank and greasy, as she struggled with the heavy buffalo paunch. She wasn't bound in any fashion, though. There was no need. This far from civilization, any attempt at escape would mean certain death.

Without appearing to notice her plight, Lance strode past her toward the stream, as if to drink. He didn't dare approach her or show undue concern, yet even from a distance he could see the vivid bruises on her face and fresh burns on her thighs. She paid him no heed as they passed. She looked neither right nor left, but stared out from eyes that were dull and lifeless.

He had witnessed worse, but even though he'd never liked Amelia, it hurt him to see her suffer like this. *Hold on,* he urged silently, clenching his fists in helpless rage. *It will be over soon, I swear.*

He paid close attention to which tepee she entered, then made friends with an old warrior who sat nearby and initiated a conversation about the band's plans for the fall buffalo hunt. Finally Lance returned to his temporary lodging to discuss the situation with his brother.

He found Fights Bear lounging beneath the brush arbor, combing his long black locks. "I cannot leave her here," Lance said in a low voice when he had settled himself beside the Comanche war chief.

For a long moment Fights Bear remained silent. "What are your plans, Kanap-Cheetu?"

"I intend to take her back from Tuhsinah."

His brother frowned. "It is not done to steal a possession from a member of the People."

"The circumstances in this case are not clear. The white captive is not only a Comanche possession, but a member of my family. It is my obligation to protect my family."

"Are you losing your manhood, brother? You do this for the white woman you call Summer."

"I do it for myself as well as my wife. I could not live with myself if I took the coward's way out."

"I do not like this decision you are making."

Lance waited, not replying.

"I cannot help you," said Fights Bear slowly. "I will not steal from a Comanche or take sides with the whites."

"I know, brother. I would not ask you. You have done much already, for which I thank you. You will not be involved. I want you to leave tomorrow. Take your warriors and ride away. I will accompany you for a short distance for appearance sake. Then I will return and wait for the opportunity to seize the captive woman."

"Do you know the risks you take with this course?"

Yes, he understood. If he was caught stealing a captive, he would likely be subjected to horrible torture before being allowed to die. But despite Fights Bear's objections and the possible consequences of failure, he had made up his mind. In addition to his own feelings of horror and pity for Amelia, he knew he could never face Summer if he abandoned her sister to such a terrible fate. Even if it meant turning his back on his own people, even if it meant burning his bridges with his Comanche family, he had to act.

"Yes, I know the risks," Lance answered solemnly. "Yet it is what I must do."

Chapter 13

~~~~⟆⟆⟆~~~~

Lightning slashed the black horizon, followed by a distant rumble of thunder. His nerves sharpened by the approaching storm and the scent of rain, Lance stealthily made his way on foot through the sleeping Comanche camp. His plan was to seize Amelia from her captor's tepee and be long gone by the time the village awoke in the morning.

The odds of success ran against him. It was the pride of a Comanche warrior to be able to slip into an enemy camp to steal horses and women without detection, but to be able to steal from the Comanches themselves would be a feat indeed.

A dog barked somewhere in the distance, but Lance kept moving. He felt his heartbeat accelerate to a heavy thudding as he neared the silhouette of Tuhsinah's lodge. In the darkness he could barely make out the entrance flap, which was tied securely to protect against wind and rain. Amelia would be just inside, as far away as possible from the rear of the tepee, the place of honor where the owner slept.

Ignoring the entrance, Lance crouched down and drew his knife from its scabbard. He had waited two days for this chance. His hope that Amelia's captor would leave with a hunting party hadn't materialized, and he had decided to act now. The brewing storm had seemed an omen, as well as a practical blessing. The gusting wind would hide the sound of his approach and, hopefully, his escape, while the drenching rain would cover his tracks within moments. The storm provided an added advantage as well. Comanches, who usually feared nothing and no one, were highly superstitious of lightning and thunder, and rarely rode out in such weather. Even if his nemesis was awakened by the storm, pursuit would likely be delayed.

If, that is, he managed to spirit Amelia away.

His senses alive as those of a hunting wolf, Lance ran his knife carefully beneath the rim of the tipi, slicing the strong buffalo sinews that pinned the hide covering to the ground. Carefully then, he began digging a stake from the earth to make room for him to slip beneath the edge.

A crescendo of thunder made him swear silently. He hoped the storm would hold off just long enough for him to free Amelia. He'd left his horses and his weapons a short distance from the camp, and if he could make it there with her, they might survive.

He unearthed a second stake and then eased himself down on his back. Slowly he raised the edge of the covering and peered beneath. A faint glow from the coal file in the center of the tepee lent enough light that he could make out the sleeping figures on the ground. Tuhsinah had only one wife, and he lay with her about twelve feet away on a bed of buffalo robes. A yard to Lance's right, Tuhsinah's captive slept naked, curled on her side.

Seeing her position, Lance swore again. Amelia's back was toward him, her head the farthest point away. He would have to cover much more distance before he could try to awaken her.

Slowly, inch by inch, he squeezed under the hide covering between two lodgepoles and eased inside. For several long moments he lay still, waiting for his heartbeat to slow and his breathing to quiet, keeping one eye on the sleeping Comanches. Then, with painstaking restraint, he began the arduous task of shimmying along the ground toward Amelia.

He could hear the wind pick up outside, and knew he didn't have much time before the storm hit. Finally, though, he reached her. Raising himself up on one elbow, Lance carefully reached a hand up to clamp it over her mouth. The danger was that Amelia might cry out when he roused her and awaken her captor at the same time.

Her body jumped reflexively when he touched her, but otherwise she showed no reaction.

"Don't be afraid," he breathed in her ear. "I'm here to help you."

He waited to make sure she understood his warning. Then slowly, with his hand still covering her mouth, he rolled Amelia over on her back. She didn't even look at him. He could see her eyes in the dim light. They held the lifeless expression of a woman beyond fear, beyond hope. He suspected she had been abused and violated enough that the threat of more no longer touched her.

"Don't make a sound, do you understand?" he barely whispered, trying to keep the pity and anger from his voice. "I'm going to take you away from here."

She simply stared at him.

Slowly Lance loosened his grip on her mouth and gestured with his head toward the opening he had made beneath the edge of the tepee. He bent to whisper again. "Summer sent me to rescue you."

A light of confusion flickered in her eyes, the first response he had seen from her. Grimly Lance took her hand and squeezed it reassuringly. He was more determined than ever to set her free of this vile captivity. It would likely cost Amelia her life if they were caught, but he wasn't going to give her the choice of remaining. He couldn't, wouldn't, leave her like this.

Pressing his mouth against her ear, he whispered instructions to her, wondering if she even understood one word in three. Then casting a glance at the sleeping Tuhsinah, Lance began the long retreat toward the opening.

At first he had to tug on Amelia's hand to keep her beside him, but she finally seemed to catch on to his intent, and he had to slow her down to prevent her from rushing ahead.

It seemed like an eternity before they reached their goal. The Comanches still hadn't awakened when Lance raised the flap for Amelia to slip through.

"Take it slow," he warned, his voice a breath of sound in her ear. When her head had vanished, he gave a push to her shoulder to aid her, then her bare hip, her knee, her ankle. Finally she disappeared altogether. With a last glance at the sleeping Comanches, Lance followed, easing himself beneath the slit.

The wind had picked up mightily while he'd been inside, and a gust buffeted him as he climbed to his feet. He could barely see Amelia. She was crawling on her hands and knees away from the tepee with blind determination, and her pitiful efforts at escape made Lance's throat tighten.

You'll get away, I promise you, he vowed silently.

She gave a cry of pain when he scooped her up in his arms, but he didn't dare take the time to see to her wounds. Another gust of wind brought a burst of rain slashing at his face, at her naked body, but Lance blessed the onslaught and the protection it offered. He tightened his grip on Amelia and ran through the camp.

She lay pliant and unprotesting in his arms, and made no effort even to shield herself from the downpour. With a silent oath, Lance pressed her face against his chest. Her spirit had been broken by the weeks of abuse, he knew, and she no longer had the strength to care what happened to her.

His two horses stood where he'd left them, pawing nervously at the ground. Setting Amelia gently on her feet, he unwrapped a blanket from his bedroll and drew it around her naked body, to cover her shivering skin. The wool became soaked in seconds, but at least it would provide a measure of modesty and protect her from the stinging chill of the rain.

She swayed as Lance looked down at her. With her scraggling hair plastered to her face, her pale face streaming with rain, she bore no resemblance to the strong, haughty woman who had always looked down her elegant nose at him. He couldn't afford the luxury of pity, though. Not yet at any rate.

A peal of thunder split the night as he tossed Amelia up on his horse and wrapped her fingers in the mane. She would have to ride with him, even if it proved a strain for the animal to carry them both, for she was too weak to sit a horse by herself.

Collecting his lance and buffalo hide shield, Lance gathered the reins of the other mount and vaulted up behind Amelia. Solicitously he tucked the slipping blanket more securely around her body and settled her back against his chest. Then with a nudge to his horse's flanks, he set out with his prize through the storm.

The journey to his brother's camp with Amelia was nothing like the one he'd made last week with her sister.

Amelia never said a single lucid word, not in protest or pain, and her eyes remained glassy and dazed, as if she were in a trance, beyond fear and exhaustion.

The storm broke by morning, and the sun came out to glisten on the pristine prairie hills. Lance stopped long enough to give Amelia his dry, fringed buckskin shirt to wear and some dried meat to eat. She stared at the buffalo jerky for a full minute before she tore into it ravenously with her teeth, wolfing it down as if she were starving—which no doubt she was.

She seemed to have no idea what to do with the herbal ointment his grandmother had made, so Lance smeared it on her cuts and burns for her, pretending not to notice her nakedness or the mewling sounds of pain she made when he touched the oozing wounds.

Her body resembled his wife's, with firm, high breasts like Summer's, the same slender limbs and curvaceous figure. But Amelia's smooth magnolia skin had been ravaged by fire and sun, by fists and lash, and her ribs showed starkly beneath the bruised flesh.

Seeing her like that, Lance felt the deep resentment he'd cherished for a lifetime against Amelia and white women like her shatter. He could find nothing in his heart but pity for the shell of the woman she'd once been.

He tried to spare her as much exertion as possible during the exhausting ride, but he didn't dare pause for long, even to rest the horses, for fear Tuhsinah was in pursuit. There was no time to sleep. Amelia dozed fitfully in his arms at times, but Lance recited ciphers learned at his mother's side to keep from nodding off while mounted. After having remained awake and alert for much of the past four days, he was straining his own physical resources to the limit. His burning eyes felt as if they'd been scratched with sand, and his aching muscles felt heavy and useless. Yet his own exhaustion didn't matter. There would be time enough to sleep once he had Amelia safe. It was possible, perhaps, that Tuhsinah would let her go without challenge, but far more likely that he was hot on their trail, seeking retribution.

It was the following afternoon when they neared his brother's camp. Fights Bear apparently had scouts out looking for them, for the war chief himself rode out to receive them.

At the sight of the approaching horde of Comanches, Amelia showed the first sign of fear Lance had witnessed in her, and cringed in his arms.

"It's okay," he murmured soothingly. "They mean you no harm."

He didn't know if his reassurance meant anything to her, but her tense body relaxed and her eyes glazed over again, as if she had retreated back into her trance.

Fights Bear drew his horse to a plunging halt and, with a glance at the white woman, nodded in satisfaction. "Welcome, brother," he said, his tone carrying approval. "It makes my heart glad to see you know how to take care of your family."

Lance grinned wearily. "No gladder than mine."

As one, the warriors turned their horses back to the camp and provided an impressive escort for Lance and his burden. Word of their arrival had doubtless spread through the camp, for as they neared the sea of tepees, Lance saw Summer running across the grass toward him. His own heart skipped a beat and settled into an accelerated rhythm, until he remembered it was her sister she was so concerned about. With unwitting bitterness he wondered if Summer would ever come running so eagerly to greet him.

He drew his horse to a halt as she reached him. Summer stopped abruptly, her hands clasped tightly before her. "Thank God, you're back," she breathed, before her gaze froze on her sister's face. Tears streamed down her own face as she whispered uncertainly, "Amelia?"

Her sister made no response, merely stared unseeingly at the ground.

"She doesn't know what's happening to her right now," Lance said quietly. "But she'll be okay with proper rest and care."

Summer made a choked sound of distress and covered her mouth with her hand to stifle a sob, but she didn't refute his judgment.

"I'd better keep her till we reach the lodge," Lance added. "She's too weak to walk."

Unwillingly Summer nodded in agreement. Turning, she walked close beside Lance's horse, her eyes never leaving her sister's face.

When they reached the tepee that belonged to Short Dress, Lance slid off his horse and reached up for Amelia, lowering her carefully to the ground.

"You're safe now," he said quietly. "Your sister's here to take care of you."

When still she made no response, Lance picked Amelia up in his arms and carried her into the tepee, where he laid her gently on the pile of buffalo hides Short Dress had prepared for the white invalid and covered her with a blanket. When he stepped back, Amelia closed her eyes in exhaustion.

Summer took Lance's place, kneeling beside her sister, wanting to touch her, to help her, but not knowing quite how. This limp, broken rag doll bore no resemblance to the strong, loving woman Amelia had once been.

Summer's throat ached with tears as she took Amelia's hand in hers. "You're safe now, Melly," she murmured, repeating Lance's words. "You don't have to be afraid of anything." Helplessly she smoothed back a lank lock of hair from Amelia's forehead, the same task her sister had performed for her countless times during her girlhood.

Amelia's eyelids fluttered opened. "Summer . . . ?" She said the name awkwardly, like a confused child.

"Yes, I'm here, Melly. I'm here."

Amelia blinked and stared. Then suddenly she shuddered, and her body started shaking uncontrollably.

"They hurt me," she complained in a bewildered, trembling voice.

Forcibly Summer bit back a sob and gathered her sister carefully in her arms. "I know, dearest. But it's over. No one will hurt you again. Now, go to sleep. You need to rest."

Obediently Amelia shut her eyes. "Don't leave me. Please . . . don't leave me."

"I won't, I promise. I'll be right here." *You don't have to be afraid, love. I'll protect you. I'll always be here for you.* How many countless times had she heard those poignant words from Amelia?

She rocked her sister slowly, while tears slipped heedlessly down her cheeks. Eventually, though, Amelia's trembling lessened and her quiet breathing told Summer that she had fallen asleep. Gently, with infinite care, she laid her precious burden down and tucked the blanket around Amelia's shoulders.

Lance, who had been watching quietly, felt the heavy burden of responsibility lift from his own shoulders. "I'll find another place to sleep for a while," he murmured. "And I'll take my nephews as well. She needs peace and quiet."

Summer raised eyes glistening with gratitude to him. "Lance . . . thank you for saving her. I know I can never repay you."

He tried to smile reassuringly, but managed only a faint twist of his mouth. It wasn't repayment he wanted from Summer. Nor indebtedness, either. What he wanted from her was far more profound, far more unattainable. What he wanted from her was love.

But he guessed he would have to make do with gratitude. That at least was more than he'd ever had from her before.

"Don't thank me yet," he replied more gruffly than he intended. "I may have managed only a brief reprieve. Her captor is no doubt riding after her right now—with the intention of reclaiming his property."

The sudden alarm that shadowed Summer's green eyes gave Lance a tiny measure of satisfaction. He ought to feel ashamed, finding hope in her fear. But the plain truth was, he couldn't regret having her dependent on him. As long as Summer needed him at least a little, there was still a change he might earn something more from her than gratitude.

Chapter 14

❦

The danger indeed was not over, Summer learned a scant hour later. Her sister might have been rescued, but the issue of Amelia's ownership was by no means resolved.

As she sat beside Amelia's sleeping form, praying for her swift recovery, Summer heard a commotion outside the tepee—men's voices raised in anger. Only when she recognized Lance's deep tones, though, did she reluctantly leave her sister's side to investigate.

The sight that greeted her made her stomach clench with dread. A war party of perhaps two dozen Comanches sat astride their sweating ponies, the glistening blades of their lances blazing as they caught the sun. The men looked barbaric and altogether frightening, with streaks of black paint adorning their cheekbones and broad foreheads.

Their leader seemed the most angry. He was arguing fiercely with Lance, who stood in front of Fights Bear's lodge. The conversation ended suddenly. Just as abruptly the warriors swung their horses around and rode away.

Summer glanced around her with growing fear, certain the altercation hadn't concluded so easily. A small crowd of Comanches had gathered to observe, but Short Dress was nowhere in sight, and Summer had no one to translate for her. When Lance turned on his heel to enter Fights Bear's tepee, she followed him inside.

She found him stripping off his leggings. "What is it, Lance? Who were those men?"

He barely gave her a glance. "Amelia's captor and friends. Tuhsinah wants to avenge his honor."

Summer stared. Lance had warned her what to expect, but she hadn't wanted to believe the nightmare still wasn't ended. "What . . . do you mean, avenge his honor?"

"It isn't over yet. I stole Amelia from him, and he's come to claim her."

Panic seized her at the thought of turning Amelia back over to that vicious brute. "You won't let him take her?"

Lance shook his head grimly. "He'll have to fight me first."

"Fight you?" Summer echoed, her wits suddenly sluggish as molasses.

"Yeah, with knives. Hand-to-hand combat. Normally we would use lances on horseback, but that would give me too great an edge. The lance is my namesake, and powerful medicine for me."

She heard him calmly explaining the rationale behind the choice of weapons and wanted to scream. What difference did it make when either could kill him?

She watched with growing alarm as Lance prepared to do battle, removing all adornment and excess clothing, till he stood before her clad only in his long breechclout and moccasins, armed with his knife.

"Lance, no!" Summer exclaimed, suddenly terrified. "You can't fight him. You could be hurt."

His black eyes sought hers. "Would you care?"

"Of course I would care! How can you say such a thing?"

He smiled faintly at her adamance. "You got a better plan, princess?"

"We could leave. . . . Right now, this minute. We could take Amelia with us—"

"And get how far? Tuhsinah would be after us in a heartbeat, and he wouldn't hesitate to kill us when he found us."

"But we might be able to elude him."

Lance shook his head. "Summer, luck was on my side when I rescued Amelia from him. I counted on the superstitious fear Comanches have of thunder and lighting to postpone pursuit, and it worked, but now I have to make a stand. I'd be branded as a coward if I ran. And to a Comanche, that's far worse than death."

"What . . . happens if you lose?"

He was silent for a long moment. "You have to decide whether Amelia would be better off dead than living as Tuhsinah's captive."

Summer pressed a trembling hand over her mouth, to keep from shrieking out her horror.

"If I lose," Lance continued, his tone soft but relentless, "she'll belong to Tuhsinah again. I know what my decision would be, but it's not my choice to make."

He bent to rummage in a parfleche, then crossed to Summer and handed her another knife, smaller but just as razor-sharp.

"You'll have to be strong enough to use this if you must." Solemnly, holding her tear-filled gaze, he raised a hand to touch the side of Summer's throat. "Draw the blade across the vein here . . . swift and hard. It'll be over in a minute."

The tears spilled over, flooding her pale cheeks and stabbing at Lance's heart. "There are things worse than death, Summer," he said softly. "I don't think you want Amelia to suffer like she has the last three weeks. Either way, you'll be safe. If I die, you'll be under Fights Bear's protection—"

"I don't *care* about being safe!" she cried in a broken voice.

"I care. I didn't go to all this trouble just to get you killed."

When she would have protested, he cast a glance over his shoulder at the entrance. "Summer, I have to go. I'll be back if I can."

He bent to kiss her lips gently, the caress bittersweet and poignant. In response, Summer raised her hands desperately to twine her fingers in Lance's black hair, drawing his mouth closer, pressing harder, this leave-taking even more urgent than the last because of the imminent danger he faced.

Finally, though, he pried her fingers loose and lifted his head. He stood looking at her for one long, final moment before he turned away.

Summer followed him to the entrance and watched as Lance strode swiftly toward the village arena. She cast an anguished glance at the tepee where Amelia slept. She didn't want to abandon her sister, and yet Lance had greater need of her. She had to be present at the battle, to give Lance moral support if nothing else. And to discover the outcome, whether he won or lost. *No, she wouldn't think of that.* He had to win. She wouldn't lose her sister again. She wouldn't let Lance die.

His enemy was already waiting for him when he stepped

into the clearing, along with a crowd of observers from both bands. An air of tension flowed from the women and children, but the warriors were gesturing and arguing, much the way Summer's brothers often had before a horse race when they'd wagered a sizable sum. Dear God, were the Comanches actually betting on the outcome of the fight? When men's lives were at stake?

Summer saw Lance's grandmother at the front of the crowd, her wizened face impassive, her piercing black eyes trained on the two combatants, and went to stand beside her. If Wasp Lady's medicine was good, then Summer wanted to make every possible use of it.

The two men faced off in the grassy clearing and began to circle one another, each clad in a long breechclout, each wielding a knife whose wicked blade flashed in the sun. Summer dug her nails into her palms as she focused her gaze on her husband. If the stakes hadn't been so terribly high, she might have admired Lance's sleek, economical movements, the animal grace of his half-naked body, the lean muscles playing under sun-dark skin. As it was, she could only pray.

She drew a sharp breath as the opening feint and parry began. The knife blades flashed in a blur as each man looked for a weakness in his opponent. Tuhsinah was the first to make a serious move, but Lance dodged the brutal thrust, the ivory gleam of his teeth catching the sunlight as he grinned fiercely.

His taunting amusement seemed to infuriate the other warrior. Without warning, Tuhsinah struck overhanded, yet at the last second Lance grabbed his wrist, his own teeth gritted now as he struggled to avoid the weapon wielded by his foe. The knife point was so near his eyes that the slip of a single inch would have blinded him.

Abruptly they disengaged and began anew, circle and feint, lunge and slash, each trying to gain an advantage.

Tuhsinah drew first blood. Lance didn't sidestep quickly enough and the blade grazed his bare abdomen, the long, thin cut instantly welling blood. He parried the next vicious thrust, and returned one of his own, managing to nick his opponent's upper arm close to the shoulder.

Both men were already breathing hard with exertion. It had become a battle of Tuhsinah's brute strength and sheer rage against Lance's superior cunning and dexterity. To Summer's mind, there didn't seem to be any honorable rules of engagement. Any tactic was counted legitimate, any target fair game. Lance leveled a well-aimed kick at the Comanche's groin, which for an instant doubled him over, but Tuhsinah promptly recovered and delivered a return blow to Lance's thigh that nearly felled him.

Incredibly, Lance laughed—and said something harsh that must have been an insult, for Tuhsinah gave a bellow and charged like an enraged bull, grasping Lance about the thighs in an assault that sent them both hurtling head over heels.

They wrestled there for a moment, struggling for dominance, but in another heartbeat, they broke apart and sprang to their feet.

The deadly dance went on for an interminable interval. Lance seemed hesitant at times, appearing to calculate the risk of his every move, while Tuhsinah seemed to grow in confidence, the cold steel blade an extension of his arm. His next offensive targeted Lance's heart, slicing diagonally across the chest from breast to waist—and barely missed.

Summer wanted to scream in fear, yet she didn't dare breathe. Instead she shoved her knuckle between her teeth and bit hard, terrified more of disturbing her husband's concentration.

His foe stabbed again, and this time the razor point pierced Lance's left side, tearing smooth flesh and muscle, even though a rib deflected the knife blade, which would have slid deep into his chest. Lance drew back, clutching his side, his wound dripping blood.

A cruel gleam of triumph shone in the Comanche's black eyes. Again he attacked, moving in for the kill.

Summer stood paralyzed with fear, unaware that she had grasped his grandmother's arm until Wasp Lady shook off her grip with a sound of contempt. She almost missed seeing when the two combatants tripped and fell. They sprawled in the grass, rolling together over and over.

A deafening hush settled over the watching crowd. The two opponents grappled on the ground, muscles straining, dark skin glistening with sweat. Lance gave a grunt of pain when, lying on his back, he caught an elbow across the throat, but incredibly, he managed to twist out from under his foe and somehow gain the upper position. Straddling Tuhsinah's broad chest with his knees, he pressed his blade against the Comanche's throat.

Summer's breath caught on a sob. Had Lance won?

She couldn't understand the hissed command that Tuhsinah uttered, but his expression clearly said, *Kill me, if you are not a coward!*

His eyes burned wildly into those of the man above him, daring him to act. Unwillingly Summer remembered the explanation Lance had given her only a short while ago, about how easy it was to slit a throat. All it would take was a single deep slice of the knife, and death would come swiftly.

Incredibly, though, Lance slowly drew his blade *away* from Tuhsinah's throat and climbed to his feet.

One hand to her trembling mouth, Summer gaped in disbelief. The fight was supposed to have been to the death, but Lance had chosen to spare Tuhsinah's life, an act of mercy for which the Comanche didn't seem at all grateful, not if his smoldering glare of hate was any indication.

Summer shook her head in stupefaction. She had no idea if Comanche custom allowed a man to walk away from mortal combat without establishing complete victory, but she had to believe it was foolish in the extreme for Lance to turn his back on his sworn enemy, leaving himself totally unprotected and open to attack.

Her fear came true. With speed that was blinding, Tuhsinah leapt to his feet and charged, his head bent low, his knife thrust at Lance's bare back.

Whether Lance heard her cry of warning or Tuhsinah's howl of rage first, Summer never knew, but Lance suddenly stepped sideways and spun on his heel at the same instant, holding his own knife out. The forward momentum carried Tuhsinah directly into the path of the blade, and his body came to a jerking halt. His fierce expression went stiff with shock, then slowly drained of all emotion.

Lance's own features still and cold, he let the Comanche's lifeless form slump to the ground. Bending, he drew his knife from Tuhsinah's chest and wiped the blade clean on the grass.

Summer shuddered, even as she released a sob of sheer relief. Lance had survived! Dear God, it was over. Except that he was wounded, perhaps terribly.

She would have run to him except for Wasp Lady's restraining grasp—a grip so tight, it was painful. She waited impatiently as the Antelope Eaters collected the body of their fallen leader and mounted their horses. To her bewilderment, they rode away without a backward glance. And yet she couldn't concern herself with them when Lance might be bleeding to death.

She shook off his grandmother's grasp and hastened to where Lance was standing, holding his wounded side. Yet she couldn't get near him. He was surrounded by warriors, obviously offering him congratulations. Summer was ready to scream with frustration by the time the crowd thinned out, but as a woman—a white woman, at that—she didn't dare interrupt them.

Fights Bear was the last to speak to him. He clasped his brothers shoulders, pride shining in his eyes, and said something in Comanche that she knew was praise. Lance replied at length, perhaps thanking Fights Bear for his part in the successful conclusion. Only when the war chief finally left him alone did Summer step forward.

"You're hurt!" she exclaimed in dismay, trying to see the wound beneath Lance's bloody fingers.

"It's nothing." His gaze found hers, searching her face, trying to determine if her concern was genuine.

Before he could decide, his grandmother came up behind Summer and launched into an angry tirade in Comanche, scolding the white woman's behavior, saying she would never make him an adequate wife.

Lance listened patiently for a moment, out of respect for Wasp Lady's age and venerable position, but cut her off sharply when she accused Summer of violating the ways of the People.

"If she errs, grandmother, it is out of ignorance, not willful disregard of our customs. She has told me that she yearns for your good opinion."

Somewhat mollified, the old woman grunted. "Your wounds should be tended."

Lance glanced at Summer, his face shuttered. "I thank you, Grandmother, but my wife will see to me."

Wasp Lady scowled, but nodded slowly and handed a small pouch to Summer. "It is good."

"What did she say?" Summer asked as soon as they were alone.

"She agreed that you should be the one to tend my wounds."

Summer looked at him blankly. "Yes . . . of course." His grandmother no doubt would be more skilled at caring for injuries, but she wanted to be the one to help him. She owed Lance that much. He had fought and won a terrible battle for her, risked death for her—more than once.

They turned together, heading back toward the tepee belonging to Fights Bear. Summer found herself gazing in the direction the Antelope warriors had disappeared with Tuhsinah's body. "Is it over finally? Have they gone for good?"

"Yes, it's over. They won't be back. The Comanches don't have extended blood feuds."

Relief shuddering through her, Summer let out her breath slowly, knowing the ending could have been very different.

They went to Fights Bear's tepee, since Amelia was sleeping in the one they normally used. Lance sat on a buffalo hide while Summer gathered the things he told her she would need.

She knelt before him to examine his injuries. The cut on his abdomen was not too deep, but a stream of blood still ran from the wound in his side, where his rib had deflected Tuhsinah's knife.

Summer winced and made a soft exclamation of sympathy. "It must pain you terribly."

Lance shook his head. "It's only a scratch. I've suffered far worse, believe me."

She did believe him, to her sorrow. Lance's life had been more difficult than anything she wanted to imagine.

She cleaned the cut on his abdomen and applied the salve his grandmother had given her. His stomach muscles contracted at her gentle touch, but Lance didn't make a sound. Instead, he watched Summer as she concentrated on her task. She had caught her lower lip between her teeth, clenching the pink flesh so hard, he knew it had to sting. He had the sudden powerful urge to replace her teeth with his own, to nip that soft lower lip till she opened eagerly for him. He wanted to cover her body with his own, wanted her kiss, wanted her . . .

Yet Summer didn't even seem aware of what she was doing to him.

When she had finished with the minor cut, she looked up and smiled faintly. "That wasn't so bad. But I'm afraid the next one is much worse. . . ."

He had to smile back. His beautiful wife was brave enough to risk death to rescue her sister, but she couldn't bear to see someone else in pain. "Go ahead."

She dribbled cool water over his side, washing the ugly wound carefully and then applying the ointment. "Lance, this really should be stitched."

"Just bandage it. It'll be okay."

Obediently she tore away the hem of her shirt and made a bandage to cover the wound. Then she wrapped a length of buffalo sinew around his rib cage to hold the pad in place.

When she leaned close, surrounding him with her soft scent, Lance closed his eyes and gritted his teeth.

"Am I hurting you?" Summer asked in concern.

Yes, she was hurting him. Her tender care was torture. The swelling in his groin had become a brutal ache. His racing blood felt hot and savage, his body throbbing with the heated lust warriors often experienced after battle.

Gently he grasped her hand and drew it down to his loincloth, letting her feel the thrusting ridge of his manhood. He heard the sharp breath she drew, saw her lips part in surprise, and his body tightened. He wanted to hear that same feminine gasp, see that same sensual reaction, when he entered her, when he filled her.

"Yes, you're hurting me," he said softly, hoarsely. "Ease my hurt, Summer."

She stared at him. Was he demanding payment for what he had done for her? This was hardly the place or time to be making love. This was Fights Bear's tepee. There were dozens of people close by, and any one of them could enter at any moment.

And yet, if Lance wanted her, she had no right to deny him. He was her husband. He had upheld his end of their bargain. He had saved her sister, at the risk of his own life; he had fought for her and won. The use of her body was a small price to pay in return. She owed him her submission, owed him whatever he wanted of her.

But truthfully, obedience wouldn't be her foremost reason for surrendering. She wanted to make love to this hard, courageous man. Her questioning gaze slid slowly downward. She could remember vividly their violent coupling, the play of those beautiful, sculpted muscles beneath her fingers, the feel of that strong, sinewy body thrusting against hers.

A sudden flush of heat burgeoned in the lower regions of her stomach and spread throughout her body, upward to her breasts, downward to pool between her thighs. Her fingers clenched reflexively, pressing against his erection, and she saw the smoldering leap of flame in his ebony eyes. His grasp on her hand was not tight; he would have allowed her to pull away. But she didn't. She would willingly accept Lance's lovemaking, out of gratitude, if nothing else, but also because she wanted it.

"Yes," she whispered, her breath a bare murmur of sound.

She saw his expression soften into a thousand readable and unreadable emotions. Releasing her wrist, he reached up to touch her face. His fingertips skirted the high plains of her cheekbones, gently tracing the softness of her skin, defining the curve of her lips.

"Lance . . . what . . . do you want me to do?"

Her mouth shaped the words against his fingers, but he quieted her immediately. "Hush, let me do everything."

He saw to her hair first. He unfastened the rawhide ties of her braids and then the braids themselves, smoothing out the waving tresses that gleamed like rich coffee. Summer had closed her eyes, as if willing to let him have his way uncontested.

She was surrendering to him for a purpose, Lance knew. She was letting him make love to her as payment for saving her sister—and he was claiming his victory. But he could pretend otherwise. He could make believe she truly cared for him, that she was his wife in more than name only, that she wanted him nearly as much as he wanted her.

Need shuddered through his body as he undid the buttons of Summer's shirt and pushed aside the lapels to bare her breasts. The sight of those swelling white mounds, their nipples so rosy and taut, made him stiff with wanting. He was already iron-hard and throbbing, and yet he clamped down on his impatience, instead forcing himself to savor the delay, the anticipation of burying himself in her sweet warmth. He reached out to stroke her bare nipple, tauntingly, with the slightest of pressures.

Summer gasped and shivered. Her eyes remained closed, and yet she was vitally aware of Lance's nearness, his barely clad body, the sudden eagerness in her own body. The feeling was so primitive, so ... needy. She suddenly wanted to be closer to Lance. She wanted to absorb his heat and sweat and man-smell and to have him absorb her.

She heard a soft rustle and then a long silence. When she forced herself to open her eyes, she saw that he had removed his breechclout and was lying nude, powerfully lithe, on the bed of buffalo robes.

Abruptly her attention was drawn to the masculine flesh jutting long and thick from a nest of wiry hair at his groin. Shyly Summer raised her gaze and found it colliding with Lance's. Those black fathomless eyes were unreadable, and yet smoldered with a flame so hot, she could almost feel it. Without quite knowing what she was doing, she reached out to touch him.

Her knuckles brushed the surging, hard, silky flesh, and Lance groaned as if in pain. He wouldn't let her continue, either, but shifted his hips to pull away.

"Summer ... come here," he commanded, his voice dipping into hoarseness.

He drew her down on top of him with total disregard for his bandaged ribs. Summer tried to spare him her weight, but he was having none of her hesitation. His arms came around her to hold her tightly against him.

"Lance, I'll hurt you. . . ."

"Hush, princess. . . ."

He started to kiss her, and her mouth went warm and yielding against his. Suddenly, though, he broke off the kiss. "You're right. . . . Not this way."

"What way, then . . .?"

He showed her what he wanted. Easing her onto her back, he loosened the bone button of her skirt and drew the bunched deerskin down over her hips, till she lay naked before him except for her open shirt.

His heart seemed to swell at the sight. She was so beautiful, his chest ached. So lovely, he thought he might die if he didn't have her right then. He wanted to thrust hard into her, to claim her, to whisper, "You're mine, you've always been mine," but he controlled the fierce urge. Instead, he moved over her, resting his weight gently between her parted thighs. This wouldn't be a brutal taking like the last time. This would be a new beginning, a new start for their marriage.

Lowering his head, he buried his face against her breasts. Summer couldn't prevent a soft whimper. His whiskered cheek was warm, abrasive, making her sensitive nipples prickle and tingle. He kissed her then, his lips nibbling at the tips of her breasts, his tongue tracing burning kisses around her fullness.

She tried to clutch at his hair, but he shook off her clinging hands and rose up on his knees. Looking along the naked length of her body, he slowly smoothed his hands up the insides of her bare, silken thighs, till his thumbs nestled in the dark curls that covered her femininity.

"Lance . . . no . . ." Summer protested breathlessly, and yet her entire body clenched with nervous anticipation.

His lips curved in a way that was not quite a smile, but rather an expression of triumph. They both knew he could compel her surrender; they both knew he would.

"Last time was way too rough," he whispered. "Let me make it better for you."

Those were the only words he spoke for a long while. Purposefully he lowered his mouth to her and began the sweet torment, brushing his lips over her, kissing her most intimate, dewy places, savoring, arousing her in the most primitive way possible. For a while it was all she could do to keep from moaning, and then the hot stroke of his tongue found her and she didn't care who heard her cries.

He caressed her till she thought she might scream with the pleasure of it. His fevered lips made her writhe, his tongue drove her to the point of madness. When her climax came suddenly, the surge was so explosive, she shook with the power of it.

She lay quivering beneath him, vaguely wondering if her shattered pieces would ever mend.

Then she felt him move over her. Her eyes were almost blind with passion, but when she looked up, she could see light and darkness moving in his.

He settled his body over hers carefully, poising above her. She saw the anticipation in him, and it went beyond uncomplicated lust. She saw determination and desire and fierce longing.

He entered her slowly, with as much care as if she were still his virgin bride—and yet she felt the hardness of his sweat-slick body contract against her, as if the effort at control was almost too much for him. When finally Lance lay sheathed tightly inside her, her breath shallowed to a sigh. The feeling was so sweet, so satisfying, that she never wanted it to end. Except that it did end, and she was glad. When he withdrew in a slow, lingering stroke, he rekindled the passion fire that had only been smoldering in her.

She whimpered his name pleadingly as he came into her again. His tenderness was too gentle for her, too tame, too unsatisfying. Wanting, needing, to draw him deeper, Summer moved her clutching fingers down his sinewed back, over his narrow hips, till she could hold him closer. She felt his masculine buttocks harden in her hands as he thrust faster, deeper, with more gratifying fierceness.

"Summer . . ." Her name was a hoarse plea as he fought for control.

"Please . . ." Her reply was just as rasping as she responded to his passion, urging him on.

With a low, primitive growl of need and dominance, his control broke. His hot, hungry mouth found hers as he drove into her relentlessly.

Sobbing, Summer clung to him. She didn't care about his violence, his crushing weight, the pounding force of his assault. She was too wrapped up in the drugging heat and man-smell of his body, too overwhelmed by the sensations exploding through her to feel anything but need.

They came at the same moment, their bodies contracting and shuddering together, his hoarse shout mingling with her gasping sobs.

Lance came to his senses first, to find himself collapsed heedlessly on Summer. Still panting for breath, his flesh wounds burning, he rolled partially onto his uninjured side, still joined to her, not letting her go. He buried his face in her hair, wondering if the urgency would ever lessen, if his need would ever diminish. He had practically raped her again, when what he really wanted was to safeguard and pleasure and worship her with his body.

Contritely he pressed his lips against the smooth, damp skin of her temple, and cursed himself silently. He didn't have much practice caring for someone, but he knew a lot about control, about keeping his feelings under tight rein. He sure as hell didn't know himself when he was near Summer, though. He acted like a damned rutting stallion around her. She was his wife, for Crisssakes, not some whore he could take roughly any time he felt like it. He ought to treat her more gently, but every time he got close to her, he exploded like a sex-starved kid.

He had to get control of himself. Summer was his now. He had won her fairly. There was always the chance that she would renege on their bargain, but he hoped to God he didn't have to fear such betrayal from her. He had upheld his end, and she would do the same with hers. Summer might not love him, but she would honor her word.

And maybe, in time, she might come to feel something for him, some fraction of the gut-deep, heartsick longing that had tied him up in knots ever since he was a kid.

"Kamakuna." He spoke softly in Comanche, but he didn't realize what he'd said until he felt her stir in his arms.

"What did you say?" Summer murmured, her voice sleepy, replete.

Lance remained silent, regretting that he had let the endearment slip out.

"You said something . . . just now . . . I didn't understand."

"Nothing, it wasn't important."

He wasn't willing to answer with the truth, that he had called her his love. He couldn't admit his weakness to Summer. A Comanche warrior was supposed to be strong, invincible, unafraid. He wouldn't divulge his terror of earning her scorn.

His private thoughts would stay secret—unless he voiced them in Comanche. In Indian language he could reveal all the things he felt for Summer. He could tell her how beautiful she was, how much he wanted her, needed her. How glad he was to have her for his wife. He could bare his love-sick soul . . .

As long as she couldn't understand what he was saying.

Chapter 15

The immediate danger was over, but the struggle to save her sister was more difficult than Summer ever expected. Amelia lay in a stupor of exhaustion, unable or unwilling to come out of her trance. Summer began to fear for her sanity. More than anything she wanted to take Amelia home to Sky Valley, where she could be safe, but at Lance's insistence, they remained at the Comanche camp for nearly a week to give Amelia time to recover for the long journey ahead.

Summer never left her bedside, hour after hour speaking softly to her, stroking her hair, holding her if she wanted to be held, washing and anointing her wounds, but it was two full days before the ill woman even recognized Summer as her sister. And then she lay listlessly beneath a blanket, docile and quiet except for frequent trembling fits of terror. She started at the slightest sound, and awoke with nightmares.

All the Comanches terrified her, even gentle, round-faced Short Dress, whose native language, Spanish, Amelia understood fairly well. She couldn't stand the sight of any male at all, even her brother-in-law, who was half-white and had rescued her from a life of degradation and terror. When Lance entered the tepee merely to speak to Summer, Amelia cringed and started whimpering, burying her face against her sister's shoulder.

Summer held her soothingly while she wept silently inside. "Melly, it's only Lance. You've known him most of your life. He would never hurt you."

"He . . . he's one of *them*."

Summer glanced at him apologetically. Lance's face had gone stiff with the expressionless mask she was coming to recognize as his defensive shield. "No, Melly. He's the man who rescued you."

Shaking now, Amelia shook her head violently. "He touched me, he put his filthy hands on me."

"Only to dress your wounds. You needed his help, Melly."

Amelia started crying then, piteously, with short, wrenching sobs. Summer looked helplessly at Lance, who turned on his heel without a word and left the lodge. She wanted to go after him, to ask his forgiveness, but just then her sister needed her more.

After that, Amelia cried often. She wouldn't speak of her ordeal yet, but frequently she would let loose a flood of what Summer hoped would be healing tears.

Short Dress was not as sympathetic to the white woman's fear. Once she shook her head contemptuously and muttered, "She should show more courage."

Her head snapping up, Summer almost retorted that Short Dress would not be so heartless if she'd endured what Amelia had—until she remembered that the Mexican woman *had* doubtless suffered such horrors when she was taken captive. She bit back the remark and settled for a milder defense, saying only that tears would help Amelia recover.

"You should take her home," Short Dress observed pragmatically. "She should be among her own people. And for your husband's sake as well, it is good if you leave this camp."

Summer eyed her in puzzlement. "What do you mean?"

"The People understand why Sharp Lance killed Hanging from the Belt, but they do not like it. It is not good that he killed one of us over a white captive. It would be better if he left."

Summer's frown turned from one of puzzlement to dismay. She had thought the Comanches pleased when he won the fight, but she could see why she might have been mistaken. They were proud of Lance's skills and courage, but resented his motivation for using them, for siding with the whites against them. Had Lance burned his bridges with his own people to help her? If so, then she owed him an even greater debt of gratitude.

The Mexican woman started to leave, but Summer remembered a remark Lance had made the other day and stopped her for a moment. "Short Dress? Lance said something in Comanche to me recently. It sounded like . . . ka-ma-kune. Do you know what it means?"

The Mexican woman suddenly beamed. *"Kamakuna.* It means 'beloved' in our language. It is a term of honor and affection."

She left Summer with a profusion of distressing thoughts to dwell over.

Beloved. Had Lance truly called her that? Did he really love her? More complex a question, what did she feel for him in return? Could she love a man she didn't understand, a man she had once been half-afraid of?

She didn't fear him anymore, that much was certain. And much of her anger toward him had softened. Her resentment at being forced into marriage had vanished the instant he had brought her dazed, pale sister into the camp. Her gratitude toward him was overwhelming, blocking out any of the more negative feelings she had once cherished toward him.

And she was attracted physically to him; that was also entirely too true. His touch made her tremble, his kisses made her burn. She went wild in his arms when he made love to her, acting like an unprincipled wanton, blazing with a passion she had never dreamed herself capable of.

But love? She didn't think so. And it would take a good deal of objective private reflection to sort through the tangled bittersweet, complicated emotions she really felt for Lance.

One thing more was certain, however. She was ashamed of her sister's reaction toward him.

The next morning when Lance entered the tepee, Amelia screamed and started crying. "Go away, get away from me! Leave me be! Summer, make him leave!"

Lance froze and, with a grim glance at Summer, backed abruptly out the entrance.

Mortified that he should be treated so badly after all that he had done for them, Summer jumped up and followed him outside. She caught up to him as he was preparing to mount his horse.

"Lance, I'm sorry! Amelia doesn't know what she's saying."

A muscle worked in his jaw as he stared into the distance. "I know. But I could take it better if she hadn't always treated me like I've no right to come near her. I wasn't going to attack her."

"Of course not. But she's terrified of men, Lance. Especially Comanche men. Please, don't be angry at her. She was never like this before. You know what she's been through. She doesn't realize yet what you did for her. She'll come around." When he remained silent, Summer placed an imploring hand on his arm. "I don't want your feelings to be hurt."

"A half-breed isn't supposed to have feelings," he said harshly, the pent-up anger of years goading him.

"Lance, please . . ."

The pleading look in her emerald eyes whittled the edge off his anger, and his reply wasn't as gruff as he'd intended. "I came to tell you I'm going hunting with Fights Bear, and I may be away all night. It may be the last time I have with him for a while."

"Yes, well . . ." She smiled at him tentatively. "I hope you enjoy your time with your brother."

His gaze arrested at her sweet expression, and for a minute Lance forgot what he'd intended to say. Her damned sister could scream at him all she liked as long as Summer looked at him that way, offering that soft, tender smile that made him feel as if he were the only man in the world. It was a female ploy she had developed with practice, of course, but still he couldn't help falling for it.

"Will you be okay here?" he asked finally.

"Yes, certainly. Don't worry about me."

When Summer smiled again to reassure him, he felt his heart trip inside like a newborn, stumbling colt. Without volition, he reached up and stroked the pale curve of her cheekbone. The circles still remained beneath her eyes, dusky smudges of weariness and strain, but her beautiful face looked less haunted than it had anytime during the past month.

He didn't kiss her. If he had, he knew he wouldn't be able to stop. Instead Lance flashed her a faint smile in return and swung up on his horse.

He could feel her watching him as he rode away, and his pulse rate quickened to a gallop. His heart felt absurdly light, soaring like a hawk over the mountains, even though his loins burned with the sweet ache of need. She had cared about his feelings. Summer had defended her sister's actions, not only for Amelia's sake, but because she hadn't wanted *him* to feel hurt.

Lance closed his eyes, remembering that tender, pleading smile Summer had given him. She was concerned for him, he would swear it. Was it possible she felt something more for him than gratitude?

He knew better than to let himself get his hopes up, but he couldn't help it. Maybe Summer might really be coming to care for him a little bit, after all.

Two days later they left for Texas, escorted by several of the band's warriors. Fights Bear sent them as protection, and to collect the thirty horses Lance still owed his brother— twenty for assisting in Amelia's rescue, ten for not sleeping with Summer. The Comanches would accompany them to the edge of Indian Territory, as far as the Red River, and then wait at Deek's Trading Post for Lance to return with the horses.

Summer said farewell to Lance's family with a genuine sense of regret. She had grown especially fond of Short Dress, who had been a tower of strength during the recent weeks of fear and uncertainty. And she would always feel a profound gratitude toward Fights Bear for the tremendous effort he'd made to save her sister.

The journey south was far more difficult than the one north had been, because of Amelia. They rode in easy stages with frequent rests, and even then she collapsed in exhaustion at the end of each day. She couldn't stand the company, either. The Comanches mainly kept out of sight, but she started crying whenever one of them came near to speak to Lance.

She would only ride double with her sister. After her experience, she couldn't bear being touched by a man. The first day when Lance tried to help Amelia down from her horse, she began screaming, "Don't touch me! Don't touch me!"

"Melly!" Summer exclaimed, trying awkwardly to turn in the saddle and put her arms around her quaking sister. "He was only trying to help."

"I don't want his help! I can't stand him—"

"Melly, listen to me," Summer replied more harshly than

she should have, given her sister's shattered nerves. "Lance risked his life for you. He killed a man for you."

Amelia burst into tears.

Immediately contrite, Summer gave in. "I'm sorry, Melly," she murmured soothingly, gently rubbing her back. "Don't cry, please."

"I can't stand him to touch me."

"He won't touch you, I promise. Now, come, you have to lie down. You need to rest."

She helped Amelia slide down from the horse, and with an impotent glance at Lance, dismounted herself. He didn't offer to assist her. Instead he stood watching her with hooded eyes. When she handed him the reins, he took the horses down to the creek to water them.

Summer put an arm around Amelia and led her out of the October sun, beneath the shade of a cottonwood tree. When she had settled her sister on a blanket and given her some water, though, Summer followed Lance.

He was immediately aware of her, she could tell by the subtle tightening of his body. He still wore his Indian garb, and his bare back looked darkly bronzed in the morning sunlight, except for the strip of sinew holding the bandage in place against his wounded ribs.

"I'm sorry about Amelia, Lance. You don't deserve to be treated that way."

He shrugged without looking at her. "Don't worry about it."

Doubtless he was used to it, Summer thought sorrowfully. This was how he'd been treated all his life, with rejection and scorn and fear. "It isn't fair," she murmured rather helplessly.

His short laugh was more of a grunt. "Life isn't, most of the time."

"I just want you to know . . . I appreciate everything you've done for me . . . your patience, especially."

He wondered if she meant his patience about their marital relations. As hard as it had been, he'd left her alone the past week. Even though Summer was his wife, he hadn't forced her to share his bed or accept his lovemaking, allowing her instead to spend all her time caring for her injured sister. "Sure," he said finally.

He thought she would go, but her next remark surprised

him. "When you're finished here, I would like to look at your wounds."

Lance turned his head to eye her skeptically over his shoulder. "Why?"

"To make sure they're healing properly."

"They are."

"I want to see for myself."

His eyes narrowed uncertainly. "I can dress them myself."

"I know. But you've done so much for me, I want to do something for you for a change."

"I don't want you fussing over me," he replied with typical male offended dignity.

She gave him a feminine smile that was almost coquettish—the familiar Summer that he'd thought vanished after the hell she'd been through the past month. "Sometimes even the strongest man needs fussing over. And I want to take care of you."

With that wifely statement, Summer turned and walked away, leaving Lance to stare after her.

He staked out the horses, letting them graze on the tall buffalo grass, while his gaze strayed to where Summer sat beside her sister. She had her back to the tree trunk, her knees drawn up, her face raised to the sky. Her eyes were closed, though, her expression relaxed and peaceful.

A quiet ache of longing filled him at the sight, so powerful, it made his chest hurt. Did she really want to take care of him? To shield him from the hurt her sister had dealt him? Only his ma had ever cared enough about him to protect him like that. Summer seemed willing to try, even if it was only to repay a debt of gratitude. But . . . would her generosity last once they got back to civilization?

Lance stroked the roan's neck absently, wishing it were Summer's neck he was caressing. She'd been wrong when she'd thanked him for his patience. He was impatient as hell—with the lack of privacy, with being unable to touch her, to hold her, to bury himself in her sweet warmth.

His sexual satisfaction could wait, though. He might be denied Summer's presence in his bed, but it was a pain worth enduring. She had obligations elsewhere right now. He wouldn't hold her to her marriage vows for a while longer.

He wouldn't push her to choose between himself and her sister.

Her sister's reaction bothered him, of course, but if he tried, he could forgive Amelia's invectives. She wasn't in her right mind after what the Comanches had done to her.

What worried him was whether she would ever get over her ordeal. Amelia always had been half-afraid of him, even before her captivity, yet he didn't know how Summer would take it if her sister held on to such stark terror and hatred of him.

For now, though, he could put up with Amelia's ranting. He was a grown man. After all these years he was hardened to the slights white women offered him, no matter how much they cut. It was enough that Summer sympathized with him, enough that she had taken his side against her sister.

As long as he was on his side, he could bear anything life threw at him.

Amelia's manner toward Lance only grew more hateful as they traveled farther south. She seemed to blame him for everything the Comanches had done to her. She wouldn't acknowledge his name, referring to him as *he* or *him,* her frightened tone suggesting he was some sort of monster. She screamed at Lance every time he so much as looked at her, and pleaded with Summer to make him go away.

Knowing the horror Amelia had endured, both Lance and Summer tried to make allowances, but it was hard.

On the fourth day, they reached Deek's Trading Post on the Red River. Amelia wouldn't look at the burly trader when he came out to greet them, or even acknowledge his existence. Deek was the first white man to see her after her degradation, and apparently she couldn't face him. Finally, though, after much pleading, she allowed Summer to persuade her to enter the trading post, where she could bathe and change into white women's clothing and sleep in a real bed.

She shrieked when she saw his Comanche wife, Topusana, but Summer, appalled by her rudeness, finally lost patience and gave her shoulders a hard shake. Amelia collapsed in a fit of sobbing and allowed herself to be supported into the spare guest room, where she fell immediately into an exhausted sleep.

Supper was a sober affair, even though Deek tried to liven it up with his tall tales and jokes about their trials in Indian Territory. When Lance sparingly related the events of the past month, Deek seemed to know just when the danger had been understated and prodded Lance to confess more of the details about the rescue and the knife fight afterward.

At the conclusion, Deek raised his glass of whiskey in a salute to Lance. "The Comanche'll be making legends about you, ya know. What you did was nigh impossible. I'm damned proud of you, boy."

Lance smiled somewhat cynically, but watching him, Summer thought nothing Deek could have said would have pleased her husband more. And indeed it pleased her, too, hearing someone she respected give Lance the praise he deserved.

Deek's friendship was obviously good for him. She had never seen Lance so relaxed, so at ease, than at this moment. All his defenses seemed to be down, all his smoldering hostility banked. When occasionally he met her eyes across the table, the affectionate intimacy in his look included her.

The feeling warmed her so much that she hated to leave just now, yet she needed to check on her sister and be there if Amelia was awakened by nightmares. After a polite interval, Summer bid the two men good night and retired to the spare bedchamber, leaving them to discuss Lance's plans to deliver Fights Bear's horses.

When she emerged the following morning, it was to find Lance dressed in the garb of a Texas mustanger—buckskin trousers and boots, blue chambray shirt and leather vest, red bandanna and tall hat. His appearance seemed strange after the past month of thinking of him as a Comanche warrior, but he looked almost as dangerous with his side guns strapped to his hips.

Amelia pretended not to notice the transformation in him. Both she and Summer, however, looked vastly different. Gone were the calico shirts and deerskin skirts of the Indian woman. Instead they were gowned as genteel ladies, which included the usual layers of underwear—corset and camisole, drawers and crinolined petticoats—beneath their voluminous skirts.

Amelia seemed less pitiful, less broken, in her new attire. She had stopped weeping and held her shoulders straighter, and her freshly washed hair had been combed into a simple coiffure beneath a wide-brimmed bonnet.

Summer, in her coffee-striped traveling costume, put her older sister in the shade, though. Her complexion was no longer pure ivory, but tanned by the sun—a crime for a well-bred lady—yet Lance thought she looked more beautiful with that golden-honey hue.

They set out early, without their Comanche escort. Amelia wanted to return immediately to the Truesdale ranch, to her late husband's family, and wouldn't listen at all to Summer's gentle warning that they might not be welcome.

The return journey to Fort Belknap took two full days instead of one, but other than Amelia's verbal attacks on Lance, it was fortunately uneventful. The endless miles of prairie grassland interspersed with patches of scrub timber assumed a monotony that was heartily welcome after the difficulties of the past month.

The tension rose in all of them, however, as they approached the Truesdale ranch, perhaps Lance most of all. It scared hell out of him to think Summer might lose her past easiness with him once she was back in civilization, and worse, that she would have to face much of the scorn and rejection his mother had faced.

Summer was more worried for Amelia than herself. The Truesdale boy had said her in-laws would take her back, but Summer wasn't at all certain of their reception.

They arrived at the ranch in late afternoon, weary and saddle-sore. As before, Billy came out to greet them, brandishing a shotgun, but when he saw Amelia, his mouth dropped open.

"Aunt Amelia! Cripes . . . Ma, come out here! They found Aunt Amelia!"

He hurried forward, and Amelia, much to Summer's surprise, allowed the boy to help her dismount. She fell into his sturdy arms sobbing, while Martha Truesdale came out onto the porch, carrying her own shotgun. She didn't look as crazed as she had the last time, but her face twisted with hatred when she laid eyes on Lance. "I thought I told you, you stinkin' Injun, you aren't welcomed here. Get off my land."

"Ma, he found Amelia!" Billy protested, while Lance sat unmoving in the saddle.

"I don't care. I want him to get. And her, too." She punctuated her command by waving the shotgun at Summer.

Amelia spoke up then, showing more backbone than she had since her rescue. "Summer's staying, Martha. I don't know where *he* is going, but my sister is staying with me."

Mrs. Truesdale turned her malevolent gaze on Summer. After a brief inspection that made Summer want to shudder, she turned away. "Suit yourself—as long as he goes," she muttered as she stalked back into the house.

"*He* can't stay here," Amelia echoed triumphantly. "He has to go."

Ashamed of her sister's appalling injustice, Summer pressed her lips together as she strove for patience. "Lance didn't intend to spend the night, Melly. I explained all that to you. We owe the Comanche quite a few horses for helping rescue you, and Lance has to deliver them."

"You owe that red filth nothing!"

"Lance gave his word—"

"What does that matter?" Amelia replied with contempt. "He's one of *them*. His word isn't worth spit."

"Summer, leave it," Lance interrupted quietly. "I need to be on my way."

She clenched her teeth in frustration, but gave up, seeing how pointless it was to argue with her sister just now. It would take time for Amelia to come to her senses and stop seeing Lance as her enemy, as a cruel brute who wished her harm.

With that issue apparently settled, Billy sent a cautious glance at Lance and helped Amelia into the house, leaving Summer alone with him.

"I'm sorry, Lance," she said at once, in a weary voice.

He gave her a brief shrug, masking his own bitterness. He was grateful to her for championing him, but it galled him that she should have to do it—and terrified him that someday she might stop.

Dismounting, he walked around his horse to Summer's and reached up for her. Without hesitation she placed her hands on his shoulders and let him assist her down.

For a moment, however, they stood facing each other, feeling the awkwardness of the moment, both aware of the people in the house behind them.

"I'll only be two days," Lance said finally. "I'll ride into Belknap now and pick up the herd at the stage station. Burkett should have them waiting for me. I can get a few miles before dark if I push it."

Summer's expression softened with concern as she searched his face. "Don't push too hard. You must be almost as tired as we are, after all the hard riding you've done."

Surprisingly, his mouth twisted wryly. "Those are insulting words to a Comanche warrior, princess. I'm used to long hours on horseback, remember?"

"Lance, I didn't mean to imply—"

He raised a finger to her lips, shushing her apology. "It's okay, I know what you meant."

And he thought he did. Summer still felt a strong sense of gratitude toward him, and accordingly felt obliged to worry about his welfare. Even knowing her reason, though, it couldn't stop his heart from warming at her display of concern.

He wanted to express his own feelings in return. He wanted to take her in his arms, to hold her close, to remove that fancy bonnet and bury his face in her hair. But he forced himself to be content with surveying Summer's face, memorizing it all once again—the emerald eyes with their sweeping dark lashes, the delicate cheekbones, the soft pink lips. . . .

"You do have enough money to purchase the horses?" she asked pragmatically, interrupting his fanciful musings.

He smiled briefly. "Yeah, plenty. We got off cheap, considering."

His eyes flickered, as if he'd just remembered something. Reaching into his vest pocket, he pulled out a wad of Union bills and handed it to her. "This is what your brother gave me to ransom Amelia. I won't be needing it."

Summer eyed the money hesitantly. "Reed wanted you to have it."

All expression left his face. "I don't care what he wanted. Our bargain was between you and me."

In the eternity before she took it, Lance felt his heart contract with a feeling almost like panic. Summer had her sister back now. She didn't need him at all, except maybe to escort her safely back home. But he wouldn't let her off the hook. He wouldn't take money in exchange for finding her sister. Summer was still his wife. She still owed him.

When she took the bills, he felt his taut muscles relax the slightest degree. "You're going to be here when I get back?" he asked, trying not to let his worry carry in his tone.

She looked at him blankly. "Of course."

At her answer, his heart stopped its slow slamming and eased into a more normal rhythm. "If there's trouble, take your sister to the stage station in Belknap. Jeb Burkett will look after you. I'm leaving you one of my rifles." He turned to heft one of the Henrys from its saddle scabbard and handed it to her.

"Lance . . . please take care."

He looked at her, wondering if she really meant it. Would she be sorry if he didn't come back? Or would she be relieved to be spared a future with him, a lifetime of living on the outskirts of society as the wife of a half-breed? If he didn't return, she could pretend this was all a bad dream.

Shifting his gaze away, he forced his doubts to crawl back under the rock where they belonged. Summer was his wife. She would keep her word.

"Is Amelia going back to Round Rock with us?" Lance asked gruffly.

"I don't know. She wouldn't tell me what she wants to do." Summer hesitated. "I may have to stay here with her for a while, to make sure she's all right."

"She has a few days to decide."

He didn't kiss her. Instead he gathered the reins of the other horses, including Summer's, and swung up on his own. "I'll take your mounts back to Burkett. They don't need to be eating their heads off in the Truesdale barn while I'm gone."

Or provide you a way home, his suspicious thoughts insisted on adding. Without horses, Summer would have to wait for his return.

He felt her gaze on him as he led the horses away, and was struck by how similar this leave-taking was to those between them in the past—him riding away, Summer watching him go.

But this would be the last, Lance swore silently to himself.

If he had anything to say to it, this would be the last time Summer was separated from him.

He glanced back over his shoulder, his heart leaping at the sight he found. Summer was still standing where he'd left her in the late afternoon sun, her hand raised in farewell. If he didn't know better, he would think she looked almost like a true wife waving good-bye to her husband.

Or maybe he just wanted so bad to believe it that his imagination was playing tricks on him again.

When Lance was finally out of sight, Summer smoothed her skirts and forced herself to enter the Truesdale house, although she dreaded it.

Finding the three of them in the kitchen, she paused in the doorway. Mrs. Truesdale bustled around the large room, straightening things that didn't need straightening, while her son, Billy, sat at the table, his expression stony. Amelia cradled a mug of coffee in her shaking hands, but she wasn't drinking. Instead she simply sat there, tears streaming down her face, as if, having come this far, she had reached the end of her strength.

When Summer heard mention of Mary, she realized they were discussing the daughter who had been killed in the same raid in which Amelia had been taken captive.

"I sent Nan back east to her grandma's," Mrs. Truesdale was saying bitterly. "Where it's safe. I couldn't bear to lose her the way I lost Mary. We're leaving, too. Soon as I find a buyer for this place."

Summer doubted that anyone else would be foolish enough to risk the danger of settling here, although she didn't say so. With all the raids and Indian depredations, the Texas frontier had been steadily retreating since early in the war, when most of the available fighting men and resources had been expended on fighting the Union rather than protecting the farmers and ranchers.

"Do you know what happened to Tommy?" Billy interjected grimly. "His folks will want to know. The last anyone saw, he was carried off with you."

"Tommy ..." Amelia whispered to herself, her face contorted as if remembering some unseen horror. "They killed him. I couldn't do anything to help him. . . . They wanted him to be quiet, but he wouldn't stop crying, so one of them . . . They . . . they killed him with a spear and left him there on the side of the trail. . . . They just left him there. . . ."

She was sobbing openly now, mourning the murdered child who had been taken captive with her. It was the first time Summer had heard her sister speak about the raid, but she didn't think it could be good for Amelia to dwell on it.

Entering the kitchen, she crossed to Amelia's side and put her arms around her. "Melly . . . please don't cry. It's over now. You have to forget."

Martha Truesdale whirled, fixing her venomous stare on Summer. "What do you know about it? You didn't lose anybody to those vicious devils."

Summer clenched her teeth in an effort to keep her voice calm. "I know what it's like to lose someone I love, Mrs. Truesdale. My mother was killed in a Comanche raid when I was very young. Amelia needs time to grieve, yes, but she needs more to get on with her life. It won't help her to dwell on what happened."

"You stinkin' Injun lover, what do you know?" The older woman picked up the closest object at hand, which happened to be an iron frying pan from the stove. "Squaw! Comanche squaw!"

"Ma!" Billy exclaimed, leaping to his feet, while Summer froze.

Billy took the skillet from his mother, who turned away, shaking with rage. In the silence that followed, the boy stood shuffling his feet, looking uncomfortable. The tension in the kitchen had suddenly swelled to an explosive level.

"Summer, what is she talking about?" Amelia asked plaintively. "Why did she call you a squaw?"

Summer took a deep breath. "Lance and I were married last month, Melly."

Her sobbing suddenly arrested, Amelia raised her head to stare at her sister in horror. "Dear God . . . you didn't. Summer, tell me you wouldn't."

She shook her head. "It's true. Lance is my husband."

Amelia recoiled in her arms. When Summer tried to reach out for her, she let out a shriek. "Don't touch me! Oh, God, don't touch me. All this time . . . you and he . . ."

She buried her face in her hands and started weeping again.

Billy shuffled his feet even harder, looking as if he would rather face a Comanche war party than a group of feuding women. Summer stood helplessly by while Martha Truesdale flashed her a malignant look of triumph.

Amelia was the first to speak. "I think . . . I need . . . to lie down. . . ."

"Yes, of course," Summer said quietly. "I'll help you—"

"No! Martha will help me!"

The pain that shot through Summer was swift and cruel. It cut her to the quick to be spurned by her only sister, a sister who until now had always loved her unconditionally. And for such a reason. She had only married Lance in order to save Amelia.

Summer felt herself trembling as she watched Martha Truesdale support Amelia up the wooden stairway to the bed-chambers above. Billy mumbled something about needing to see to the animals and made his escape. Alone, Summer sank weakly into the chair her sister had vacated.

Amelia didn't know what she was saying. She was simply reacting to the shock, that was all. When she'd had time to adjust to the idea of their marriage, she would accept it.

She would have to, because it was now a fact that couldn't be changed.

To Summer's vast relief, Amelia relented. Or at least, she appeared to. At supper that evening, Amelia pretended she'd never heard about her sister's marriage to a half-breed.

Instead she chatted about mundane things, quizzing the Truesdales about their neighbors and events that had occurred during her absence. She even made an effort to include Summer in the discussion with pleasant comments such as "You would like her, Summer; she's the sweetest child," and "Did I tell you about the time Limmel took me to the dance in Belknap?" She spoke a lot about her late husband, Limmel, and even laughed once or twice about her memories of him.

Even so, supper was a strained affair. Martha hadn't allowed Summer to help with the preparations, and she sat in sullen silence throughout the meal, her hateful gaze fixed on Summer, as if she could drive her away by mere wishing.

Just as Amelia had taken her pain and fury out on Lance, Martha Truesdale seemed to blame Summer for all the losses the settlers had ever suffered, especially the raid in which her daughter had been killed. Summer was glad to escape the hostile atmosphere.

She thought she might have to sleep in the barn, but Amelia claimed to want her presence. As she'd done for the past week, she cleaned and salved Amelia's burns and cuts, which seemed to be healing, and helped her sister into a nightgown.

She was tucking Amelia into the small tester bed, the way Melly had always done for her during her childhood, when Amelia suddenly turned a pleading gaze on her. "I want to go home, Summer. To Sky Valley."

"Yes, of course." She bent to kiss her sister's forehead. "Whatever you want, Melly."

"I don't want to stay here any longer." Tears filled her eyes. "Too many memories . . ."

"Yes, I know."

"Will you take me home?"

"Certainly, Melly."

"Tomorrow? I can't—"

She broke off as a rap sounded on the door. Martha Truesdale shuffled in, garbed in a black nightcap and woolen wrapper. Even her nightdress was black, and she hovered at Amelia's bedside like some malevolent crow hungering for carrion. Summer wanted to cringe, but she maintained her position by the bed, in case Amelia needed protection.

It was *she* whom Martha wished harm, however, Summer realized. Mrs. Truesdale said good night stiffly to Amelia, and then added with a venomous glance at Summer, "I hope for all our sakes you know what you're doing, Amelia, inviting *her* into our house. I just hope she doesn't take it into her head to murder us all in our beds."

A streak of fury raced through Summer, but she forced herself to take a calming breath. It hurt, though, when her sister lowered her eyelashes and looked away instead of coming to her defense.

"I assure you, Mrs. Truesdale," Summer managed to reply evenly, remembering the reply Lance had once given to a similar accusation, "I haven't murdered anyone recently, as I recall."

Martha stared for a moment, and then her mouth took on a contemptuous sneer. "How can we be sure? What kind of heathen tricks have you learned, married to that savage Injun?"

"My husband is not a savage, Mrs. Truesdale."

"You're a liar!" Her eyes turned a bit wild, while her voice rose to a near shriek. "He is so—and so are you, copulating with that stinking devil! You'll just get yourself a litter of half-breeds and turn them loose to murder and rape."

With a virulent scowl, she turned and stalked from the room, shutting the door forcefully behind her.

Trembling at having such hatred directed toward her, Summer looked at her sister, hoping Melly hadn't paid any mind to the woman's viciousness.

Amelia was clutching her stomach, staring down at herself. "Oh, God . . . no . . . I may be pregnant," she breathed, her shaken voice barely audible. "What if I'm pregnant? What if I'm breeding one of those savages? God wouldn't do that to me, would He?"

Her own thoughts similarly stricken, Summer held a hand to her own stomach. She might be carrying Lance's child even now.

But she couldn't think about herself right then, not when her sister had suddenly turned hysterical. Amelia had curled her hand in a fist and was beating her abdomen. "I won't have it, I won't have a Comanche baby!"

"Melly, stop, for God's sake, please stop! You'll hurt yourself."

She grasped her sister's hands, pinning them to her sides, which only made her more frantic. Writhing, Amelia began screaming, pleading for her to stop. It was only when Summer released her altogether that her panic lessened and her shrieks turned to gasping wails. Turning her face to the pillow, Amelia curled in a ball beneath the covers, weeping piteously. "I don't . . . want a . . . a breed baby. . . . I don't!"

"I know, dearest, I know. But maybe it won't happen." Her heart aching, Summer brushed Amelia's damp hair off her forehead. It was possible Amelia had been impregnated by her Comanche captors, but perhaps unlikely. She had never conceived during her four-year marriage.

"We'll face that situation if we come to it, Melly. Now, please, you have to quit thinking about it. You'll make yourself sick."

"Summer . . . I want to go home."

"Yes, I know, Melly. And we will. Just as soon as Lance returns, we'll leave."

"No, I want to go *now.*"

When Summer didn't answer at once, Amelia suddenly ceased crying and reached up to grab her sister's hand.

"Please, Summer, tomorrow . . . Promise me you'll take me home tomorrow. Promise me. . . ."

She tried to look away from her sister's bleak eyes, her tearstained cheeks, but she couldn't. Nor could she deny Amelia whatever she asked for, no matter how irrational or difficult. "Yes, Melly, whatever you want. We'll discuss it in the morning. Now, go to sleep, darling. I'll be here if you need me."

Her hope that Amelia would forget about her promise never had a chance to take root. Amelia woke her at daybreak, eagerly making plans for the journey. She wanted to go home to Sky Valley that very day and wouldn't listen to reason or rational arguments.

"You, promised!" Amelia cried when Summer tried to explain why she couldn't leave just yet.

"I know, Melly, but Lance expects us to be here when he gets back."

Amelia's eyes brimmed and her lower lip started quivering.

Summer bit her own lip. She had promised her sister, but she had also promised Lance to wait for his return. What would he think when he arrived to find her gone?

"I never imagined," Amelia said accusingly, "that you would care more about a half-breed than your own flesh and blood."

"Please, don't call him that. Not after all he's done for us."

Amelia started crying. "I hate him! I don't want to wait for him."

Torn between her sister and her husband, Summer agreed at least to inquire about the stage schedule.

She wished she hadn't. Billy knew exactly when the stage was due to head south—at one o'clock that afternoon.

"See, Summer?" Amelia pleaded. "We have to leave today. the stage won't come through town for four more days, and I can't stand to wait that long. I hate it here! Please? Billy will drive us into Belknap, won't you, Billy? If we can't afford the price of the tickets, we can borrow the money from Martha."

"That isn't it. Lance gave me money."

"Then why can't we go? You promised!"

Amelia alternately cried and pleaded until Summer finally gave in. Reluctantly she helped pack Amelia's most prized belongings—the remainder of which Martha agreed to send by stagecoach later—and watched as Amelia said a tearful good-bye to her mother-in-law.

Her last hope that the stage would be filled came to naught when they arrived at the station. They were the only passengers expected. They had no trouble buying tickets from Jeb Burkett, even though he looked at Summer oddly.

"Strange," Jeb said slowly, as if not wanting to be caught prying. "Lance didn't mention you'd be wantin' to take a trip."

"He doesn't know about it. My sister doesn't feel she can stay here any longer. I am taking her home."

Summer borrowed a sheet of letter paper from Jeb and left a message of explanation for Lance, telling him she was taking Amelia back to Sky Valley. She left the note in Jeb's care, not trusting the Truesdales to deliver it or in any way help her and her half-breed husband.

The stage arrived only an hour late, with the same two drivers as on the trip north. Shep and Petey both greeted Summer as a bosom friend, and promised to take good care of her and her sister on the long trip home.

Amelia shrank from them both and wouldn't accept their assistance in boarding, but as the stage pulled away from the station, she looked out the window with more interest than she'd shown in all the time since her rescue.

Summer couldn't help but feel glad for Melly, but her own heart sank with every mile they traveled. She sat blindly looking out her own window, wondering if she had done the right thing, hoping that Lance wouldn't consider her leaving him behind a betrayal.

Chapter 16

Home. Sky Valley. From a rise in the road, Summer looked out over the cedar-studded limestone hills with their lush, grassy meadows and bands of grazing horses, and her heart swelled at the sight. They had made it. Amelia was safe.

Her sister sat silently next to her in the buckboard borrowed from Lance's livery, while his young hired hand drove the team and filled the awkward moments with artless prattle—a prattle Summer encouraged. Amelia felt keenly self-conscious about her return to civilization, and she needed to be treated as if nothing eventful had happened to her. There would be enough people who would condemn her for having been a Comanche captive, but she needed to know there were some who would not.

She took Melly's hand and pointed in the distance, describing the difficulty they'd had last spring when the creek had overflowed its banks. She hoped to interest her sister in the ranch, in the simple tasks of everyday living, and turn her thoughts from the terrors of the past.

Her own heart lighter than it had been in weeks, Summer drew in a deep breath of fresh air. It was so wonderful to be home! The land looked the same as she'd left it, except for the changing season. It was only the second week in October, but evidence of autumn was beginning to crop up here and there. She could see fields whose hay had been cut, and closer to the ranch, acres of drying cornstalks whose crop had been harvested. There were no immediate signs of the vaqueros who guarded the herds, though, and no one rode out to meet them.

Summer felt uncomfortable at this lack of caution after weeks of living with her nerves on edge. A war party could have raided the ranch and burned it to the ground before any of the occupants could arm themselves. It was not often that Comanches raided this far south, but it still happened. During the war, horses had been stolen and countless head of cattle driven off, for sale to Federal Army contractors in the New Mexico Territory.

The sprawling white clapboard house looked exactly as it had when she'd left five weeks ago—had it only been that long? It seemed like an eternity since she'd first gotten word of Amelia's capture, since she'd pleaded with Lance to help her, since she'd married him in exchange for attempting her sister's rescue.

The intrusive memory sobered Summer's thoughts. She was a married woman now. She was the wife of a Comanche half-breed. Her future was likely to be even more difficult than her sister's. A captive who survived imprisonment by Indians was considered dirty and disgraced, an object of pity and embarrassment, but a woman who would willingly ally herself with the Comanche would no doubt be subjected to outright contempt and scorn.

When the buckboard clattered to a halt in the sweeping drive, one of the Mexican maidservants noticed them first. With a cry of delight, Estelle ran out on the porch and called excitedly for the *patrón* to come quickly, that the señora and the señorita had returned.

Hobbling outside, Reed bounded down the steps as fast as his crutches would allow, and dropped them altogether when he reached the buckboard. With a sound that was half shout, half sob, he hauled Amelia down and into his arms.

"Oh, God . . . Melly . . . you're safe."

Tears of joy streamed down his face as he clutched Amelia in a grip that threatened to crush her. From the look of her shaking shoulders, Amelia was crying also. Summer felt an ache in her own throat, watching her brother's relief as he rocked their sister in his embrace. She was grateful to Nate Jenkins, the lad who'd driven them, for his sensitivity, when he climbed down from the buckboard and moved away, leaving them in privacy.

It was a full minute before Reed looked up to meet Summer's eyes. "You really did it. You found her. I feared . . ."

"I know." She smiled. "I feared the same thing. But it's over. Amelia's safe."

His gaze narrowing, Reed looked around him. "Where is Calder? Didn't he return with you?"

At the mention of the man who'd saved her life, Amelia stiffened visibly and pushed out of her brother's embrace. "I want to go inside now." She turned to the Mexican women who were waiting on the porch, eager to greet her. "Estelle, Consuala, Maritza, how *are* you? It is so good to be home!"

Summer's smile faded as she watched her sister being welcomed by the laughing women.

"What happened?" her brother demanded. "What's wrong?"

"She wants to pretend Lance doesn't exist. She blames him for what the Comanches did to her."

"He *was* the one who found her, wasn't he?"

Summer sighed. "Of course. I could never have done it on my own. He risked his life for her twice, Reed. But she hates him because he's part Comanche."

Reed turned to watch Amelia get swept into the house by the Mexican women. "I'm not sure I understand. Where is he?"

"On his way home by now, I hope. He had to drive some horses north in payment for his brother's help. The next stage was supposed to leave from Belknap today. If he caught it, he should be here in a few days."

Her brother suddenly scowled up at her. "You traveled all that way *alone?* Without an escort?"

"I didn't have any choice. Melly was determined to come home, and I couldn't change her mind. I don't think even you could have persuaded her. But it wasn't too dangerous, Reed, truly. The stage drivers are Lance's friends, and they looked out for us." When her brother's frown didn't diminish, Summer gave him an imploring look. "Don't be angry. I couldn't refuse her, Reed. She was hurt badly by the Comanches, and her nerves were fragile enough to snap. I had to risk it."

"All right." Reed closed his eyes for a moment, his agony showing on his face. "Oh, God . . . poor Melly."

"Don't think about it. It's over, she's safe now. We'll have to help her go on with her life."

"We'll have to help her heal, won't we?"

"Yes," Summer agreed softly.

He reached up to help her down from the buckboard, and then apparently remembered he was standing on only one leg. Cursing under his breath, he shook his head. "You'll have to get down on your own, blast it."

She flashed him a smile reminiscent of the old Summer as she climbed down. "I don't mind fending for myself. If you'd seen all the chores I had to perform in the Comanche camp, you would have been astonished. I vow I developed muscles I never knew I had." She gave a short laugh. "Lance doesn't even call me princess much anymore."

She saw the start Reed gave, saw his features tighten in a grim expression, but she waited until he had picked up his crutches before placing a restraining hand on his arm. Looking up at him imploringly, she held his gaze. "Reed, Lance is my husband now. We owe him a huge debt. You won't forget that, will you?"

Her brother's lips pressed together in a bleak line, but he nodded brusquely. "I know exactly what we owe him. And I feel obligated to honor the bargain you made with him—even if I think you made a deal with the Devil."

She thought she would have to be satisfied with that disappointing answer, but Reed paused before turning toward the house. "Summer, I want you to know . . . I appreciate the sacrifice you've made for Amelia. And that . . . whatever you want to do . . . I'll stand by you."

"Thank you." Her eyes shimmered. "That means a great deal to me."

And it did, Summer realized as she matched her steps to her brother's slower plod-hop. She didn't think she had the strength to fight Reed as well as Amelia.

The coolness of the house was welcoming after the heat of the afternoon sun. Summer would have relished a refreshing glass of lemonade or a cup of water from the spring, but she could hear the murmur of voices coming from upstairs and knew Amelia must have retreated to the bedchamber they had shared as children. Excusing herself from Reed, she followed the sound.

As she climbed the stairs, though, she let her weary gaze drink in her surroundings, cherishing the familiar sights and smells of home.

Home. Memory closed around her and filled her with longing. How she wished things could be the same as they'd been before the war, when her brothers and father were still alive, when Reed and Amelia were still whole, when she herself had no decision more difficult to occupy her time than which party dress to wear and which beau to favor with her attention.

Those carefree days were gone. The uncertain future spread out before her like a murky swamp, with untold dangers to be negotiated, not the least of which was resolving her relationship with the man who was now her husband.

That man sat his horse the following afternoon, staring at the big white ranch house with uncertainty and resentment. Any pleasure Lance had felt at his own homecoming, any joy he'd found in being on Sky Valley land again, had faded at the prospect of entering that big house.

John Weston had taken two years and a small fortune to build it, determined to provide his large family with something better than the rough log cabin that had supported them when they first settled the land.

A familiar, cold heaviness swallowed Lance up as he sat there hesitating. He remembered being a kid gazing up at the fancy mansions in Austin, remembered his mother drawing him away as she gently explained why he would never be accepted in any of those fine homes. *You aren't like them, Lance. They can't accept your Indian blood. They can't accept me. But it doesn't matter. We don't need them. Not as long as we have each other.* He remembered the anger that had burgeoned inside him, the anger that, like smoldering embers, only grew hotter. He remembered the savage hurt.

That pain hadn't been as raw, though, as what he'd felt when he'd learned Summer had betrayed her promise to wait for him. She had left him to follow her, as if he were some sort of unwelcome afterthought.

Setting his jaw, Lance tore his gaze away and swung down from his horse. There was no point in waiting. He was here to lay claim to his wife, and nothing was going to stop him. And unlike five years ago, he wouldn't be run off.

To his surprise, when he knocked he was admitted at once by a Mexican woman, just as if he'd been expected. He was shown into the front parlor and told that she would fetch the *patrón* if he would wait, *por favor.*

Left alone in such elegant surroundings, Lance belatedly removed his hat. He didn't take a seat on the blue chintz settee or the velvet armchairs or even the wooden rocker. Not when he was so dusty and unshaven, with three days of trail dirt clinging to him. He hadn't even taken the time to change clothes before riding out here to settle the issue of his marriage with his errant bride.

She and her sister had made it back unharmed, he'd learned from young Nate when he'd arrived at his livery in Round Rock. But once he'd known they were safe, the relief he'd felt had quickly been overshadowed by smoldering anger . . . and fear. Anger that Summer would risk making such a dangerous journey unprotected. Fear that she'd only used her sister's condition as an excuse to be free of him.

His claim to Summer wasn't indisputable, not by a long shot. Her sister was safe, and without that leverage, he had no real hold on her. If Summer wanted to disavow their marriage, she could do it. She could demand a divorce, and any judge in the land would grant it to her, Lance had no doubt. Certainly her family would have preferred it that way.

Vowing it would be a cold day in hell before he gave her up, Lance glanced around the parlor. He had never been inside the Weston house before, and he found himself looking for glimpses of Summer, unwillingly comparing the elegance she had grown up with to the rugged simplicity he'd always known.

When his gaze roamed over the stone fireplace, his eye caught the small gilt-framed portrait sitting on the mantel—and his breathing suddenly seemed to stop. Summer. How did he always manage to forget how beautiful she was?

The portrait was Summer as he'd known her five years ago—laughing, face upturned, innocent green eyes dancing with that feminine come-hither glance that could tempt a man's soul from his body. Even then she'd been sure of her own power.

He hadn't heard much laughter from her lately, nor had he seen that alluring look directed at him, but she still held that same devastating power over him. She could wound him without even trying.

Was that what she'd done? Her note had said she'd been forced to leave Belknap at Amelia's insistence, that she was sorry but she had to take her sister home—but was that the truth? Was her regret real? Or had she simply been running from him, trying to postpone the moment of reckoning?

His dark musings were interrupted just then when Reed limped through the door. Lance looked up—and tensed as he met the other man's gaze. Reed's blue eyes were unsmiling, his expression as solemn as a funeral.

Mentally Lance girded himself for battle, but to his surprise, Reed balanced one crutch under his arm and held out his hand. Lance looked at it warily for moment, then reached out his own to accept the handshake.

"I can't ever repay you for what you did, Calder," Reed admitted in a low voice. "Thank you for saving my sister."

"I don't want your thanks," Lance retorted more gruffly than he'd intended. "I want my wife."

Reed tried to smile. "Of course. Summer should be down in a minute. I sent Maritza to fetch her."

Lance's stiff stance relaxed the slightest degree.

"You made good time. Summer said you wouldn't be here for several more days."

"I didn't wait for the stage."

Reed's eyebrow rose. "You rode all that way?"

"Yeah, what of it?"

This time Reed managed a reluctant chuckle. "You haven't changed one damn bit, have you, Calder? You're still just as prickly as you were when you hired on five years ago. But there's no reason to take my head off. I meant no insult. Indeed, I'm envious you can sit a horse that long. This damned stump of mine"—he glanced down at what remained of his left leg—"won't let me even climb on one, let alone ride hundreds of miles. Ten minutes in the saddle would put me on my back for a week."

It was said lightly, not at all a plea for sympathy or pity, yet Lance felt both. The Comanches had no place in their society for crippled warriors. He couldn't imagine living as Reed was trying to do, being forced to hobble around, being dependent on others, especially a household of women. But then, Weston didn't need his pity. He had plenty of servants and hired hands to do his bidding. All he had to do was crook a finger and his wishes were met. A damned far cry from the way Lance himself had been raised.

Still, Reed was obviously making an effort to be amiable,

not as if he intended to kick his unwanted visitor off his land.
Lance felt some of his resentment, his age-old hostility, drain
away. If Summer was going to divorce him, would her
brother be standing here now, acting so polite? Unless Reed
was trying to soften him up—

He heard the silken rustle of a woman's skirts, and looked
beyond Reed to find Summer poised in the doorway. Lance
was aware of his heart thudding slowly against his ribs, of
anger and hurt and fear swelling again in his chest.

"Lance." Her voice was a soft murmur as she offered him
a tentative smile. "I didn't expect you back so soon."

Without waiting for a reply, she swept into the parlor, offering
her hands to him graciously—the lady of the manor to the hilt.
Except that Summer went one step further. Raising on tiptoe,
she tilted up her face and planted a gentle kiss on his cheek.

It startled him so bad that the gruff retort he'd meant to
make died in his throat.

"How is your wound?" she asked, then glanced over her
shoulder at her brother. "Reed, I told you about the terrible
knife fight Lance was in." She turned back to Lance. "It isn't
any worse, is it?"

If he didn't know better, he would swear Summer sounded
nervous. And to his surprise, her unexpected reception threw
him off balance. He'd come here prepared to battle for his life,
but he didn't know how to act in the face of her insecurity.

He wanted to haul her into his arms and shake her till her
teeth rattled for taking off the way she had. He wanted to
crush her to him and strip off her clothes and his own and
take her right there in the parlor—except that her brother was
hovering protectively nearby, and his own clothes were much
too filthy for any well-bred lady to get close to.

Instead of doing either, he brushed his hat against his thigh
in a gesture of restrained impatience. "The wound's fine."

"I know you must be unhappy with me," she began,
sweetly reasoning. "And you have every right to be, but truly,
I had no choice but to come home when I did. If you had
heard Melly's sobs, you would have done exactly the same
thing. I know you would have, Lance. Beneath that fierce
scowl of yours lies a kind and generous heart."

He knew what she was doing with her flattery—trying to
wrap him around her little finger—but dammit, she was suc-

ceeding. And her explanation did mollify him a bit. He knew what dealing with that hysterical sister of hers was like.

"Maritza said you rode in," Summer went on at his silence. "I'll have her husband take your horse to the barn and carry your things up to your room. You can sleep in our brother Jamison's old bedchamber—"

"*We* can sleep in your brother's old bedchamber, princess."

A flush of warm color spread over her cheekbones, and she avoided looking at Reed. "Well, yes, if Melly doesn't need me."

"Summer ..." Lance said warningly.

She obviously wanted to delay this particular conversation. "You must be hungry and tired—and in need of a bath," she said with a glance at his attire. "I'll have Estelle fix you something to eat while I heat some water." She gave him a brilliant smile. "And don't tell me I shouldn't go to the trouble. I fetched enough water in the Comanche camp to know what I'm doing. Did you bring some fresh clothing? If not, I'm sure Reed wouldn't mind if you borrowed some of his. You're about the same size—"

"I brought a change of clothes in my saddlebags," Lance interrupted.

"Good. Then come to the kitchen when you're through here. I'll leave you two alone to get reacquainted." She flashed another smile, which included her brother, and swept out in a rustle of skirts.

Lance glanced at Reed, who was looking solemn again. "I guess I'll be staying here," Lance said contentiously, determined not to mince words.

"I guess so," Reed replied. "I just hope ... It ... won't be easy for her, being married to you, Calder."

His jaw hardened. "It was Summer's choice."

"I know. I just don't want her hurt."

"She's my *wife*, Weston. I don't want her hurt, either."

Reed nodded slowly, and Lance felt the worst of his tension ease. It was clear he wouldn't get a warm welcome into the family, but they weren't going to try to kick him out, either. It was probably too much to expect anything more.

The kitchen stood at the back of the house, Lance discovered when he went looking. It boasted an iron stove, but the big fireplace apparently was used for most of the cooking, judging by all the hooks and tripods suspended over the coals.

Several large kettles hung there now, and one of the Mexican women was stirring the contents of a pot—some kind of soup, Lance figured from the delicious odors wafting his way. The smell made his stomach grumble. Summer was right. He was damned hungry, after the lengthy journey. He'd ridden hell-for-leather and hadn't taken the time to eat anything but jerky the whole trip.

Summer came up behind him just then, carrying a pile of snowy white towels. She smiled as she passed him, and addressed the Mexican woman.

"Maritza, this is the man who rescued the señora. My husband . . . Lance Calder."

To his surprise, the woman bobbed him a curtsy and grinned broadly. "Welcome, Señor Calder. We are very glad you bring the señora home."

A small storeroom off the kitchen held a copper tub, and Summer deposited the towels in there. "I told Pedro to bring your saddlebags in here," she said when she came out. "Sit down, Lance, and we'll feed you."

Lance took a seat at the large wooden table, waiting while the women served him a steaming bowl of beef-and-vegetable soup and a plate of fresh cornbread, with a crock of sweet butter and some homemade apple marmalade to go along.

Summer filled the tub while he ate, making small talk and listening as he told her about delivering the horses to Fights Bear's warriors, and expressing her relief that everything had gone smoothly.

She wouldn't attend his bath, though. Not even when some devil inside prodded Lance to remind her of the time he'd taken her to the creek to bathe.

"You weren't so shy then, as I remember, princess. What's wrong? You afraid to see me without my clothes on now? After all the time we've been married?"

Her cheeks flushing with color, Summer sent an embarrassed glance toward the Mexican woman standing at the fireplace and murmured an excuse about needing to prepare his room. Before he could stop her, she had fled from the kitchen.

Lance stared after her, his mouth tightening. It seemed Summer was ashamed to have anyone know they slept together as man and wife. But she had better get over her offended sensibilities pretty soon. He wasn't going to let her deny him his marital rights any longer.

Telling himself there would be time enough to press the issue, though, he shut the door to the bathroom behind him and began stripping off his filthy clothes.

Upstairs in the bedchamber that had once belonged to her brothers, Summer felt the warmth gradually fade from her face as she busied herself arranging the flowers Consuala had brought in from the garden.

She'd already checked to see that there were fresh sheets on the bed, but her glance kept straying to the large four-poster, where in all likelihood she would be sleeping with Lance tonight, where in all probability he would take her body with the kind of passion he'd shown her during most of their marriage.

Faith, she wished he hadn't reminded her of how abnormal their relationship was. In the Comanche camp, their lovemaking, while wild and primitive, had seemed almost natural, part of the untamed setting. But what had been an earthy mating between husband and wife there would seem entirely wanton here, depraved even, now that they'd returned to civilization. What had been acceptable there just wasn't done between ladies and gentlemen. Why, Amelia had once confessed she'd never even *undressed* in front of her husband, let alone let him do the kind of scandalous things Lance had done to *her*.

Summer felt unwelcome heat steal back into her cheeks, and scolded herself for allowing it. She would have to learn to quell the hot feelings Lance aroused in her before she turned into a complete hussy. And hide her embarrassment. All he had to do was *hint* at the things that had happened between them, and she flamed up like a torch. If she kept that up, soon everyone would know just how appealing she found her husband's lust and—

"Summer, what are you doing?"

She gave a guilty start at the plaintive sound of her sister's voice. Amelia had been napping in her own room, but obviously had just awakened.

Turning slowly, Summer hesitated to answer. She dreaded the upcoming discussion, but it couldn't be put off any longer. Lance was here, and demanding his rights as her husband, and she couldn't, wouldn't, turn him away.

She gave her sister a bright smile, or tried to, as Amelia entered the room. "I'm putting out flowers, Melly. You know how much you enjoy fresh-cut flowers."

"But why *here?*"

"Because . . ." Summer took a deep breath. "Because Lance has come home. And this is to be his room. Our room."

"This . . . ? He means to live *here?*" Amelia's voice had grown high and breathless. "In our *home?*"

"Yes, in our home. He's my husband now—"

"No! I won't have him in this house!"

"You don't mean that, Melly," Summer said stiffly. "You—"

"I do so mean it! He can't stay here!" Her face flushed with fury as she stamped her foot. "He's a savage! I won't allow it. I won't eat or sleep in the same house as one of those horrible creatures, even if he is your husband!"

Summer sighed as an impossible tiredness flooded her. Reminding herself of all her sister had been through, though, she tried to restrain her impatience. "I should think you would be grateful for all he did for you, Amelia. Lance risked his own life *twice* to save you—"

"I don't care what he did! He's a rutting beast! God, I don't see how you can bear to have him touch you!" Amelia shuddered violently while her tone held revulsion. "How *could* you? How could you have married a heathen like him?"

"It was easy," Summer retorted, losing a measure of control as well as her temper. "He promised to try and rescue you if I became his wife. I chose you, Melly. If you want the truth, I only married him for *your* sake. I think you should be grateful that I was willing to make such a sacrifice!"

The words had scarcely left her mouth when she caught a flicker of movement out of the corner of her eye. Jerking her head up, Summer gazed beyond Amelia in dismay.

Lance stood in the doorway, his wet hair slicked back, his face frozen in an expression that was no expression. Except that she could see the anguish in his eyes, stark and raw and excruciating to watch. It was gone in an instant, replaced by a grim defiance, cold and hard as granite, but it was clear he had overheard their argument.

"Lance . . ." Summer breathed.

Amelia whirled, clutching the lapels of the wrapper to her throat. Her gaze fixed on Lance, she backed up a step, then another, as if expecting him suddenly to attack her. "Get out! Get out of this house! You aren't welcome here!"

His gaze, so piercing and insolent now when a moment before it had held agony, shifted slowly from Summer to Amelia. "I'd say you've made that real clear, ma'am. I'd say both of you have."

"Lance, no . . . !" Summer cried softly.

Her sister retreated another step but stamped her slippered foot. "You aren't staying in this house!" She turned to Summer, her eyes wild. "I won't live here with him! I won't! I won't." Abruptly she burst into tears.

Reflexively Summer put an arm around Amelia's shoulder, trying to console her, even though she wanted more to reach out to Lance. He didn't look, however, as if he would accept consolation from anyone, especially her.

"Don't worry, ma'am," he said with a cynical drawl—to either or both of them, Summer wasn't certain. "You won't have to put up with me any longer."

Spinning on his heel, he quit the room.

Horrified by his obvious misinterpretation of her words, knowing she was greatly to blame, Summer nevertheless turned her frustration on her sister. "Melly, how *could* you!"

Amelia began crying harder, but Summer couldn't summon the will or take the time to comfort her. She owed her husband more than that. "Lance, wait!" Calling after him, she brushed past her sister and followed him.

By the time she gained the stairway, Lance had already bounded down the stairs and was striding down the hall in the direction of the kitchen. A moment later, as she reached the bottom step, she heard the back door slam.

He was heading for the barn, she knew with instinctive certainty. He was going to leave, to ride away just as he had five years ago when her father had driven him off the ranch. He would leave just like last time, thinking the worst about her, that she was cruel and selfish and totally heartless.

No, she wouldn't let it happen again! She wouldn't let him go. Not this way. Not at all. Not after all she owed him.

Her heart pounding in her throat, Summer picked up her skirts and ran.

Chapter 17

When her father was still alive, the barn had been filled with livestock—Sky Valley's prize thoroughbreds primarily, but also broodmares and milk cows and saddle mounts of visiting guests. Now the large stone structure stood two-thirds empty. The days of the gay house parties that went on for days had ended with the start of the war, and racers were an expense the ranch could ill afford. Those animals that couldn't earn their keep had been sold, and the three remaining stallions had been turned loose on the range to mix their blood with the smaller, hardier mustang mares in hopes of gaining the best of both breeds.

Lance's horse was the same roan that had carried him from Belknap into Indian territory and back, Summer saw when her eyes adjusted to the dimmer light, which meant he must have ridden straight here. It had been tied in a stall near the center, rather than turned out in the corrals with the working horses of the remuda.

There was no immediate sign of Lance, but she noticed the saddlebags draped over the stall side rail. If they were his, he must have picked them up on his way through the kitchen.

Just then he came out of the tack room behind her, hefting his saddle. He didn't look at her as he brushed past her silently, but his jaw was set in a rigid line. He slung the saddle over the rail, then threw a blanket pad over the roan's back. He meant to ride off, she was certain. Unless she could prevent him.

Summer took a step toward him, then stopped uncertainly, twisting her hands together in regret and shame. How could she have hurt him so? No matter how unintentional, she had shattered his pride, delivered a devastating blow to a man

254

who had only pride to sustain him against a white world that had always tried to beat him down.

"Lance . . . please, don't go. Please?"

When he glanced briefly over his shoulder at her, she almost flinched at the hostility in his eyes. "Don't go? What the hell did you expect me to do? Stay there with your sister screaming at me to get out? With her looking at me like she expected me to rape her? With you telling her what a great *sacrifice* you made for her?"

The fury, the bitterness, in his tone lashed out at her like a whip, cutting her as she had cut him. Summer couldn't defend herself, either, not against the bald truth.

He shook his head. "It'll be easier to calm her if I'm not around," he muttered bitterly. "If she doesn't have to be afraid of the murdering breed." His chin dropping to his chest, he shut his eyes, as if weary of fighting.

Watching him, Summer felt a fierce ache well up in her throat. He seemed to her at that moment to be utterly alone, utterly desolate.

But how could she expect him to be otherwise? She thought about the crushing life of rejection he'd endured as a child, so bleak, so without hope. How had he borne it? How had he come through it with his soul intact? Lance was proud and hard and harsh-tempered, yes, but he was a good man, too, worthy of respect and loyalty. He didn't deserve the grim fate that life had thrown at him. He should have someone to stand up for him—and she desperately wanted to do it, to let him know that he wasn't alone anymore. He needed to know. . . .

"Lance . . . you don't have to leave."

He stiffened, and seemed abruptly to remember her presence. His head jerking up, he threw another fierce glance over his shoulder. "You're damned right about that. I hate to break it to you, princess, but I've got no intention of leaving this ranch. I'm going back to the livery and get my things and make arrangements for Nate to take over full-time. Then I'm coming back here. You're stuck with me, princess.

"Don't worry," he added harshly before she could reply. "I'll bunk with the vaqueros. I'll spare your sister the horror of living with an Injun right now, until she gets better, but I'll be damned if I'll be driven off like five years ago! I'm sure as hell not gonna crawl out of here with my tail between my legs like last time. I'm staying. You're my wife, whether you like it or not."

Wincing, Summer clenched her fingers together to keep from reaching out to him. Did he think she was trying to be free of their marriage? But of course he would. She had left Belknap so abruptly, betraying her promise to him, even though she hadn't wanted to. After that, he wasn't likely to believe she hadn't seen an opportunity to be rid of him. And her declaration about sacrifice would only have confirmed his suspicions.

But he was wrong, Summer reflected. She considered herself honor-bound to live up to her end of the bargain. No matter how difficult it would be for her to live as the wife of a half-breed Comanche, she would see it through. In all honor, she couldn't go back on her word. Yet obviously she needed to reassure Lance of that. She took a step closer, carefully choosing her words.

"Lance . . . what I said a moment ago . . . I didn't mean it the way it sounded. I was only attempting to make Amelia acknowledge what we *both* had done for her. I . . . I did sacrifice for her, it's true. But I would do it again if it meant saving her life, if it meant keeping my family together, keeping this ranch together. I don't regret my decision. I don't regret marrying you, Lance."

His bronzed features turned hostile again. "Don't lie to me, Summer! You can't tell me you're not ashamed of me—of being married to a breed."

That wasn't entirely true. She was afraid of what the future held, yes. And she was ashamed of the wanton way Lance made her feel. But she wasn't ashamed of him.

"No," she asserted with as much fervor as her unsteady voice would allow. "I'm ashamed of my sister's behavior, of my own, but I'm not ashamed of you, not at all. I'm grateful to you."

"I don't want your goddamned gratitude!"

"Then . . . what do you want?"

He was silent for a moment, and when he answered finally, his voice was so low, she could scarcely hear. "I want you to honor our wedding vows."

He stood waiting with that bleak stillness, waiting for one more rejection, expecting a response she wouldn't give.

"I mean to, Lance."

He turned to look at her, his face hard and still, his eyes narrowed and burning. "Your sister's safe," he reminded her. "You don't need me any longer. You've got no reason to remain my wife."

"I won't break my word."

"No?" The word was a cynical drawl. "Why should I believe that?"

"Because it's true," Summer said simply.

He gazed at her, his eyes still wary, distrustful, still wounded.

Summer took another step toward him, moving close enough to touch him. There seemed only one way to make him believe, one way to heal his hurt. Reaching up, she pressed her palm gently against his cheek and raised her lips to his.

He didn't really kiss her. His mouth was cool and hard and angry, a conscious defense against more pain.

When he lifted his head, his gaze narrowed threateningly. "Don't start something you're not willing to finish, princess."

She recognized the dangerous note in his warning, but still she ignored it. She knew Lance well enough now to know what would happen if she continued to press him, if she tested his control further. He would explode with fury, with passion—which was precisely what she wanted. She might be playing with dynamite, but just now he desperately needed proof of her willingness to honor their marriage vows. He needed evidence of her pledge of loyalty. And she would give it to him.

Determinedly she slid her fingers around the nape of his neck, pulling him closer. "I know exactly what I'm doing, Lance."

"Damn you. . . ." The hoarse groan was barely audible.

As if against his will, he lowered his head again and took her mouth, this time savagely. Yet within that brutal kiss, there was pain, an aching vulnerability that touched her soul in a way nothing else ever had. Summer returned his kiss wildly, opening to him fully, to his thrusting tongue, to his hungry need.

She was startled when Lance abruptly broke off their embrace. Without a word he grabbed her hand and pulled her behind him toward the rear of the barn, and Summer let out her breath in relief and triumph. She knew what would follow. When he pushed her inside a large box stall filled with clean, sweet-smelling straw, she went willingly.

Her heart was pounding as Lance shut the door behind them and turned to her. They would cause a scandal if they were caught coupling in public in broad daylight, where any one of the hired hands could discover them, but she didn't care. Her body felt hot and tight and eager, and she wanted exactly what Lance wanted. To have this clamoring sexual hunger eased by his physical possession.

Summer gasped softly when he hauled her into his arms and kissed her hard, but she responded eagerly, her sharpened senses assailed with the hot, thrilling scent of him. She gasped again when, abruptly, unexpectedly, Lance pushed her backward across the width of the stall, until her back was pressed against the far wall. His hard body crowded her, intimidating her, and she had to grasp the soft chambray of his shirt to catch her balance.

"So you think you know what you're doing?" he demanded mockingly, his eyes hard and bitter.

"Yes," Summer answered, panting for breath.

"You're gonna let me take you right here? Like some whore I paid to fuck?"

She winced at his crudity, but she didn't back down. "Yes— I mean no—"

"I didn't think so." His drawl was harsh, cynical.

"What I mean is, not like a . . . a fancy woman. I'm your wife, Lance. And I'll thank you to remember it when you make love to me. Now, hush up and kiss me."

Reaching up, she tried to pull his head down, but he held himself back, his eyes sparking with fury. "You want me to act like a savage so you can hold it over me."

"No . . . I don't care if you act savage."

"You wouldn't want me to take you like this, standing against this wall."

Her eyes widened fractionally in surprise at the realization that it could be done that way, but then she smiled at her ignorance. "Yes, I would. I wouldn't care."

His mouth curved in a sneer. "You don't know what you want, princess."

"I know I want you," she murmured, half-shyly, half-defiantly.

His obsidian eyes, so threatening and angry, flared with predatory heat. "Yeah? Well, you're going to have me." A fiercely male intent was plainly written on his harsh features, yet Summer hesitated out of concern for him, not herself.

"Are you sure it won't hurt your wounded ribs?"

"What's wrong, princess? Losing your nerve?"

"No. Are you losing yours?"

Her challenge was like throwing oil on a fire. Those black, piercing eyes held hers as he slid his hand between their bodies. She could feel him unfastening the buttons of his pants, feel him shoving up her skirts and the bulky crinoline petticoat she wore, searching for the slit in her cambric drawers.

She sucked in her breath sharply when his probing fingers found the folds of her femininity, but she didn't try to escape. Instead she opened her thighs to accommodate him and closed her eyes against the shameful excitement and delight of it, the anticipation of having Lance enter her body, become fully part of her. Her nipples were so tight, they ached, and within the deepest part of her an empty throb had begun to torment her.

When Lance wrapped one strong arm around her waist and lifted her up, Summer caught at his shoulders with a little whimper, her nails digging into the corded muscles beneath his shirt. She felt the burning heat of him jabbing at the softness of her inner thigh, the fierce strength of him demanding entrance.

Finding it, he thrust upward into her hot, silky sweetness.

She made a wild sound in her throat, clinging as Lance impaled her on his thick shaft. Her entire body quivered from the pleasure and pain of it. Then he stilled.

She said his name in a raw, shaking voice and tried to move her hips, but he only held her more tightly, crushing her breasts against his hard, muscle-layered chest, grinding her hips against his, spreading his legs to control her.

She arched her back against the rough wooden wall behind her, oblivious of the discomfort as she tried to get closer. "Lance, please . . ."

"Please what, princess? Please you?" Deliberately he withdrew partway, making her feel an aching emptiness where his hot, throbbing tumescence had been. "Please me?" The muscles of his shoulders bunched and flexed beneath her clutching fingertips as he thrust slowly, making her sob in relief at the exquisite pleasure of having him fill her again.

"Yes . . ." she breathed feverishly. "Please, yes . . ." He was rigid inside her, and she trembled at the enormous pulsing size of him, but it wasn't enough. She moved again, trying to meld her flesh to his, seeking release for the restless clamoring inside her.

Lance shuddered convulsively, grinding his teeth to hold back the deep primal sound rumbling in his chest. "Wrap . . . your legs around me."

She obeyed—just then she would have done anything he asked—and clutched her arms around his neck as well. A gasping moan escaped her throat as he surged hard into her.

And then a violent hunger, primitive and raw, seemed to take control of her body. Her hips jerked spasmodically, her head thrashing side to side in fiery pleasure.

Lance seemed suddenly to feel the same wild urgency. He drove himself into her, big and hard, his powerful body trembling with angry need.

For a score of heartbeats they strained together in frenzied pleasure, Summer meeting the driving need of Lance's body, matching her movements to his in frenzied abandon, her hips writhing under his pounding force. He was slamming into her with fierce rapidity, and she bit his shoulder, sobbing from the power of it, from the shock of the impact.

And then abruptly it was too much for her to bear. Her senses crested and shattered at the wild magnificence of his possession.

Lost in shimmering heat and blind ecstasy, she finally regained awareness to find his hips jerking in the final spasms of completion. His breathing was harsh in her ear and he collapsed against her as if he could scarcely support her clinging weight.

With what seemed a valiant effort, he turned with Summer and sank into the straw, depositing her limp body in the softness, moving with her to cover her body with his and bury his mouth in the curve of her neck.

Summer made no protest whatsoever. She felt dazed by what had just happened, and yet totally replete. He was hard and heavy and hot on her, crushing her down in the straw, but she wanted him this way, wanted the intimacy, wanted him still joined to her. She could feel the heat emanating from his body, smell the musky odor of sex mingling with the warm male scent of his freshly bathed skin, and it made her feel powerfully female and deliciously weak.

"Is your wound all right?" she managed to ask weakly.

His grunt she took to mean that he would survive, which was more than she might do. She might never get up again.

"You aren't going to leave the ranch," she murmured sleepily after another long moment.

Lance stiffened at the sharp pain of remembrance—and cursed himself again for his lack of control. He had taken her again without preliminaries, without gentling her body to arousal, treating her like the basest of whores instead of the lady she was. She hadn't seemed to mind. Hell, Summer had seemed to want him as much as he had wanted her. But it was small consolation. She was more than capable of pretending to be all hot for him in order to get her way—whatever that was at the moment, he wasn't certain.

"You won't have to sleep in the bunkhouse with the vaqueros," she said more firmly, snuggling against him as if she wanted the closeness.

He was a long time in answering. "Your sister ordered me out of your house, or didn't you hear?"

"So? Amelia doesn't speak for me . . . or Reed, either, for that matter."

Slowly he raised his head to stare down at her. "You're telling me you're willing to fight your sister to let me live there?"

A small frown appeared between her eyes. "I don't think I can go that far, Lance. I have to think of her, too. Amelia is so terrified, she isn't rational. But I won't allow her to drive you away, either."

His harsh features remained totally expressionless. "It doesn't matter. A featherbed would be too soft for me, anyway."

It did matter to him, she knew. It mattered desperately.

Holding his gaze, she shook her head. "We'll find someplace else to live."

"We?" The word was wary, disbelieving.

"Yes, *we.* As your wife, my place is by your side. If you've been banished from the house, then I have been, too." When he remained tense and still, she glanced around her lazily, musing out loud. "Perhaps we can move out here to the barn. This is nice, don't you think?"

His mouth twisted in a frown that was almost a sneer. "You want me to believe you're going to live in a *barn?* A pampered princess like you?"

She offered him a pouting smile that was pure coquettishness. "I don't think you can call me that any longer, Lance Calder. I just spent an entire month as an unpaid drudge in a Comanche camp, remember? But I suppose you're right. The barn wouldn't do, for we wouldn't have any privacy. But don't worry, I'll think of some place. If nothing else, we can use one of the servants' cabins—

"Oh—I have it! The old house, the one Papa built when he and Mama first settled here. It's only used for storage now, and for guest quarters, but it would be *perfect* for us. It's only made of logs—not as fancy or as large as the big house—but if you don't mind, I wouldn't. It will need a lot of work, I'm afraid—no one's touched it since the war started, and it's probably filthy and in need of repairs—but we can fix it up, I'm certain."

He stared down at her, doubt and shock warring with outraged pride. "I'll be damned," he said stiffly, his voice gruff with renewed fury, "if you're going to sacrifice any more for me."

She reached up to touch his cheek, so tenderly, he almost winced. "That's what being a wife means sometimes— sacrificing for your family. You're my family now, Lance. My husband. You would do the same for me, I know. You *have,* in fact. Many times. What's fair for you is certainly fair for me."

Easing his weight off her, he rolled onto his back and stared up at the loft overhead. Part of him wanted to throw Summer's magnanimous gesture back in her face. He didn't want her sacrificing anything for him, goddammit—the mere word speared a raw, festering wound that had tormented him all his life, because his mother had sacrificed so much for him. Summer didn't want to have him for her husband, he knew. She only felt an obligation to him.

And yet her avowal was balm to his bitter fury. She wasn't going to try to get out of their marriage. She was going to keep her end of the bargain. She was even going to try and build a home together with him. *If* he was willing to swallow his hot-tempered pride.

But did he have any choice? Could he bear the cold emptiness of his existence without her?

He laughed harshly to himself, covering his eyes with his arm. The question was downright moronic. He couldn't live without Summer filling his days and nights. Not now, not after knowing the wonder of possessing her.

Just then she turned toward him and nuzzled her face against his side, as if she wanted the closeness. Hesitantly he lifted his arm and let her snuggle against him, her head resting in the curve of his shoulder. She sighed as if content.

The icy knots of tension inside him slipped a bit, loosening a tiny inch.

They unraveled another degree at her next murmured words. "We're married now, Lance, for better or worse. All we have now is each other."

He felt his heart stop beating for breath of time. "*Do* I have you, princess?" he asked quietly.

"Yes, you have me," Summer answered sincerely. He didn't quite believe her, she could tell. Or trust her, either. Lance was a man who had been alone too long to trust easily.

But she would prove to him she meant what she said. She intended to honor their wedding vows, no matter what it cost her. He had earned her loyalty, and he would have it—for as long as he wanted it and her.

Chapter 18

It was a new start for their marriage. They slept in the barn that evening, and in the morning, began to make their new home habitable—Summer cleaning and sweeping while Lance repaired the roof and sagging shutters and hauled their belongings in.

The cabin that John Weston had built for his family twenty-five years before sat facing the creek, the farthest west of all the ranch buildings. The dwelling actually consisted of two log structures joined by a common room, with a breezeway in between and a gallery extending across the front. The half now used for storage was crammed with old furniture and equipment, but the other half had two serviceable rooms that would serve as a bedchamber and a kitchen/parlor/living area.

"It isn't nearly as nice as the big house," Summer told Lance apologetically as she stood back to view their efforts on the exterior.

"It'll have to do till I can build you something better," he returned gruffly, setting a wicker rocker down on the front porch.

Realizing he had misinterpreted her remark, Summer wiped her sweating brow and sent him an exasperated frown. "That isn't what I meant at all, Lance Calder. I only meant that I'm sorry you have to live here instead of up at the big house. Heavens, you're as prickly as a cactus."

His stiff features seemed to relax, and he gave her a rueful grin. "Okay, so maybe I overreacted."

"I think perhaps you did."

"Sorry, princess."

Lance hitched a hip up on the porch rail as he gazed out over the yard. Joining him on the porch, Summer sank wearily into the rocker, grateful for the chance to rest. She didn't remember much about living here in this house, since they'd moved when she was eight, but the memories she had were fond ones. And by many settlers' standards, the cabin was luxurious. Besides spaciousness, it offered privacy and a pretty setting, with redbuds and persimmon bushes dotting the yard, and wild plum trees and mustang grapevines covering the sandy banks of the creek.

"I think we'll like it here," she mused aloud.

"It's a lot nicer than the place I grew up in back in Austin," Lance agreed.

At his quiet admission, Summer remembered what he had told her about his childhood, about the terrible way his mother had been forced to exist. They had lived in poverty, outcasts from society, enduring hardships she herself had never known. *She* had been raised in comfort, never experiencing want or need. Even now, when she likely faced social ostracism for marrying a half-breed, she wouldn't have to whore in order to survive.

No, Summer reminded herself, Lance had good reason to be touchy about his past. She would just have to make allowances for his lingering hostility, while trying to prove to him she was on his side.

"This'll do fine, princess," she heard him say absently. "At least till I can build us a real house."

Summer shook her head. The days when luxury dominated her life, when expense and sacrifice had no meaning to her, were over. "I'm not a princess any longer, Lance. I don't need a fancy house."

His jaw hardened before he turned away. "Well, maybe I do."

She watched him stride toward the barn, hearing the echo of his defiant marriage proposal in her ears. *That's all I want. A wife who can help me become a respected member of the community.* He had wanted to marry her because of the advantage her background and family connections might bring him. And after experiencing firsthand the contemptuous treatment Lance had always been accorded, she had no trouble understanding why respectability and acceptance might be so important to him. She only hoped she could help him achieve it. She would try at least.

And Reed would, too, she knew. When she'd spoken to her brother last night, informing him they planned to live in the cabin, Reed had repeated his vow to support whatever decision she made and offered to send some of the hired hands and their wives over to help fix up the place—an offer that Lance stubbornly had refused.

Summer wasn't nearly as certain of her sister, or that she would ever be able to persuade Amelia to see reason where Lance was concerned. When she'd tried once more, Amelia had again declared hysterically that she wasn't staying with a "red devil" in the house. It was all Summer could do not to lose her temper.

With a sigh at the unpleasant remembrance, she rose from the rocker and carried her broom inside the cabin to tackle refilling the rope-bed mattress with clean straw. She hoped her sister would relent, but if not, then she would have to live with it. She intended to stand by her husband, no matter what the future held.

The first few days of that future were unexpectedly difficult as she and Lance adjusted to living with each other in close quarters, as man and wife. Accustomed to having the Mexican women as household servants, Summer was unused to keeping house totally by herself, let alone caring for someone else. And Lance wasn't used to having to consider someone else's welfare.

He was a loner, by choice as well as by circumstances, and had a hard time shedding his hostile defiance, even when he knew Summer was trying her damnedest to make their marriage work. He saw an ulterior motive in every gesture of tenderness and helpfulness she made, and viewed with suspicion any attempts to charm him. And she, weary from the exhausting work, tended to snap at him with alarming frequency, forgetting the old adage about catching more flies with honey and her own cardinal rules about using sweetness and flattery to get her way—not that it would have worked with Lance, in any case.

They often danced around each other, being scrupulously polite, testing one another, frequently misunderstanding, sometimes arguing. It was only in bed that they seemed to be of one mind, sharing a passion that was explosive and abandoned and totally satisfying. In the privacy of their bedchamber, they met as equals, both hungry and possessive as they learned to please and be pleased. In the sensual darkness, Summer lost any pretense of genteel inhibitions, and Lance lowered his own defenses in return.

It was three days after his arrival at the ranch, when their cabin was finally clean and comfortable enough, that Summer turned her attention to more difficult matters. After breakfast that morning, she went up to the big house and spoke to her brother about her husband's place on the ranch.

It took a little doing, but despite Reed's reluctance to relinquish the reins of power, she managed to persuade him to give Lance a chance at assuming greater responsibility with the herds. Afterward she talked to Dusty Murdock, the Sky Valley foreman, about the situation as he came in from the range.

"I've got no problem taking orders from Lance," Dusty admitted easily. "And I doubt many of the boys will, either. He's a regular hero for rescuing Miss Amelia, you know."

Summer looked at Dusty in surprise. "No, I didn't know."

"Sure is. Most of the boys are right proud of him, though they might not let on."

"And you think they would accept having him as boss if he takes over part of the ranch?"

"The Mexes won't be a problem, for sure. Lance is the best man with a horse anybody around here's ever laid eyes on, and the vaqueros respect that. And they know what it's like, being looked down on 'cause of their skin color. But the white fellas ... There'll be a few who'll object to working for a mix-blood Comanche. Some might quit or even try to cause trouble, but Lance can take care of himself. Always has." The foreman hesitated. "I guess I'm a lot more worried about Miss Amelia."

Summer frowned; she was worried about her sister as well. In the past few days, some of their neighbors had come to call, but Amelia had refused to see any of them, even the women who had been her closest friends. "What are people saying, Dusty?"

He looked down at his feet, as if reluctant to meet her eyes. "They feel sorry for her, I reckon. But nobody blames her for what happened."

"They wouldn't dare say it to her face, at any rate," Summer said sadly.

Dusty abruptly raised his head, his usually calm blue eyes

suddenly blazing. "They do and I'll beat the livin' daylights out of 'em."

Summer was a bit surprised to hear the easygoing ranch foreman champion her sister so vehemently, and even Dusty seemed embarrassed by his outburst. His ears turned red, and he tugged on his hat, pulling it way down over his eyes as he squinted off in the distance.

"Well, anybody would," he mumbled, before he excused himself, saying he had work to do.

Summer sighed. She would have to deal with Amelia's problems eventually, but right now Lance deserved her concern more. She had won Reed's and Dusty's support to involve him more in the workings of the ranch. There remained only to convince Lance to agree—which might indeed be the hardest part. She ought to be able to charm any man into doing her bidding, but her husband was not just any man.

A short while later she found Lance out back of their cabin, where he was chopping a load of firewood he'd brought in off the range. He was shirtless, exposing a great deal of bronzed skin glistening with sweat, and the sight brought Summer up short. Lance was hard, uncompromising male, and she was always exquisitely conscious of being female when he was near—and yet just now she was shocked by the sudden surge of desire that streaked through her.

Right then Lance looked up and smiled at her, his teeth flashing white in his harsh face, as if he was glad to see her. Summer felt raw color rush to her cheeks. She had never been overly concerned with propriety, but still, it wasn't proper to feel such fierce lust for one's husband.

She had brought him a dipper of water from the spring, which he accepted gratefully. When he'd finished drinking, though, she didn't leave. Instead she settled herself on a log.

"Something wrong, princess?"

"No, I just wanted to talk to you."

He turned back to his work. "What about?"

For a moment she didn't reply. Fascinated, she watched the powerful play of sleek muscles moving in his shoulders and chest as he swung the axe. His rib injury had improved enough so that the bandage covered only the healing flesh, held on by sticking plaster.

"Summer?"

Flushing, she made herself remember what she had come here for. "About your taking over my part of the ranch. I've discussed it with Reed, and he's amenable to you starting right away."

His harsh features had suddenly gone expressionless. "You can tell your brother I don't want his charity."

"It isn't charity, Lance. When you married me, my interest in the ranch became yours. And besides, Reed *needs* you."

A snort of disbelief was Lance's only answer.

"He *does,*" Summer insisted. "You know Reed is crippled. He can't even manage to sit a riding horse, much less break in a wild mustang. Not only are you more mobile, but your skill with horses is unequaled. And there's more than enough work for both of you to handle. Reed can manage the books like he's been doing, while you supervise the range work. I expect he'll be grateful for your help, but even if he's not, *I* will. The ranch hasn't operated at even a quarter of its capacity in years, but with you here, we can build it back up."

"I think you're forgetting one thing, princess. Your drovers aren't gonna take orders from a breed."

"You're wrong," Summer said triumphantly. "I've already spoken to Dusty about it, and he's more than willing—and he thinks the others will be, too. You've earned their respect, whether you wanted it or not."

He turned to eye her with a smoldering gaze, but he didn't answer.

Rising to her feet, Summer placed her hands on her hips. At the same time her mouth curved in a provocative smile, while her tone turned teasing. "What are you going to do if you don't take over the ranch? If you think you can just laze around the cabin all day, Lance Calder, you can think again. You may be a hero, but you still have earn your keep."

His brows drew together. "I may be a *what?*"

"A hero." Summer smiled smugly as she sauntered over to him. "Dusty says everyone thinks you're one for rescuing Amelia. And frankly, so do I."

A muscle twitched warningly in his jaw as he stared down at her. "Flattery isn't going to work on me, Summer."

"No? Then will you tell me what will?" She smiled coaxingly, which only brought an answering scowl to Lance's features. She took a step closer. "Reed is waiting in his study to talk to you about the arrangements."

"You're forgetting another thing, aren't you? Your sister won't let me in the house."

"I haven't forgotten. But Amelia is likely to be asleep. And even if she's not, Reed won't let her interfere with something this important. Won't you at least speak to him, Lance?"

Her sweet, wheedling tone could make him forget his own name, but this time it only served to stiffen his resolve. She was the perfect coquette, confident of her power, certain of her allure, damn her. It was all he could do to resist. "Dammit, Summer . . . . quit trying to work your blasted wiles on me. It's not going to work. I'm not some tame pansy you can ride herd on."

"Gracious, I never thought you were, not for a single, solitary instant, I promise." Reaching up, she wrapped her arms around his neck. "Will you at least *talk* to Reed before you say no?"

He held his head away and glowered at her.

"What can I do to convince you?" she asked softly.

"You might try honesty instead of your female tricks."

"I tried that, Lance. I've persuaded . . . I've pleaded . . . I've used reason. But you're so muleheaded and proud that nothing works." Her smile took the sting out of her accusation. "All I have left is feminine wiles."

He muttered a curse under his breath, but he could feel himself weakening. "I don't suppose you can help it," he said grudgingly. "Playing the flirt comes as natural to you as breathing."

Summer pouted attractively. "That certainly isn't very complimentary."

"You don't need compliments, princess. What you need is a good paddling."

"Lance . . . shame on you! You wouldn't raise a hand to a lady, would you?"

Her dancing emerald eyes told him very clearly she knew she had won—and so did he, though he didn't want to admit it.

With a harsh jerk, he hauled her against his body. "Maybe I would. Just don't push me too far."

She could smell his skin, smell the dust and sweat and heat of him, and she wanted more. Raising her lips to his, she tried with a sweet caress to draw his anger from him. Her tactic succeeded . . . partially. Only somehow Lance turned the tables on her, and it was she who found herself trembling and on the defensive. She drowned in the dark seizure of his kiss, and knew a profound disappointment when he abruptly let her go.

"Now, get the hell out of here before I forget it's broad daylight."

"Broad daylight never stopped you before," Summer murmured wickedly, and laughingly scurried out of his way when he pretended to lunge after her. "I'll tell Reed you're coming after you finish here."

She wanted to be there during their discussion, but she knew her presence would be unwise. Her husband and her brother needed to come to know each other without her interference, and to realize they needed each other. She hadn't lied about that. Reed did urgently require help with the ranch, even if he wasn't willing to admit his limitations. And Lance needed to be accepted into the family, without feeling like he was surrendering his manhood by taking charity. He needed the responsibility and challenge that running an operation like Sky Valley afforded. And he needed to believe the Westons trusted him to oversee such an endeavor. Her husband was a strong, proud man, too proud to walk in anyone's shadow— and special tact was required in handling him.

Remembering Lance's capitulation just now Summer felt her mouth curve in a self-congratulatory smile. Finally, after all this time, it seemed she was learning how.

The interview with Reed was as uncomfortable as Lance knew it would be. He hated coming hat in hand like some beggar looking for a handout. And so when he was shown into the parlor that was Reed's combination study/bedchamber, he refused to remove his hat at all, and he remained standing, even when Reed politely offered him a seat in front of the large oaken desk. His stance exuded belligerence, and his expression might have been carved in stone, so stiff were his facial muscles. He knew it, and yet didn't attempt to change it. Instead he said through gritted teeth, "Summer asked me to talk to you."

Reed's blue eyes surveyed him coolly. "I know. She asked the same of me."

"So talk."

"You aren't going to make this easy for me, are you?"

"Should I? I don't recall you Westons ever making anything easy for me. Fact is, I distinctly remember your pa trying to make my life hell."

Reed sighed. "I know. And I'm sorry for that. But I'm not my pa." When Lance remained stubbornly silent, he ran a hand roughly through his dark hair. "All right. I'll just spit it out. My sister made a contract with you, and I feel obligated to honor it."

"You're gonna let me into the Weston family, is that it? You're going to let your sister stay married to a breed?"

"Actually, I don't have any say in the matter. Summer is of age. She makes her own decisions. I can't say I like it, but it's done. You're her husband now."

"She's likely to be shunned by all your fancy friends, staying married to me. Nobody around here is likely to accept me as a social equal."

"Probably not. But there's not much I can do about that—except stand by her. If we stick together, then perhaps we can keep the wolves at bay. I'm not without influence in this county, despite my Union sympathies. I can have a talk with the ranchers in the area . . . try to encourage them to accept you."

"You're willing to stick your neck out for me? Why the hell should you do that?"

Summer's brother ground his teeth. "Because I'm a man of my word, for one thing. And I would be doing it for Summer as much as you. If they accept you, they'll accept her. And last—most of all—because I owe it to you both for what you did for Amelia."

Lance still didn't believe Reed was willing to accept him as a brother-in-law, and a devil drove him to press the point. "I can't give her all this." He waved a hand, indicating the luxury that surrounded him. "I can't support her in the manner she's accustomed to."

"None of us can have what we're accustomed to," Reed retorted with a bitterness Lance recognized. "The war saw to that."

"Summer said the ranch was part hers," Lance said finally, his lips stiff.

"Yes. Which means it now belongs to you, too. You can

have your share now, if you want, but I'd rather . . . It would be better to keep the place together."

"Better for who?"

"Perhaps for both of us. Certainly for the ranch."

Lance stared coolly.

"The fact is, I can't . . . I'd be obliged if you'd lend me a hand." When Lance continued silent, he lost his temper. "Look, dammit, I don't like this any better than you do, Calder. I didn't like being beholden to you for saving my sister, and I sure as hell don't like being in this position. It galls me to have to ask for help. But Summer's right. I can't continue to manage the place alone. The ranch will only continue to go downhill if I try."

"Seems to me Summer did well enough by herself during the war."

"Perhaps so, but she says she won't do it any longer, that it's your place now. Besides, she's a woman. She wasn't brought up to ride the range and supervise an operation of this size. I can't do it myself now, either, with only one goddamned leg."

"What about your foreman?"

"Dusty's a good man. And we've got good hands. Summer made do with the vaqueros during the war, and since then we've hired more men to build up the operation—Sky Valley is nothing like it was when my father was alive. But hired hands can't make the thousands of decisions that make the difference over the long haul between a first-class ranch and a run-down one. They don't care about this place, not like an owner would." He held Lance's dark gaze. "You're part owner now. You have a say in how Sky Valley is run. So what do you say?"

"You really want my help on the ranch?" Lance asked slowly, as if still not believing.

"Yes, I really want it. I mean it when I say I'd be grateful to be relieved of some of the burden."

"So . . ." Lance took a slow breath, finding it hard after all the years of being an outcast to commit his trust. "What needs doing?"

Reed's mouth curved in a rueful smile. "The most pressing is to round up several hundred head of the least valuable horses and sell them before winter sets in. There won't be enough grazing to support all the herds once the grass goes dormant. And they'll need to be broken to saddle if we're to get the best price. Can you see to all that?"

It was Lance's turn to break into a grin. "With one hand tied behind my back."

"Would you like to shake on our new partnership?"

For a long moment, Lance looked at the hand Reed had stretched out to him. And then slowly he reached across the desk and clasped it with a firm grip. "To our partnership," he replied solemnly.

Reed relaxed visibly. "I'd say this calls for a drink to celebrate. You prefer whiskey or brandy?"

The result of their interview gratified Summer. Reed and Lance settled into a truce of sorts, apparently willing to let bygones be bygones. It was awkward at first, and a bit uneasy because of their past relationship, but Summer held out the hope that from partners, the two men eventually might become friends.

Amelia showed no sign of relenting, however, much to Summer's sorrow. She scarcely spoke to Summer when their paths crossed, and looked at her as if she considered her a traitor. The night Reed invited Summer and Lance up to the big house for dinner, Amelia stayed in her room. And the following afternoon, when Summer found her crying in the kitchen, she wouldn't accept consolation or comfort.

Otherwise, Lance seemed to be fitting in fairly well as the new boss. As Dusty had predicted, a few of the hands quit outright, but the others were willing to give him a chance, and the Mexican vaqueros seemed pleased to be working with a man of Lance's knowledge and skill.

That he was skilled with the horses, no one could dispute, and he more than proved his worth in the roundups.

"You ought to see how he breaks those mustangs, Miss Summer," Dusty told her a few days later. "He downright charms 'em. It's a sight to watch."

"I'd like to see it," she agreed, warmed to have someone finally appreciating Lance for his abilities rather than condemning him for the copper color of his skin.

She rode out with Dusty that afternoon to the north end of the valley, and found a ridge where she could watch without getting in the way. In the distance she could see where the vaqueros had constructed a wide-mouthed corral of brush and post oak timbers near a watering hole and had driven part of the herd inside.

The wild mustang was a tough, wiry, mobile animal, smaller than the warm-blooded American horses of the East, and more ungainly, but with great endurance and the ability to subsist on grass and cover great distances between water holes. John Weston's strategy for the ranch had always been to encourage selective breeding, maintaining the best qualities of the mustang stock but adding the thoroughbred traits of beauty and speed. More than a few of these wild mustangs joined Sky Valley's herds each year and had to be culled out so as not to dilute the bloodlines and contribute to overgrazing.

Summer watched at a distance as Dusty explained what was happening. Lance, mounted on his sorrel gelding, a coiled lasso on his arm, entered the corral and rode through the restless herd. When he picked the horse he wanted, he and the other vaqueros drove it away from the band and back through the opening in the fence, which was quickly closed. Then the chase began, Lance alone following the racing mustang over the valley.

"It won't be long now," Dusty said confidently from beside her. "And you'll get a better view. They're headed this way."

True enough, the galloping pair had moved close enough for Summer to see the flecks of foam on the horses' coats. After a mile or so, when the mustang was weary and blowing hard, Lance uncoiled the thong of braided rawhide and flung the lasso noose over its neck, choking off its breath. Immediately he dismounted, running with the animal, holding the rope taut as he ran.

Moments later the horse fell to the ground for want of breath. Lance advanced slowly, keeping the lasso tight, till he could fasten a pair of hobbles on the animal's forelegs and slip a noose around the underjaw. Then he loosened the rope so it could breathe.

The dazed animal struggled to its feet, and having gotten its breath, began a desperate effort at escape, rearing and plunging and whirling till it was covered with foam.

Finally, at last, the mustang's power was exhausted and it stood trembling and wild-eyed. Lance advanced hand over hand toward the horse's head. From her position, Summer couldn't hear what he was saying, but she knew it must be something and that his low murmurings obviously had a calming effect. The mustang stood obediently as Lance gently placed his hand first on the horse's nose, then over its eyes.

"What is he doing?" she asked Dusty curiously when he saw man and horse standing nose to nose.

"Breathing in its nostrils. It's the darnedest thing you ever saw. Watch and you'll see what I mean."

Bending down, Lance carefully removed the hobbles. Then catching a handful of mane, he swung himself gently up on the animal's back. The mustang moved off without protest, as docile as a lamb.

"See? And it doesn't break the mustang's spirit. We'll keep it tied to a gentle mare for a few days, and give it a lot of handling. Then one of our boys will be able to break it to saddle without much trouble. We already have two dozen green-broke horses like that ready for market, thanks to Lance. Come on, let's go meet him."

He led Summer down off the ridge, while down below, some of the vaqueros assumed control of the mustang and returned Lance's sorrel to him. Lance must have spied her, Summer realized, for he turned and rode directly toward her. When he reached her, Dusty excused himself, giving them some privacy.

Lance looked tough and supremely masculine with his black hair drenched in sweat and plastered to his skull, and streaks of dust lining his face, she thought. He also looked guarded as his dark eyes surveyed her warily. "Something wrong, princess?"

Summer smiled demurely as she offered him water from a canteen. "Why do you always thing something's wrong whenever I come out to see you?"

"I guess I still think of you as being too fancy to get your fine clothes dirty, coming near us filthy hands."

Since she was wearing a brown calico gown that had seen far better days, she wasn't particularly worried about her clothes. And besides, the war had done a lot to change what she considered important in life. Pretty, smudgeless dresses were no longer very high on the list.

"Gracious, Lance. I grew up on this ranch—with three brothers, no less. I'm entirely accustomed to dirty men, including you. And you're no longer a hired hand. You're the boss, remember?"

He ignored her last remark. "Why'd you come, Summer?"

"I told you, I wanted to see you. Actually I wanted to see you ride. Dusty said it was fascinating watching you break a mustang, and it was. I've never seen anything so incredible. And I'm not trying to flatter you either, Lance Calder! You're proud enough as it is. You don't need your ego puffed up. However did you learn to handle horses that way?"

Her gentle teasing combined with her frank curiosity disarmed him, Summer thought. He still looked wary, as if he couldn't quite accept her reasoning, but he gave her a half smile that was a bit rueful and self-consciously pleased. "The Comanches taught me, but I've always had a knack with horses."

"Well, it certainly is impressive. And productive. Dusty says we wouldn't be half as far along if it weren't for you."

"Maybe," Lance replied modestly.

Summer flashed him an arch smile. "I'm glad it's working out so well, your taking over here. I don't suppose I need to say I told you so?"

"No, you don't," Lance retorted with a mock growl. He glanced over his shoulder. "I need to go. The boys will be waiting for me."

"All right. I need to get back to my own work, anyway. I'll have supper waiting for you when you get home. Pedro caught some bass in the creek, and I thought I might fry it, if that's okay with you?"

Lance's mouth curved dryly. "Are we having rocks or biscuits to go with it?"

Summer flushed. She'd forgotten to put any yeast in the biscuits she'd made for breakfast two days ago, and they'd turned out as hard as granite. "I thought I would heat up some stones from the creek and see if you could tell the difference."

To her surprise, Lance threw back his head and laughed, a deep, rusty laugh that caught at her heart. It pleased her that he could laugh like that, that he could share the humor of her mistake. It gave her a comfortable, pleasant, *warm* feeling to know she had given him some pleasure in his hitherto cheerless life.

She said good-bye and, accepting one of the armed vaqueros as escort, rode back to the ranch, feeling content and satisfied with her progress. She had tried to carry through with her promise to make her marriage to Lance work, and her success buoyed her spirits.

Her return home, however, forcibly reminded Summer just how unfounded her optimism was. When she rode into the yard, having dismissed her escort to return to his work, she discovered, to her surprise and dismay, a visitor she'd never expected. Will Prewitt, one of the neighboring ranchers who'd been so offensive to Lance last month when they'd met to discuss Amelia's rescue, was just mounting up.

The look he gave her as he addressed her held insolence and smug contempt. "I hear tell you went and married yourself to our resident Injun, Miss Summer."

Summer stiffened at his rude tone. She had temporarily forgotten the world beyond Sky Valley and how unfavorably it would view her marriage to Lance. She wanted to tell Prewitt to mind his own business, but it would do no good to respond with ire. Grinding her teeth, she forced herself to smile sweetly. "I am now Mrs. Lance Calder, yes. Have you come to congratulate us on our marriage, Mr. Prewitt?"

He snorted. "Not hardly." He moved his horse closer to hers, giving her a leer that made her skin crawl. "What's a pretty lady like you want with a stinkin' breed?" His voice lowered suggestively. "You like it rough, do you? If you were so hot for it, you should've come to a real man."

She gasped at his crudity, while her chin snapped up. "You are disgusting, sir! I'll thank you to go. And to keep off Sky Valley land in future."

His grin made a mockery of her indignation. "All hoity-toity, ain't you? Seems mighty odd for a squaw to be putting on airs."

"Get out of here!" Summer said through gritted teeth. "Before I call someone to teach you some manners."

"I reckon I got a right to visit here. Your sister sent for me."

"Amelia?" The revelation shocked her. Two years ago Amelia wouldn't have given a man like Prewitt the time of day, and that was before her ordeal. If her sister couldn't bear to be near men now, why had she chosen to invite this trash to be her first caller? There had to be some mistake. "I don't believe you," Summer said flatly.

"Oh, yeah, Miss Amelia asked me to call," Prewitt said with a secret glee. "You just go ask her."

"I intend to!" Summer said tightly. "In the meantime, I suggest you leave. I assure you, you don't want to be here when Lance returns from the range."

"I ain't afraid o' no half-breed Injun," he retorted defiantly, but he glanced over his shoulder all the same. Not seeing anyone around, he tipped his hat to her, the epitome of mockery. "You tell your sister good day for me." Turning his horse toward the road, he spurred it into a lope.

Summer stared after him a long moment before she forced herself to dismount. She wasn't surprised to find herself shaking; she had known she would be subjected to scorn and contempt because she was Lance's wife. Her only surprise was that Amelia had wanted to speak to someone like Prewitt. She couldn't imagine what her sister had been thinking.

Knowing she had to talk to Amelia, Summer put up her horse and then went in search of her. She found her sister in the front parlor, rocking herself slowly in the wooden rocker while she hummed tunelessly to herself. How many countless hours had they spent here together when they were younger, working samplers and mending clothing while Amelia lectured her on manners and ladylike behavior?

"Melly," Summer began uncertainly. "Are you all right?"

"Oh, yes, I'm fine."

"I just saw Will Prewitt out in the yard. Did you really invite him to visit?"

"Yes, I asked him here." Amelia's lips curved in a secretive smile that Summer didn't understand at all, and that worried her no small amount.

"Why?"

"That really is none of your business, is it?"

"Melly . . ." Summer faltered, not knowing how to get through to her sister. This cold, bitter creature was a stranger to her, nothing like the strong, generous-hearted woman who had raised her, whom Summer had cherished like a mother. "Do you know he insulted me?"

"Did he? Well, I expect you'll just have to live with it. You brought it on yourself, after all, marrying that savage."

She wanted to protest the unfairness of her sister's accusation, but she suspected it would be futile. And Amelia's next words sent her thoughts spinning along another track.

"I'm not pregnant."

"I'm glad for you, Amelia," Summer said slowly.

"Yes, you can't know what a relief it is, knowing I won't have to bear a bastard redskin. I only hope you're as lucky."

Involuntarily Summer's hand went to her abdomen. She had refused to let herself think too much about that complication. She wasn't certain she was strong enough to withstand the tribulations she would face as the wife of a half-breed, let alone the implications of bringing an innocent, defenseless child into the world to brave the same adversity. No child deserved the fate Lance had endured.

When she remained silent, Amelia leaned her head back and shut her eyes. "Now if you would only get rid of that terrible man."

"What man?"

"Why, that disgusting half-breed, of course."

"Melly ... I've told you before, Lance is my husband. I can't go back on my word."

"You could if you wanted to." Amelia looked at Summer directly for the first time, her eyes filling with tears. "I can't bear him, don't you see? He'll always be a reminder of what happened to me."

"Amelia ..." Her sister's plea raked her heart, but she couldn't give in. "I'm sorry, but ... Lance is a good man. I won't betray my vows to him." Her own voice quivered. "Please, don't make me choose between the two of you."

Amelia rose regally to her feet. "I think you've already chosen, Summer. It's certain you're no longer my sister."

She swept from the parlor in a rustle of black skirts, leaving Summer to sink unsteadily onto the chintz-covered settee.

That Amelia considered her a traitor made her heart ache, in addition to rendering her resolve to honor her marriage vows that much harder to keep.

And yet, as she'd told Amelia, she had no choice in the matter. She had made a bargain with Lance, and she owed it to him to keep up her end.

Chapter 19

S he didn't tell Lance of the incident with Prewitt, knowing it would have aroused her husband's dangerous temper. And two mornings later, she was glad she hadn't, since it would have spoiled a beautiful day.

She was in bed, fast asleep, dreaming of nothing in particular, when a warm, suggestive voice murmured in her ear, "Wake up, your highness." Strong arms slipped about her waist, dragging her flush against a male body.

"Lance?" she mumbled, reluctant to leave her comfortable nest.

"Who else? Come on, sleepyhead, open your eyes."

Obeying, she blinked at the bright sunlight streaming through the open shutter. "What time it is?"

"Early. Now, wake up."

The smell of fresh coffee filled the cabin, and when she sat up, she saw that Lance was fully dressed in denims and chambray shirt. It was Sunday, she remembered, brushing her hair out of her eyes. "We're not going to church, are we?" Her family used to attend a Methodist church service near Round Rock at the home of one of the ranchers, but she hadn't dared face the outside world yet, and she hadn't thought Lance would ever wish to.

He grinned. "Nope. We're going for a ride. You have five minutes to get ready."

"A ride? But . . . have you forgotten that Reed invited us to Sunday dinner this afternoon?"

"Nope. We'll be back before then. Now, get going."

He gave her mouth a quick, hard kiss and her fanny a gentle swat, but Summer could only stare at him. Lance had an air of eagerness about him that she had never seen before, almost like a little boy with a secret—although she couldn't imagine that he had truly ever been a little boy.

It was only when he stripped her of her warm covers that Summer at last obeyed. Her curiosity aroused, she shrugged off the last dregs of sleep and climbed out of bed.

He had fixed a picnic breakfast, she realized once she had washed and dressed and drunk a hasty cup of coffee. And he had saddled their horses in preparation for a long ride.

The early morning sparkled. The October air was chilly and crisp, with a vast blue sky overhead. They rode west through the valley, across dew-covered meadows glinting with sunshine, while all around them stood rugged hills, studded with stands of post oak and evergreen cedar brakes.

Summer reveled in the beauty. On such a day she could forget any worry she'd ever had, any thought of war and pain, prejudice and despair. All she had to do was close her eyes and put her head back to let the gentle breeze blow her memories away.

Lance seemed to share the sentiment. His gaze traveled over the land, drinking in the sight, his expression silently declaring his pleasure.

He led her up a steep incline, to a ridge where the ground flattened out and the view was spectacular. Down below they could see much of the huge Weston spread, and the flying herds of horses whose hooves beat out a song.

Summer suspected Lance had brought her here for a purpose, and she wasn't wrong. Resting his forearm on his saddle horn, he pointed to the east, down in the valley, perhaps a mile or so this side of the main buildings.

"See that bend in the creek? That's where I'm going to build our house," he said in a low voice.

Caught by surprise, Summer parted her lips to issue a protest—but then she thought better of it. The cabin where they lived now was adequate for *her* needs, but perhaps not for her husband's. A man as proud as Lance would chafe at being unable to provide his wife with her customary standards of wealth and luxury, even if she would be satisfied with far less.

"It's perfect," she murmured quite truthfully.

He had chosen a beautiful site, and practical as well. The great cottonwoods and pecans that lined the creek would provide shade in the heat of summer, and shelter against the fierce northers that swept off the plains, while the surrounding pastures would provide lush grass for grazing their livestock. In spring those meadows would be carpeted with wildflowers—bluebonnets and Indian paintbrush, wine-cups and goldenrod and wild verbena.

The setting presented so pristine a picture that Summer could imagine what her parents had felt, arriving as some of the first Texas settlers to carve a way of life out of the wilderness. And in a way, that was what she and Lance were. They would have to carve their own place in the valley, make their own life together.

"Think Reed'll mind if we claim that piece of land for our own?"

"No. I think he'll be pleased you finally want something. He's been fretting to repay you for all the help you've given him." And her sister would be glad to see them move farther away, Summer added silently to herself.

"I hope to start the foundation next week. I thought maybe I could work on it a few hours each day, in between rounding up mustangs. I'll send to Austin for supplies."

She considered asking Lance if they could afford building a house just now, after all the money he'd spent buying horses to compensate his brother, but she figured he might take offense. Besides, he was unlikely to propose such a grandiose scheme without considering the cost.

She allowed Lance to help her dismount and then spread the blanket he'd brought over a patch of grass while he hobbled the horses. The fare she found in his saddlebags was simple but delicious—apples and sausage and a loaf of wheat bread he said he'd persuaded Estelle to bake for them. They joked about Summer's cooking and then hungrily devoured the meal.

When they were done, Lance lay back on the blanket, one arm behind his head, as he gazed up at the warming sky. Summer, who sat beside him with her chin resting on her updrawn knees, thought she had never seen him so at ease with himself, so carefree.

"This reminds me of when I was a kid in my father's camp," he said wistfully after a long, comfortable moment of silence. "He would take me hunting sometimes . . . partly to show me how to survive in the wild, but mostly to teach me about the spirits that dwell in the rocks and trees and especially the animals. He would make me sit still for hours while I tried to feel them."

Summer eyed Lance curiously. "Do you miss that life?"

He thought about the question. A part of him would always be Comanche. Like them, he understood the craving for freedom. Away from them, he felt tied down by too many restrictions, still felt a restlessness that his civilized life couldn't satisfy. And yet he was too civilized really to be one of them. Sometimes when he thought about his years with the Comanche, when he remembered the times he'd gone against every stricture his mother had taught him, he winced. He'd done things she wouldn't have been proud of. Things he wasn't proud of himself.

"Sometimes," he said finally.

Another moment passed before Summer realized he had turned his head and was watching her.

"I guess I owe you an apology, princess," he began in a low voice. "I didn't really think you would honor our marriage vows."

Summer went still, not knowing quite how to reply to his solemn admission. She thought she knew what it cost Lance to admit he was wrong—but perhaps it was wiser not to make too much of it.

Impudently Summer wrinkled her nose at him, forcing a light reply. "Well, at least you admit now that you misjudged me."

"I didn't make it very easy for you."

"That you didn't."

"I guess I'm not used to this husband business. It'll take some time, I reckon."

Summer smiled. "I'm not exactly accustomed to being a wife, either."

"I have something for you," he said quietly as he reached in his vest pocket. When she looked at him questioningly, he handed her a small leather pouch. "I never gave you a real wedding ring, so maybe this will do."

Inside was a small seed pearl mounted on a thin band of silver. "It belonged to my mother."

"Oh, Lance, it's lovely."

"It isn't much—"

"Oh, but it *is.*" Slipping it on her left ring finger to find it a perfect fit, Summer held out her hand to admire the delicate filigree mounting. Strangely, his gift pleased her far more than any expensive jewelry could have done, for it meant Lance might finally be coming to trust her, at least a little, if he was willing to part with a ring that, while not worth much in monetary terms, had profound sentimental value to him. "I shall cherish it. I know how much your mother meant to you."

"Yeah. She did," he responded gruffly.

Reaching out, he took Summer's hand, his fingers closing tightly around hers. She saw a softness in his hard face that she'd never seen before. She felt the callused skin of his palm, strong as leather, warm against her own, as he slowly drew her down to him for his kiss.

The careful brush of his mouth caught her off guard. Surprisingly, there was nothing lustful about his caress. Instead it was a mingling of quiet breath, a tentative exploration. She tasted uncertainty, a mute questioning, as if all his defenses were down and he were lying bare a vulnerable and lonely soul.

It made her feel oddly humble, having this wary, mistrustful man open himself to her.

When he pulled her down beside him, Summer went willingly. He tucked her against his body, her head on his shoulder, as if he simply wanted to share the closeness. As if he wanted to hold and be held. She knew that need. There had been countless times during the past five years when she'd longed for someone to turn to, to lean on and help lessen the pain, a compatriot in the struggle merely to get through each day.

And perhaps that was what Lance really needed from her, after all. He had claimed he wanted a wife who could help him become a respected member of the community, but perhaps what he wanted was more basic, more essential. What he wanted, what he needed, was acceptance of the most elemental kind: the simple human warmth he had never had except from his mother and his Comanche family.

They rode home reluctantly, not eager to spoil the intimacy of the day, and discovered an unexpected visitor awaiting them in the stable yard. Summer tensed when she spied the man standing beside her brother, dreading another encounter with Will Prewitt, but relaxed as soon as she realized the visitor was much taller and bulkier than Prewitt.

Harlan Fisk, their closest neighbor and owner of one of the largest cattle ranches in the area, had been a good friend of her father's, as well as one of the countless malleable, soft-hearted males to spoil John Weston's youngest daughter rotten. Summer had always liked him, and not just because he let her have her way.

Harlan greeted her now with a fond smile, although the glance that flickered over Lance was less welcoming as he dismounted and helped Summer down.

"There you are," Reed said jovially. "I didn't know where you'd gone, so I couldn't say when you'd be back."

"Lance was showing me the site for our new house he means to build," Summer replied purposefully, determined to show their guest her solidarity with her husband.

Her brother raised an eyebrow, but didn't follow up on the opening. "Lance, you know Harlan Fisk. Harlan rode over to welcome you to the neighborhood."

Immediately the man stepped forward, his hand outstretched. "Hello, son."

His face shuttered, Lance stared down at the proffered hand. "You want to welcome me?"

Summer drew a sharp breath at his hesitation, but Harlan had obviously been expecting it, for he didn't seem to take offense. "Yes, that, and to say thank you for getting our Miss Amelia back. I want you to know how grateful I am—we all are. You took on a job that none of the rest of us had the gumption to face."

Stubbornly he kept his hand out, and Lance seemed to sense a determination as strong as his own. Warily he extended his hand, which the other man shook firmly.

"Nice to have you as a new neighbor, Calder."

Disbelief in his expression, Lance nodded carefully.

Reed cleared his throat. "Harlan and his wife plan to hold a barbecue next Saturday, and he brought our invitations personally."

"Why, Harlan, how thoughtful!" Summer said brightly, thinking it was time she intervened. "A barbecue! What a

splendid idea. I'm certain we would be delighted to attend."
Stepping forward, she stood on tiptoe to kiss him on the
cheek.

"Amelia is to be the guest of honor," Reed told his sister.

"Oh?" Summer said in surprise. "Melly really means to
leave the house?"

"She says no," Harlan replied, "but I hope she'll change
her mind."

With a smile, Summer took the older man's arm. Steering
him toward his horse, she asked after his wife, Becky, and
stood chatting with him for a moment, answering his concerned questions about the difficulty they'd had rescuing
Amelia.

By the time he mounted his horse and rode off, both her
husband and brother had disappeared into the barn to unsad-
dle the horses.

Or rather, Reed was leaning on his crutches, watching
Lance do the work. When Summer joined them, Reed handed
her the invitation, which had been written on expensive
pressed paper.

"He really means to include Lance?" she asked skeptically.

"Yes. See, it specifically says Mr. and Mrs. Calder."

"Did you put him up to it?" Lance demanded, glancing
over his shoulder with narrowed eyes.

"I spoke to him last week, yes, and convinced him to give
you a chance. There's no one else in the county who could
do you more good. If it's seen that Harlan and his wife accept
you, you'll have won half the battle."

Lance didn't seem to appreciate the efforts on his behalf.
Instead his jaw had hardened in that stiff, belligerent way
Summer knew so well.

"It would be fun to go to a party," she acknowledged. "It's
been so long since we had much to celebrate. What about
you, Reed? Do you mean to go?"

Her brother gave her a grim smile. "Absolutely—although
I doubt I'll be much more welcome than Lance is, Union traitor that I am. But I have some fence mending to do. And I'll
have to escort Amelia, if she attends."

"Do you think she will?"

"I don't know. I'll do by darnedest to persuade her." Bal-
ancing on one crutch, he put his arm around Summer's shoul-

der and squeezed. "Come on, sis. Use your powers of persuasion to convince this ungrateful grizzly to accept Fisk's invitation. We'll all be outcasts together. Strength in unity and all that." Shifting his crutch back beneath his arm, he turned and hobbled away, calling over his shoulder, "I'll see you at dinner in a little while."

Alone with Lance, Summer watched him in silence, wondering exactly how far she could push him. His reaction to the invitation was as cynical as she'd expected, and just as bristling. When it came to dealing with whites, Lance was like a half-tame wolf, bearing his teeth and raising his neck fur, ready to attack before being attacked, hating to accept the slightest show of kindness, yet at the same time dependent on that very kindness. He had needed such defensive measures in dealing with a hostile white world till now, but it was time to lower his defenses and give people a chance to accept him.

"I think we should go," she said finally.

"Do you?" His tone was far from agreeable.

"Yes, I do. Reed was right. Harlan's support will make it much easier for others to accept you."

"You think anyone's going to welcome me just on his say-so?"

"Perhaps not, but they certainly won't if you don't try."

When Lance didn't answer, Summer bit her lip. She wouldn't use the argument that they should attend for Melly's sake. Lance had done more than enough for her sister, with too little thanks to show for it. Besides, she wanted him to go for his own sake. "Lance . . . please?"

A muscle clenched in his jaw at her pleading tone. "If you want to go so bad, then have your brother take you," he muttered.

Summer shook her head. "If you think I intend to face all those people alone, you're greatly mistaken. Reed was right about sticking together. We go as a family or not at all."

"Then we don't go."

"You're not afraid, are you?"

A spark of fury kindled in his eyes, but he didn't rise to the bait.

She tried a different tact. "Lance, it won't be so bad, truly; you'll see."

"For you, maybe. You're one of them." His mouth curled

at the corner. "But your neighbors sure as hell wouldn't agree with you. And I wouldn't want to spoil their fancy party."

"Stop that, Lance Calder!" Summer stamped her foot in irritation. "You're as good as any man in this state!"

His narrowed gaze fixed on her. "What does that have to say to anything? Red skin has a way of blinding people. To the upstanding citizens around here, I'll never be more than a breed."

"You could make them accept you. Prove to them you belong."

Not replying, he picked up a piece of burlap and began giving the horses a light rubdown.

Summer took a deep breath, prepared to toughen her arguments. "You married me to help you gain respectability. Well, this is your chance."

That brought absolutely no response.

She tried again. "If you turn your back on all our neighbors, they'll have no reason to welcome you. It will get awfully lonesome year after year, with no one to talk to, to share joys and sorrows with."

"I don't need them or their favors," he ground out, his voice rough with emotion.

"So you mean to remain an outcast all your life?"

"Maybe not, but I'll be damned if I'll grovel!"

His dark eyes glowered at her, fierce and smoldering, but Summer stood her ground. "Did I hear anyone ask you to grovel?" Before he could reply, she tossed her head. "All right, do as you like. But . . ." Her expression softened, as did her voice. "Do you really think it's fair to make me an outcast along with you?"

This time she didn't give him a chance to respond, but turned and left the barn, leaving Lance to stare after her.

It was a low blow, he thought, squeezing his eyes shut. His beautiful, manipulative temptress of a wife didn't need feminine wiles as long as she could play on his guilt. All Summer had to do was remind him of the difficult position he'd put her in by marrying her, and he felt like pond scum.

She was wrong about why he'd married her, though. He'd done it, not just because he wanted respectability, but because he loved her, because he'd seen a desperate chance to grab his dream and he'd taken it.

She was right, though, about his stiff-necked pride. He was too proud to let himself in for the reception he'd get if he went to her damned barbecue. Too proud to let Summer know how he felt about her. To let her see how much he wanted her— Hell, who was he kidding? The line had long ago vanished between what he wanted and what he needed. He needed her like the air he breathed.

She was right about him being afraid, too, but his fear wasn't really for him. He was afraid of how Summer would be received by their neighbors. He didn't want her to have to face what his mother had endured. At least here on the ranch she was surrounded by her family and hired help who loved her. He couldn't keep her safe forever, yet he owed it to Summer to make the effort. To make something of their marriage.

She sure had tried. She had done her best to hold up her end of the bargain. She'd proved as stubborn as she accused him of being, fighting to hold her family and ranch together, challenging him to take his rightful place as her husband and part owner of Sky Valley.

She'd denied him nothing, not even in bed. Sex with her had only grown in intensity and passion and boldness—and God help him, it had only made his need for her worse. His hunger for her body had only increased. He was aroused by nothing more than the straight, slender line of her back, or a careless smile sent his way.

And yet he wanted more than just her body. He wanted all of her. He wanted to know how she felt, what she thought, what she cared about. He wanted to learn about *her* hopes, *her* dreams.

And God knew he wanted to see her happy. She was far too serious since war and death had ripped her life apart. He wanted her back, the beautiful, vital girl he had fallen for so many years ago. He wanted to see her laughing and teasing and even flirting, just like the old Summer. *A party would make her happy.*

He had done little to make it easy for her up till now. But it wasn't too late. He could meet her halfway. He could try to give her reason to be, if not happy, then at least content with their marriage. Hell, he'd already planned to do just that. Just yesterday he'd vowed he would make an effort to change. He would do his damnedest to control his vicious temper, at least. And he would try to woo Summer with tenderness, if he could.

He knew she didn't love him—not yet, anyway. But maybe, one day, she might come to look upon their marriage as something other than an obligation she regretted.

An honorable man would have given her up before putting her through the hell she would face as his wife. But he couldn't make himself do it. He might as well cut out his heart while he was at it. Summer was the one thing in his life that was warm and real and made life worth living. When he held her in his arms, he could almost believe his dreams were in reach. A place of his own where he could do work he loved best. A wife who would stand by him. Acceptance by the white community. But more important than any of that, Summer. His Summer.

This morning, when he'd taken her to see the land where he hoped to build their house, he'd felt so close to achieving everything he wanted. For a few hours he had forgotten all the things that threatened him. His Comanche blood. Their neighbors. Her sister.

He could see the hurt in Summer's eyes whenever she thought of her sister. It was because of him that Amelia had turned against her. He only hoped to God his presence didn't cause a permanent break between them.

And if it did? Would Summer come to hate him for it?

He couldn't make himself think that far ahead.

Still, he had to decide how to answer her. What she wanted from him was simple enough. Take her to a barbecue. Endure the disdainful looks and maybe the slurs that were sure to greet him. Keep a tight rein on his temper, no matter what the provocation.

Simple enough.

Goddammit, he couldn't deny her this one thing.

With a curse at her blasted tactics, Lance turned the horses out in the corral and stalked over to their cabin. He found Summer in the bedroom, getting ready for Sunday dinner, pinning up her hair.

When she looked up, he spoke through clenched teeth. "I'll go to your damned party," he said grudgingly.

He was rewarded with the response he had longed to see.

Summer smiled—a smile so joyful, so radiant, it seemed the sun had suddenly broken through the clouds.

His pulse surging, Lance propped a shoulder against the doorframe, suddenly worried that his weakened knees might not support him.

Amelia didn't come down to dinner, her empty place a silent reminder of her revulsion for Lance. And yet the atmosphere around the elegant dining table was less strained than anyone expected. Summer provided a steady supply of cheerful conversation, Reed played the convivial host, and Lance dusted off his best manners and made a determined effort to respond in kind.

He answered guardedly when Reed questioned him about the house he meant to build, and was more than mildly surprised when the other man offered to work on the plans.

"I studied a little architecture before the war," Reed admitted somewhat sheepishly. "A hobby I indulged in."

"It was more than a hobby," Summer interjected, her tone warm with praise. "You should have seen his drawings, Lance. They were beautiful."

"Well, adequate perhaps," her brother countered modestly. "But it was something I loved. As the youngest son, I figured Ty and Jami could take over the ranch, but Pa was outraged that I might want to do something other than raise horses. Pa and I didn't agree on a lot, actually."

He looked directly at Lance, who understood the implied message: John Weston's deep prejudice was not his son's.

"If you know the kind of house you want, I could help with the design," Reed offered.

"I'd like that," Lance replied truthfully. "I know as much about building houses as a cotton planter knows about raising stock."

He found himself relaxing and letting down his guard, even when they discussed the price of such a venture. When Reed tactfully probed about how much he was willing to spend, Lance surprised himself by answering honestly.

"I don't have to worry much about the cost, not unless I try to pave the floor with gold. I made a lot of money selling mustangs over the years, and saved most of it." He glanced at Summer. "I never had anybody else to spend it on before."

"Do you mean to tell me I married a wealthy man?" she demanded, her green eyes dancing. "Shame on you, Lance, for keeping such a secret from me. I suppose you thought a princess like me would drive you into bankruptcy with her extravagant habits."

That she was teasing him was clear, but her tender smile puzzled him—until he figured out that she was simply glad he had finally shared something personal about himself. He had never made such an admission before, not even to the woman who was now his wife. He'd deliberately kept it from her, in fact. But Summer deserved to know he could support a wife, even if she had expensive habits.

Reed was watching them with a frown. "You told me just last week that you couldn't give her the luxuries she was accustomed to."

His mouth curved in a rueful grin. "Well, maybe I shaded the truth a bit."

"Which occurs frequently," Summer said in an arch tone. "Lance has the annoying practice of making himself seem less than he is. He doesn't *want* to convince anyone to think well of him, you see. What he really meant, though, is that he wants to be accepted for who he is, however rich or poor."

Black eyes locked with green in understanding, Lance's self-conscious and amazingly meek, Summer's smug and amused, as if she was pleased to have figured him out and determined to prevent him from using such tactics. It was an intimate moment, though, as comfortable as a worn moccasin, and one that satisfyingly lasted well into the evening.

Lance was also surprised a while later to find himself offering to fit a saddle for Reed to use comfortably with only one leg.

"I think you could ride well enough if you had a brace for your missing limb and a horse trained to respond to just one spur."

"Oh, I could probably ride," Reed responded with a bitterness he couldn't hide. "If I could get on. Mounting is what's nigh impossible."

"It'll be a problem," Lance agreed thoughtfully, "but we can figure out something."

They dined on fried chicken and sweet potatoes and gooseberry tarts, and then had coffee and brandy in the front parlor.

It had grown dark by the time Summer and Lance said goodnight and strolled silently the two hundred yards or so to their own cabin. Pale moonlight cast a gentle glow over the ranch buildings; a horse whickered in the corral as they passed.

Still acting the gentleman, Lance guided her through their front door and shut it softly behind them. By feel, Summer lit the lamp that sat just inside and then turned to look at him.

A long, quiet, sensually charged spell filled the silence.

Lance was lounging casually against the door panel, but his black eyes shone with a stark sultriness that was unmistakable.

"Come here," he murmured, roughly impatient.

When she moved into his arms, he bent his head at once, his mouth latching on to hers, his fingers laced behind her nape to hold her captive while his tongue thrust deep in a hungry claiming. This was the taste he'd needed, craved, all evening.

Summer felt the same craving. Eagerly she rubbed her body against him, feeling her nipples harden and the now familiar quickening between her legs.

To her surprise, though, Lance broke off the caress. With a questioning look, she led the way to their bedchamber, setting the lamp on the small table that served as a dressing table and writing desk. Removing the black knit shawl from around her shoulders, she folded it and stored it on a self inside the armoire. Lance was already pulling off his clothes and tossing them on the rocking chair that sat in one corner.

In only a moment he was naked, beautifully naked— wearing only a gauze bandage over his healing ribs that contrasted starkly with his bronzed skin. Summer drew a sharp breath, captivated by the beauty of his dark, sleek animal body illuminated in the lamp's glow. Just the sight of him made her own body tremble and grow heavy and sultry with wanting.

He caught her watching him, and his manhood reacted, filling, swelling, engorging, till it stood thick and rigid and ready.

He didn't offer to help her undress as a gentleman would. Instead he tossed back the covers of the rope bed and carelessly sat down, his shoulder propped against the headboard, one leg stretched out, the other foot resting on the wooden floor. His swollen shaft rose nearly straight up. Summer found she couldn't tear her eyes away; she could only remember the exquisite feel of that hard flesh moving inside her, impaling her, filling her, and she wanted to moan.

When finally she managed to look up, her gaze locked with Lance's, and time seemed to falter. She was aware of the most potent sense of anticipation she had ever felt.

"What are you waiting for, princess?" he murmured, his voice low and husky.

What indeed?

Her cheeks flushing, she unbuttoned the bodice of her gown with shaking fingers, aware that Lance was deliberately making it harder for her. He lay powerfully lithe on the bed as he watched her, his gaze hot and possessive.

With awkward haste, she removed her gown and petticoats and hung them in the armoire. Her underclothes followed, but she modestly kept her back to him, until Lance commanded softly, "Turn around. I want to see you."

Almost quivering, Summer obeyed. She could feel the slow, hot sweep of his gaze linger over her bare breasts, her belly, the juncture of her thighs.

"Take down your hair," Lance commanded.

Dazedly she raised her arms, her fumbling fingers searching for the pins. Finally free of restraint, the heavy mass fell down her back, and Summer distractedly raked the tangled locks through her fingers. Lance's heated look made the simple task somehow even more intimate than undressing before him.

He moved then. She heard the soft creak of the bed ropes as he rose, magnificent and virile, from the mattress. Her breath caught in her throat as he soundlessly crossed the floor to her. His harsh features dark with passion, he stood over her for a moment, his shining blue-black hair sweeping forward across his high cheekbones. To her bewilderment, though, he didn't kiss her or take her in his arms. Instead, he gently turned her around and pushed her down to sit on the stool before the dressing table.

She was aware of the cool polished oak surface against her bare buttocks, the radiant heat at her back as Lance moved behind her, the irregular thudding of her heart. In the mirror's golden reflection, she could see his arms come around her, feel his callused hands glide down her chest to cup the swollen mounds of her breasts.

The sight was keenly erotic: his hands dark and powerful against her pale jutting breasts, the nipples hard and distended as his thumbs flicked the aching peaks. The feeling was exquisite. Summer arched, shuddering, but his palms closed around her, holding her still.

The expression on his face was absorbed, focused, as he watched his ministrations, a man intent on giving pleasure, on seeing that his woman was pleased. His hands moved over her skin in a languid rhythm, stroking with delicacy, slowly rubbing her taut nipples between thumb and forefinger. Summer bit back a whimper at the lush heat that was swelling in her, at the delicious flush suffusing her body.

"I want you," he said softly, hoarsely.

She wanted him, too. Her woman's body craved the maleness of him.

But it seemed that Lance was in no hurry. In a moment, his hands relinquished their pressure, fell away from her breasts, leaving her skin chilled where his fiery hands had been. As if he had all the time in the world, he picked up the silver-backed brush from the table and, in a long, measured stroke, drew the bristles gently through her dark hair. An intimate act, leisurely and sensual. And yet incredibly erotic, too: such a feminine, servile task performed by such a virile, independent man.

His slow, rhythmic motions were quiet and gentle—and implausibly arousing. The languorous repetition of the brush should have lulled and soothed Summer, and yet it only built the rampant desire pulsing through her. Sensation seared along her nerves: the gentle tug against her scalp, the cool silkiness of her hair against her bare shoulders, the knowledge that Lance's hard, lean body was so close and yet so far away.

He seemed immune to her feverish need. He was studying her tresses with half-closed eyes, as if fascinated by the mahogany length. When several crackling strands tangled with his wrist, he loosened them with infinite care, as if handling something precious.

Watching the way his obsidian eyes softened, Summer

could almost believe he was two different men. One a dangerous warrior, defiant, unforgiving; the other a sensitive, sensual lover, eager to be tender.

Who taught you gentleness? Summer wondered. *How, with the brutal life you endured, did you ever, ever, manage to keep your humanity?*

"I love your hair," he murmured reverently. "I love the way it feels . . . like satin."

"Lance . . .?" she said breathlessly.

"Mmmm?"

"Do you think you could feel it later? After . . . ?"

He looked up then, met her gaze in the mirror. And smiled. Slowly he set the brush on the table. Placing his hands on her shoulders, he turned her on the seat so that she was facing him, one of his iron-muscled legs between her slender ones. His jutting arousal, darkly flushed and swollen with desire, was so close to her face that she could bend just a little and touch it with her lips, take it in her mouth. She wanted to—it shocked her how desperately she wanted to.

What would Lance do if she kissed him there? If he felt her mouth pressing against him? If she stroked him with her tongue, licking and caressing him the way he often did to her? Would he go wild the way she did when he put his mouth on her?

What would that heated, velvet-covered granite taste like? Like the rest of his skin? Like his tantalizing masculine scent, hot and musky, that surrounded her now, making her lightheaded with longing?

Only the long hours of training as a well-bred lady prevented Summer from acting out such wanton impulses. And Lance himself seemed to have other ideas.

"I love your breasts," he remarked almost casually as he reached down to stroke her. "I love the way they tighten up when I touch them." His palm was hot and rough, the callused skin rasping over her swollen nipples.

"Lance . . ." The word was a breathy whimper as she arched her back, pressing against his caressing hand.

"What, princess?"

"You're torturing me."

"Maybe so. Maybe I just want to make sure you're good and ready for me."

With thumb and forefinger he gently pinched her left nipple.

Summer gasped and quivered.

"Are you ready for me?"

His tone was quizzical, detached, almost amused, damn him. He knew she was ready, she thought dazedly. The hot scent of sexual arousal emanating from between her aching thighs had to tell him how much she wanted him.

"Touch yourself, and tell me if you're ready."

She shut her eyes at his brazen command.

When she hesitated, Lance reached down and closed his hand deliberately over hers, imprisoning her in his grasp. Gently, inexorably, he forced her fingers between her thighs, till they pressed against her woman's mound.

Summer shivered at the feverish rush of pleasure that flooded her senses.

"Touch yourself, princess. Tell me how it feels."

She obeyed, suddenly too aroused to care how scandalous her action might be. At his direction, she slid her finger through the heated dew gathered between her thighs, over the throbbing nub of her womanhood, and flinched at the powerful arrow of delight that shot through her.

"Tell me how it feels."

"G-Good."

"That's all? Only good?" The pressure of his cupping hand increased, sending streaking heat shuddering through her body.

"No . . . better?"

"Much better?"

"Yes . . ."

"Are you wet there?"

"Y-Yes . . ."

"Are you hot there?"

"Yes . . . !"

"Are you hot for me?"

"Yes . . . Lance!"

"Let me feel." He bent and dipped his finger into the spirals of dusky hair, finding her slick heat. Slowly, maddeningly, he rimmed the entrance to her body, circling, stroking her there with a leisurely, bewitching rhythm, till her breath shallowed and seemed to vanish. Then his finger entered her, impaling her lingeringly, thrusting unhurriedly within her.

A whimper dredged from her throat, Summer jerked and arched her hips, her inner muscles clenching instinctively around him. "Lance, please . . ." she panted.

"What do you want, princess?"

"I want you . . . please!"

He let her have what she wanted . . . partly. Clutching her hair with his free hand, he leaned close and kissed her in a hard, sensual caress, his lips moving roughly over hers while his fingers plied her throbbing depths. The combination left her half-dazed with hunger.

She had had enough of games, though, no matter how intoxicating. Nearly desperate, Summer reached blindly out to curve her moist fingers around his thrusting manhood. A flaring sense of excitement and triumph claimed her when she heard his sharp rasp of breath. Lance wasn't nearly as cool and detached as he would have her believe. His body had gone rigid, while his eyes kindled like twin coals.

She could feel him pulsing and burning in her hand. Her heart hammering in her breast, Summer squeezed her fingers lightly, delicately, around his blatant erection. If he wouldn't end his sensual torture, she would make certain he endured a similar agony.

Lance's face twisted in a grimace of fierce pleasure at her startling touch. For an instant he thrust his throbbing shaft against her sheathing grasp, straining against the jolt of sensation so strong, it made him shudder. Yet he wouldn't, couldn't, allow her to do more.

Gritting his teeth against the surge of need, he abruptly pulled away, making her release him, knowing if he didn't, he would go off like a sex-starved kid. He wanted to be the one in control tonight. He wanted Summer writhing for him. He wanted her trembling and hungry. He wanted to watch her go crazy in his arms, and when it was done, he wanted it to happen again.

Abruptly he pulled Summer to her feet. When she swayed dizzily, he held her rigid, his hands on the curves of her hips, staring down into her passion-hazed eyes. In a single smooth motion then, he lifted her onto the dressing table.

Instinctively her hands clutched at his shoulders, but her

startlement quickly changed to acquiescence when she realized his intent. Pliantly, eagerly, she leaned back, her shoulders against the wall. Lance met no restraint when he spread her legs wide so that she lay open to him.

She was visibly shaking now, her arousal flame-hot, which was just how he wanted her. His hands braced on either side of her thighs, he lowered his head, breathing in her wonderful fragrance, her female heat. With deliberate speed, he planted a soft kiss on her woman's mound, and Summer groaned out loud.

Lance smiled grimly, reveling in his own power. All he had to do was stroke her with his tongue and she would come apart. But he didn't want her to come without him. He wanted to be inside her when she shattered, deep, deep inside her.

Sliding his hands beneath her buttocks, he lifted her hips onto his thighs and lowered her onto the throbbing erection pulsing against his stomach. Summer surged toward him, desperate to feel him inside her, to feel the wild beat of his heart match the wild beat of hers.

With a hard thrust of his hips, he crowded into her on one heavy stroke, impaling her to the hilt. Summer shrieked, and climaxed instantly, shuddering, quaking, her breath coming in panting moans.

When a staggering moment later she regained consciousness, it was to find herself draped limply against Lance, her arms, clinging to his neck, her face buried in his smooth, sweat-damp chest, his body's heat and smell enveloping her. She had melted around him—and he was still huge and hard inside her.

He wasn't moving at all, yet his breath was coarse in her ear, as if he were making a valiant effort at restraint.

Fighting off an exquisite languor, Summer experimentally moved her hips a fraction of an inch, and had to smile at the way every corded muscle in Lance's body contracted involuntarily.

"Are you ready for me?" she murmured, her tone exhausted but smug.

"Shut up, witch," Lance growled.

With the stiffness of rigid control he reached down and drew her legs around him, holding himself inside her shimmering heat. Lifting her in his arms, he turned and strode across the room to the bed, where he lowered them both to the mattress, still joined.

His black eyes held her gaze as his hands came up to roughly tangle in her hair, destroying the just-brushed neatness of her smooth, shining tresses. That was how he wanted her, with that regal image of hers shattered, with her emerald eyes soft and liquid with desire.

He began to move then, with an urgency as intensely primal as anything he had ever felt. Summer. His woman. He would never get his fill of her, the wild sweetness of her body, her lush, welcoming warmth.

Groaning in tender anguish, he took her, claiming, conquering, worshiping all at once. Soon she was responding with the same fierceness, her head thrown back in rapture. And when the flood came, all heat and light and motion, it held an intensity of pleasure as profound as pain.

His hard body buckled against hers, helpless in the throes of fulfillment. And when the shuddering contractions at last faded, Lance shut his eyes, satisfaction and desperation warring in his heart. He loved her, this beautiful, fiery lady who could tie his insides into knots and make every breath feel like his first.

And somehow, someway, he had to make her love him in return.

Chapter 20

~~~◯◯~~~

The first sign of real trouble came the following morning, when Lance's livery stable in Round Rock was vandalized. The boy who looked after the livery, Nate Jenkins, galloped up to the cabin after Lance had already left for the range, almost beside himself with distress. Summer sent Nate after her husband while she conferred with Reed and had the buggy harnessed.

By the time she and her brother arrived in Round Rock, Lance was already there, and Nate was showing him the damage. The vandals had cut the leathers on all the harnesses and broken the backs of the riding saddles, scattering them in the yard, as well as driving the stage horses out of the corral. The carcass of one of the animals lay in a pool of blood, a hundred yards from the gate, its throat slit, the wound covered with feasting flies.

Summer stared in horror as Lance hunkered down beside the dead horse. From his expressionless features, she couldn't guess what he was thinking, and yet she knew him well enough now to sense his rage. And for a moment, when he looked up and met her gaze, she thought she could read grief in his eyes over the senseless loss.

"I'm *sorry*, Mr. Calder," Nate Jenkins said for perhaps the twentieth time. "I don't know how they could have done this without waking me. I was here all night—"

"I don't hold you to blame, son," Lance assured him grimly. "You can't stop people determined on destruction. The last time they stole all the horses instead of turning them loose."

"You mean this has happened before?" Summer asked in outrage.

Lance gave her a sardonic glance. "You sound surprised,

princess. This is white Texas, remember? Somebody thinks this the best way to run me out of the county."

"What are you going to do?" Reed asked quietly.

With a sigh, he stood up, looking around him at the destruction. "Clean up this place and get on with my work." He glanced at his wife. "Go on home, Summer. There's nothing you can do here."

"But I could help clean—"

"I don't want you involved."

She would have protested further, but Reed placed a restraining hand on her arm. "Lance is right—you should stay out of it. It might even be dangerous. He'll deal with it better if he doesn't have to worry about you."

Reluctantly Summer allowed Reed to escort her back to the ranch, and yet she saw her retreat as cowardly. The monstrous warning had been directed at Lance, but he was her husband, and she should stand by him, despite the danger. Besides, she didn't think anyone would actually hurt *her*. On the other hand, she couldn't dismiss the possibility. The Weston name no longer provided her much protection, now that she was Lance's wife. She could become the target of viciousness, just as Lance was.

The knowledge left her furious and more shaken than she cared to admit. She would never forget the ghastly, pitiful sight of that dead horse. And nothing could have driven home to her more thoroughly the ugly hatred Lance had faced all his life. She felt so helpless. So impotent. As if she were fighting a foe she couldn't see, against whom she could never win.

Lance wouldn't discuss the incident with her, she discovered to her frustration. He seemed intent on pretending it had never happened, or at least shielding her from the ugliness. Summer couldn't be so sanguine.

For a few days, however, life seemed to return to normal. Reed started work on the plans for the new house, and Lance, after discussing the design and material construction with him, rode the twenty miles to Austin to order building supplies. While he was gone, Summer made another attempt to mend her relationship with her sister, or at least persuade her to attend the barbecue.

Amelia rebuffed both. When Summer knocked on the open door to her sister's bedchamber, Amelia stiffened in her rocking chair and told her tightly to go away. Summer remained out in the hallway, but refused to be driven away.

"Melly, you don't have to speak to me if you don't wish to, but please . . . for your own sake, you have to stop doing this to yourself. You can't spend the rest of your life hiding in your room."

"Can't I?"

"It isn't healthy to sit here day after day, dwelling on the past."

"Do you expect me to forget what happened to me?" Her tone was cold, angry.

"No, of course not. But it would be good for you to get out some. I think you should go to the barbecue Saturday night."

"*No.*"

"Why not? You know you've always enjoyed a party. And Harlan says you are to be the guest of honor."

She made a contemptuous sound deep in her throat. Summer bit her lip. Amelia had always loved parties, because they were the only times she could shirk the heavy duties thrust upon her at their mother's death. It grieved Summer to see even that small pleasure denied her. She tried again.

"All your friends are anxious to see you and welcome you home."

"Th-They won't."

"I think they will, if you give them a chance. And there will be lots of gentlemen there who want to dance with a pretty widow."

A bitter silence greeted her speculation.

"Melly, I know you think your life is over, but it isn't, not at all. You're still young. You could marry again, have children."

Amelia shut her eyes, a look of anguish twisting her features. "I've been raped by savages," she said in a voice so low, Summer could barely hear. "Do you honestly think any white man is going to look at me after that?"

"Yes," Summer replied quietly. "No man worth his salt would hold your assault against you."

"No? Name a single man who could overlook what happened to me."

"Dusty Murdock, for one."

Amelia seemed startled. "Our foreman?"

"Yes. You may not have known it, but Dusty was sweet on you before you married Limmel."

"He . . . he never said anything."

"I should think not. You never gave him the slightest encouragement—and he worked for us, for goodness' sakes. If he had dared make unwanted advances, Papa would have fired him on the spot. You know that."

Amelia made no answer, but Summer left satisfied at least to have given her sister food for thought.

She was more satisfied by her brother's relationship with her husband. Reed and Lance had begun to get along even better than she'd hoped.

On Thursday morning, the day after Lance's trip to Austin, as Summer carried a basket of laundry to wash up at the house, she spied the two of them in a side corral and stopped to watch. Lance appeared to be teaching the crippled Reed how to mount with only one leg. His methods seemed unorthodox, but they brought results.

His well-trained sorrel stood patiently while Reed, positioned on the right, grabbed a handful of mane and tried to lever himself up onto the animal's back. All he managed was to catch the stump of his left leg, which had been padded with a blanket, on the back of the saddle.

Swearing brutally, Reed fell back to the ground, but Lance prodded and taunted him to keep trying.

"You'd damn sure never make it as a Comanche. They wouldn't put up with a one-legged man for a day. Fact, a warrior would rather be dead than live as a cripple."

Summer gasped at the cruelty of the observation, even though she was certain it was true, but Reed merely gritted his teeth and tried again, putting every ounce of energy into hauling himself up. He didn't make it this time, but he came close, so close Summer found herself leaning forward in silent encouragement.

"Use the one leg you do have," Lance advised him. "Quit trying to pull yourself up and spring from the calf."

Breathing hard, Reed rested a minute before he attempted it. This time he made it, much to Summer's delight and obviously his own. Dragging himself upright in the saddle, Reed gave a shout of triumph and pumped his arm in the air.

Lance seemed unimpressed. "Time to celebrate when you can do that ten times out of ten."

Walking around to the sorrel's left, he adjusted a loop of buckskin to support Reed's severed leg. A crutch had been tied to the saddle, Summer noticed, but she was surprised when Reed unfastened it and tucked it under his left arm, letting it hang straight down.

Under Lance's supervision, he directed the sorrel around the corral, using the end of the crutch in place of a left spur. Eventually he put the animal through its paces, both horse and rider becoming more familiar with the unusual aid. It was a child's lesson, reminding Summer of when her brother Tyler had taught her to ride, but Reed, instead of being offended, concentrated as if his life depended on learning this knew skill.

And after a time, when he trotted back to Lance, he was grinning from ear to ear. "By God, it works!"

"On my sorrel, yeah, because I taught him. We'll have to train a couple of other horses to respond to you, though. And to come when you whistle. Wouldn't want you caught out on the range without a mount."

"Would you consider selling this fellow?"

"Sorry, he's not for sale." Lance patted the animal's neck fondly. "We've been through too much together. I'll loan him to you for a while, but I want him back." He looked up at Reed. "Think you can get down without falling on your face? You need more practice mounting."

"Sure."

He hooked the crutch over the saddle horn, where he could reach it once he'd dismounted, then tried to slide off.

Despite his confidence, though, as soon as his right boot touched ground, he lost his balance and fell, landing hard on his right side.

Alarmed, Summer took an automatic step forward, but Lance's sharp drawl stopped her. "Good thing you're a rich man, Weston. You can pay somebody to pick you up and wipe your skinned knee."

Astonishingly, Reed grinned up at him. "Somebody should

have washed your smart-ass mouth out with soap a long time ago, Calder."

Lance grinned back. "A lot of fellas have tried."

"Get back. I don't need your damned help."

"I didn't think you did," Lance returned smugly. "Use the stirrup leather."

As ordered, Reed sat up and half slid, half crawled to where he could grab the stirrup leather and pull himself up to stand beside the horse. When he finally made it, he stood panting for a moment, then said in a voice so low, Summer could barely make out the words, "Lance ... I'm grateful to you. More than you'll ever know. I've felt so blasted trapped, being unable to get around."

"Oh, I know, all right," Lance retorted gruffly. "But there's no call for you to feel beholden. Fact is, I'd say we're even. You just better do a damned good job drawing my new house." They grinned at each other in complete accord. "Now, get moving. I've got work to do out on the range. Can't spend all my valuable time mollycoddling you."

As Reed tried again, Lance caught his wife's approving eye. Summer gave him a smile of such brilliance that it dazed him for a full minute.

She had just picked up her basket of laundry from the ground where she'd set it, and turned toward the big house, when the distant sound of galloping hooves disturbed the calm, cool morning. Out of the corner of her eye she saw Lance quietly check the action of the six-shooter he wore strapped to his hip. Reed, who had managed to mount, turned the sorrel toward the approaching riders.

A group of a half dozen men came pounding up in a cloud of dust. Summer felt her heartbeat falter when she recognized Will Prewitt as the leader.

Prewitt raised his hand and brought the group to a halt near the corral, then sat staring with undisguised animosity at Lance.

Reed broke the silence with a cautious greeting. "Will, what brings you boys out our way?"

"Somebody stole two hundred head of prime stock off my north range yesterday."

Reed adopted an expression of polite concern, while

Lance's features remained totally closed. Summer felt the knot of tension in her stomach tighten.

Prewitt held up an object—an Indian arrow, by the looks of it. "This was found in place of my beeves. Looks like a Comanche arrow to me," he added, addressing Lance directly.

Lance's black gaze swept the arrow casually as he hooked his thumbs on his gun belt. "Could be. What of it?"

"That's a right good question. How do you figure them stinkin' Comanche knew to raid my place?"

Reed shook his head. "I'm not sure that's a fair conclusion, Prewitt. With all the vagrants on the loose nowadays, it could just as well be whites who stole your stock."

That was possible, Summer knew, but not as likely. During the war, with the frontier crumbling, cattle raids by Indians had occurred frequently, even as far south as Williamson County. The Comanche and Kiowa especially had made off with thousands of head from Texas ranches and exchanged them for blankets and weapons with the ruthless Mexican traders known as Comancheros, who in turn traded the livestock to Federal Army contractors in the New Mexico Territory. After the war, the Federal market had dried up, but there was still a big demand for Texas longhorns by ranchers in New Mexico. Summer had heard of huge Comanche camps to the northwest serving as trading stations for the illicit enterprise.

"It was Injuns, all right," Prewitt countered. "Where this arrow was found, there was a mess o' horse tracks—all goin' barefoot. Them Injun ponies ain't shod. Looked like maybe two dozen of 'em. It was Injuns; I think maybe they had good reason to come visitin' here."

Reed's eyes narrowed. "I don't think I like what you're implying."

Prewitt spat a stream of tobacco juice on the ground, a scarce foot from Lance's boots. "I ain't implyin' nothing. I'm statin' facts. Them Comanche stole my cattle. And I think maybe *you* know more about this than you're lettin' on."

"What's your point, Prewitt?" Lance demanded.

"I think maybe you drove off my beeves to give to your red nigger kin."

Summer didn't know whether to be more incensed by the ugly slur or the ridiculous accusation. "Why, that's absurd!"

she exclaimed indignantly, stepping forward. "Lance would never be part of such a raid."

"Oh, yeah?" Prewitt gave her a narrow look before shifting his attention back to Lance. "Where were you all day yesterday, Calder?"

Lance tipped his hat back, eyeing Prewitt steadily. "I rode down to Austin to order some supplies."

"Time enough to swing by my place to lift my beeves and meet up with them red devils."

"That's enough," Reed broke in. "You've no call to come around accusing innocent men."

"How can you be so damned sure he's innocent?"

"Think about it. It doesn't make sense, Lance stealing from our neighbors." Reed made a sweeping gesture with his arm, encompassing the Sky Valley ranch. "Why would he jeopardize everything he has here?"

"How the hell should I know? Maybe he wanted to pay somebody back for what happened to his livery t'other day."

"How do you know about what happened to my livery?" Lance asked, his tone grim.

Prewitt smirked. "Everybody heard about that. Could be you blame me."

"You're clutching at straws," Reed insisted.

"I sure as hell don't think so. It's a fact Comanches'd rather steal horses than steers. I didn't hear tell of any of your stock goin' missin'. Why would they bypass your place lessen *he* was in on it?"

"You'll have to have more proof than that, Prewitt."

"I'll get you your proof. And then he's gonna pay." He looked directly at Lance. "Around these parts a man gets strung up for stealing beeves. I don't give a shit what your Yank traitor and your purty squaw say to protect you—"

Lance struck faster than a rattler. Ducking through the rails of the corral, he had Prewitt by the shirt collar and was dragging him from the saddle before any of his henchmen could even think of reacting. His fist made a sickening *thwick* as it contacted with Prewitt's jaw and sent the man sprawling face-first in the dirt.

Flexing his knuckles, Lance stood over him threateningly. "You can say what you like about me, but you talk filthy about my wife and you'll find your face rearranged."

Working his jaw gingerly, Prewitt turned his head and spit out blood, although still keeping a cautious eye on the dangerous man above him. "Who the hell are you to threaten me?"

Lance's mouth twisted in a not-very-nice smile. "Not a threat, Prewitt. A fact. You're so big on facts. Keep it in mind—and get the hell off our land."

Prewitt, finding no one among the men he'd brought willing to push the issue, picked himself up off the ground and climbed back into his saddle. With a malevolent look at Lance, he jerked the reins and turned his horse. "You ain't heard the last of this," he called over his shoulder before he galloped off, his men following.

The silence they left behind seemed hollow and ominous.

"I wouldn't let Prewitt get to you, Lance," Reed said finally.

"It's not me I'm worried about." He was looking at Summer.

Reed nodded grimly. Considerately then, he backed the sorrel away to resume his training, giving them some privacy.

"I'm sorry about what he called you," Lance said in a low voice.

Summer, finding her knees strangely weak, put a hand out to hold on to the corral fence. "It's all right."

"No, dammit, it's not all right." He took a step closer, but stopped, as if afraid to touch her.

Summer closed her eyes, feeling somehow violated by Prewitt's ugliness. She had known the attitudes of some of her neighbors would be poisoned against her because of her marriage to Lance, but she had thought she would be safe at Sky Valley. "Sometimes I wish . . ."

"What?" Lance demanded quietly when she faltered.

"I just wish the world would go away and leave us in peace."

He closed the distance between them then, his arms a protective weight as they slid about her waist. Blindly she turned and melted into the shelter of his embrace.

He held her like that for a while, his throat closing on old and familiar emotions . . . sick helplessness and impotent rage. *Squaw* was such an ugly word the way whites meant it. An Indian's whore. He'd learned to despise that word, watching his mother shrink a little more each time some holier-than-thou bastard taunted her with it. But the sensation that gnawed deepest in his gut was fear. Summer was being treated just the way his mother had been—and sooner or later she would come to hate him for it.

"I guess I've let you in for a hard time."

She stiffened in his arms. "It isn't your fault!"

"I made you marry me," he said quietly.

"I've told you before, I consider my sister's life a fair exchange—but that is entirely beside the point. Oh, I wish I could have been the one to hit that horrible Will Prewitt!"

It was Lance's turn to stiffen. "This isn't your fight, princess."

"It is now," Summer vowed grimly. "You took on my battle for my sister, Lance. It's only right that I take on yours now."

"Uh-uh. I don't want you involved."

"I already am involved. I'm your wife. For better or worse." She gave a small, mirthless laugh. "I guess this is just the 'worse.'"

He was silent for a minute. "I'd rather you didn't go to that barbecue Saturday night."

She shook her head violently against his chest. "Wild horses couldn't keep me away now."

"It may get rough."

"Just let it."

The grit and determination in her voice sounded so much like his ma that it took him aback.

"Besides," she added adamantly, "you should know better than anyone that you can't escape bigotry and hatred by doing nothing. The only way to deal with it is to face it squarely."

"Maybe, but I don't want you having to face it at all."

Suddenly drawing back, she looked up at him with shimmering eyes. "I know what you're trying to do, Lance Calder. But you're not wiggling out of Harlan's invitation. We are *going* to that barbecue."

He searched her face for a long moment, relief stealing through him like a guilty thief. As long as Summer was fighting mad at bigoted bastards like Prewitt, she wouldn't be thinking about how she could get out of her marriage to *him*.

He just wished like hell she could hold on to that anger. She would need skin as tough as rawhide if she meant to stay his wife.

"We are going, Lance, and that's final," Summer repeated.

"Yes, ma'am," he said with unaccustomed meekness. He reached up and brushed the dampness from her cheek with his thumb. "I guess you ought to know something about me I never told you, though."

"What?"

"I can't dance."

"Oh." She smiled tremulously at his faintly sheepish expression.

"I never got invited to parties, so I never learned."

"It doesn't matter. Reed can't dance either now. And in any case, we aren't going for the dancing. We're going because we have as much right to be there as the next person."

Lance forced his lips into a semblance of an answering smile, though his thoughts responded differently. *Sure, princess, and I hope you go right on believing that. You're going to need every ounce of grit you have if you're to stick by me when the going gets rough.*

And unless I miss my guess, if Prewitt has his way, the going is about to get mighty rough indeed.

Chapter 21

The Saturday of the barbecue dawned clear and cool, but held a nerve-racking tension that, for Summer at least, only built as the day wore on. She spent the morning at the big house, baking four sweet potato pies to take to the party, and the afternoon getting ready for the evening.

They left for the Fisks' ranch while it was still light. Determined to use every advantage at her disposal, including her beauty, Summer wore an outdated yet stunning gown of forest green silk that brought out the red highlights in her dark hair and exposed a great deal of pale white shoulders, which she modestly covered with a black lace shawl. If someone dared condemn her because she had shed full mourning, she intended to respond that her brothers and father would not have wanted her to dwell on their deaths forever. Maritza had come to the cabin to help her dress and to arrange her hair up in soft ringlets—which, to Summer's delight, made Lance's gaze narrow in heated speculation.

Lance, to her great surprise, had allowed Reed to unearth for him a handsome suit of black wool that belonged to their late brother Tyler, along with a white cambric shirt and black tie. The colors looked striking against Lance's dark skin, but the civilized tailoring only seemed to accentuate the harshness of his features. And for once, his air of defiance was gone. In its place was a quiet uncertainty, a vulnerability that absurdly made Summer want to wrap her arms around him and hold him close, protecting him from the cruel world.

She settled for a gentle kiss and placed her hand on his sleeve, allowing him to lead her to the buckboard waiting outside.

To her further surprise, Reed was handing Amelia into the

buggy. Or rather, Dusty was, while Reed fiddled with storing his crutches.

Summer wondered what had made her sister decide to attend the party, but she doubted it was a change of heart toward Lance. Most likely they were taking separate vehicles because Amelia refused to associate with him.

Lance did not seem in any hurry to reach the Fisks' place. He let the buckboard fall behind to avoid the dust and maintained a plodding pace, but Summer didn't mind. Not with the glorious sunset turning the hill country gold and red. She rested her head on her husband's shoulder, letting contentment steal over her. If only every day could be so peaceful, life could not offer much greater happiness.

They spoke little on the drive, neither of them wanting to consider the approaching ordeal. By the time they arrived at the Fisk ranch, Reed had slowed the buggy he was driving in order to wait for them. Strength in numbers, Summer remembered her brother saying. If they were to win over their neighbors, they would need to stick together, for they were all outcasts. Lance, with his Comanche blood. Summer, who had married him in defiance of society's mores. Reed, who had fought for the Union when Texas declared for the Confederacy. And Amelia, a gentlewoman cruelly violated by her brutal captors. Only Dusty Murdock had no past to live down. Summer found herself murmuring silent thanks for his quiet strength and his determination to stand by them.

The Fisks' home, built of whitewashed weatherboard, was even bigger than the Westons', for Harlan had prospered raising stock as one of the first settlers. The barbecue was being held outdoors, on the front lawn, where already a crowd of gaily dressed people milled about.

To one side stood tables groaning with dishes brought by the guests, and beyond, smoke rose from the cook fires, where whole steers were roasting on giant spits. Above the murmur of laughter and conversation, Summer heard someone warming up a fiddle in preparation for the dancing.

Parking the carriages, Dusty and Lance tied their teams to the temporary picket line and then helped the ladies down. Summer, collecting two pies and giving the others to Lance to carry, led the way toward the gathering, allowing Amelia to hang back with Reed.

Their hosts must have been watching for them, for as soon as they had deposited the pies on a table, Harlan and his plump wife, Becky, strolled over to meet them. Summer held her breath during the exchange of greetings, remembering Lance's rudeness the last time the two men had met. But her husband seemed to be on his best behavior, or at least he allowed Harlan to pump his hand with no show of animosity.

"How do, Mr. Calder, sir. Glad you-all could come. You know my wife, Becky?"

Mrs. Fisk, although looking nervous, smiled and offered her fingers politely. Just as politely, Lance bowed over her hand. "Good evening, ma'am. It's kind of you to have us at your party."

She looked a bit surprised by his polished manners, but after a courteous response, she seemed to forget Lance altogether. Brushing past him, her arms outstretched, she exclaimed in delight, "Amelia! Oh, dear Amelia, praise the Lord you're safe. We were so worried about you."

Summer watched in concern as Amelia momentarily seemed to shrink back, but Becky's arms came around her in a motherly embrace, refusing to be denied, and her disarming chatter soon had Amelia responding with a tentative smile.

The warm welcome for her sister didn't end there, either. Dozens more of their friends came over to greet Amelia, surrounding her and accepting her back into the community while Dusty hovered protectively nearby. Summer felt the tight knot in her stomach relax a degree. If Amelia could see that her life truly wasn't ruined, then perhaps she would stop blaming Lance for the violence the Comanches had committed against her.

Summer was about to ask Lance if he wanted to join the crowd when Reed hobbled over to them. "Looks like she's going to be okay."

"Yes," she murmured gratefully.

"That leaves the rest of us." Reed gave Lance a friendly cuff on the shoulder. "You ready to beard the lions with me?"

Lance's mouth curved in a wry grin. "I rather face a dozen real lions, but yeah, I guess I'm ready."

They strolled toward the crowd, intent on mingling. They were met with looks of hostility and wariness, but also of curiosity and welcome. Some of the guests gave them a wide berth, but one by one, others—those willing to overlook Lance's ancestry and forgive Reed's political persuasions—began to gather around them. They were mostly young men, the boys Summer had known all her life, all eager to get back into her good graces, as well as a few older women, those who had known her mama and still felt a responsibility toward raising a motherless girl.

Lance watched in unwilling admiration as his beautiful young wife worked her magic, slowly gathering her court, charming and wooing them to her side. The males were like bees buzzing around a rose, unable to resist her alluring scent.

Only one man dared to challenge their presence, and then it was to hint that Reed should have stayed up north with the Yankees.

"Sounds like sour grapes to me, J.T.," Reed retorted with an unapologetic smile. "But the war is over, and you lost."

"Reed, shame on you!" Summer scolded gently, bestowing a bewitching smile on the unfortunate J.T. "I'm certain Mr. Wilkes didn't mean to imply you had no right to come home. In any case, you should be more gracious in victory. J.T. fought just as bravely for the Confederacy. I'm sorry, Mr. Wilkes. You must forgive my brother. His missing leg pains him so that his temper gets the better of him." She raised entreating eyes to him. "Can't we forget that horrid war and be friends again?"

Lance shook his head with cynical amusement as the young man's scowl faded under her appealing warmth. Summer's wiles were still potent as ever, the hapless males who came within her sphere as defenseless as he had always been.

No one said a word about Lance himself. There was no doubt he was being shunned by many of the guests, but no one yet was willing to challenge him to his face. Summer introduced him to all and sundry as her husband and the courageous man who had rescued her poor sister. And from the grudging looks sent his way, it was clear that many of them were jealous of her praise.

When the music started and sets began forming in a clearing, she refused all invitations to join the dancing. "My husband doesn't dance," she said firmly, "and I plan to keep him company."

Amazingly, her coterie of admirers were willing to stand on the sidelines with her. They obeyed slavishly when she suggested they ask her sister to dance, and scurried to fetch her cups of lemonade, returning to her side directly afterward.

When the fiddles struck up a lively reel, one of her former beaux cast a sour glance at Lance and muttered under cover of the music, "It isn't fair, Miss Summer. We always thought you would marry one of us."

Summer dimpled. "But I did, Paul. Lance belongs to Williamson County. His mama was one of the first settlers in Austin, and he came to live here when he was just a boy."

"Drat it, Miss Summer! You know what I mean."

Her smile turned cool. "Yes, I believe I do. Really, Paul, I expected better of you. If you judged a man by his character rather than his kin, Lance would come out miles ahead of any man here."

Paul flushed resentfully and turned away.

Summer met Lance's gaze. He was looking at her with grim humor—or was it loneliness?—in his eyes. It made her heart ache to see how he was being treated. People were being scrupulously polite to him for her sake, and yet no one had truly welcomed him or shown any pleasure at his company. And she doubted that her consequence was high enough to force his acceptance. Indeed, fully half of the guests had ignored her own presence, either avoiding her gaze or staring right through her, as if, by pretending she didn't exist, they could delay dealing with her betrayal of their social creed. She could only hope that in time, with familiarity, that would change—that she would be forgiven and Lance would come to be tolerated. If not, they could contemplate a grim future.

At least it appeared her sister had been accepted back into the fold. Summer looked across the clearing where the dancers were engaged in violent foot stomping, to find Amelia conversing with a group of guests. Dusty Murdock stood near her, watching her out of distant, hungry eyes. Amelia had danced once with him, but seemed intent on ignoring him now.

Her distance seemed all the more strange when compared to the welcoming smile Amelia bestowed on Will Prewitt when he ambled up. Summer felt her stomach muscles tense as she watched. How could Melly show favor for the likes of Prewitt when Dusty was so much the better man?

Prewitt bent to murmur something in her ear, which made Amelia nod. He moved away again shortly, but Summer's tension turned to definite unease. Amelia had turned to stare across the way at Lance, a bitter expression on her face, full of resentment and spite.

She could have been mistaken about her sister's malevolence, Summer hoped. Dusk had fallen, and although lanterns had been set on the tables and hung at intervals from the nearby trees, lending a golden glow to the scene, the shifting shadows made by the dancers were deceptive. And yet she couldn't shake the sensation of impending trouble.

Her concern proved out some ten minutes later. From somewhere behind her, she heard a man's voice say in a sneering drawl, "The stench round here is gettin' might bad."

"Yeah, know what you mean," another voice replied. "I can smell a red hide from miles away."

Stiffening, Summer glanced over her shoulder. Some half dozen men, Will Prewitt among them, had gathered to one side to smoke cigars and were passing around a jug of what no doubt was whiskey. Summer had no doubt, either, that they had deliberately raised their voices to make their conversation audible over the music.

In concern, she looked up at Lance. Seeing the rigid set of his jaw, she placed a restraining hand on his sleeve. Prewitt wanted to start a brawl, obviously, but no matter how skillful a fighter Lance was, with one man against so many, he would come up the loser. Not to mention that a fight would create a scandal and destroy any progress they'd made toward getting their neighbors to accept them.

It was hard to ignore the slurs, though, and the rough sniggering.

"What's Harlan thinking of, letting them red devils sidle up to our womenfolk?"

"Never figured Harlan for a Injun lover."

"That breed sure as hell don't belong here. I say we oughta run 'im off."

"How you gonna do that? Them Comanche bucks don't scare for nothing."

Summer forced a smile and gazed appealingly up at her

husband. "Lance, I just realized how famished I am. Would you escort me to the buffet tables so we can get some supper?"

He looked at her a long moment, his black eyes smoldering dangerously. But he didn't resist when Summer took his hand and led him away from all the hostility.

Instead of heading for the supper tables, though, she bypassed those and drew Lance around the side of the main house, into the shadows. Alone, she turned to him and wrapped her arms around his neck, pressing her body close.

Lance held himself stiffly, refusing to succumb to her wiles. "I know what you're doing, princess."

"Do you?"

"You're trying to take my mind off their talk so I won't light into them."

Summer smiled in the darkness. "I don't care a whit about *them.* I would prefer you didn't hurt them, of course—not because they don't deserve it, but it would be sure to spoil the party. But"—she raised her face to his—"I really brought you here because I think you deserve to be rewarded for your forbearance, and I couldn't do it in front of all those people."

He watched her, his eyes narrowed.

"Well, are you going to kiss me, Lance Calder? Or do you intend to stand there all night, refusing a lady?"

At her impatient demand, he lowered his head slowly and took her mouth. His kiss was softer than usual. Strangely poignant. She tasted reluctance, desire, need, but more than anything else, she tasted an intense and powerful loneliness. A vulnerability that tore at her heart.

Feeling it, Summer tightened her arms about Lance and, after a moment, felt him do the same to her. They pulled each other close, drawing strength from the contact. To hold and be held, she understood his need. A simple human craving that they could fulfill for each other. And yet somehow it seemed more than that. It seemed to her as if Lance had somehow become part of her.

When he would have pulled away, she wouldn't release him. "Would you dance with me?" she asked.

"I told you I don't know how."

"It doesn't matter. Just hold me."

He complied, hesitantly following her lead when she began to move slowly, gently, from side to side.

The night had quieted. The fiddles had ceased temporarily, but it made no difference to either of them. In the silence, they swayed slowly to their own inner music, in their own private dance, a slow, languid motion, sensual but not entirely sexual.

Summer sighed as Lance's hard arms tightened tentatively, possessively, about her. She loved this side of him: this gentleness, this rare and tender sweetness. He held her with as much care as if she were fragile crystal, and yet she could feel his controlled passion ... a dangerous man restraining his lover's hunger. His unspoken need aroused an answering longing within her, made her feel soft and achy inside. Nestling in his embrace, she closed her eyes, breathing in the warm, musky scent of him.

Lance breathed in her own sweet fragrance, desperately savoring the soft body filling his arms. She created such an ache within him, he thought he might break. He wanted her so bad. Wanted so much to lose himself in her. Wanted her to heal the hurt. Summer was everything to him. She was his weakness, his sanity. His heartbeat, his wishes. His hopes, his dreams. With a hoarse exhalation, he buried his face in her hair, feeling as if his heart were splintering with love for her.

It was only his damnable pride that had kept him from letting her know how much she meant to him. But he could tell her now. He could shed his pride, his defenses, and bare himself to her, open himself up.

"Summer?" he began hesitantly, his tone roughened by a wealth of unwelcome emotion.

Her quiet "Yes?" made his heart start pounding.

He swallowed hard, girding himself for the confession. In the brief interval, though, he had time to realize that the rhythmic thudding was not only his heartbeat, but the distant sound of galloping hooves. Lance raised his head, a wolf scenting danger.

Summer heard the sound a moment later and stiffened apprehensively. The hoofbeats stopped suddenly, as if a rider had come to a plunging stop, but then the sudden lull was followed by voices raised in alarm.

She and Lance drew apart, exchanging frowning glances.

Turning as one, they made their way around to the front of the house, back to the party.

A total silence had fallen over the crowd, and the air held a live tension, the kind of dark, ominous atmosphere before a twister hits.

At the edge of the crowd, a rider sat astride a sweating, heaving horse—a man she recognized as Bob Blackwood, one of the ranchers who lived some five miles northwest of here. One of the men who had come to Sky Valley the other day to accuse Lance of stealing Will Prewitt's stock.

Her dread grew when she heard someone mutter the word *Comanches*. She pushed through the crowd, toward the front, in order to hear the conversation fully, although Lance held back.

"Was anybody hurt?" a man asked Blackwood.

"Not yet, far as I know."

"Maybe it was some white varmints who ran off your beeves."

"It was Comanches, I tell you!" Bob vowed. "I saw a whole passel of 'em, driving my stock off toward the west."

"I guess maybe we should get a posse together, go after 'em. We could catch 'em in the act—"

"They'll be long gone by now," someone else said, which started a free-for-all discussion.

"No, they won't. They'll be slowed down by the cows."

"We can't just stand by while them red devils steal our stock!"

"Maybe that's what they want, to draw off our menfolk and leave our homes undefended."

"Yeah! Maybe they mean to attack."

A sudden silence fell over the crowd, a wave of fear running through it that was palpable. Lance, standing toward the rear, had to admire Prewitt's tactics. It was a setup, of course. In all likelihood, Blackwood's stock had no more been stolen than Prewitt's had last week. Certainly not by Comanches. If they had, they wouldn't have let anyone live to tell about it. No, Prewitt simply needed somebody else's word that cattle raids had occurred, to bolster his own case. No doubt Blackwood's arrival at the barbecue had been staged for the greatest possible effect, with the largest possible audience. And if it was his intention to whip up the crowd, he was doing a fine job of it. There was nothing like the threat of a Comanche raid to strike terror in the heart of a Texan. Already there was a tangible aura of panic among the guests, a panic that was edging toward hysteria.

"We'd do better to try to protect ourselves," someone said. "Stick close to home, in case they come back."

"Yeah. Those stinkin' killers are liable to circle back and murder us all in our beds."

"I don't believe they intend murder," a woman said quietly.

Everyone looked around to see who had spoken. Lance felt his gut tighten when he recognized Amelia Truesdale's voice.

"They only want the cattle," Amelia said in a small voice. "You see . . . Mr. Calder invited them."

He heard a gasp that he suspected came from Summer, while a murmur of outrage ran through the crowd.

So that was what Prewitt intended, Lance thought grimly. The man wouldn't need actual proof of any cattle thefts if he had a character witness. It was enough that Amelia Truesdale was willing to testify against him.

He could see people turn to stare, could feel the hostile, horrified eyes directed at him. They started inching back fearfully, the crowd parting slowly like a sea, giving him a clear view of his accuser.

Harlan Fisk stepped forward then, looking uncomfortable but determined to take responsibility for the proceedings. "You better explain, Miss Amelia."

"When I was . . . at the Comanche camp, I heard him tell those savages which ranches would be best to raid. His brother . . . the chief . . . said they would follow him here."

Lance clenched his jaw in an effort at control. Vaguely he wondered if Summer would come to his defense—and she did instantly. She closed the distance between herself and her sister, and stood directly before Amelia.

"That is absurd! Melly, you're entirely mistaken." Her voice sounded carefully controlled, as if she were trying to keep a rein on her fury. "You couldn't possibly have overheard any conversation Lance had with his brother, at least nothing you could have understood. Fights Bear doesn't speak English."

Lance shook his head, knowing she wouldn't be believed. The crowd was in no mood to listen to logic.

"I . . . I know what I heard. Perhaps it was someone else."

Summer's fingers curled into fists. "It's an outrageous lie to suggest Lance would invite his kin to raid."

Harlan interrupted grimly. "Are you sure, Miss Amelia? You're accusing Lance Calder of being behind these cattle thefts?"

"I . . . I only know what I heard. He invited his kin down here. He told them where to find cattle, which ranches to steal from."

"I told you he had a hand in it," Will Prewitt said in a contemptuous drawl. "I was jest wrong about how. I figured Calder stole my herd and gave them to his red devil friends, but he let them do all the work."

"Stop it!" Summer demanded, stamping her foot. "This has gone far enough!"

"Summer, let it go," Lance commanded, his tone cutting through the night.

She whirled to face him, her expression anguished. "I won't stand by while men like Will Prewitt spread lies about you."

He had to be grateful to Summer for sticking up for him, but he knew better than anyone else that her denial wouldn't make a difference. She was his wife. Of course she would take his side. Nobody would listen to her, not with her sister damning him. The damage was done.

His faint smile held bitterness. "You can't stop it. I'm already guilty in their minds, and nothing's going to change that."

"Lance—"

"No, Summer, it doesn't matter."

His gaze moved over the crowd till he found her brother. "Reed, take her home."

When Reed, after a slight hesitation, nodded solemnly, Lance turned and walked away, leaving a hushed crowd behind him.

Summer whirled on her sister with fury. "Do you hate him so much? After what he did for you?" Then picking up her skirts, she ran after Lance.

He was heading toward the line of carriages, she realized. By the time she caught up with him, he had already untied the team of their buckboard.

"Where are you going?" she demanded breathlessly, halting so close that she prevented him from backing the horses.

"What difference does it make?" His voice sounded brittle and distant.

"If you're going home, I'm coming with you."

He stopped suddenly and exhaled a soft gust of bitter laughter. "Home." He bowed his head, his hand clenching on the harness. "You know what's really funny? I really believed I had a home here. A future. For a minute I let myself hope. . . . God, I was a damned fool."

Summer felt her heart break. He was so alone. So vulnerable and terribly alone.

"Lance," she said carefully, her throat aching. "Don't give up. We'll fight this. We'll prove that Melly—"

"No." He shook his head harshly. "It's gone too far. This isn't your fight."

"It is. I'm your wife—"

"I want you out of it. It's gotten too dangerous."

"Do you think I care about that?"

He turned to look at her, his expression unreadable in the faint moonlight. "*I* care. Do you think I could live with myself if you came to harm?"

"Lance, please . . . wherever you're going, let me come with you."

"No." He reached for the nearest horse's bridle.

Desperately she moved closer, wrapping her arms around him to hold him to her, pressing her body against his.

For a brief moment, as if against his will, Lance's arms came around her, tightening as if he would bring her inside him if he could.

His eyes shut in agony. He'd known want before. He'd known need and physical fear. But he'd never known anything like this savage twisting in his gut. This craving for something he knew now he couldn't have. This raw, stark terror that he was about to lose the one thing in his life that meant anything to him. Summer. He was going to lose her. As sure as Indians and white men were mortal enemies, he wasn't going to have any kind of future with her.

Unwinding her arms from around his neck, he pushed her away, distancing himself more than just physically.

"Summer, go back to your brother. He'll keep you safe. I can't manage it any longer."

Chapter 22

The party broke up quickly with the festive mood shattered by the threat of Comanche raids. The guests scattered to their various vehicles, wanting to get home to their ranches and protect their stock and to prepare for the worst.

Summer, still furious over her sister's betrayal of Lance, refused outright to ride home with Amelia. Instead, she borrowed a buggy from Harlan and had Reed escort her home, while Dusty drove her sister.

Summer fumed the entire way. "Why, *why* would she be so cruel and lie that way? She's ruined his chances to become accepted into the community. Destroyed whatever trust he'd begun to develop—and she did it *deliberately,* maliciously."

"Perhaps it wasn't deliberate, Summer," Reed temporized. "Perhaps she truly believes Lance is her enemy. You know what an ordeal she went through. Her mind is so . . . fragile nowadays that she could have talked herself into it."

"I don't *care* why she did it. I've made allowances for weeks for the terrible way she's treated him, Reed, but I can't forgive her this time. I *can't.* And he won't either."

Lance didn't come home that night, or the next—or any night during the following week. He hadn't left the ranch altogether, Summer discovered to her profound relief. Although he was apparently no longer herding mustangs with the vaqueros, Dusty saw him occasionally during the days. Summer could only conclude that he was avoiding her. She spent the interval vacillating between fear for his safety, fury and despair at her helplessness to change the situation, and hurt that he was shutting her out.

For some time now she'd known her feelings for Lance had been changing gradually—had grown beyond gratitude and simple loyalty, beyond mere physical desire. The hollow ache that pulsed in the vicinity of her heart only confirmed her suspicions. Lance meant far more to her than she had ever allowed herself to admit. His presence fulfilled a need in her; his absence created a great emptiness. And his deliberate withdrawal from her left her in a turmoil of guilt and frustration.

Perhaps he only wanted to protect her by staying away, but he had no right to make such a decision for her, no right to spurn her help. He had been there when she needed him. She should be there for him now.

The building supplies started arriving for the house Lance had planned to erect—finished lumber from Bastrop, nails and bricks and plaster from Austin. Summer directed the deliveries to the homesite, but she was no longer certain that there would even be a house, or that they would have a future that required it. Reed had finished a preliminary set of drawings, but she couldn't answer questions about Lance's preferences for the small details, or make decisions for him in his absence.

Those unresolved questions, however, were minor compared to the terrible tension that permeated the rest of her life. Not only was her marriage in limbo, her future with Lance in doubt, but she felt as if she were waiting for an impending explosion. She jumped at shadows, froze at the merest creak of a floorboard.

The uncertainty was beginning to wear on her nerves, so much so that she was almost grateful when an incident occurred at midweek that allowed her to vent her temper. She had ridden into Round Rock with Reed in order to purchase some miscellaneous household supplies and sewing notions at the general store when she ran up against the kind of prejudice Lance had lived with all his life, coupled with genuine fear.

She had known the store owner, Jeb Parker, and his wife, Mary Sue, all her life, but incredibly, they refused to serve her and ordered her out of the store.

"We'll fill your order, Reed," Mrs. Parker said stiffly. "That woman isn't welcome."

Summer drew herself up, bristling. "That suits me fine, Mary Sue Parker. I don't care to associate with blind, small-minded, bigoted people like you, either."

Turning on her heel, she walked out. Reed found her a moment later, standing by the buggy, shaking with sick fury.

"That is exactly what Lance's mother had to deal with all her life, what Lance had to put up with. Oh, it makes me so mad, I could scream!"

Not answering, Reed took her arm and urged her into the vehicle. "We'll drive to Georgetown next week to buy what we need."

"If they'll serve us. No doubt they've heard about what's happening down here by now."

"Then we'll go to Austin," Reed said quietly.

"You shouldn't have to go to all that trouble." She hesitated. "Mary Sue said she would serve you."

Reed shook his head. "You're my sister, Summer. I told you I'd stick by you. It's no more than you've done for me since I came back from the war."

She was glad of her brother's support but regretted that he should be made to suffer. Even so, she didn't intend to argue.

With a contemptuous glance at the store, she turned around in her seat to stare straight ahead over the horses' heads, determined to forget the entire incident.

Yet she couldn't dismiss her concerns as easily the following day when Harlan Fisk rode over to talk to Reed. Summer learned of the visit after Harlan had left, when she walked over to the big house to share supper with her brother and sister, preferring even Amelia's traitorous company to eating alone. Amelia had refused to retract her accusation, and Summer refused to speak to her until she did. After a virtually silent meal, Summer followed Reed to his study, where he told her about Harlan's call.

The previous night several hundred head of prime stock had gone missing from the Fisk ranch, and Comanche arrows had been found at the site.

Summer sat numbly, wanting to deny Reed's solemn disclosure, knowing she would be grasping at straws. She might have accused Will Prewitt and even Bob Blackwood of lying to gain their own ends, fabricating stories about cattle rustling, but Harlan Fisk was as honest as a man could be. If he said his stock was gone, then it was gone. It seemed that cattle really were disappearing from neighboring ranches. And the evidence pointed to Comanche involvement.

"Maybe the Comanches really are behind it," Reed observed quietly. "And maybe"—he took a slow breath—"Amelia didn't lie about Lance."

Summer lifted her head to stare at him in horror. "Surely you don't believe *Lance* is involved?"

"Honestly?" Reed ran a hand distractedly through hair. "I don't know what to believe. The evidence looks pretty damning."

"What possible motive could he have for stealing from our neighbors?"

"Revenge for what happened to his livery, maybe?"

Summer shook her head, trying to keep calm, her tone reasonable. "Not only isn't it logical, but it's impossible. Think about it, Reed. Lance didn't know his livery would be vandalized. If he invited his brother to raid as Amelia suggests, then he had to have done it before he left the Comanche camp. Why would he have arranged for them to steal from this area when he planned to settle here?"

"I don't know. Maybe he didn't trust you to keep your word about your marriage. You left him behind, remember? Maybe he thought you owed him, that the people here owed him for all the hell they'd given him over the years. Maybe he's getting back at them. Or maybe he only wanted to repay his brother for helping him find Amelia."

"Lance paid his brother already, in horses and money."

"Maybe that wasn't enough."

"No." She shook her head furiously. "It's impossible."

"It isn't *impossible,* Summer." Reed gazed at her with sympathy, but also with unwavering determination. "Nobody's been hurt so far. That isn't like the Comanche. Maybe Lance told his kin to lay low, to leave the ranchers alone and only take their stock."

"And maybe it's the whites who are stealing and blaming it on Lance!" Her eyes grew pleading. "Think about it, Reed. Will Prewitt hates Indians. He would like nothing more than to drive Lance out of the county, like Papa did five years ago. Think about it—"

"Perhaps you're the one who should do the thinking, Summer. I realize he's your husband. . . . Of course you feel a certain obligation toward him for coming to Amelia's rescue.

But what do you really know about him? How do you know he can be trusted?"

"I just know. And you would, too, if you gave him a chance. Lance hasn't been back here all that long, not enough time for you to come to know him well. Or anyone else for that matter." She laughed bitterly. "And now Amelia has ruined any chance he had of earning their trust."

"Has she?"

"Yes! It's her fault—"

"Loyalty is admirable, Summer, but stubborn blindness is stupid."

"What are you saying?"

"Where has Lance been the past few days? What has he been up to?"

Summer remained silent, unable to answer.

"He's been gone every night since the barbecue, and during the day, too. He could be riding with his Comanche kin."

"No."

"I think you at least have to consider the possibility."

"If ..." She swallowed with difficulty. "If he is ... involved, then there have to be extenuating circumstances."

"Yes." Reed's eyes hardened. "But if he is stealing from our neighbors, then your obligation to him is at an end. Married or not, if he's guilty, you don't owe him anything more. And you have to consider what to do about it."

Summer did consider her brother's suspicions. She thought of nothing else for the rest of the week, waking or sleeping. In her morbid contemplations she began to envision the worst, while her dark dreams were filled with raiding Comanches, with Lance as their leader. She saw him riding at the head of the war party, bare-chested, his face streaked with black paint, eagerly spurring on his galloping mount, brandishing his long, wicked lance. . . .

She couldn't believe he was guilty, and yet . . .

She couldn't help the niggling doubts, couldn't help wondering if there might be something to Amelia's accusations after all.

No, her sister had lied. Amelia had never overheard Lance plotting to steal cattle from the ranchers.

Yet no matter how many times Summer told herself the possibility was absurd, she couldn't deny that Reed's arguments made sense. Lance *had* been disappearing at night. And he hadn't defended himself the night of the barbecue. Perhaps because he didn't have a defense?

Had he invited his Comanche kin south to raid? Was he aiding them even now?

Was he distancing himself from her now to prevent her from learning the truth? Or in order to protect her? Because if he was caught, he didn't want her involved?

She had to know. The nerve-shredding uncertainty was almost worse than the truth. She didn't know what she would do if he was guilty, yet she would rather know clearly what she was facing. She had to discover what Lance had been up to this past week, where he had been.

If he ever came home, she would question him. If not, she would have to search for him. To demand answers he wouldn't want to give.

In the end she didn't have to search for him. On Friday afternoon Summer walked back from the big house to their cabin and found Lance in their bedroom, stuffing a change of clothing into his saddlebags.

He didn't speak when she paused in the doorway. Didn't even look at her. Summer felt her heartbeat falter. He seemed well enough, until she saw the dark-shadowed eyes rimmed with fatigue. Worried, uncertain, she drank in the sight of him.

"Lance?"

He didn't answer as he folded a shirt.

"Where ... have you been?"

His expression was hard, shuttered, when he glanced up. "What difference does it make?"

"I ... I'm your wife. I've been worried about you."

His mouth curled at the corner, but he continued to work in silence.

"Are you hungry? I haven't started supper yet, but—"

"Don't bother. I'm not staying."

His response was sharp and unyielding, distancing, shutting her out. Her heart sank. "At least let me fix you something to eat."

"I can feed myself."

Of course he could, Summer thought with regret. He could

care for himself better than she could. He had always been a loner. Self-sufficient in ways she could never dream of being. He didn't need her, didn't want her. . . .

She searched his face, which was set like flint, hearing the grim, deep echo of his last remark. This was the old Lance, the hard-bitten, unforgiving stranger she had once been half-afraid of. She could see no hint of the tender side he'd recently shown her. None of the gentle, vulnerable, sensitive lover she had come to know. *Where had all the sweetness gone?*

She drew in a shaky breath. "Lance . . . about this week. You've been gone a good deal. And . . . some people are beginning to wonder where you've been, what you've been up to. They suspect . . . Lance, please . . . I have to know."

He froze in the act of fastening a buckle, not looking up.

Aware of the sudden, dangerous tension in the room, Summer twisted her fingers together and hastened to reassure him. "I could understand, Lance, truly. If you were trying to get back at Prewitt . . . if you wanted revenge for what he did to your livery . . . But please. I hope . . . I hope you'll reconsider. It isn't worth it. You'll destroy everything you've worked for—we've worked for—if you keep this up."

He heard her words as if from a great distance, as if he were outside himself looking on. But his body felt the physical impact. His gut tightened with every damning word of accusation and defense, locking the air inside his chest.

"You think I did it." His tone was controlled, uninflected, but she caught the rawness in the quiet words.

"I . . ." She faltered.

"You think I've been out rustling cattle for my brother." His whisper was knife-edged, but he held himself rigidly, determined to keep the sick disbelief, the numb acceptance, at bay. At least until he could get out of the room. With effort, Lance gathered his control and his saddlebags and started to walk out.

"Where are you going?" Summer was startled into asking.

"Out to steal some more cattle, where else!" His fierce retort rang with fury.

"Lance, you can't just leave—"

Summer clutched his arm as he passed, trying to prevent him from going—a mistake, she learned at once. With a violent oath, he dropped his saddlebags and turned on her, grabbing her shoulders in a tight grip and pushing her up against the wall adjacent the door.

Shocked, unnerved by his violence, she stared at him in fear, at the hostile eyes that flared darkly above her. He had grown white about the mouth, while the muscles in his jaw knotted, but his words held a blistering force.

"You want me to stay, do you? *Why,* princess? What do you want from me? This?" His hand roughly covered her left breast, pressing through the layers of cloth and whalebone.

"You said you missed me. Well, I missed you, too. I missed what's between your legs. I missed having you bucking and moaning beneath me."

She whimpered, trying to pull away from his hurtful grip.

"What's wrong, princess? Are you afraid of the savage Injun?"

"Lance . . . what are you doing?"

His fingers worked the buttons of her gown, ripping the cloth. "If you can't get over thinking me a savage, I might as well act like one."

"No . . ."

"No?" His dark eyes seared her with a blazing look, full of aggression, and yet they betrayed a bleak pain that the harsh fury couldn't completely hide.

"Lance . . . don't . . ."

"Don't touch you? Don't fuck you?" His hand left her bodice and fumbled for her skirts. "Come on, now, princess. You enjoy what I do to you. You like my touch. You like it when I fuck you—"

"Stop it!" She turned her head away, unable to bear his ugliness, his making what had been beautiful seem base and lewd. "Stop being so crude!"

"Crude? You don't know what the word means. Crude is the drunken slobs who used to rut on my mother. Crude is listening to their grunts as they forced themselves on her."

"Is that what you mean to do to me? Force me?" She turned her anguished gaze on him. "This is your answer to everything, isn't it? Violence. Physical force. Do you mean to rape me?"

His angry expression shattered . . . wilted abruptly . . .

eaving desperate vulnerability in its wake. He stared at her, his features stricken.

Suddenly he squeezed his eyes closed, realizing what he had almost done. He had assaulted Summer, hurt her, when he would have cut off his hands before he harmed a single hair of her head. When she'd voiced her suspicions to his face, he'd snapped—

God, you savage bastard.

Now that he was still, he felt the faint tremors of her body, the thundering of her heart. He took a slow, deep breath.

Carefully, as if handling fragile crystal, he removed his hands from her body and stepped back, feeling as if he were severing his heart from his chest. A moment before, he'd been all knotted up inside with anger and hurt. Now he only felt empty, a bleakness that was soul-deep.

Summer leaned weakly against the wall, her hand pressed against her throat protectively, her green eyes wary.

Lance cursed himself again. "You want to know what I've been doing the past week?" he asked in a voice so low, it was almost inaudible. "I've been searching for a ghost band of Comanches, the ones Prewitt claims stole his stock. To see if I could find any tracks. I figured if there really were Comanches in the area, then I'd best get to them first and convince them to leave. But if Prewitt was just making the story up to frame me, I might be able to challenge him with the lack of evidence." He exhaled a gust of ugly laughter. "Fool notion, huh? Even you thought I was guilty."

He bent to retrieve the saddlebags he'd dropped and turned to go. At the door, though, he stopped and glanced back over his shoulder.

"Just tell me one thing, Summer." He waited till she looked directly at him. "Why would you think me fool enough to jeopardize the life I've made with you here? The kind of life I've always dreamed of living?"

Tears welled in her eyes when she saw the despair in his. "I ... I'm sorry. What was I to think with you shutting me out of your life at every turn?"

He chuckled, the bleak sound a travesty. "You might have trusted me."

He left quietly then. Turned and walked through the main room, shutting the door softly behind him.

Her knees weak, her heart hollow, Summer sank into the rocking chair. She could still hear the echo of Lance's boot-heels on the floorboard, still remember his raw gaze when he said she might have trusted him, his face drawn as though in pain.

A sharp ache rose in her throat as she realized the full scope of what she'd done. She had turned her back on Lance. She had acted as whites usually did, banding with their kind against him. She had taken their side, refusing to believe in his innocence. She had let him down, disappointed him cruelly—at the very moment she'd come to realize how very much he meant to her.

Summer pressed a hand over her mouth to hold back a cry of despair. For some time now she had known she was in danger of losing her heart. But until this moment she hadn't realized it had already happened. She had fallen in love with her husband. With a hard, hostile, defiant half-breed who had opened himself up to her, only to find himself betrayed.

She loved Lance. She didn't know when it had happened, or how, yet she knew why. Lance was a good man. With an honor and integrity that most men couldn't hold a candle to. With a grit, a heart-deep courage, that most whites couldn't even understand, let alone emulate. He deserved better than a wife who lost faith at the first trial.

Shame crawled through Summer's belly, gnawing at her. If she had truly loved him, she never would have doubted him.

But then, she had been wrong about Lance frequently. She had prided herself on her magnanimity, on her self-sacrifice in agreeing to marry him. She had condescended—stooped—to become his wife, telling herself it was the only way to gain what she wanted from him. She had braved the censure of their neighbors, even daring them to snub her and him, all the while feeling a self-righteous anger at being forced to renounce her future because of Lance. She had been afraid for herself, her future, *her* needs, *her* consequence. She hadn't been concerned for Lance at all. She had thought Lance lucky to have won her hand—but she was the lucky one.

Fool! Arrogant fool.

She hadn't trusted him enough—no, that wasn't quite true. There was no one she trusted more than Lance to keep her safe, to protect her physically from harm. But she hadn't *be-*

ieved in him. She hadn't taken his side when all the evidence pointed against him. She hadn't given him a wife's loyalty.

And now her lack of faith might have destroyed whatever softer feelings he had begun to feel for her. She deserved it if he couldn't forgive her, if he hated her.

Shaking, Summer wrapped her arms around herself to hold back the tremors. Dear God, she couldn't bear it if he hated her. She wanted him to love her. She wanted to own his heart, as he owned hers. She wanted to become the center of his universe, his hopes, his dreams. She wanted him filling the emptiness inside her, just as she wanted to fill it for him. She wanted him standing beside her, against the rest of the world if need be. Just as she should have stood beside him when he'd needed her.

She closed her eyes tightly, wishing she could deny her betrayal. Lance had been right to condemn her. She had done nothing this past week to help him clear his name. She had sat at home waiting, while he had tried to prove his innocence, while he had faced his enemies alone.

But he wouldn't be alone any longer.

With determination and a bleak hopefulness, Summer raised her head. Lance needed help. *She* needed to find him help. She would do everything in her power to provide it for him. She would show him that she was on his side, totally, irrevocably.

And this time when he asked for her trust, she wouldn't let him down.

Chapter 23

A half hour later, Summer spoke to Reed, telling him exactly what Lance had been up to during the past week. She believed totally in his innocence, she declared, and never should have doubted him. She also demanded that they do everything possible to help Lance in his search for the real cattle thieves, and that Reed put all resources of the Sky Valley ranch behind the effort. Reed, in the face of her adamancy, swallowed his skepticism and capitulated.

Summer confronted her sister abruptly afterward, demanding that Amelia retract her lies about Lance. Amelia, however, remained stubbornly silent, her hostility undiminished.

Frustrated, Summer went out to the corrals to look for Dusty. She had to wait until he returned from the range, though, to implement the main part of her plan. She wanted to enlist his help, as well as that of the vaqueros who could be counted on to be loyal to Lance.

When Dusty rode in, Summer followed him into the small office he used for record keeping and forced herself to sit in the wooden chair he offered, determined to remain calm and logical. The foreman seated himself behind the small desk, heard her out in silence, and agreed to her plan without hesitation.

"You don't believe Lance is guilty?" Summer asked, relieved.

"Nope." Dusty shook his head. "I never thought for a minute he'd do something stupid like stealing beeves. Lance might have the disposition of a grizzly bear, but he's always had brains."

"Lance told me he was hunting for Comanche tracks, but he never said whether or not he'd found any."

Pushing back his hat, Dusty frowned in thought. "I doubt he did. Leastwise, not any that belonged to his kin. He'd be a damn fool to invite the Comanches into this territory—he knows he'd be blamed for anything any Indian did."

"But if the Comanches aren't stealing, then someone else is."

"Yep. I'm inclined to think maybe Will Prewitt had a hand in it."

Green eyes met blue in complete understanding. "So am I."

"Well, then . . ." Dusty grinned, making Summer feel infinitely grateful to have someone on her side. "I guess we better figure out how to catch us some cattle thieves."

They talked for a time about various options and what men they could put out riding the range. Dusty finished by expressing regret that Lance was trying to do it all alone.

"I wish he had come to me. I would have done my darnedest to help him."

Summer smiled bitterly. "Lance wouldn't ask anyone for help, not even me. You know how proud he is."

Dusty nodded. "That, he is. And after the barbecue . . . I guess now he feels like everybody's against him."

"My sister didn't help matters with her accusation. She refuses to admit she could be wrong."

"I can't figure why Miss Amelia is so set against him."

"I suppose because she blames him for what the Comanches did. I'm not really certain. I feel like I don't know her anymore."

They both fell silent, reflecting on the unfairness of the situation.

"Dusty . . . would you consider talking to Amelia? Perhaps you could influence her where I've failed."

"You think she would listen to me?"

"I don't know. I hope so. She likes and trusts you."

"She does, really?" He averted his gaze, as if suddenly ill at ease. "Do you think . . . someday maybe . . . Miss Amelia might consider getting married again?"

His color was high, his eyes lowered—the signs of a man enamored of a woman but reticent to admit it. Summer, acutely sensitive to such nuances with her own affairs of the heart in such disarray, replied gently. "I don't know. Perhaps to the right man, she would. After what happened . . . she's afraid of men. And at the same time she's afraid no man would want her."

"I'd want her. I'd take her as my wife in a second."

She smiled. "Perhaps in time. I wouldn't give up."

"I won't." He adjusted his hat and stood up. "Well, I guess I better go talk to some of the boys so we can get started tonight."

"Dusty . . . thank you."

"No need to thank me, Miss Summer. Even if I didn't like Lance as much as I do, I'd still help him. I figure I owe him for bringing Miss Amelia back safe."

He left then, relinquishing the small office to her. Alone, Summer let her head sag wearily. The strain of the past week was beginning to tell on her physically. And if she was suffering, how much more was Lance enduring?

God, please let it be over soon.

She rubbed the ache in her temples with both hands, wondering where Lance was at this moment, wondering if he was thinking of her, and if he possibly knew how desperately she regretted hurting him with her doubts.

The nausea began the following morning. Summer woke Saturday feeling listless and overhung, as if she was coming down sick. Her stomach settled as she lay there worrying about Lance, but she had barely left the bed before she felt the remains of last night's supper start to well in her throat.

For a full minute she retched into a basin, an attack that left her weak, as well as puzzled and concerned. She was rarely ill, and just now she couldn't afford to be sick. Not now when Lance's troubles demanded her best efforts, when his situation remained so uncertain.

She felt better once she'd chewed on a crust of bread. Following her new plan, she went up to the big house to iron her best day gown and choose a suit for Reed to wear. If she meant to drag her brother all over the countryside, paying a call on every woman in the neighborhood in order to plead Lance's case, she wanted her finest armor. It was possible such a venture would come to naught, that they would be refused entrance before being given a chance to explain why they thought Lance innocent of the charges against him, but

Summer thought making the attempt better than sitting at home doing nothing to help the man she loved.

She was heating the irons at the kitchen fire, working alongside Maritza and Consuala as they did morning chores, when the nausea struck again. Clapping a hand over her mouth, Summer whispered, "I think I'm going to be sick."

Maritza had enough command to hastily guide Summer to the sink and hold her shoulders while she retched, while Consuala wet a cloth and held it to her flushed forehead.

"Thank you," Summer murmured gratefully. "I don't know what's come over me. This happened earlier this morning, too."

In the silence that followed, Summer looked up to find both Mexican women watching her with dancing black eyes.

"What is it?" she asked, bewildered.

"You are to have a *bebé, sí?*" Maritza said happily.

"A baby?" She stared unseeingly at the woman. "You mean I am *pregnant?*"

"That is usual when these signs come to a woman. I myself was very sick when I carried my first son. The next two were not so difficult." Her smile faded. "Are you not glad about *el niño?*"

"I . . . yes . . . I'm just . . . surprised, that's all. I haven't been married very long."

Consuala laughed. "You should not be surprised with such a magnificent *hombre* as Señor Lance. He is one lusty lover, I would guess. This baby will have a fine *padre,* no?"

Summer felt color flood her cheeks at the woman's frank supposition.

"It is warm in here, señora," Maritza observed. "Perhaps you should go outside where it is cool. I will make you a cup of tea to ease your stomach. You will be all right once you grow accustomed to the idea of bearing a baby."

"Yes . . . thank you . . ." Summer said distractedly.

She let herself out of the kitchen onto the back porch, hardly knowing where she was going. Apprehension, shock, joy, wonder, all warred inside her.

A baby. Lance's child. A child of mixed blood. White and Comanche.

Blindly she sank into a wicker rocking chair, her hand pressed uncertainly to her stomach. Was there truly a new life growing inside her? If so, it would only compound a complex situation.

And yet she couldn't bring herself to regret it. She *wanted* this child. Even knowing the difficulties she would face bringing a mixed-breed baby into the world. Even knowing the trials a young child would suffer as an innocent victim of bigotry and hatred. She would have to shield him, teach him to defend himself against the slurs and innuendos, the baiting and physical assaults, to hold his head proudly, without shame. . . .

At the thought, Summer felt a surge of protectiveness rip through her, an instinct so fierce, it took her breath away. No one, *no one,* would ever harm this child as long as she had a breath left in her body. She pressed her hand possessively over her abdomen. She knew, in that moment, what a mother lion felt defending her cub. She thought she understood what Lance's mother must have felt when she'd chosen a life of shame and poverty as the price of keeping her infant son.

She herself would be willing to pay that price, Summer thought. As long as she had Lance, she could face anything a hostile world threw at her. Love engendered strength, and she loved him deeply, irrevocably—more than enough to brave whatever future lay before them. As long as she had Lance—*if* she still had Lance. Which really was not so certain at the moment.

Remembering his painful departure yesterday, how terribly she had wounded him with her suspicions, Summer gazed blindly out over the buildings of the ranch.

She wouldn't allow herself to believe she had lost him for good. She owed him an abject, humble apology, yes, but she would make him accept it. She would admit how wrong she'd been, how weak and foolish she'd been to be swayed for one instant by the arguments against him. She would make Lance see how much she loved him, that she believed in him.

And she would make him love her in return. She had never met a man yet who could resist her charms when she truly put her mind to it. Not even Lance, as fiercely proud and unyielding and defensive as he was.

How would he react about the baby? Should she even tell him yet? With such flimsy evidence as two instances of a sick stomach? No, she could be mistaken. She didn't think so; in her heart she knew it was true. She was carrying Lance's child. But she would wait for a time. For the moment she would hug the secret to herself, at least until she was certain.

She was so wrapped up in her thoughts about the baby that at first her consciousness didn't register what her eyes were seeing. In the distance, near one of the barns, a man and a woman stood engaged in intent conversation.

Summer had no trouble recognizing her sister, but the man was more difficult to place. It looked like one of their young ranch hands, Calvin Stapp. But whatever would Amelia be doing talking to him? For that matter, why was Calvin here, instead of out riding the range?

A chill swept Summer as a suspicion struck her. Amelia had spoken secretly with Will Prewitt shortly before he began his campaign to discredit Lance. Could this be connected somehow? Could Calvin be in league with them? Could, perhaps, they be plotting a further offense against Lance?

Summer's fingers clenched into a fist, but she willed her heart to settle down. There was an innocent explanation, surely. Amelia couldn't hate Lance that much. All the same, it would be wise to warn Dusty about this rendezvous, to ask him to keep an eye on Calvin.

Her sister was too far away for Summer to hear what was being said, but she appeared upset about something. When Calvin spoke to her earnestly, gesturing, Amelia shook her head once, twice, then took a step back, as if trying to distance herself from him. He seemed intent on arguing a point, or perhaps persuading her to do something she wasn't eager to do.

A moment later, he left her, heading toward the hitching rail and his horse, while Amelia stood watching. He had mounted and ridden away, toward the range, before she finally turned and moved slowly toward the house, her head lowered as if deep in troubled thought.

She had climbed the porch steps and was about to enter the back door when she saw Summer sitting in the rocker. Giving a start, Amelia came to an abrupt halt.

"Is everything all right, Melly?" Summer asked in a cool tone.

"Y-Yes . . . of course. Why wouldn't it be?"

"I thought you could tell me. I'd say you've been acting rather secretive of late."

Amelia gave a small laugh, which sounded a bit forced. "That's absurd."

"Why were you talking to Calvin Stapp just now?"

"I . . . I wanted to ask him about the herd they are rounding up for market."

"You're finally taking an interest in the ranch?"

"Yes. Is there something wrong with that?"

Summer shook her head sadly. "Do you know what hurts the most, Melly? We used to be friends, sisters. Not strangers. Not enemies. You never used to lie to me."

Amelia winced, and for a moment, her gaze looked anguished. But then she stiffened, straightening her shoulders. "I am not your enemy, Summer."

"No? You are doing your best to drive my husband out of the county. I think that makes you my enemy."

"If I am . . . it's only because he shouldn't be here. Lance Calder doesn't belong."

Pulling herself up out of the rocking chair, Summer rose slowly to her full height. "You've made yourself believe that, but he *does* belong here, Amelia. Lance has every bit as much right to stay here as you or I. He owns this ranch now, my part of it anyway—"

Amelia shook her head bitterly. "What would Papa say if he heard you?"

Summer raised her chin, holding her sister's gaze unwaveringly. "I don't care what he would say. Papa is dead—and I can't honestly say I'm sorry. While he lived, he was too blinded by hatred to give Lance a fair chance." She ignored the shock on her sister's face. "Just as you are blinded now. I warn you, though, Amelia. I mean to stand by him, no matter how difficult you and Prewitt make life for us. If I must choose between the two of you, then I'll choose Lance. Without question."

"You would turn your back on your own family?"

"Not entirely. Lance *is* my family now. He's my husband. And the father of the child I'm carrying."

Shock turned to horror as Amelia stared. "You're. . . ."

"Yes, I am going to have his baby."

"Oh, God . . . a Comanche . . ."

Summer's jaw hardened as she stepped close to Amelia. "Yes, Comanche. Feel this, Melly." She grabbed his sister's hand to press it hard against her stomach. "There is a *life* growing inside me! My child and Lance's. And yours, too, in part. You are going to be this baby's aunt."

"No . . ."

"Yes. He is *your* family, *your* flesh and blood, whether you like it or not."

"No!" Amelia recoiled, jerking her hand away.

Summer smiled coldly, relentless in her scorn. "I'd even go so far as to say you share responsibility for his conception. In order to save you, Lance married me—and this baby is the result. This child will be born because of you."

Amelia covered her mouth with her trembling hands.

Summer's fierce glare softened. "I don't think you mean to be so cruel, Melly. I can't believe you would condemn an innocent child to the terrible life of an outcast."

Amelia's eyes filled with tears, but her only response was to turn and grope blindly for the door.

Summer's quiet voice stopped her from leaving, however. "Don't do this to Lance, Melly. Please . . . I'm begging you. Don't hurt him any more than he's already been hurt. I love him, Melly. It may not have started out that way. I resented him at first, for forcing me to marry him. But that's all changed now. I *want* Lance as my husband. I *want* him as the father of my child."

With a choked sob that was almost inaudible, Amelia pushed open the door and fled.

When Lance faced Amelia some ten hours later in the front parlor of the Weston house, she looked pale and subdued. In the deceptive lamplight, he found it hard to tell whether sleeplessness or weeping had caused the dark circles under her eyes.

Amelia wouldn't meet his gaze, although now and then she risked a fearful glance at him. Lance watched her with similar wariness as he stood inside the parlor door.

To say that he had been surprised by her peculiar summons would have been an understatement. Calvin Stapp had found him out on the range just before dusk and told him that Miss

Amelia wanted him to come to the house, that she had something to show him. She wouldn't say what it was, though.

His first reaction, absurdly, had been hope. The irrational, foolish hope that the woman had somehow relented in her attitude toward him and was willing to take the first step toward making amends.

A stupid hope, obviously, he realized as he recognized that look of fear and contempt twisting her features.

Now, as he'd done too many times to count when confronted with white prejudice, he masked his disappointment behind a hard stare. If he was making her nervous, he didn't much give a damn. His own unease at being here was only increasing, the longer she remained silent.

Amelia was clutching a crumpled piece of paper between her fingers, and kept looking at it, as if she couldn't quite make up her mind about what to do with it. She didn't immediately satisfy his curiosity, but instead, asked him in a small voice if he knew how to read.

The cold fury he thought he felt for this woman dissipated into weariness. What difference did it make what the ignorant savage knew or didn't know? "Well enough," he replied gruffly.

She handed him the paper, careful not to let his fingers touch her. When he unwadded it, he could see a message printed in uneven block letters.

Miss Summer, If you want proof *that your Injun stole all them beeves, meet me at midnight at the old Paxly place near the three oaks.*

His gut clenched at the damning words. Somebody was going to a lot of trouble to pin the blame for the stolen stock on him—and dragging Summer into it. A note like this would only make her believe the worst about him—and somehow that hurt more than knowing her sister hated him enough to plot his downfall.

"Did Summer give you this?" he asked Amelia.

"N-No, she doesn't know about it yet."

The relief he felt was absurd, considering the danger he was in. "Then where'd you get this paper?"

"I ... I found it ... lying on the front porch, tied around a rock. I thought ... you would want to do something about ..." She faltered, as if unable to continue the lie.

He looked at her a long moment. "About destroying the evidence, you mean."

"Y-Yes."

"That's right kind of you, Miss Amelia. You wantin' to help me and all."

His tone was cool, drawling, and made her flush. The note was a setup, Lance knew. Amelia Truesdale hadn't suddenly had a change of heart and become willing to embrace him as her brother-in-law. If he went to the Paxly place, he'd be walking into a trap. He knew it, as sure as whites hated red men.

But he no longer was certain he cared how this trouble ended. His life here was over. His dream of building a place with Summer was just that, a foolish dream. Clearing his name was likely beyond his reach with so many of the good citizens of Williamson County in league against him. So he'd settle for what he could have. Finding out who was behind the thefts—and making sure whoever it was paid.

"Why the change of heart?" Lance asked Amelia softly, without emotion.

"What ... what do you mean?"

"A week ago you did your best to get me run out of the county, telling those lies about me in front of the entire community. Why are you suddenly willing to help me out now?"

She didn't answer. Instead, Amelia covered her mouth with one hand while her eyes filled with tears. "I ... I ..." With a broken sob, she turned and fled from the room.

Lance stood looking after her for a long while, slapping his hat against his thigh, weighing his choices.

He rode cautiously through the darkness, his guns loaded, his knife loose in the scabbard at his waist. The old Paxly homestead had been deserted some twenty years ago, burned out by raiding Comanches, but the land, which had been bought up by John Weston, now made up the southwest corner of the Sky Valley spread. The three oaks mentioned in Amelia's note were a familiar landmark to anyone in the county, since they'd been planted beside the graves of the Paxly family.

There was enough moonlight to see by. Lance's gaze swept the surrounding hills, noting any of a dozen places that would make a good location for an ambush. He didn't think they would spring one on him yet, though. They would wait to catch him with the evidence.

There were still three hours to go till midnight, but he'd decided not to wait. Prewitt and his gang—if it was Prewitt—would likely be prepared for him in any case, not knowing if and when he would show, but any element of surprise was better than none.

He'd ridden straight from the Weston house, passing the cabin he'd shared with Summer without stopping, ignoring the light burning inside that told him she likely was home. The need to see her one last time had burned in him like fever, but he'd refused to acknowledge it. He didn't think he could take facing her again, not with her suspicion, the pleading accusation in her eyes. The last time had near killed him.

Too, if he went near her, he wouldn't be able to stop himself from holding her one last time. And then he would have to tear himself away. And when he tried to leave, she would ask questions. She would want to know where he'd been, where he was going, and then there would be explanations to make, her reaction to deal with. If she knew what he planned, she might try to stop him. And he didn't want her to stop him.

His jaw clenched, Lance kept his horse at a steady walk as he rounded a rocky outcrop. Up ahead lay the meadow with the three oaks where the Paxlys were buried. It was surrounded by hills that offered plenty of places for a man to hide. He didn't want to hide, though. He wanted to draw Prewitt out. If he was going down, he would go down fighting. And if he was going to die, he intended to take Prewitt with him.

The cold gust of wind blew in his face, carrying with it the scent of livestock. A prickle of awareness traveled up his spine at the smell. Silently Lance slipped his six-shooter from its holster and thumbed back the hammer.

He heard the cattle moving restlessly in the dark before he saw them. There had to be two or three hundred head, grazing peacefully. He would bet his life they would be marked with Harlan Fisk's brand, and maybe others as well.

He skirted the herd slowly, keeping away from the long, wicked horns that could rip a horse's belly with a single stab.

It was maybe a minute later when his instincts told him he wasn't alone with the steers. He brought his horse to a halt, waiting.

In the silence, he could feel the slow, harsh pounding of his heart, the gathering of nerves as he waited for a possible attack.

"Okay, Prewitt," he called out finally. "I'm here. Now what?"

A group of shadows peeled away from the hill to his right. He counted four riders, but he suspected there were more.

Prewitt wasn't one of them, he saw as they approached him cautiously, pistols and rifles down. He recognized Bob Blackwood, and one of the Weston ranch hands whom Reed had hired recently, a kid by the name of Calvin Stapp. That hurt, knowing a man he had worked with had turned on him.

"Put your hands on your hat," Blackwood ordered as they came to a halt, half surrounding him.

"Where's Prewitt?" Lance asked, keeping his hands right where they were.

A disembodied voice came at him from the darkness to his left. "Here, Calder." Will Prewitt slowly rode his horse into view, followed by some half dozen other silhouettes. "What'd I tell you, boys? I said he'd show."

No one answered the rhetorical question.

Prewitt halted his horse behind Blackwood, out of range. "Do as Bob says, breed. Raise your hands."

Lance casually rested an arm on his pommel. "I thought I'd find you here."

He raised his rifle menacingly. "You red bastard, get your hands up!"

"Why should I?"

"Because you're under arrest for thieving stock. We caught you in the act."

"That so?" Lance's mouth curled. "How do you figure?"

"You're here, ain't you?"

"And so are you. You set this whole thing up."

Prewitt smirked. "You'll never prove it."

"And you'll never prove I had anything to do with stealing Fisk's livestock."

"We don't need to. We got all the evidence we need right

here." He waved his arm in the direction of the herd of long-horns.

"I'm supposed to have herded all these beeves here by my-self?"

"Your stinkin' Injun friends helped. And you'll hang for it, breed."

"I don't think so," Lance said in a low, deadly voice.

"Maybe we better get Fisk," somebody said nervously—the kid named Stapp, Lance thought.

"Yeah, get Fisk here," Lance said aloud. "Make it look all legal-like when you do murder."

"It won't be murder," Prewitt retorted as he moved his horse closer. "Stealing stock's a hangin' offense."

Blackwood glanced at Prewitt. "Maybe we should. Have Fisk here, I mean. It won't take long to fetch him. We should have a trial."

"There's no need for a trial!"

"I don't like this," someone else said. "Maybe a trial's best."

A tense moment followed before Prewitt shrugged. "I can wait. Calvin, you ride for Fisk. In the meantime we'll ready the rope."

"You're planning to take the law into your own hands, Prewitt?" Lance drawled.

"Damn right. We're gonna have us a lynch party. You're gonna hang, Calder."

"You'll have to take me first."

There was a brief silence while Prewitt stared at Lance. "Suits me."

Without warning, he took aim with his rifle and fired.

Lance ducked low over his sorrel's neck and raised his own six-shooter at the same instant. He got off a shot as he dug in his bootheels, heard Prewitt cry out at the explosion, felt a long, tearing pain along his own upper right arm. As his horse leaped forward, he managed to fire another round in Prewitt's direction before the other startled men reacted and raised their weapons.

Lance felt sharp pain in his right side as a volley of gunfire exploded in his ears.

A nearby steer bellowed as riders scattered.

Then chaos followed as all hell broke loose.

Chapter 24

Too tense to sleep, too weary to work, Summer rocked herself slowly in the parlor rocking chair. The calls she and Reed had paid on some of their neighbors this afternoon had yielded little results. No doors had been slammed in her face, but neither had her visits been welcome. She'd been unable to persuade anyone of Lance's innocence. His ties to the Comanche were too powerful to ignore, and the suspicion that he might have invited the vicious marauders to pillage the countryside was enough to put a lifetime of friendships at risk.

Gently Summer laid a caressing hand on her abdomen. This was the treatment she could expect for herself and her child. And yet she knew she would endure it gladly if only Lance would come home, if he would forgive her for her faithlessness and give her a second chance to prove to him that she wanted to be his wife.

She gave a start when a soft knock sounded on the cabin door. *Lance,* was her first thought.

Leaping to her feet, she fairly flew to the front door. To her dismay and bewilderment, Amelia stood there in the dark passageway.

"Is something wrong?" Summer demanded in breathless alarm.

"I . . . no . . . May . . . I come in?"

Her sister had never visited her at the cabin before, and Summer didn't know what to make of it. Amelia looked pale and nervous as she stepped inside.

Feeling a sudden chill that had little to do with the November night air, Summer drew her shawl more tightly about her. "Why are you here?" she asked warily. "I don't imagine this is a social call."

Amelia wouldn't meet her eyes. "I . . . couldn't sleep. I just wanted . . . to see you."

Gesturing to indicate the small, chintz-covered settee that served dual purpose as a spare bed for visitors, Summer kept her tone cool, polite. "Please sit down. Would you like some coffee, or tea?"

"No . . . no, thank you."

Amelia didn't take the proffered seat. Instead she let her gaze wander around the room. "The cabin . . . you've fixed it up. It looks very nice."

"Thank you. I've made it into a home. It's not large or elegant, but it's ours. And it was shelter when you refused to allow us to live in the house."

A fleeting look of anguish crossed Amelia's features, but she didn't reply. Moving carefully over to the settee, the way an old woman might, she slowly sat down. Rather than making conversation, though, she clutched her fingers in her lap, staring at her hands.

Summer resumed her seat in the rocker. She refused to ease this awkward situation by playing the congenial hostess, or to help her sister with whatever she'd come to do.

Amelia didn't look up when she said finally, in a small voice, "Are you . . . really going to have a baby?"

"I believe so. Lance's baby. But of course, you won't want to acknowledge it. It will be a mixed breed, you know."

Amelia shut her eyes, her face contorting for a moment. "Summer . . . I . . . I'm sorry."

"Whatever for, Melly?" she retorted with cynical sweetness. "Why should you feel the least bit sorry? Just because you've made Lance's life hell? Destroyed any chance he has of becoming part of this community? Destroyed our children's chances of being accepted as anything but savages? Subjected them to a life of scorn and hate? Why*ever* should you apologize?"

Tears welled in her sister's eyes as she mutely shook her head. "Yes . . . for all that. I'm s-sorry."

"It's a bit late for regrets now," Summer observed bitterly. "I kn-know. . . ."

Fiercely she gave herself a push in the rocker, but then abruptly stopped the sway. "Just tell me one thing. Why did you tell those lies about Lance in front of everyone? Now the whole county believes him to be a monster."

"I ... I only ... I didn't want ... people to accept him." The tears were streaming down her cheeks by now. "I didn't want him to fit in ... b-because ... then he would stay. At the barbecue ... people were acting so friendly. . . ."

"So you deliberately ruined his chances."

"Y-Yes ..."

Summer leaned toward her sister, pinning her with a fierce gaze. "Lance risked his *life* to save you, Amelia? If not for him, you would still be a Comanche captive, enduring the horrible things they did to you. You might even be dead by now! I think you owed Lance more than treachery."

Her sister flinched, cringing in her seat.

"I begged you ... *begged* you to think about what you were doing, to see how obsessed you were with hating him, but you wouldn't listen."

Amelia lowered her face into her hands and sobbed.

Summer clenched her fingers, refusing to relent, to offer comfort for this belated attack of conscience. She was glad Amelia felt a measure of remorse for what she'd done— Melly deserved to suffer—but Summer wasn't certain she could ever forgive her. Perhaps if Lance returned, if he could somehow put all this behind him, then she might someday consider accepting her sister's apology.

It was during that righteous reflection that Summer heard the distant shouts and then the sudden staccato of hoofbeats outside, as if someone had galloped up to the cabin. Rising quickly, she went to the door—this time to admit a grim-faced Dusty.

"You've got to come," he said without preliminaries. "Lance is in big trouble. Gather up any guns you have and bring them. The boys are saddling up. I'm going to find Reed."

He started to turn away, but Summer stopped him by clutching his arm. "What kind of trouble?" she asked hoarsely.

"He's been shot, but he's still alive. But they're talking about hanging."

"*Who?*" Summer cried.

"Prewitt and his gang. I was keeping an eye on Stapp like

you said—followed him to the old Paxly place and waited. Lance showed up and then there was a gunfight. I was too far away to help, and alone, to boot. I figured I'd better fetch some backup."

She was grateful to Dusty for his succinctness, but her pounding heart had lodged in her throat, and she could do nothing more than nod.

"Hurry up. If we don't get there fast, there's gonna be a lynching."

With shaking hands, Summer turned blindly to lift the loaded rifle that was always kept hanging by the front door, and then started to fetch the one in the bedroom. Only then did she notice or even remember her sister. Amelia was standing, staring white-faced at Dusty, her tears arrested.

He gave a start when he saw her, and hesitated for an instant.

"No . . ." Amelia said in a breathless whisper. "They weren't supposed to hurt him."

Summer froze in the act of clutching the rifle. "What . . . ?"

"He said . . . I thought . . . they would just make him leave. Not try to hurt him. He said they wouldn't hurt him."

"Who said?"

"S-Stapp."

Summer felt panic like a knife in her stomach, but she tried to force it down. "Melly . . . tell me what happened."

"I . . . I gave Lance the note . . . so he would go to the Paxly place . . . just like Prewitt wanted. They were going to catch him with the stolen cattle, but that was all, I swear it."

Summer stared, reeling at the enormity of what Amelia had done. Slowly, as if sleepwalking, she moved to stand before her sister.

"Don't look at me that way!" Amelia cried suddenly. "I didn't mean . . . I never intended for him to be killed! I only wanted him to go away and leave us alone! I only wanted him out of our lives!"

Blindly, hardly knowing what she was doing, Summer drew back her hand and struck Amelia across the face with her open palm. The stinging blow made her sister recoil and elicited a protest from Dusty, but Summer ignored both. "Lance *is* my life, Amelia! And if he dies . . ."

She couldn't continue the thought. Swallowing the burning

ache in her throat, she glared at her sister, who was cringing as she held her cheek. "You are coming with us."

Amelia took a startled step back. "No . . . I can't!"

"You can and you *will!* You devised this plot to incriminate Lance, and you'll get him out of it."

She threw a glance over her shoulder at Dusty. "Get Reed, and hurry. And bring Amelia with you. I don't care if you have to tie her hand and foot, just get her there! I'm taking your horse."

With grim determination, she turned and swept past Dusty, out into the night. The terror was almost manageable now. A frozen calm had settled over her, numbing her.

She stumbled as she ran down the porch steps, but scarcely noticed. Quickly she caught the reins of Dusty's horse and hauled herself up into the saddle, cradling the rifle in her lap. He could bring Amelia and Reed in the buckboard. Just now she had to reach Lance before it was too late.

The pain took his mind off his other troubles.

His right side burned like hell; his wounded arm stung; his shoulder sockets ached from when they'd wrenched his arms behind his back to tie them. His balls throbbed from being dragged across a saddle when they'd shoved him onto a horse, and his bruised jaw felt broken from the punches Prewitt had thrown after they'd both survived the gun battle. His lip was split in at least two places, filling his mouth with blood. And his forehead was bleeding, too, making it damned difficult to see. And if that wasn't enough, the noose around his neck was tight enough to make breathing rough.

His only regret, though, was that he hadn't hurt Prewitt nearly bad enough. The bastard only had a flesh wound in his thigh, which he'd tied off with a tourniquet.

Lance squinted through a haze of blood and fury, trying to locate Prewitt in the crowd. There was plenty of light— somebody had lit a couple of torches in honor of his lynching—but he found it hard to shift his head with his neck stretched by the rope. The exploding gunfire had stampeded the cattle, a turn of events that had caused more damage than the flying bullets. Two of Prewitt's boys were lying on the ground with various injuries, neither of them too serious.

Lance blinked when he found Harlan Fisk's solemn face

staring up at him. Oh, yeah. Fisk had arrived minutes ago, he remembered. The older man was trying to get him to answer some questions, while the others wanted to get on with the hanging.

Even as Lance had the thought, Harlan Fisk shook his head sadly. "I didn't believe it, son. I didn't believe you'd steal from *me*, even if you might from Prewitt."

Lance felt the blood welling in his mouth and tried awkwardly to spit it out.

"Well?" Fisk demanded impatiently. "What do you have to say for yourself?"

What could he say? That he hadn't done it? That he'd been set up? That he'd been stupid enough to walk into Prewitt's trap because he'd wanted a fight? All true, but he wouldn't be believed.

"Go to hell," he mumbled instead.

"See there?" Prewitt demanded. "That arrogant bastard thinks he's above the law." He raised his voice to address the crowd of men. "I say there's no need for a trial. We got six men who will testify they found Calder with the evidence."

"Yeah," a chorus of voices agreed.

"I say finish him," someone else called out. "One less red hide won't hurt the world none."

"The outcome wouldn't be any different if we waited for a trial."

"Jerk that rope tight around his neck, boys," ordered Prewitt, "and tie it off."

Harlan looked reluctant but resigned. "The evidence against you is mighty strong, son. I can't help you if you won't help yourself."

The rope was pulled taut over a limb of one of the three oaks, and Lance winced in spite of himself as the abrasive noose dug into his throat.

"You got any last prayers?" Prewitt taunted. "Last chance to cleanse your soul before you meet your Maker."

He managed to aim a mouthful of spittle in Prewitt's direction. He would never beg for his life, not from the likes of Prewitt at any rate. Without Summer, he wasn't sure life was really worth living anyway. And she would be better off without him, for certain.

Lance closed his eyes and said a prayer, not for himself,

but for her. He hoped to God that she would be okay without him and get on with her life. That she would forget about how he had ruined her future. That she would remember him without hating him.

When he heard a distant drumming, he thought it was blood pounding in his ears. It took him a second to realize that it wasn't, that it was hoofbeats instead. He squinted at the sound, and thought he was imagining what he saw: a woman bent low over a heaving horse, her long, dark hair streaming behind her as she raced across the field. *Summer,* he thought with weary regret. *Go away.*

She came to a plunging halt at the edge of the crowd, but had eyes only for him. Lance closed his own eyes, wishing she hadn't come, wishing she'd never found him like this— beaten and battered and at the mercy of white trash like Prewitt. He'd rather die.

She was breathing hard as she urged Dusty's sweating horse through the group of silent men toward Lance. Her anguished gaze took in the blood on his face, his shirt sleeve, the hem of his vest, then turned contemptuous as it traveled accusingly over the crowd. "Dear God, are you all animals? Treating a wounded man like this?" She lifted the rifle nozzle, aiming it at the crowd. "Cut him down."

"Now, just a minute there—" someone protested.

Summer swung the rifle in the direction of the voice. "If you want to hang him, you'll have to kill me first! I advise you not to try it, because I'll shoot every last one of you." She gestured with the rifle. "I have fifteen rounds. And Reed should be bringing more."

A tense silence followed her threat.

She found Calvin Stapp's youthful face in the crowd. "You're in on it, Calvin, I know. You'll be the second one I shoot, right after Will Prewitt. Now, *cut him down.*"

Lance, as bad as he felt, couldn't help but also feel a measure of pride at her defiant defense of him.

Stapp even started to obey her fierce order, before Prewitt stopped him. "Hold on. We ain't gonna let anybody interfere with the carriage of justice. Calder's a cattle thief who deserves to hang."

Summer turned on Prewitt in fury. "My husband no more

stole any livestock than I did! I'm willing to swear my life on it. And so will my sister."

"Miss Amelia?" Harlan Fisk asked.

"Yes, Amelia! She'll be here any minute, along with Dusty and Reed. You can wait that long to carry out your unlawful justice."

Prewitt, however, apparently didn't care to wait. He lunged forward with a shout and struck Lance's horse with the butt of his rifle. The startled horse squealed and bounded sideways, leaving its rider behind: Lance's body jerked as the rope took his entire weight.

Summer choked on a scream, paralyzed by horror. It was sheer terror that made her kick her mount viciously, forcing it between Lance and the ground.

He appeared half-dead, but he managed somehow to try and save himself. Wildly swinging his leg, he hooked it over her horse's neck, relieving his neck of some of his weight.

Desperately Summer abandoned the rifle to wrap her arms around Lance—which was a mistake. Rather than supporting him, she was only helping the rope kill him with the added strain.

Sobbing with fear, she groped for the knife he always wore around his belt and whimpered out loud when her fingers closed around the hilt. Crying too hard to see, she raised her arm and blindly sawed at the rope.

When it finally gave way, Lance slumped forward on her horse's neck, choking and coughing. Still weeping, Summer pressed her face against his back and held him, murmuring his name over and over and over again.

She didn't even hear the arrival of the vaqueros from Sky Valley, even when they came thundering up. She felt gentle hands urging her down from her horse, but she didn't want to turn loose of Lance for an instant. Only when Harlan Fisk's quiet voice explained that Lance needed care did she relent.

Practically falling into Fisk's arms, she allowed him to support her while two men carefully laid Lance on the ground. They took the noose from his neck and cut the bonds from his hands; then, by the light of a torch, they stripped off his vest and shirt to examine his injuries. Lance lay with his eyes closed, unmoving, except for the harsh rise and fall of his chest as he dragged short breaths of air into his lungs.

"The arm is not too bad, señora," Pedro pronounced. "The side, it is bleeding, but the patrón, he will be okay."

Summer wanted to scream a denial, that Lance *wasn't* all right, that he was hurt, but she couldn't force the words past her raw throat. She watched as Pedro made a bandage from Lance's shirt and tied it around his bleeding waist.

As soon as the task was complete and someone had covered Lance's bare torso with a bedroll blanket, she dropped to her knees beside him, laying a tentative hand on his shoulder. She felt the shudders ripple through him, felt the clenching and unclenching of his muscles as he struggled to draw breath. Carefully she took his hand and pressed her lips against his palm, wetting it with her tears.

She heard the buckboard arrive a moment later, but was too shaken to acknowledge it. A wild trembling had invaded her limbs. She had lost her shawl on the mad ride, and perspiration soaked her gown, but it wasn't the chill night air that froze her blood. It was realizing how very close she'd come to losing Lance. She had never known such desperation.

The crowd of men parted slightly, allowing a path for the buckboard. Dusty brought the vehicle to a halt, a mere three yards from Lance.

"Is he all right?" Reed asked sharply.

Summer managed a tearful laugh. "If you call being shot and nearly hanged 'all right.' They tried to lynch him."

"Put him in the buckboard. We'll get him to a doctor."

Summer shook her head. Just now she wanted nothing more than to protect Lance, to take him home, away from these people who wished him dead. Yet a more urgent task prevented her. She couldn't leave until the cloud of suspicion hanging over Lance's head was destroyed for good. She had to prove his innocence, make them believe. She lifted her gaze to her sister. "After Melly tells the truth about what happened."

Amelia sat totally still, her eyes shut, her head lowered.

Summer was grateful when her brother took the lead. Reed remained in the buckboard beside Amelia, holding her hand, and cleared his throat. "My sister has something to say," he announced to the crowd. "Amelia?"

She gave a choked sob, and then mumbled something no one could hear.

"Louder, Amelia," Reed urged gently. "Lance's life depends on it."

"Mr. Calder didn't do it!" she cried. "It's *my* fault."

"What's your fault, Miss Amelia?" Harlan asked kindly.

She looked up, focusing on him, while tears streamed down her face. "I . . . asked Will Prewitt to help me get rid of him."

"Him? You mean Calder?"

At Harlan's question, Summer shifted her gaze to glance at the faces of the men above her, the ones who stood as Lance's judges. Every one of them looked skeptical.

"They don't understand, Melly," she said in a low voice. "Tell them why you wanted to be rid of Lance."

"Because . . . because . . . he was one of *them*. I was afraid of him."

Summer watched the faces. Her sister's tormented confession was too real not to believe, but still they weren't convinced.

"She wanted revenge," Summer explained quietly. "She blamed Lance for the trials she endured at the hands of his Comanche kin and wanted him to pay. Isn't that right, Amelia?"

Amelia covered her face with her hands, but she nodded. "Y-Yes . . ."

"There never were any Comanches here, were there? You lied about that, too."

"Y-Yes," she said, her shoulders shaking with sobs, "I l-lied. There never . . . were any Comanches."

Beside her, Dusty put a comforting arm around her, as if he couldn't stand her anguish.

After a minute, the uncertain voice of one of the men broke in. "But somebody stole all those cattle. If Calder didn't do it, who did?"

"Amelia?" Reed prodded. "You have to finish."

She swallowed a sob, then took a deep, shuddering breath. "Prewitt. Will Prewitt . . . stole all the cattle . . . and left behind evidence to make it look like Indians at work . . . so Lance would be blamed. But I didn't know. . . . He told me they would just make sure he left. He never said ... they would try to hang him."

The garbled, tearful admission of conspiracy was difficult to follow, but Summer could see it sinking in on every face: shame for nearly lynching an innocent man. Growing anger at being duped into it. All of them turned to look at Will Prewitt.

"We still got a rope," someone observed. "We could make us of it."

"No!" Summer surged to her feet. "We're civilized citizens, not savages! Will Prewitt deserves justice, but there are adequate laws to punish him for what he did. He should be put in jail."

"You're right," Harlan Fisk seconded. "We should stay within the law. We can take him to Georgetown until the district judge can get to him—"

"I ain't going to any jail!" Prewitt retorted. He took a limping step backward, brandishing his rifle. "You won't pin the blame on me. You try, and Miss Amelia's going down with me. She's the one told me to do it."

All eyes turned on Amelia. She sat sobbing softly, her head bowed, while beside her, both Dusty and Reed stiffened.

Summer could feel the crowd's hesitation: No one could possibly want to make Amelia suffer more, not after all she had been through.

"Well, now," Harlan began awkwardly, evidently searching for words. "Miss Amelia wasn't really in her right mind when she got back from up north. ... And she's sorry now for what she did, aren't you, Miss Amelia?"

"Yes," she murmured in a raw whisper.

"I bet Lance would forgive her if she asked him to. But you, now ..." Harlan looked piercingly at Prewitt. "There's always been bad blood between you two. Even if he could overlook being framed, I don't think he could forget how you tried to hang him just now by shying his horse. You almost killed him."

Harlan glanced around him, as if gauging whether he had the support of the crowd. When several of the men nodded, he pushed back his hat to rub his forehead thoughtfully. "Fact is, I don't believe there's room for you both in the same county. I guess it's up to Lance to press charges, but if it were up to me . . . I'd just as soon see the last of you, Will. Nobody wants a man they can't trust for a neighbor."

A murmur of agreement rose from the crowd, and Summer could almost sense their relief at having so reasonable a solution presented to them.

Prewitt must have sensed the same thing, for he looked around him wildly. "I wasn't the only one! I had help driving them beeves." He looked directly at Bob Blackwood, who was standing rigidly. "Bob was in on it as much as me."

"It's up to Lance," Harlan replied.

Summer looked down at her wounded husband. She was certain he was conscious, but he kept his eyes closed and remained silent. Perhaps he was in too much pain to care, or too indifferent. Perhaps he merely hated them all.

She took a deep breath, making the decision for him. There were too many people involved in the plot against him to banish them all, at least without increasing the enmity and resentment the rest of the community felt toward him. In the long run, forgiveness would win Lance more converts than stark justice. "I think Lance would be satisfied if only Mr. Prewitt were gone."

Blackwood looked visibly relieved, and Harlan nodded. "You sell your place, Will, and move on. I'll give you a fair price if no one else will. Otherwise we take you to jail right now."

Prewitt gave one last desperate glance at the others, then spun on his uninjured leg and limped over to his horse.

Summer pressed her lips together tightly as she watched him ride off. With only a leg wound and banishment, Prewitt had gotten off too lightly, but at least it was over. He wouldn't hurt Lance anymore. It was over, except that Lance was still badly hurt.

Shaking herself, she glanced at Pedro. "He should have a doctor."

She stepped back while they lifted Lance and put him in the back of the buckboard. Climbing in after him, Summer cradled his head in her lap and tucked the blanket around his bare shoulders.

It made her heart sink when he refused to look at her. Lance kept his eyes shut, not acknowledging her—or Harlan

Fisk, who came to stand beside the buckboard, twisting his hat in his hand.

"We owe you an apology, son," Harlan said quietly. "A mighty big one. I guess none of us deserves it, but if you could find it in your heart to forgive us . . . Well, I just want you to know I'm damned sorry."

Reed answered for Lance, and Summer, as well. "If you really mean it, Harlan, you'll make sure the whole state finds out that he's innocent. And that there never was any danger of Comanches."

"I'll see to it," Harlan replied solemnly.

Reed nodded at Dusty, who, with a backward glance at his passengers, snapped the reins and urged the team forward.

Summer put her arms around Lance, bracing him against the jolt and sway of the buckboard. She felt no response, not even the slightest softening. Lance lay stiff and silent in her embrace, his eyes closed, his lips pressed together in a grimace.

Summer closed her own eyes as dread curled around her heart. Perhaps his continued silence had little to do with physical pain. Perhaps he simply wanted nothing more to do with her—because she was one of the people he couldn't forgive.

Chapter 25

T he Round Rock doctor patched up Lance's wounds and declared him lucky. The bullet had pierced his side but failed to hit any organs or ribs. The arm wound, too, could have been much worse, splintering bone instead of tearing only muscle. His other injuries, though no doubt hurting like hell, were superficial. Summer was allowed to take Lance home with only a warning to yell if there were complications.

She would have been relieved, except for his continued silence. Lance had a high tolerance for pain, she knew, but he hadn't made a sound through all the jostling and jolting of the buckboard, or when the doctor had poked and prodded him or stitched him with a needle. Nor did he curse or rant or even mention the incident just past that had nearly cost him his life. He merely maintained a grim silence that none of the Westons dared breach, not even to ask forgiveness for the part they'd played in doubting him. Only Dusty was entirely blameless. *His* graveness seemed directed at Amelia, who sobbed softly from time to time.

Summer felt like weeping as well; tears would have been a welcome relief to the self-reproach that ate at her stomach like acid. But they wouldn't come.

It was nearly two o'clock in the morning when they reached the ranch. Dusty and Reed helped Lance into the cabin and put him to bed, then took their leave. Summer, bone-weary and filled with growing dread, settled into the rocking chair with a blanket to be near if Lance called her in the night.

He didn't.

She dozed fitfully now and then, and started awake to gaze wildly around her, finding solace at the sight of his poor, bruised face whose bronzed hue was mottled with shades of black and blue. Lance was home, with her, battered but safe.

He woke at midmorning, showing no signs of fever. He drank some soup that Summer warmed for him, but he didn't speak to her, or even look at her, and he insisted on feeding himself.

Her heart ached hollowly at his distancing silence. His manner wasn't hostile, or even cold, but it aroused a terror in her nearly as great as when she'd watched him struggle helplessly against a deadly, strangling rope. There was an air of defeat about him, a supreme indifference, as if he no longer cared what happened to him, or between them. As if he'd lost the will to fight, to continue his defiant battle against a hostile white world. As if he'd decided he couldn't forgive her for not believing in him, for not trusting him.

Afraid to press the issue, Summer couldn't find the nerve to disturb the silence. What Lance needed most now was sleep, healing rest. When he had recovered enough, then she would be forced to face the welling fear that had already woven knots in her stomach.

He had gone back to sleep when Reed stopped by to ask how he was faring. Summer put on a brave face, assuring her brother that Lance seemed to be recovering and that she would call if he took a turn for the worse. It was only when Reed was gone that the tension of the past few days finally got to her and she broke down for a bout of weeping. She felt somewhat better afterward, but only in the way numbness is preferable to pain. When Dusty called a short while later, she was able to force a smile and thank him profusely for the part he'd played in saving her husband's life.

She was there when Lance woke again in late afternoon—and so was the wall he'd erected between them. When she offered to wash him, Lance clenched his jaw and refused her help with a terse shake of his head. He took the wet cloth from her and performed his own ablutions, and when he was done, he turned his head on the pillow to watch the window, shutting her out. He seemed so far away, so unreachable, so unutterably alone.

It was all Summer could do to keep the tremor out of her voice when she asked if he wanted something to eat. He refused that, too, and made no reply when she offered to bring him a glass of lemonade. Helplessly she turned away, escaping into the next room on the pretext of fixing him a drink, unable to bear his remoteness any longer.

While she was gone, Lance watched the shaft of late sunlight streaming in the window. The warm brilliance made mock of the bleakness in his heart; the dancing dust motes taunted him with their cheerful gaiety.

He felt empty inside. Drained. Wrung-out. Hollow. Except that the clamoring ache in the pit of his gut had little to do with physical hunger.

It was shame, pure and simple. Gut-wrenching, soul-writhing, heart-sickening shame. Shame at his weakness.

What kind of man couldn't protect himself and his woman? What kind of warrior had to be rescued from mortal danger by his wife? What future could he offer Summer if he could no longer hold his head up? If every time he looked men in the eye, he saw his defeat in their expression, his humiliation?

All his life he'd endured scorn and degradation, and spit in the face of any man who'd dared press too hard. But he couldn't face this. Something had snapped inside him last night. The noose that had nearly hanged him had ripped away his self-respect even though it hadn't taken his life.

Summer came back a while later with his glass of lemonade, and approached his bed tentatively, as if she feared to get too close. He took it and drank, but his throat still felt full of gravel when he lowered the glass from his swollen lips.

His voice was low and hoarse, but his tone uninflected when he finally spoke. "I'll be leaving just as soon as I can ride."

Summer froze, staring at him as if she hadn't understood what he'd said. "L-Leaving? What . . . do you mean?"

"Just what I said." He turned his shuttered black gaze on her for a fleeting interval. "I'll be leaving the ranch. Leaving Texas, in fact."

"Why? Where . . . ?" She started to ask where he intended to go, but broke off stupidly. *Where* wasn't nearly as important as *why*. She could barely force the question past her tight throat. "Why? Is it to punish me for not . . . for thinking you . . . You can't forgive me for having so little faith in you?"

His dark brows drew together in a scowl. "You don't have to feel guilty for that, princess. I never expected your faith, not really." His lips twisted. "Don't look so stricken. I'm sure you'll be glad to be rid of me—"

"Lance . . . no . . . that isn't true!"

"Isn't it, princess? You never wanted to marry me, you know damn well you didn't. Well, you won't have to put up with a savage redskin as your husband any longer. You'll be free of me. You can get a divorce easy enough. Any white judge would jump at the chance to 'sever our union.' "

He said the last formal words mockingly, with a bitterness he didn't try to hide as he turned his face toward the window again.

"I don't want a divorce," she whispered rawly. "I don't want to be free of you."

He shook his head, obviously not believing.

"I don't want you to go. Lance, please . . . I'm asking you to stay."

Lance shut his eyes. A few days ago—for most of his lifetime, in fact—he would have sold his soul to hear those words from Summer. He had dreamed about it so long, he could almost believe he wasn't imagining her saying the words. What he couldn't believe was that she meant them. He couldn't *let* her mean them. Whatever her reasons for asking him to stay—guilt, remorse, compassion—he couldn't accept them. He wouldn't stay on those terms. Not as half a man.

"*Why?*" she cried softly when he was silent. "What have I done?"

The hollowness inside him swelled to a throbbing ache. "It's not you," he retorted, his voice so low, she could hardly hear. "It's me. I don't have the right to stay."

"What . . . what are you talking about?"

He rubbed his fingers absently over his temple, gingerly touching the line of stitches in his scalp. "The Comanches would call me a weakling. Hell, so would the whites." Lance gave a low, mirthless chuckle. "For once, they would agree. A man who can't protect his woman isn't much of a man."

Pressing her trembling hand over her heart, Summer stared at him. So that was it. For a man as proud as Lance, defeat at the hands of his enemies would have a shattering effect.

His pride had suffered a mortal blow. But that at least wa something she could fight.

She took a step closer, her gaze pleading. "There is n shame in standing up to a mob of bullies, Lance. What the did to you . . . they could have done to anyone."

She saw his eyes close, saw the bleak grimace that con torted his features for an instant, and her heart squeezed She'd already sensed his loneliness, but this was beyon lonely. This was a man in pain.

But he could get over it. He had faced hatred before an survived it—and he could this, as well. Lance was a survivor He was a fighter, just as she was. Except that he seemed t have given up his will to fight.

"Don't . . . don't be foolish." Fear made her tone shrill "It's just your stubborn pride talking."

"So what if it is?" His retort was low, hostile—and it gave her courage. Deliberately she tried to inflect scorn into he own voice.

"So . . . so I don't really think you're being too objective at the moment. You're not the victim you're making yoursel out to be. What those men did was wrong, shameful, bu you're not entirely blameless either. You brought some of i on yourself for taking them all on alone. You could have waited to go after Prewitt until you had help."

Lance's eyes narrowed in fury. "I could have waited?" The sudden fierceness that claimed his harsh features was the firs show of emotion other than resignation she'd seen since hi near brush with death. "For help? Just who was I supposed t ask for help? Who believed me?"

"I know. . . ." She hung her head, choking back a sob. "I'n sorry, Lance. . . . I'm sorry I ever doubted you. . . ."

She broke off her pleading when she saw the coldnes overtake his expression again. He wasn't listening.

Desperately Summer searched her mind for some way t get through to him. She stood near the bed, her hands tightly clasped over her stomach in an effort to calm herself. Sh would tell him about her hope that she was pregnant, tha their baby would likely be born in the summer—except tha Lance wouldn't be here next summer, she realized dazedly He had just said he was leaving. . . .

"Lance ... you can't ... you can't leave. I ... I think I'm pregnant."

His head snapped up; his black gaze pierced her with startled awareness.

Summer flinched at his expression, all her words rushing together as she tried to explain. "I'm not certain, not really, but I've been sick the past several mornings, and Maritza says that's what it is, that I'm breeding, and I know it's true, I can't really say how, but I'm sure of it.... I'm going to have your baby."

He didn't reply. Didn't make a sound. The ache that ripped through him had made his breath cease.

Summer swallowed, hard. "Lance ... you can't leave us. I don't want to bear a child alone, the way your mother was forced to. You can't leave now. It wouldn't be fair to him ... or to me, to make me rear him alone."

"My ... baby?" The word was scarcely a rasp of sound.

"Yes, your baby. And mine. Ours." Summer dashed a stream of tears from her eyes, vaguely aware she was crying. "Do you want us to face the hardships your mother had to endure? Do you want your child to suffer the way you did?"

"No ..."

"Neither do I. So you have to stay. It will be difficult enough with two of us protecting him. I want him to have a chance for a good life, not the terrible one you had to live. And I'll do everything I can short of murder to see that he gets that chance."

Lance stared, doubt scoring his features. "You ... want my baby?"

"Yes, yes, of course I want him." Her tearful expression grew indignant. "You can't think I would abandon him?"

"A lot of women would."

"That ... has to be the cruelest thing you've ever said to me." The tears spilled over again. "I would no more abandon my child than I would abandon you. I love you, Lance."

He went totally still, his expression blank. Now who was being cruel? He didn't believe her claim. Not for a second. But at least he understood now why she didn't want him to leave. She didn't want to be left alone with a half-breed kid to raise. That was why she'd professed to love him.

Summer could hear his disbelief in his silence. She wrung

her hands, clenching her fingers so tightly, the knuckles showed white. She had gone about this all wrong. It had been a mistake to tell Lance about the baby, trying to force his hand without telling him what was in her heart. Perhaps he didn't care what she felt for him, but he deserved to know. If he still wanted to leave her ... No, she wouldn't think in that defeatist vein. She would get down on her knees if that would make Lance listen.

"Last night ... when I thought I had lost you ... I thought I would die. But it was before then—when you walked out the last time—that I realized how much I loved you. I was wrong not to trust you, I know that. But even then ... even when I thought you might be guilty, I still loved you. I do ... I love you, Lance. I don't care about anything else, anyone else. Lance, please ... I'm begging you ... don't leave me."

He couldn't answer her. The oxygen seemed trapped in his lungs.

Summer took a gulping breath, trying to stop her tears. "All right. If you truly want to leave ... if you can't bear to live here any longer ... then I'll go with you. Wherever you want."

"You'd leave here with me? You'd leave your ranch? Your family?"

"I'm your wife," she said simply, her voice quavering. "My place is with you, beside you. You're more important to me than anything, anyone."

And she knew as she spoke the solemn words, they were true. She was willing to face a hostile world at Lance's side, wherever he chose to go, whatever he chose to do. And yet they now had something else besides themselves to consider.

Her voice lowered to a shaken murmur. "I would like ... our children to grow up here at Sky Valley. This land ... the life we could have here together ... are worth fighting for. But if that isn't what you want, then I won't ask you to stay. Just ... don't leave me behind."

Blindly Lance turned his head toward the window, the disconnected emotions of hope and fear and joy crashing through his mind. Could he dare believe? Was Summer working her wiles on him for some ulterior purpose of her own, or was she telling the truth? Had she really come to love him, as in his most cherished fantasy?

A shadow passed in front of the window just then, blocking out the sunlight. Lance reached for his guns beside the bed, slipping his six-shooter into his palm with the ease of long practice, while Summer froze.

A moment later they heard footsteps on the connecting porch, then a quiet knock on the front door. Summer could have screamed. Nothing short of an Indian raid should be able to interrupt this crucial, critical moment, when her future and Lance's hung in the balance.

Spinning on her heel, she went into the other room and flung open the door. Reed was standing there, his arm around a subdued Amelia.

"Is he awake?" Reed asked quietly.

Regretfully, curtly, Summer answered, "Yes."

"We came to offer our apologies. My we see him?"

Summer hesitated. She still couldn't face her sister with anything approaching equanimity, but one glance made Summer reconsider slamming the door in her face. Amelia looked terrible, almost as devastated as when Lance had rescued her from her Comanche captors, although without the ugly cuts and bruises. There were puffy dark circles under her eyes, which were red from weeping, and her complexion was splotchy with tears. Her head drooped in shame, and she wouldn't meet Summer's eyes as she twisted a handkerchief nervously between her fingers.

Silently Summer stepped back to allow them entrance. She couldn't deny Amelia this moment of healing—or Lance either.

"I don't know if Lance will want to see you," she warned. Shutting the front door behind them, she preceded them into the bedchamber.

In order to gather his crutches, Reed had to release Amelia, but she remained close beside him, like a child afraid to stray from her parent.

They stopped just inside the door, as far away as possible from the man on the bed.

Lance had put aside his six-shooter and had drawn the blanket up far enough to cover most of his bare chest. "Excuse me if I don't get up in the presence of a lady. I'm not quite up to such exertions." His tone was cool, uninflected, but amazingly, lacked the hostile edge Summer had expected.

Reed took off his hat and met Lance's eyes directly, his own blue ones somber and sincere. "I owe you one heck of an apology, Lance," he began without preliminaries. "It was wrong of me to suspect you, especially after all you've done for us. My only excuse is that I was worried for Summer's sake. I couldn't take the chance ... well ... if you were guilty, you might drag her down with you."

Lance's black gaze flickered over her. "I understand."

Reed looked cautiously relieved. "I want you to know ... I was the one who doubted you. Summer didn't want to believe you had anything to do with those cattle thefts. I spent a damn hour trying to convince her while she defended you at every turn." He hesitated as if to give Lance a chance to respond, but Lance remained silent. "You have every right to kick my butt—and you're welcome to, as soon as you're able. But if you'll forgive me, we'll go on as before."

For a long moment, Lance didn't reply—and when he did, Summer didn't know what to make of it. "As soon as I'm able ... I'll think about it."

Reed eyed him quizzically, as if not knowing whether his apology had been accepted or not. Apparently deciding not to press the issue, though, he edged aside so that Amelia could step forward.

She did so, her head lowered, her lower lip trembling, her fingers clenching and unclenching her handkerchief. She took a deep, shuddering breath as if she were about to speak, and for a brief instant, she even risked a glance at Lance. But then suddenly she turned away, sobbing, and covered her face with her hands.

Summer took an involuntary step toward her, feeling the need to offer her sister comfort despite Amelia's treachery, but Reed raised a hand, making her halt. And he was right, Summer knew. This was something Amelia had to do on her own.

"I'm ... I'm s-sorry ..." she finally managed to get out between deep, gulping sobs, "... for what I did to you.... For lying. I'm so sorry.... I would ... I would ... understand ... if you never forgave me ... but I never meant for ... them to h-hurt you.... I never ... I didn't w-want you to d-die...."

She stopped explaining then, and wept for a long while,

while everyone else in the room remained silent. Reed, looking grim but determined, rubbed her shoulder in solace, but he evidently didn't yet consider her apology adequate. When Amelia's sobs had quieted to shuddering breaths, he turned her back to face Lance, saying gently, "All of it, Melly. Tell Lance everything you told me. You asked Prewitt to get rid of Lance for you, but then you changed your mind because things went way too far."

"Y-Yes. I never wanted him to be l-lynched. I just didn't want . . . him to stay. . . ."

"Why didn't you want him to stay?"

She raised her head slowly then, daring to look at Lance. "I thought you might . . . h-hurt me. I was . . . I was . . . afraid of you."

"Am I really such a scary fellow, Miss Amelia?" Lance's tone was quiet, softer than Summer had ever heard it, the gentleness incongruous coming from so hard a man.

"N-No . . . I don't r-really s-suppose so. It's just that . . ."

"That I look like the Comanches who hurt you."

"Y-Yes . . ."

"I may look like them, but I'm half-white, too. And I'm human, just like you." He patted the bandage covering his wounded right arm. "I bleed just like everybody else."

She gulped, wiping absently at a tearstained cheek. "I know . . . but you . . . you saw my shame. I wanted to die. . . ."

"It wasn't your shame I saw, Miss Amelia. It was your courage." The light in Lance's eyes was almost tender. "It takes a strong, brave woman to survive what you did. I always thought my ma the bravest person I knew, but you Weston women are right up there with her."

"Some people would say . . . I should have . . . I should have killed myself."

Summer drew a sharp breath, but Lance shook his head. "Some people would be wrong, Miss Amelia. As long as you have family behind you, you can get through anything. That's what my ma would have said.

"I'm sorry about what the Comanches did to you," he added quietly. "If I could have prevented it, I would have. But—I know you find it hard to believe just now—but not all of them are bad. My brother's not. He helped me find you,

Miss Amelia, at no little risk to himself. He wouldn't have hurt you. Just like I wouldn't. I want you to believe that, Miss Amelia. I would never, ever hurt you. Not in a million years."

She started crying again, but more softly this time. "I'm the one who's bad.... You saved my life ... and I never even thanked you ... for rescuing me."

"Well ..." Lance gave her an awkward smile. "Consider it done. And we'll forget what happened after. All's forgiven."

"No ... no, it's not." She sent a sad look toward her sister. "Summer won't forgive me. She won't speak to me any longer."

"Melly ..." Summer began uncomfortably, but Amelia shook her head.

"No, you were right. What I did to Lance ... to you, was terrible. You risked your life to come after me ... and all I did to repay you was nearly get your husband killed. I'm sorry, Summer ... truly. I wasn't in my right mind."

Summer couldn't refuse such a humble, heartfelt apology. Not if Lance was willing to let Amelia off so easily. Her own eyes filling with tears, she went to her sister and put her arms around her. "I know. I'm sorry, too ... Melly. I'm sorry for striking you. I had no right."

"What's that?" Reed asked.

"Summer hit me ... when she found out that I had helped ... lure Lance into a trap. But I deserved it," Amelia added quickly, as if her admission might be construed as an attempt to shift blame.

"No, Melly, you didn't," Summer interrupted. "I shouldn't have hurt you. I would never have, either, if I hadn't been out of my mind with fear."

Her sister pulled away, looking at her intently. "I know. But, Summer? You were wrong ... about the baby. I wouldn't cast out an innocent child. I want to be a good aunt to him, Summer. I promise, I'll be the best aunt a child could ever have."

"Summer told you?" Lance demanded softly. "About the baby?"

Amelia looked worriedly from one to the other, and stammered, "I'm sorry, I shouldn't have said anything, I didn't know it was a secret—"

"It's all right, Melly," Summer soothed. "I told Lance already. Besides"—she forced a small laugh—"we all have too much to be sorry for. I think we should do as he says and consider the past forgotten."

Amelia sniffed and nodded. After using her handkerchief to mop her swollen eyes, she turned once more to Lance. "I was wrong . . . to force you out of the house. You can live there . . . with us . . . if you want."

Lance's mouth curved in a forced smile. "Thank you, Miss Amelia. That's a mighty fine offer. But I don't guess I can take you up on it. I won't be living here, you see."

The sharp ache that sliced through Summer's heart could not have hurt worse if Lance had physically struck her. She was certain it showed in her expression. She wanted to cry out, to protest, to issue a desperate denial, a plea for him to give her another chance. But all she could do was stand there dumbly. Her face felt numb, and the dull roaring in her ears nearly drowned out his next words. And even then, it took her a moment to comprehend.

"You see, I won't be needing a place to live. I plan to build your sister a fine house of her own about a mile from here. Reed's been working on the plans. This cabin will do fine till then. That is . . . if Summer's agreeable."

With a soft exclamation, she took a faltering step toward him and stopped, afraid to believe what he was saying. His black eyes were watching her, intense yet wary, as if he was still uncertain about lowering his defenses to her. Her knees suddenly felt weak; her heart had leaped into an erratic rhythm.

She was hardly aware when her sister and brother took their leave. She didn't know what she actually said in farewell; she only knew that she was left alone with Lance, was only aware of the quiet tension in the small bedchamber.

"Did you mean it?" she breathed, her voice a hoarse whisper.

"Mean what?"

"About building our house? Living here with me?"

In answer, he tossed the blanket aside and struggled to swing his legs over the edge of the bed.

"Lance, you shouldn't get up! You're hurt!" In an instant Summer had crossed to his side, but she couldn't manage to prevent him from standing up. On the contrary, he grasped her arm and used her to lever himself to his feet, holding on to her tightly to maintain his balance.

"Hush, princess," he warned as he hauled her close. "You always did baby me too much. A real Comanche warrior would be ashamed to be lying on his back for as long as I've been out of commission."

He kissed her then. His mouth came down on hers with a strength that captured her breath and filled her with hope. She tasted desperate loneliness. And need. And want. All the powerful yearnings that clamored for expression inside her, as well as a determination that settled all the terrible doubts that had tormented her for days.

When, a score of heartbeats later, he raised his head, Summer clung to him weakly for support.

"Say it," he whispered, his voice as hoarse as hers had been, his ebony eyes kindled with a fierce flame.

She couldn't possibly misunderstand what he needed to hear. "I love you, Lance. I always will."

He shut his eyes, his face contorted with what looked like pain.

"Please . . . your injuries . . . At least sit down."

"Hell, I'm okay." His grimace had more to do with the shocking culmination of his most cherished dream than his physical wounds, but he complied, sinking onto the mattress. Refusing to let Summer go, he drew her down with him, keeping his good left arm tightly around her.

She didn't protest, but laid her head on his bare shoulder, cherishing the closeness, the warmth, the way his lips were buried in her hair.

"I was so afraid. . . ." she said after a moment. "Afraid I had lost you."

"I didn't think I ever had you to lose," Lance said quietly.

Summer drew back and reached up to tenderly touch his bruised jaw with its faint shadow of stubble. "You do have me. I think you've always owned a little piece of my heart. I was just too blind to see it."

His eyes searched hers, dark and intense, as if still not totally convinced of her sincerity, and yet desperate to believe.

She smiled, tentatively, wishing she could smooth away that crease between his brows, wishing she could take away his hurt, wishing he would ease hers. His somber silence was not at all the response she'd yearned for. She'd offered her heart to Lance, and his lack of a reply left her feeling suddenly shy and in need of reassurance.

"Lance ..." Summer faltered, finding herself in the awkward position of not knowing what to do or say next, or how to handle this crucial, intimate moment. With any other man, she might have wheedled a reciprocal admission of love from him. But Lance was not simply any man. All her feminine wiles were less than useless; indeed, they were as welcome as poison. Any attempt at manipulation on her part, she knew, would only arouse suspicion and doubt on his. No, if Lance was to trust her, she had to be totally honest. And the same was true of him. Summer found herself wanting, needing, the truth from him—even if it confirmed her worst fears.

"You aren't ... really going to leave, are you?"

"No." He knew he could no more walk away from her now than he could cut out his heart. Not if she really loved him.

"I had always hoped ... to have a husband who loved me in return," Summer murmured hesitantly.

"Love?" He scowled suddenly and looked away. "I don't know anything about that."

"I think you do, Lance." She waited hopefully, but he remained silent.

Watching the way his jaw clenched, she thought she understood his struggle. Looking deep, beyond the grown man he was now, she saw the defiant young boy inside, the one who'd always guarded himself so fiercely against rejection that he'd never allowed himself to love—or to believe that anyone could love him. That certainty, that no one wanted him, had been ingrained in his soul. It would take far more than a single confession of love to erase all the scars, to make Lance forget all the years of pain. She would have to fight for every inch of progress, perhaps for the rest of their lives. But it was a battle worth fighting.

"You once called me *kamakuna*. Short Dress said it was the Comanche word for 'beloved.' Did you mean it, Lance?"

"Maybe," he replied gruffly.

His refusal to commit himself should have worried her, but it only confirmed what she should have known all along. Deep down, her fierce, invincible warrior had his own fears.

Lance was afraid—to feel, to hope, to love. To acknowledge his own loneliness or need.

"Is it so hard to say?"

His eyes turned to glower at her. "Are you fishing, princess?"

"Well, yes . . . I suppose I am. I'm not the heartless flirt I once was, Lance. My heart can be broken, too. But only by you. I need to know that you love me. Unless you really don't? Do you, Lance? Do you love me . . . at least a little?"

"You already know the answer to that."

"No, I don't."

"Okay, dammit, I love you! Are you satisfied?"

"Truly? You love me?"

"I've always loved you," he said harshly, his confession barely audible. "Ever since you were old enough to bat those long eyelashes of yours at me—and you damn well know it."

Summer shook her head. "When you proposed our bargain, you said it was because you wanted a wife who could help you become a respected member of the community."

A muscle in his jaw clenched tightly. "I don't give a damn about respectability or community, not as long as I have you." He stopped, suddenly looking hesitant. "I know those things are important to you, though—"

"No . . . they aren't. I once thought they were, but I was wrong. They don't matter, as long as you love me. It's only that . . . acceptance would make it easier for our children."

Lance looked down, his gaze fixing on her flat abdomen. Reverently, as if he feared he might hurt her, Lance reached down to touch her stomach. "Are we really going to have a kid?"

"I think so. I hope so. I'll know in another week if my courses are late." She frowned, recalling what he had once told her about not wanting to make her pregnant. "Do you want a child, Lance?"

His black eyes lifted to hers. "I . . . don't know. I don't like to think of what he's going to have to go through with me as his pa."

"Oh, Lance." Her heart ached. "We'll figure out something. Together."

"Together," he repeated, and yet his tone held doubt.

"We will. We'll start over . . . from this moment on. As long as we love each other ..." Summer raised her fingers to his lower lip, tracing the firm fullness with a gentle caress, her own features soft with love. "Will you marry me, Lance Calder? Will you be my husband till death do us part? Will you live with me as my lover, my friend, the father of my children?"

His solemn expression never wavered as he gazed at her searchingly.

"We're already married, I know," Summer added quietly. "But I want a real wedding this time. With my family in attendance. And this time when we say our vows, I'll mean every word of it."

When still he remained silent, Summer smiled up at him, a tender, teasing, alluring smile, with only the slightest hint of forced gaiety. "Well, what do you say, Lance Calder? Don't you know it isn't polite to keep a lady dangling on tenterhooks? Your mama should have taught you better."

"My ma taught me just fine," Lance growled as he turned with Summer in his arms and pressed her down on the mattress. "Will you marry me, then?"

"Yeah, I'll marry you. If you're sure you want a savage breed for a husband."

Reaching up, she entwined her arms carefully around his neck, conscious of his wounds. "I wouldn't have anyone else."

In response, Lance raised a hand between their bodies and began unfastening the buttons of her gown's bodice.

Summer's breath caught in her throat. "Lance, you can't mean ... You were just shot! Aren't you hurting too much?"

His faint grin was part pain, part hungry wolf. "Yeah, I'm hurting. And you're the only one who can make it better, princess." He winced as he tried to shift his weight over her. "But I think you're gonna have to do the honors for a while, at least till the stitches in my side stop pulling."

Her own smile held a hint of worry, but was mostly smug. "Well, finally you're going to let me help *you* for a change. It's about time you admitted you need me."

Lance's expression sobered at her artless remark. He needed her, all right. He needed her to fill the empty place in his soul, to heal the raw chasm of hunger in his heart. He needed her like the air he breathed. God help him, he needed her.

Lowering his head, Lance captured her mouth with a fierce possessiveness, intent on showing her just how much.

Chapter 26

The week that followed was a time of healing, for the body as well as for soul and heart. Summer and Lance built on the fragile trust they'd begun by declaring their love—sharing their feelings and thoughts, opening themselves to each other, exposing vulnerabilities, guardedly testing the limits of their delicate new bond.

Summer tried in countless ways to show him that her devotion was real, and Lance cautiously started to believe. Every time he so much as kissed her, she responded like a woman desperate to live, desperate to love. And he felt himself turning into a lovesick kid all over again—fiercely hungry for the sight of her, for the touch of her, for the laughing light in her eyes that came more readily now.

All the vicious hurt dealt him by others, his ravaged pride, his humiliation, his physical injuries, no longer meant so much, not with Summer there to heal him. He had her, and that was all that mattered. Maybe he was a selfish bastard for wanting her so damned much. Maybe he didn't have any right to ask her to suffer as an outcast with him. But Summer was his, and he would never let her go.

It looked as if she felt the same way. She babied him shamelessly, insisting on taking care of him after all he had done for her. And he shamelessly let her. Except in the mornings, when their roles reversed.

Summer was sick most mornings, almost certainly a sign of pregnancy. The thought filled Lance with wonder and fear. Wonder that his kid might be growing inside her. That she wanted to have his baby. Fear that he wouldn't be able to protect them both from the kind of life he'd led. It was only then that his rage returned to haunt him—rage over his helplessness, despair over his impotence.

He'd had to be satisfied with a sort of slim justice. Prewitt had left the county, run out by the same men who had nearly lynched *him*. But there was no saying it wouldn't happen again, or that his neighbors wouldn't take up arms against him and his family. He meant to live at Sky Valley as one of them, and he knew better than anybody how unlikely it was for white society to tolerate with equanimity the presence of a bastard breed settling in their midst.

At just this moment, though—the afternoon of his second wedding—Lance had no thought for the future beyond the immediate present. For the ceremony, he'd borrowed a fancy suit of Summer's late brother Tyler, and the thing was killing him. The high starched collar choked him, and the stitches in his side itched like crazy as he waited with Dusty in the front parlor for his bride to appear. Plus the air had started to turn warm, what with the audience of all the Weston ranch hands and their wives crowded into the elegant room. And yet he was willing to endure worse tortures in order to give Summer her special day.

"What's taking so long?" he asked Dusty in a low voice. "You think maybe something's happened?"

"You just asked me that two minutes ago," Dusty returned in a calming tone. "Settle down, Lance. It isn't even five o'clock yet. Nothing's happened. She's just getting spruced up. You know how women are about those things."

He couldn't settle down, though. His biggest fear was that Summer wouldn't show up for their wedding, even though she'd been the one to insist on it. Maybe she'd changed her mind about marrying him again. Maybe she regretted having to make a new commitment to him and wanted to end it altogether. It wouldn't be the first time a bride had left her groom standing at the altar.

The only thing that kept Lance from bolting out the parlor and up the stairs in search of her was the memory of Summer's look this morning when she'd made love to him, all dewy-eyed and passion-flushed and content.

He tugged anxiously at his strangling tie and counted the interminable seconds until Summer finally, at last, appeared at the parlor door on Reed's arm, a vision in lace and satin.

The Sky Valley women had gone to work making her a full-skirted ivory wedding gown whose bodice was embroidered with tiny seed pearls, and the sight of Summer standing there took Lance's breath away, made his knees weak. She'd never looked so beautiful—and she had eyes only for him.

Lance scarcely noticed Reed's limping gait when he awkwardly escorted her in, paid no attention when Amelia, as bridesmaid, held her train and arranged it lovingly, then took her place beside Summer before the same minister who'd married them two months before.

It was only when his bride smiled up at him and took his arm, turning him to face front, that Lance blinked and tried to focus his attention on his duty.

The words were a blur in his memory afterward. He vaguely recalled repeating his vows—but he would never in all his days forget the look Summer gave him when she said hers, promising to honor and obey and cleave only unto him till death parted them.

"Yes, I will." Her eyes were luminous and unafraid. "Oh, Lance, yes."

And the kiss afterward—so tender and poignant and full of forever—seared his soul and shook him to his roots.

Something of his feelings must have showed on his face, for Reed laughed and slapped him on the back and warned him about getting trod underfoot if he didn't stop acting like a mooncalf and stand up to Summer from the beginning.

He was aware of Dusty congratulating him, and Amelia, shyly but sincerely, welcoming him into the family. Then he and Summer accepted the well-wishes of the other wedding guests, most of whom seemed genuinely pleased for the *patrona* and the new master of Sky Valley.

The dinner afterward passed in a daze, the music and gaiety and laughter enveloping Lance like a healing balm. He danced with Summer—or at least he moved his feet where she instructed him to—and the ribbing he suffered as a result was good-natured and friendly enough that he couldn't take offense. Fact was, it felt good—damn good—to be part of the community, to be accepted in the celebration because he belonged instead of excluded because of who he was.

It was late when the newlyweds slipped off to their own cabin. They walked hand in hand through the chill, starlit night—Summer dreamily humming snatches of a favorite tune, Lance finding pleasure in her pleasure, and both of them stopping every few feet to indulge their ravenous need for a kiss.

They stopped for the last time at their front door. "Say it again," Lance demanded, unwilling to let her inside until she'd given him the reassurance his heart craved.

"I love you, I love you, I love you. . . ." And those were the last words she spoke for long, breathless minutes.

He carried his new bride over the threshold of their front door, despite her laughing protests and the ache in his side. One of the Mexican women had prepared the cabin for their arrival, leaving a fire burning merrily in the hearth, a lamp lit on the bedside table, the covers turned down invitingly, and a filmy nightdress spread out on the bed.

Ignoring the suggestive garment, heedless of the fragility of her wedding gown, Lance laid Summer on the mattress and followed her down, taking time only to tear off his tie and his strangling collar before sinking his mouth into hers.

Their urgent need had risen to a feverish pitch before Summer finally, regretfully, stopped him by pressing her fingers to his lips. "Lance . . . my dress. I don't want to tear it."

She saw the sudden, bitter hurt that flashed in his eyes before she could explain what she meant. "I don't care really, but I thought I would save it for our daughters to wear when they marry. And it might be awkward to have to explain how it came to be in less than pristine condition."

His mouth lost its rigid look and slowly curved upward at the corners. "I guess it might at that."

He helped her undress, or rather he got in the way with his tendency to plant hot little kisses on her bared skin. The hairpins that held up her hair got lost somewhere on the floor as Lance tossed them away recklessly. Several moments were lost as well when Lance insisted on combing out her silky, shiny tresses with his fingers. He buried his face there, inhaling the sweet perfume, making a sensual feast of the texture and scent, until Summer pulled away, laughing.

Turning, she removed the last of her underwear, giving him her naked back as she reached for the nightdress on the bed.

"You're really going to wear that thing?" Lance asked, disappointed.

"What, you don't like it?" She threw a coquettish glance over her shoulder, while her eyes danced mischievously.

"I guess it's okay, but I'd rather have you without it."

"You will. Only just not yet."

She put it on, and the sensual smile she gave him as she turned around was as alluring and provocative as the negligee she wore. The gown was white, but there was absolutely nothing virginal about it. So sheer as to be nearly transparent, it had been fashioned to arouse a man's lusts, and it succeeded with him entirely. Below the daringly low bodice that revealed most of her swelling white breasts, Lance could see the dusky hue of her peaked nipples, the narrow curve of her waist, the feminine flare of her hips, the dark inviting curls that shielded her womanhood, the slender legs that would wrap around him and take him inside her body. The sight made his blood boil.

He reached out to stroke a sensitive nipple, which made her suck in her breath, but still she refused to rush or allow him any part in his seduction. Instead, she removed his clothing: coat and shirt first, then undershirt, planting her own brand of searing kisses on his chest and abdomen as she went, driving him mad.

Need slammed through his chest by the time Summer took his hand and led him back to the bed. Lance sat to take off his shoes and trousers, but Summer insisted on taking the lead when he tried to unbutton his drawers. With an arch little smile, she made a production out of unfastening each one, stroking the hard ridge beneath the red cotton fabric, teasing his straining arousal in a way that made Lance grit his teeth. When finally she drew the garment slowly down over his hips, his manhood rose thick and eager from its nest of black hair.

She bent and kissed the rigid shaft, and his flesh reacted instantly, filling, swelling, aching for her touch. When she flicked the hot, stretched skin with her tongue, he groaned and reached for her, but Summer, with a soft, musical laugh, pulled back.

She made him lie naked on the bed and then stretched out beside him, her fingers lightly caressing his body, tracing the bronzed hues of his skin, till he quivered like a stallion, till every muscle and nerve and sinew was taut with anticipation. She was the aggressor, controlling the moment. Her arousing strokes trailed over his deep chest, his flat abdomen, down along his narrow hip, up the inside of his thigh, drawing lazy circles closer and closer to the seat of his need.

With gritted teeth and closed eyes, Lance arched his back and spread his legs to allow her stroking fingers better access, but she would do no more than tease him with her touch, offering no relief for his sex, which was heavy and swollen and throbbing with pain.

Only when Lance gave a soft groan did Summer raise herself up on her knees. Bending over him, she kissed his healing wounds and older scars one by one, using lips and tongue and breath to express her own hurt at his suffering, enticing away the pain, hazing his memory, until all Lance could think of was Summer, his beautiful Summer.

He was half-mad with desire when finally she stretched out above him, her lovely breasts nestled against his chest, her soft thighs partly straddling his hard-muscled ones, her silken hair curtaining her shoulders and his. But still she hesitated.

Lance shifted restlessly, wanting desperately to flip her over on her back and take her with savage fierceness, but wanting more to give her whatever she wanted.

What she wanted was to torment him, to postpone the moment of joining until his desire was razor-sharp. What she wanted was to make him need her as much as she needed him. What she wanted was to fulfill his dreams.

There'd never been any softness, any ease, in his life, and she wanted to give him that. There'd been so little love in his past, and she desperately wanted to change his future. He'd been alone too long, with too great a loneliness in his soul. She wanted Lance to know he wasn't alone anymore, to make him believe that the love she felt for him was strong and enduring. She thirsted to show him her love, hungered to express how huge her feelings were. And she wanted reassurance in return.

"Do you love me?" Summer demanded, her tone more serious than playful.

Lance gazed back at her with eyes that were solemn and smoldering with heat. God, yes, he loved her, with a fierce and proud intensity that filled his soul.

Catching her fingers, he put her palm against his chest where his heart was thudding painfully. "Feel this." His hoarse, whiskey-rough voice washed over her like a caress. "This belongs to you."

"Yes," she agreed, "but do you love me?"

"I've loved you so long," he said finally, simply, "I can't remember what it's like not loving you."

"Oh, Lance . . ." Her soft voice said his name as no woman ever had, as he knew no one ever would, with pride and desire and deep, deep devotion. "I love you."

She moved over him then, craving his granite hardness inside her to seal their vows, gripped by the primitive need to possess and be possessed. He reached up roughly to pull her nightdress from her body, but she welcomed his impatience, welcomed his hands, which came up to clutch her naked buttocks and guide her down onto his thick, straining shaft.

Summer sighed at the exquisite penetration, in the relief of having Lance finally home. He thrust deep, and the jolt of sensation made her entire body clench with an unbearable surge of pleasure.

Their gazes locked.

"I want you," Summer whispered solemnly. "I want to be part of you . . . make you part of me."

The fierce light that entered Lance's obsidian eyes seared her and gave her all the reassurance she could want.

"*Kamakuna,*" he whispered in return as he began slowly to rock his hips and fulfill her heart's desire.

They made love in the true meaning of the word, confirming their new commitment to each other. Summer held nothing back, offered everything, as did Lance. His roughly muttered words of love and lust and need mingled with her gasping cries.

And when the shattering climax came at last, it somehow felt as if night and day had merged into a glorious, splintering burst of dawn, portending a dazzling, blindingly bright future.

Even when morning came, the feeling persisted. Lance lay quietly in bed, his arms around a naked, sleeping Summer, savoring the knowledge that she was truly his, and the peace that his possession brought his soul.

When she stirred drowsily, he snuggled her closer, keeping her soft bottom nestled against his loins. His shaft was half-erect, despite the physical demands passion had made on his body last night, but he was content simply to hold her and let her wake naturally, knowing there would be time enough in the years ahead to enjoy each other.

It was perhaps ten minutes later when she finally came awake. Turning with a dreamy yawn, Summer curled her arms around his neck, pressing her body against his in a suggestive, totally adoring way, and blinked up at him. In the pale light slipping through the shutters, her green eyes were soft and welcoming as clover, her lips swollen from his passion. She wore, Lance thought, the look of a woman in love, a woman who had been thoroughly loved.

She brushed her mouth over his in a sweet greeting, before suddenly ducking her head and burying her nose in his chest with a muffled laugh.

"What?" Lance demanded, curious to know the cause of her humor.

"Nothing. I'm just happy." She drew back to look up at him. "It feels different being married this time."

He knew what she meant. It did feel different. *He* felt different somehow. Stronger, better, more able to take on his hostile neighbors. Summer had become his wife in front of her family and friends, declared her intent to love and cherish him in front of the world, and then proven it last night with her eager body.

He lowered his mouth to hers, taking it in a kiss that turned hungry and lusty as need rose strong and fierce to seize him. Summer returned his kiss with willing fervor—until suddenly she pulled back. She had turned a pale shade of green, he saw with a sense of alarm.

She hastily clamped a hand over her mouth, but barely had time to turn and lean out over the bed before retching into the chamber pot she'd begun keeping there for just that purpose.

Lance held her head and stroked her damp nape, the gesture tender but awkward in his need to support her.

When she was done, Summer wiped her mouth on a towel and lay back weakly on the pillows, her eyes closed in embarrassment.

"How romantic," she murmured, and despite their tangled emotions, they both chortled.

In a moment she opened her eyes to gaze at him apologetically. "I'm sorry, Lance, but I don't think I feel very passionate just now."

"I'm not sorry." His own eyes softened as he placed his hand over her still flat stomach. "No woman's ever wanted to have my baby before. I can put up with a little queasiness if you can."

"I can, willingly."

His brows drew together in a thoughtful frown. "Will it hurt the baby if I'm inside you?"

"Martiza said no. We don't have to worry for months, at least. And not even then if we're careful."

"Well, then," Lance said with a grin, "I guess we'll just have to be careful."

They rose eventually, and lazily took turns bathing each other, then even more lazily dressing one another. Lance did the cooking in honor of their honeymoon. He fixed a huge breakfast of ham and eggs and pan biscuits, which he wolfed down, having eaten hardly a thing the day before because of wedding nerves, while Summer watched him jealously, nibbling on a soda cracker and drinking herbal tea to settle her stomach.

They cleaned up the dishes together, and it was then that Lance noticed Summer kept glancing at her watch.

"Would you like to go for a ride?" she asked when the last skillet was dry.

"A ride? On a horse?"

She flushed and laughed when she realized where Lance's mind had been. "Yes, on a horse. Not me."

His mouth curved dryly. "That isn't exactly how I thought I'd spend today."

She went to him and wrapped her arms around his neck, pressing her body suggestively against his, while giving him a smile that could charm a grizzly. "Please, darling? I think the fresh air would do me good."

He saw through her, even though he hadn't yet figured out what she wanted from him. Summer was trying to work her wiles on him again—and succeeding all too well. Despite his vow to remain indifferent when she used those female tactics on him, his body had responded instantly to the feel of her rubbing up against him. Still he was content enough to be amused rather than angry.

"Where would we go?"

"It's a surprise."

He gave in gracefully, not wanting to disappoint her or see that sparkle in her emerald eyes fade. When he asked her what she was up to, Summer would only smile secretly and say, "I'll tell you when we get there."

They took coats, since the weather had turned chilly, but Lance felt warm enough, seeing her eagerness and delight.

The yard seemed deserted, with none of the hands in sight. Lance saddled his sorrel and lifted Summer up onto the horse's back, then swung up behind her. At her direction, they headed out to the open range.

It was a blustery day, cloudless but with a hint that winter would soon be coming, but his arms kept her warm. Indeed, Lance's hands wouldn't leave her body alone. And with all the attention his lips gave her, it was clear he found the left side of her neck and the shell of her ear fascinating.

When they'd ridden half a mile or so from the ranch and were sheltered by the relative privacy of a stand of post oaks, Lance left off nibbling Summer's skin to murmur huskily in her ear, "You've never made love on horseback before."

Summer turned her head to glance at him with wide eyes. "Can you do it that way?"

His grin was wickedness itself. "A Comanche can do anything on horseback."

Summer returned a wicked smile of her own, but declined his scandalous invitation. "Someday we should try it—when it's not so cold, and when we have the time—but not right now. Now, behave yourself, Lance Calder, and stop distracting me."

Which, of course, he took as a challenge to see just how distracting he could be.

He thought at first she was taking him to the site of what would be their new home, but she guided their mount up into the hills, toward the same high point he had once shown her, the day he'd talked about them building a future together. She halted the horse just before the promontory, though, where they could look out over the rugged, rolling land of Sky Valley.

"I'm glad you decided we should stay here," Summer murmured, drinking in the magnificent view. "This land is worth holding on to."

"I know," Lance said quietly. "I always wanted this land for my own."

The look she turned on him was teasing yet faintly hesitant. "I always suspected that was the real reason you married me."

"Dammit, princess, you know that's not true."

"Do I?"

"You should."

Keeping his arms tightly around her, Lance took her hands, interlacing his fingers with hers, while his voice wrapped her in a velvet cloak. "Have you ever really yearned for something you couldn't have? Ever wanted something so bad, you ached for it? That was how I wanted you. But you were beyond my reach, untouchable, like a precious dream."

Summer smiled softly. Some untamed part of her heart had always wanted Lance, too. Even when she'd thought him a dangerous, forbidden savage.

She'd conquered her prejudices since then. Lance was half-Indian, true, but she wouldn't change him for all the civilized, purebred gentlemen in the vast state of Texas. Except maybe his stubborn pride. That could stand softening. She only hoped—fervently—that Lance had learned not to let his difficult past destroy his future. That having a child to consider would make him temper his hostility toward the whites he would have to live among.

Deciding it was time to put her hopes to the test, Summer nudged the sorrel forward, bringing them to the crest of the ridge. From that vantage, they could look down and see the site where Lance had planned to build their home.

She watched him anxiously, and so knew the instant he realized there was something different about the place, that there was activity in progress down below. From this distance the people and animals looked like scurrying ants.

Lance's eyes narrowed grimly. "What's going on?" he demanded, his tone hard, his reaction not at all what she'd hoped it would be.

"Those are our neighbors, Lance. They're building our house for us."

"Our . . . neighbors?" He turned his harsh look on her.

"Yes." Summer hastened to explain, so that the terrible light in his eyes would fade. "It was Amelia's idea, really—a wedding present for us. And an apology from her and everyone else for the terrible mistake they made last week. Melly asked them all to pitch in, and Harlan Fisk organized it all. It's like a barn raising, only this is for our house. They mean to set the frame and the roof today, and the outside walls tomorrow, so we can work on the interior during the winter. Most of the supplies you ordered came last week, and Reed finished the drawings. . . ." Her voice trailed off at the last. "I hoped you would be pleased."

"I don't take charity," he replied stiffly, but she thought his tone might have softened just a bit.

Summer shook her head. "It isn't charity. It's their way of saying welcome. This is what neighbors do for one another, for members of a community. And you're part of this one now—we are."

Without a word, he took the reins from her and backed the sorrel away from the ledge, turning the way they'd come.

The ride to the valley below was silent. Summer could feel the tension in Lance's body, but she was afraid anything she said would only make the situation worse. Lance would have to decide on his own whether he wanted to make peace with their neighbors. They were willing to meet him halfway, but he would have to rein in his stubborn pride and accept their offer of friendship.

There must have been over a hundred people present, they saw as they rode up, and every one of them, man, woman, and child, was hard at work hammering and sawing, lifting and toting. Teams of oxen and horses shifted wagonloads of lumber and bricks and moved beams into place, while to one side stood tables loaded with food and drink brought by the women. Whole families had driven dozens of miles to be here, Summer knew, giving up their Saturday workday and their Sunday day of rest to help the newlywed couple set up home. She wondered if Lance realized the significance of their generous gesture.

It seemed as if he did, for he pulled up and sat staring at all the industry, his expression wary, as if not quite believing his eyes, or knowing quite how to react.

The choice was taken from him.

Amelia must have been on the lookout for them, for she immediately came out to greet them, offering Lance a shy smile of welcome, although her eyes were a bit anxious. "I hope you don't mind, having to work on your honeymoon, but it seemed best to get started."

Dusty was right behind her, a big grin on his usually calm face. "Howdy, Lance ... Miss Summer. Good to see you made it through the wedding night. Lord, I thought you were gonna come out of your skin yesterday, Lance, waiting for the ceremony to start."

Lance's bronzed features relaxed slightly at his good-natured ribbing, Summer saw with relief. She also noticed the way Dusty had placed a proprietary hand at Amelia's waist, and that her sister didn't seem to mind the contact.

Summer gave him a grateful smile. Perhaps Amelia's recovery wasn't so doubtful after all.

Dusty stepped forward then and reached up to help her dismount, but Summer held back. She wouldn't get down unless Lance chose to.

He had stiffened again, his eyes fixed on the large, older man striding toward them.

Harlan Fisk stopped beside their horse and looked up at them with a smile. "Hello, folks." While his greeting was jovial, his expression remained entirely serious. Nor did he mince words. "I'd take it most kindly if you'd accept my apology, son. I always thought myself a fair man, but what happened last week ... Well, I'm downright ashamed. There's no excuse for nearly killing a man, but, well ... I'm damned sorry."

After a moment's hesitation, Lance gestured with his head toward the skeleton frame that was springing up before their eyes. "You didn't have to do this."

"Sure I did. You think I want to live with that night on my conscience? No, sir—and every man here feels the same way. You've got a lot of us squirming, son." Reaching up, he stretched out his hand, offering it to Lance. "If you'd accept my apology, maybe I'd quit feeling like a yellow-bellied snake."

Slowly, coolly, Lance took the proffered hand, allowing Harlan's handshake.

Beaming with what looked like relief, Harlan turned to

face the crowd, calling for silence. "Hey, everybody! The Calders are here." When the work stopped and all eyes had turned toward them, he added, "What do you say we give the newlyweds a cheer?"

From the shouts and applause that suddenly erupted from the crowd, it seemed as if some great event had occurred.

Reed limped up on his crutches just then. "It's about time you two got here." His blue eyes scanned them both, going from Summer to Lance. "She been keeping you in bed all day? I warned you, Lance. Summer'll turn you into a lazy good-for-nothing if you let her."

"Reed!" Summer protested, her cheeks flaming in response to her brother's ribald comment.

Reed chuckled and cocked a thumb toward the emerging new house. "I appointed myself chief supervisor, but there are a dozen decisions I didn't want to make for you. You better get started or they'll be finished before you can get a word in."

Not replying directly, Lance turned to look at Summer. "This is what you want, princess?"

She returned his gaze solemnly, love and loyalty shining clearly in her eyes. "If it's what you want. It's your decision, Lance."

"So," Reed demanded, "are you going to let us do all the work on your house, or are you going to pitch in?"

Lance's hard mouth tentatively, reluctantly, curved in a slow grin. "I guess I better, if I mean to have any say at all in how it's built."

The collective relief his small audience evidently felt showed on all their faces: Amelia, Dusty, Reed, Harlan Fisk, all smiled up at him in gratitude. Lance felt their warmth and knew he had made the right decision.

He swung down from the sorrel, then reached up for his wife. When Summer slid down into his waiting arms, he stood there for a minute, holding her, while the others politely recognized his desire for privacy and left them alone.

Not loosening his grip, Lance gazed down at her intently. "I want you to know, I'm only doing this for our kid."

Summer smiled up at him. "That's a very good reason."

"And because I love you."

"That's an even better reason."

His mouth curved wryly as he glanced at the construction. "I didn't figure on spending our honeymoon building our house."

"I know. But we can't reject the kindness of all these people. They really do want to make amends, Lance."

"Yeah." He turned back to her. "Even so, I'd rather do what your brother suggested—spend the day in bed with you."

Reaching up, Summer brushed her fingertips caressingly over her husband's lips. "I would, too, but there will be plenty of days in the future when we can be lazy together. We have forever."

His ebony eyes searched hers intently. "That a promise?"

"A solemn, cross-my-heart promise, my love."

His dark features softening at her answer, Lance took her hand and turned with Summer toward their developing house.

A dozen people called out greetings as they melded into the crowd. Lance greeted them back, even the men he recognized from his near lynching, but those were all the pleasantries he was allowed time for. Someone handed him a hammer and Summer a bucket of nails, while someone else demanded to know where the parlor fireplace was supposed to sit.

With a fleeting grin at his wife, Lance hefted the hammer and pointed to the framework for what should be the front left room on the lower floor. "You want to help me figure out what's the parlor in this fancy house, princess? I don't want to do this all alone."

"You won't have to," Summer replied softly. "I'll be with you."

Sharing a smile, they went to work, building their new future together.